Touch of Desire

*In a world of forbidden magic,
seduction is the
most powerful spell...*

SUSAN
SPENCER PAUL

ST. MARTIN'S
PAPERBACKS

U.S. $6.99
CAN. $9.99

ALSO BY SUSAN SPENCER PAUL

TOUCH OF PASSION

TOUCH OF NIGHT

**AVAILABLE FROM
ST. MARTIN'S PAPERBACKS**

ISBN 0-312-93389-4

Touch of Night

"A remarkable plot makes *Touch of Night* a bewitching sweet tale whose characters come alive for the reader." —*Rendezvous*

"Paul has created an intriguing story that's evenly balanced between magic and romance. She has a real knack for creating wonderful characters... *Touch of Night* is a wonderful first installment of what will surely be an engaging new paranormal series." —*BookLoons Reviews*

"Paul captivates readers with a story that's an entrancing, intriguing blend of magic and romance...Paul has crafted a remarkably appealing romance that is as dark in magic as it is light in its faith in the power of love...her strong characters and instinctive belief in all that is good are evident on every page of this masterful paranormal romance. A must for fans of Susan Carroll and Katherine Kingsley." —*RT BOOKclub Magazine*

"An engaging paranormal romance peppered with action and humor." —*Romance Reviews Today*

"With a historical base, this story blends magic, fantasy, and romance into one extraordinary tale...one incredible journey." —*Fallen Angel Reviews*

"This fabulous romantic fantasy will grip the audience from the beginning...the storyline enables the audience to believe in wizardry and sorcery, but even more so in the healing magic of love. Susan Spencer Paul writes a robust tale in which the worst demons are inside a person's soul." —*Midwest Book Review*

"Delightful romance at its best, this historical paranormal romance was refreshing to read...this fabulous magical tale is a must-read!" —*Romance Divas*

"Author Susan Spencer Paul has traveled down a new path with her complex and entertaining book...her fascinating characters promise future stories filled with a wide variety of mystical abilities. *Touch of Night* will appeal to every reader who likes historical romance." —*A Romance Review*

ST. MARTIN'S PAPERBACKS TITLES
BY SUSAN SPENCER PAUL

Touch of Passion

Touch of Night

Touch of Desire

SUSAN SPENCER PAUL

ST. MARTIN'S PAPERBACKS

TOUCH OF DESIRE

ISBN: 0-312-93389-4
EAN: 9780312-93389-0

Printed in the United States of America

St. Martin's Paperbacks edition / October 2006

St. Martin's Paperbacks are published by St. Martin's Press, 175 Fifth Avenue, New York, NY 10010.

10 9 8 7 6 5 4 3 2 1

Chapter 1

" '*In* conclusion,' " Niclas Seymour read aloud from the letter he held, " 'I give my word of honor that any meeting between Lord Graymar and myself will be brief and to the point. I shall not importune His Lordship for any greater period of time than absolutely necessary, and shall not press him for any but the most pertinent information. I cannot possibly render sufficient thanks for your help in this most important matter, kind sir, but please believe that I am sincerely grateful. With deepest respect, Sarah Tamony.' "

Setting the missive aside on a nearby table, Niclas looked across the study to where his cousin the Earl of Graymar reclined in a comfortable chair near the warmth of the fire, a glass of wine loosely clasped in lax fingers, his blue eyes half-closed, as if the reading of the letter had nearly put him to sleep. Niclas knew better, however, than to assume that Malachi Seymour was anything but completely awake and aware. Powerful sorcerers often looked, by long practice, far more safe and vulnerable than they were. Apart from that, Niclas knew that Malachi wasn't in the least disinterested in the contents of Sarah Tamony's latest letter, for Miss Tamony had become, in recent months, a most unpleasant thorn in the Earl of Graymar's side.

"There wouldn't be any harm in simply speaking to the woman, Malachi," Niclas said. "Grant Miss Tamony an interview, and then perhaps she'll leave you—and me—in peace."

Lord Graymar's eyes opened slightly. He gazed levelly at his relative as he lifted the glass of wine and slowly sipped from it. Lowering the glass, he replied, simply, "No."

Niclas set one hand to his aching temple. He didn't want to be where he was at the moment, at Glain Tarran, the ancient Seymour estate in Pembrokeshire, and so far away from his wife and children in London. But he wouldn't be able to go home until he'd finished with all of the business that had brought him to Wales—all of it, including the matter of Miss Sarah Tamony.

"Be reasonable, for pity's sake. The woman has been hounding you for months, undeterred by your refusals, and she's not going to stop until you grant her an audience."

"Then she is stubborn beyond all countenance," Lord Graymar stated tersely. "Her parents failed her miserably, for she was clearly spoiled as a child. I do not see why the Seymours should suffer for their lack of resolution."

Niclas dropped his hand. "Suffer? What on earth do you imagine Miss Tamony has in mind? She only wants to speak with you."

The fingers on the wineglass tightened, and Malachi's eyes narrowed. "Because she plans to write about us in her next book," he said angrily. "Because she's trying to ferret out secrets she has no business knowing and she intends to expose us—and all the ancient clans—to the rest of the world. And aye, the Seymours will suffer for it. I am the Dewin Mawr, Niclas." He sat forward and pinned his cousin with a steely gaze. "The sorcerer to whom those families give their complete trust. I'm not going to lend Miss Tamony my aid in causing magic mortals harm. It would be the worst sort of betrayal."

"That's utter nonsense," Niclas replied. "You make it

sound as if she plans to write the truth about us—as if she could even do such a thing, which she couldn't, unless someone among our kind told her our entire history. Have you ever read one of Miss Tamony's books?"

Malachi made a grumbling sound and pushed to his feet, setting the wineglass aside on a low table near the fireplace.

"The entire world seems to have been entranced by the woman's scribblings," he muttered, moving to one of the tall bookcases that lined the walls of his study. The cases, like the room itself, indeed like all of Castle Glain Tarran, were ancient, ornate, and overlarge in their medieval structure. They rose from the floor to the ceiling, dark and imposing, towering above those who happened to stand before them. Despite that, they never seemed to be able to make Malachi appear small by comparison. But then, Niclas thought, his cousin was the Dewin Mawr. It was not in his makeup to appear small, ever.

"I suppose it would be astonishing if I hadn't read something of her work," Lord Graymar said. "Society talks of little else these days. I assumed at first that the fascination sprang mainly from the fact of her father's famous works on ancient civilizations, and that the clamor would quickly dim once it was seen that her efforts couldn't possibly compare to his scholarly epics. But I was wrong. She's evidently inherited Sir Alberic's way with words. Well-meaning acquaintances find it necessary to force her publications upon one with the assurance that they shall be found absolutely riveting. I came to Glain Tarran with the hope of escaping the current, terribly annoying fascination Society has with Miss Sarah Tamony." He spoke her name as if it was distasteful even to say. "But even here I find no peace. My servants adore the woman. I can only pray the foolishness has passed before the Season begins. Here." He pulled a particular volume from among the many before him. "This one. I brought it back with me from London and promptly shelved it with the ardent hope that I would never again be made to set sight upon it. I believe it is her latest." He examined the cover more closely. "*Enchanted Heritage: Factual Accounts of Europe's Most Beloved Myths and Legends.*" His hand opened and the book floated slowly across the room to Niclas, who took it.

"Yes, this is her latest," he concurred. "A sequel of sorts to the first, *Fascinating Truths of Fantasy and Fables.*"

"Aye, that's the bothersome tome that started all this ridiculous fascination with the supernatural," Malachi said unhappily, taking his place in the chair again.

"Why, Malachi," Niclas said with a touch of surprise, examining the book more closely. "You've actually *read* this. The pages are worn."

"Of course I read it," Lord Graymar said irately. " 'Know thy enemy.' My father taught me that from the cradle, just as I know yours taught you. It's the second most important rule of our kind, next to never revealing one's magic to mere mortals. I've read Miss Tamony's books merely as a means to understanding what we're all up against in this woman's determinations."

Niclas looked at him. "And you enjoyed them, didn't you? She is a marvelous writer, just as Sir Alberic is, though I think her subjects far more engaging. Her books are wonderful."

Malachi took up his wineglass and drank before uttering, "Hmph."

Niclas gave a shake of his head. "They *are* wonderful," he insisted. "Julia and I took turns reading the second one aloud to the twins at night. They were enchanted."

Lord Graymar's eyebrows rose. "Enchanted?" he remarked. "Children who've been raised with magic all their lives? I should have thought they'd find the writing as dull as memory work compared to the reality of their lives."

"But that's precisely my point," Niclas said. "Miss Tamony doesn't tell the old stories as other mere mortals have always done, as if the tales are simply ancient history without any purpose or interest for modern society. She's unearthed nearly forgotten fables and brought them back to life, much as the elders in our Families have done throughout generations of magic mortals. Miss Tamony is giving mere mortals that same gift, save that she uses far more humor and wit in the telling. She's our English version of the Brothers Grimm."

Malachi gave a single ill-humored laugh but otherwise made no reply.

"Sarah Tamony isn't going to go away because you continue to be so stubborn," Niclas pressed. "Part of what's made her so well loved by her many readers is her tenacity in ferreting out the details of the most ancient and far-flung mysteries. Even her loudest critics admit that her research is incredibly thorough . . . as well as unusually insightful. If I didn't know better, I would almost suspect that Miss Tamony is of our kind."

At this, Malachi uttered an inelegant snort. "Aye, from one of the darker clans, as she seems to be intent upon destroying us. Perhaps she's in league with the Cadmarans. Have you ever considered that possibility?"

Niclas scowled. "She only wants to write about the lives of unusual characters in British history," he countered. "Nothing more. Do you sincerely believe that mere mortals are going to accept as true the intimation that those same characters had magical powers?"

"What I believe scarce matters," Lord Graymar told him. "As the Dewin Mawr, I cannot take such a risk. If Sarah Tamony writes the book she's proposing to undertake, a great deal of Seymour family history will be laid bare to public eyes. People will begin to wonder, and to ask questions, to poke and pry. I'm not going to lend her my aid in bringing that about. Indeed," he said, taking another sip from the wineglass, "I'm going to do everything possible to stop her."

With a sigh, Niclas set aside the elegantly bound volume he'd been holding and regarded his immovable cousin with resignation. A flash of lightning illuminated the tall windows at the far end of the study, only partly concealed by heavy velvet curtains, and a moment later a distant rumbling sounded from the direction of the ocean shore. A gust of wind caused the fire in the grate to give a sudden spark. Malachi smiled and murmured, with obvious pleasure, "A storm is coming."

Malachi loved storms, Niclas knew, and the wilder they were, the better. Where more normal individuals might find such weather daunting, uncomfortable, even frightening, the Earl of Graymar found it . . . well, the only word Niclas could think of that truly described it was "sensual." He remembered vividly those times when he and Malachi were boys, growing up in Wales, and a sudden storm would overtake their outdoor play. The same wind and rain that had Niclas running for shelter sent Malachi into raptures of delight. Something in wild nature seemed to transport him to another sphere. Which meant that his parents, Niclas's long-suffering aunt and uncle, were often obliged to forcibly fetch their son indoors, and that Malachi spent a great deal of his time—considering the frequency of rain along the Pembrokeshire coast—in wet clothes.

"I hope it passes by morning," Niclas muttered. "I don't fancy riding in the same sort of weather that accompanied me here, and Abercraf will be exceedingly put out if he's made to endure the rain again."

Malachi chuckled. "Your manservant is as delicate and particular as the highest-born nobleman. But you've nothing to fear, Cousin. It will pass. The morning will bring clear light, and you and Abercraf will find the way ready to traverse, if not entirely dry. I know how eager you are to return to London, to Julia and the children."

"I cannot go until we've discussed the next matter of import, which is the *cythraul,* and we cannot move on to that subject until we've finished with this one."

Malachi sighed. "There are times, *cfender*, when your sense of organization is far too overdeveloped. I'm weary of speaking about Sarah Tamony."

"No more so than I," Niclas replied tartly, a touch of aggravation in his voice. "Can you not reconsider, Malachi, and talk to the woman? If you're so concerned about what she'll write of us, then use your powers to persuade her to do so in a manner that you approve of."

By the look on his cousin's face it was clear that Niclas had surprised him. "Do my ears deceive me," Lord Graymar murmured, "or is my strict and saintly cousin Niclas actually suggesting that I place an enchantment on a mere mortal?"

"Don't look at me as if the idea shocks you," Niclas countered irately. "You've already thought of it yourself. I know how your mind works."

Malachi grinned. "Aye, I've considered it," he confessed. "But it would answer far better if you'd simply write the dratted woman and tell her to leave us in peace. I don't want to risk placing a secret, lasting spell on the daughter of a baronet, no matter how odd Sir Alberic reportedly may be. His writings are uncommonly insightful, and I've no doubt the man is the same in all his dealings."

"You'll have the opportunity to find out if that's true," Niclas told him. "The famous Tamonys have returned from all their wanderings this year to be in London for a proper Season, also to introduce their celebrated daughter and their niece to Society."

Malachi slowly sat forward. "At her age? I should have thought Miss Tamony to be firmly on the shelf by now."

"She's six and twenty," Niclas countered, "and still a beauty, by all accounts. But it would scarce matter if the woman was a six-headed Gorgon. The *ton* is seized with anticipation of her coming—of her entire family's coming. Sir Alberic and his wife haven't been to Town for nearly ten years. Indeed, they have seldom resided in England, spending so much of their lives traveling the world on Sir Alberic's scholarly quests."

Malachi's brows drew together in thought. He lifted a hand and made a gentle waving motion. Across the room, a crystal decanter lifted from its table and floated toward him. He waited until his glass had been refilled before he looked at Niclas and asked, "Will you have more?"

Niclas gave a shake of his head. "We must still discuss the *cythraul*. I'll want all my senses for that."

"Aye, the *cythraul*," Malachi muttered wearily. "I discerned that you've brought a package from Professor Seabolt for me, filled with warnings and advice."

Niclas nodded. "Indeed I have. He hopes to meet with you immediately upon your return to London to discuss the situation more fully. He seems to think you're not taking as seriously as you should the imminent arrival of so powerful a demon."

"Of course I take the matter seriously," Malachi countered. "I should be a fool not to. The spirits send the demon as a test for ruling wizards, after all, and it is not a test I intend to fail. But I understand the professor's impatience. It's quite a boon for a mere mortal who loves the supernatural as he does to be involved in such an event."

"It will be a boon for someone else, as well," Niclas remarked, "if you don't get to the demon first."

Malachi looked at him. "Morcar Cadmaran, do you mean?"

Niclas nodded. "The Earl of Llew will do all that he can to gain control of the *cythraul* before you've managed to banish it. And if he does, he'll possess the strength to oust you from your place as Dewin Mawr." His expression was grave. "We both know what he'll do with such power."

Malachi shuddered lightly. "He would rule the world. It doesn't bear thinking of. But it won't come to that," he vowed. "I'll reach the demon first and command it back to the spirit realm, just as the Great Dewins before me have done."

"You will both be given the signs of its coming," Niclas said. "And be required to interpret what they mean. Morcar may not be as clever as you are, but his hatred for the Seymours, particularly for you, will drive him to win the contest. He's not forgotten how you tricked him two years past, causing him the loss not only of his betrothed but also of his cousin Tauron—which has proven to be far the worse of the two. It enraged those who give Morcar their allegiance. The Earl of Llew doesn't simply wish to bring you down, Malachi. He wants to destroy you. Don't let yourself become overconfident simply because you're the superior wizard."

Malachi gazed at him very directly. "I have known almost from my cradle that I would likely live to face the *cythraul* when it came. Believe me, *cfender*, the demon will be banished."

Niclas's features relaxed. "I'm satisfied that it will be so. But we've still the matter of Miss Tamony to decide."

"Miss Tamony," Malachi said with a groan. "What a pestilential female. And to cause such a stir in England when the *cythraul* is prophesied to come. God help me." He rubbed his aching temple with his fingers. "I'll consider giving Miss Tamony an interview once the *cythraul* has been dealt with. That's the most I'll promise. But I don't want you to give her the hope of such an interview occurring. It's more than likely I'll still refuse. For now, write and tell her that I wish to be left in peace, else the chance of any private meeting at another time will be nil. I expect I'll not be able to avoid meeting Miss Tamony in Society during the Season." The striking blue eyes fixed on Niclas intently. "I don't want her making scenes or bothering me—or any other members of the Seymour family—with her requests."

"Really, Malachi," said Niclas. "I can't think a woman of Miss Tamony's intellect and talent would do such a thing. She is the daughter of a gentleman, after all."

"She's a woman who apparently can't take 'no' for an answer," the earl replied. "And that's the most unpredictable kind of female on earth. But you must make her accept my answer, Niclas, at least for the remainder of the Season. I shall have done with the *cythraul* by then, and can set all my attention toward dealing with Miss Pestilence Tamony."

"I shall do my best," Niclas vowed.

"Do more than that," his cousin insisted. "For if you can't find the way in which to convince her to leave the Seymours in peace, I shall be obliged to overcome my aversion to placing enchantments on unsuspecting members of the *ton*, and will assuredly take matters into my own hands."

Chapter 2

*Y*ou must leave the man in peace now, Sarah." Julius Tamony looked over the top of the book he was reading, pinning his sister with a stern gaze. "I insist upon it. And if you won't listen to me, then I'll make certain that Father insists as well. One doesn't continue to harass a peer of the realm after so many firm refusals, unless one wishes to find oneself the worse for it. Especially not a peer like the Earl of Graymar."

Sarah responded with an amused laugh, countering Julius's unhappy look with one of affection and patience. "You are welcome to try with Father, Jules," she said, reaching for the jam pot and pulling it toward her, "but I doubt he'll give the matter more than five minutes of attention before turning his thoughts elsewhere. He's far more taken up with preparations for his speech before the London Antiquities Society than with any of my doings. Philla, dear, pass me those sausages, will you, please? Isn't the food at this inn wonderful? I do love a good English breakfast. It makes such a nice change from what we've had on the Continent."

Lifting the platter, Philistia did her cousin's bidding,

saying, "I do think you ought to leave Lord Graymar in peace, Sarah, just as Julius says. This last letter you've had from Mr. Niclas Seymour certainly does seem to be final regarding the matter. And it can't be very ladylike to press onward with your requests. From all that we've heard, the earl is terribly powerful among members of the *ton*. You shouldn't wish to have your only Season ruined because he's taken a dislike to you, do you?"

Sarah filled her plate with a number of sausages before setting the platter aside. "I really can't see why such a thing should happen. I doubt I'll set sight on the man again after I've had my interview with him. The Seymour family is far above the kind of society that we'll find ourselves in, my dear."

"But you're so famous, Sarah," Philistia said. "And so is Uncle Alberic. Aunt Speakley wrote that Society is all eagerness to meet you both. She's already been overwhelmed with invitations for all of us, and the Season doesn't even begin for many weeks."

"Stuff and nonsense," Sarah said, swallowing a mouthful of food. "Aunt Speakley, God bless her sweet soul, has been trying for so many years to get the *ton* to take notice of her that she believes an invitation to a card party is a social boon. I doubt anyone will care a whit about a family like ours, with a bent for writing about oddities. Especially now that Julius has joined the madness and written his unique perspective on the history of the Celts."

Julius peered over the top of the book once more. "It is not unique," he stated. "It is simply none of the popular romantic rot that's being put out today."

"People like romantic rot, dear," Sarah said, spearing a sausage with her fork. "It's far pleasanter to read about gallant warriors riding out to battle on their magnificent steeds and beautiful ladies dancing beneath a full moon than heads stuck on pikes or using the skulls of one's enemies as drinking vessels."

Julius's brow furrowed. "I fail to see why that should be so. The truth should always be preferable to mere perceptions, certainly to anyone possessed of a superior sense of reason."

Sarah smiled indulgently. "You would think so, dear. But never mind. There's no question that a great many scholars will receive the work with glowing appreciation."

"Of course they will," he stated, and went back to reading.

"But *your* books have been received by the public at large, Sarah," Philistia said. "And Uncle Alberic's have always been widely accepted, as well. And he's a baronet. Surely that means something to Society."

"Perhaps," Sarah said. "I really don't know. We've been gone from England for so long that I'm not sure what to expect. Papa's estate has been well managed in his absence, thankfully, and the books have ensured enough funds to allow us to rent a proper residence while we're in Town. I don't think we'll be a complete disgrace to Aunt Speakley. I hope we shall not, anywise. Will you be a dear and fill my cup with more coffee? Thank you, love."

"All will be well so long as you keep your distance from the Earl of Graymar," her brother said, not looking up this time. "And the rest of the Seymours. You have more than enough interviews arranged for your next book without having to speak with them."

"I have had a letter from the Earl of Llew," she said. "He's agreed to an interview, and even offered to lend me his aid in speaking with other members of his family. Which is truly very kind, for there are several ancestral Cadmarans on my research list. I'm especially interested to find out about one in particular," she went on, giving her attention back to her plate. "A fellow named Prothinus Cadmaran, who lived in the ninth century and set himself up in Ireland as some kind of magician who could help rid dwellings of unwanted evil spirits. For a price, of course." She glanced up at her cousin, who was daintily sipping a cup of hot chocolate. "I told you about him, do you remember, Philla? The one who got drunk and fell into a well one night? Several local villagers who saw him fall swore that he surely died, but they never found his body at the bottom, and years later it was discovered that Prothinus was living in another village, miles away, still practicing the art of spirit expulsion."

Julius uttered a derisive snort. "What you mean to say," he said, "is that some other fellow who looked like this Prothinus was living in a village miles away and was mistaken for the dead man. Any number of deceivers took money from the ignorant by claiming the power to rid them of curses and spirits. It could scarce be wondered at if untutored country folk started such rumors and spread them about. It was commonly done, even among the Celts."

"But, Julius, what happened to the body at the bottom of the well?" Philistia asked.

He considered for a moment before speaking. "The water must have been too deep for them to recover the corpse. Either that or the fellow had gotten into some kind of local trouble and run off, leaving the villagers to devise an explanation that made sense to them. That would account for someone who looked so like him appearing in another village. You see, Phil, there's always a logical explanation for these mysteries, just as I've always told you. Sarah's readers may fall for such fables, but anyone possessed of a reasonable intellect must seek out the truth."

Sarah frowned. Julius was so painfully practical in every matter. Like the rest of the world, he thought her books entertaining but untrue. It didn't matter that Sarah, herself, knew the reality of the supernatural world. She could never convince him or anyone else of it.

Philistia was thoughtful. "I suppose you must be right, Julius. But it is a fascinating tale, nonetheless."

Sarah gave her a grateful look. "Yes, it is," she said. "But much more so are the stories I've heard of ancient Seymours. One that I find particularly interesting relates the tale of Mistress Helen Seymour. She lived in the fifteenth century, in a small village near the border of Scotland. Her father was a baron, possessed of a fine manor and many acres of land, and her mother was distantly related to the king. Mistress Helen was their only child, and accounted a great beauty. She was also said to be a powerful sorceress."

Behind his book, Julius snorted again. Philistia's eyes widened and she leaned closer.

"Was she?" she whispered. "Truly?"

"It seems very likely," Sarah said. "She was able to change her form, you see, and turn herself into various creatures."

"Oh, my," said Philistia. "And she was a Seymour—the same family that is related to the present Earl of Graymar?"

Sarah nodded. "The very same, though of course there wasn't an Earl of Graymar then, for the family hadn't received the title. But this young woman, Mistress Helen, was observed by the villagers as leaving the baron's grand manor at night to wander through the forest—in the forms of different beasts, they claimed. She performed dark and terrible rituals and brought evil spirits to life, and if anyone dared to naysay or anger her she placed a curse upon them."

"How terrible!" Philistia said.

"Sarah," Julius muttered, "stop telling Phil such nonsense. Can't you see that she believes you? Save it for your books."

Sarah ignored him. "There was only one manner in which she could be taken and held captive," she went on, "and that was by the light of the bright midday sun, for then—and only then—was she powerless. But she never ventured out-of-doors during the daylight hours, and so the villagers had to devise a trick to get her past the threshold of her front door."

"What did they do?"

"Be careful of your plate, dear," Sarah warned, and Philistia, having bent so near the table, straightened to keep from staining her sleeve on a bit of jam. "Well, first, they waited until Mistress Helen's parents had gone to London to visit at court, and then they trapped a little dog that had been seen accompanying Mistress Helen into the forest at night. They tied the dog to a tree near the manor house and whipped it to make it cry—"

"Oh!" Philistia said, both hands flying to press against her cheeks.

"Sarah, don't frighten her," Julius warned.

"—and then they called to her, saying, 'Mistress Helen, come quickly! Your little dog has broken its leg.' And, hearing the poor dog's cries and the shouts of the people, out the door she came."

"What terrible deceivers."

"The moment Mistress Helen was out the door," Sarah said, "the villagers took her and bound her with ropes. They carried her to a stake with wood piled all about it and imprisoned her there."

Philistia's hands slowly dropped to her lap. Her eyes remained wide with distress.

"They burned her *alive*?"

"That was the way to be rid of a witch, was it not?" Sarah asked. "And they were quite certain she was one, though she protested her innocence and cried piteously for her mama and papa, for she was then but a young girl of ten and three years."

Philistia's eyes began to fill with tears, and Julius murmured another warning from behind his book.

"Mistress Helen pleaded with her captors to grant her one request, and because of her youth and beauty they agreed that, within reason, they would comply. She asked only that the little dog be brought to her so that she might touch it one last time, for it had been a dear companion to her. She begged her captors to give their solemn vow that they'd not set flame to the wood until she'd been able to pet the dog's head with her own hand. The villagers did as she asked, and made their vow before God. Having made such an oath, they could not then take it back, and that was the mistake they made in dealing with Mistress Helen Seymour."

"How so?" Philistia asked.

"Because the little dog, when untied, bit the man who'd whipped it and then ran off into the forest. Once inside the trees it led its pursuers on a merry chase, first showing itself and then running away, refusing to be caught until darkness had fallen."

"Thank heavens!" Philistia declared, much relieved. "And by then Lady Helen had gained her powers and was able to escape."

Sarah smiled and nodded. "She did, and was. She transformed into a sleek black cat and disappeared into the forest, and neither she nor the dog was ever seen again. The baron and his good lady returned to the village only long enough to pack their belongings and close the grand manor. And, it's said, to also lay a curse upon the villagers who had tried to murder their daughter. For once the Seymours left that village, it slowly began to die. The land failed to yield any crops and the water in the river and village wells dried up. In time, the village ceased to exist, as all who lived there were forced to move elsewhere to find work and food."

"And what happened to Mistress Helen and her family?" Philistia asked.

"They went to London, where the Seymour family had established itself as a great political power, and where Helen's cousin, Mistress Glenys, oversaw the Seymour shipping concerns and other businesses. They had built their grand palace, Mervaille, along the Thames and become favorites of the court, despite having stood firmly with Glendower during the Welsh uprising some years earlier. But the Seymours were very wealthy, you see, and the king cared far more about that than the Welsh loyalty they so insistently displayed. When Glenys married and took up residence with her husband at Glain Tarran, in Pembrokeshire, Mistress Helen took charge of Mervaille and became famous throughout London for her great charm and beauty. She had many romances with numerous dashing noblemen before at last falling in love with a wild Scotsman named MacQueen, who swept her off her feet and took her back to the Highlands to live in his impoverished castle. They had nine children, and those children had children, and the MacQueens have been closely tied to their Seymour cousins ever since." Sarah picked up her coffee cup. "I have a great many stories about them to investigate, as well."

"How romantic!" Philistia declared happily. "And did Mistress Helen continue to transform into other creatures?" Philistia asked. "Even while in London?"

"Philistia!" Julius admonished sternly, peering over the top of his book. "She did not truly transform herself. That is an impossibility, as you very well know."

"Yes, Julius," Philistia replied obediently.

"This is particularly why you must give up on your pursuit of the Seymours," Julius told his sister, who had given her attention back to her breakfast. "You're clearly obsessed with them beyond rational thought."

"I certainly am," Sarah agreed. "But if you only knew some of what I've turned up in my research, you'd be fascinated, too. Well," she amended at his astonished expression, "perhaps not. But they are fascinating. Their history is going to make the most wonderful part of my book."

"You'll have to find some other way of ferreting out your facts about the Seymours than speaking with them personally. What about that fellow in London who knows so much about your subjects? The professor?" Julius prompted at her blank expression. "You gave me some of his books to read. Seabolt or some such."

"Oh yes! Professor Harris Seabolt. I forgot to tell you. I had a response from him last week, when you and Father left us at Bamburgh to make your visit to the Celtic sites at Lindisfarne. The professor was pleased to have my request, and has agreed to help me in any way that he can. Which is the most wonderful thing, for I doubt there's another man in all of England who knows as much about the history of the supernatural as he. And he's arranged for me to speak to the London Society for the Study of the Mystical and Supernatural—does that not sound like a wonderful gathering?" Her voice betrayed her excitement. "I vow I cannot wait to meet with others who share my passion for such things."

"It does sound exciting," Philistia agreed halfheartedly. "But I hope we'll be invited to dances and parties, as well, just as Aunt Speakley wrote."

The wistful tone in her younger cousin's voice made Sarah pause. It hadn't occurred to her until this moment that Philistia might not be viewing their visit to London in the same manner as the rest of them were. For Sarah it was an opportunity to interview the descendants of those ancient individuals she intended to write about, to do additional research for her next work, and to spend time with others, like Professor Seabolt, who shared her passion for the supernatural. For her father it was a chance to accept an award from the Antiquities Society in recognition of his work and to see old friends and acquaintances. For her mother it would mean several weeks with her sister, their Aunt Speakley, whom she'd not seen in years, and for Julius it would merely be a trip to another large metropolitan city possessed of numerous museums and galleries with which to fill his days. But for Philistia, Sarah realized, London meant something entirely different.

Philistia had lived and traveled with them since she was a young girl, after her parents had both died of the influenza. She was far more like a sister to both Sarah and Julius than a mere cousin, though she was so different from the entire Tamony family as to seem completely unrelated. She was small and delicate, rather than tall, as the Tamonys were, and was blessed with soft brown hair rather than the horrid auburn that Sarah despised. Only Julius had escaped the red-tinged hues that crowned the rest of the family, and although his dark chestnut hair wasn't the most striking aspect of his handsome person, Sarah had always thought him tremendously fortunate in possessing it. Philistia was also the only member of the family who wasn't obliged to wear spectacles, yet another blessing as far as Sarah was concerned.

Unfortunately, poor, sweet Philistia also had no bent for any of the pursuits that drove the studious Tamonys and was obliged to spend her days trotting after them as they read, researched, and wrote. But she was repaid for such drudgery by the social life that the family enjoyed. Their fame abroad had made the Tamonys desirable guests in every corner of the Continent, with the result that seldom an evening went by that Philistia didn't find herself at a ball or festive gathering. Those were the moments the younger woman lived for.

But despite such a steady diet of entertainment, London held out the promise of something far more important. These would be English people she would be in company with and Englishmen whom she would dance with. For the first time in her life, Philistia would be able to cast lures for the kind of husband she dreamed of having—a proper British gentleman who spoke her language and understood her sense of English propriety.

"I'm sure that we will," Sarah assured her. "And we'll have new gowns made, shall we? The ones we had from France two years ago are probably long out of fashion. We'll go shopping for everything we'll need—shoes and gloves and hats. Mama will enjoy that. She always does."

"What's this?" Lady Tamony said as she entered the private dining room, followed by her husband. "What is it that I'll enjoy?"

Julius stood to greet his parents, and Philistia leaped up to grasp her aunt's hands.

"Shopping!" Philistia said happily. "For the things we'll need in London. You do remember, don't you, Aunt Caroline? Aunt Speakley wrote that we'll be invited everywhere, to the most wonderful parties and balls and dinners."

Lady Tamony patted Philistia's hand. "Of course we'll be going out into Society. I've written your aunt and informed her that I intend for both of my girls to have proper come-outs."

"Oh, Mama, how foolish," Sarah said as her father bent to kiss her cheek. "I'm far too old for such nonsense. Philistia must certainly have a true Season, however. She'll catch the eye of every man in Town."

Philistia blushed and took her seat, saying, "What a shameful fib."

"Now, now, what's this?" Sir Alberic said, kissing his niece. "Sarah's quite right, as always. Our little Philla will be snatched up as soon as we reach London if we're not keeping watch, eh, Jules? What's that you're reading?"

"The *Life of Cromwell,* by Southey," Julius replied, a note of approval in his tone. "It's not so good as the one he did of Nelson, but worth reading, nonetheless."

"I should like to borrow it when you've finished," Sir Alberic said, smiling at his wife as she filled his cup with coffee. "Thank you, my dear. Well then." He looked at each person sitting at the table. "We've seen all there is to see in Cheshire, I would wager, unless there's some minor historical sight of great interest that one of you would like to propose to me. If not, shall we go into Wales, proper, next? I know you've a special interest in some of the Celtic relics there, Julius, and Sarah's been talking of nothing else since we arrived back in England." Sir Alberic glanced at his daughter. "She's anxious to do research for her next book. And, of course, I should like to see the handiwork left behind by the Romans once again."

"I particularly wish to visit Pembrokeshire, Papa," Sarah said.

"*No,*" Julius said firmly. "You're not to bother the Earl of Graymar, Sarah. Most especially while he's in residence. You shouldn't be allowed within ten miles of his estate." He turned to his parents. "She's had a letter just this morning from Mr. Niclas Seymour, cousin and man of business to the Earl of Graymar, stating that His Lordship has no desire to speak to Sarah and requesting that she leave both him and the rest of the Seymour family in peace in the matter of her research."

"We have no way of knowing whether His Lordship is in residence at Glain Tarran," Sarah countered. "It's very likely that he remained in London, rather than brave the harsh winter in the country. I should merely like to discover whether the house is open for visitors. And you'd enjoy seeing it as well, Jules, for I've heard rumors that the estate hides marvelous ancient ritual grounds similar to those at Stonehenge, and—"

"Oh, come now," Julius said. "You can't believe that's so. How in heaven's name would the Seymours keep such a thing hidden from public knowledge? Stonehenge indeed. It's ridiculous. I suppose you heard that from one of those sorcerers or witches you love to write about."

Sarah could feel herself blush. "Yes, I did," she told him. "From several sources, as it happens, and all in remarkably similar detail. I should think you of all people would want to see whether the rumors are true."

Julius gave his parents a knowing look. "Ten miles," he said. "We make certain to keep her at least that far from Glain Tarran, and keep a strict eye on her even then. We don't want to anger a peer of Lord Graymar's standing before we arrive in London. He could stop my book from being published," Julius said forebodingly, "and keep the Antiquities Society from having anything at all do to with you, sir. Not even Sarah's recent fame would be able to save us from his reach."

Sarah rolled her eyes and muttered, "For pity's sake, he's but an earl. One of many, and hardly so powerful as all that."

"Oh, my dear," said their mother, "I'm afraid Julius has the right of it. The Seymours have always been a most influential family. You've been away from England for so many years that you wouldn't know how true that is, but your father and I remember far better. Can't you find a way to leave them out of your writing, Sarah? We shouldn't want to ruin Philistia's only opportunity for a proper Season."

Philistia turned wide eyes on her cousin, silently pleading.

Sarah looked into her coffee cup. "Very well," she said after a moment of silence, choosing her words with care. "If it means so much to all of you, and if you can't have enough faith in me to let me sort the matter out on my own—as I have always done before, mind you—I shall simply have to cross the Earl of Graymar off my list of planned interviews."

"That's fine, dear," Sir Alberic declared, pleased. "Then we'll head into Wales without any fears, shall we? I'll make the arrangements after breakfast and we'll leave on the morrow. At this rate we should be in London in good time for the Season, and then all of my ladies can buy themselves some pretty new things. How does that sound to you, Philla? I know you're anxious to get to Town. Can you put up with our wild wanderings for a few more weeks?"

Philistia beamed at him from across the table. "Yes, Uncle. I shall be more than happy to do so."

"There's a good girl," he said approvingly. "Now, Sarah, remember what you've promised. Leave the Earl of Graymar in peace."

Sarah smiled sweetly over the rims of her spectacles and said, "I shall keep my promise, Papa." It didn't seem wise to point out that she'd promised only to cease planning an interview with the Earl of Graymar. She'd said nothing at all about leaving the man in peace . . . and hadn't the least intention of doing so.

Chapter 3

$\mathcal{M}$orcar Cadmaran, the Earl of Llew, surveyed his guests in silence. They stood in the magnificent great hall of Castle Llew before the dais upon which he sat, all of them clearly nervous and unsettled. Save one: Serafina Daray. She had brought them here, the heads of those clans who embraced darker magic, to face Morcar, the lord to whom they had all given allegiance, and to challenge him for his place of power.

Serafina stood with a pleasant smile upon her lips, looking as if she'd arrived to partake of tea with the powerful Earl of Llew rather than to attempt to overthrow him.

She was the most deceptive sorceress he had ever known, powerful and cunning and deadly within, and perfectly practiced innocence without. She was dainty and extraordinarily beautiful, with short blond curls and wide blue eyes that gave the impression of sweet helplessness. Men were lured by her fragile demeanor and delicate femininity, deceived by her ability to make them feel necessary to her happiness, and quickly enslaved by the enchantments she placed on them. Serafina knew precisely how long she could play with the hearts she took captive before the Guardians who ruled as judges over all magic mortals would punish her, and always willingly released her victims. If those same men went away broken, it only amused her the more. Like all who enjoyed dark magic, Serafina understood the pleasure that came from using mere mortals for her own purposes.

Morcar had always admired Serafina's methods, similar as they were to his own, and appreciated her powers. They had been lovers for a brief time and enjoyed each other considerably. She hated the Seymours as greatly as he did, especially Malachi, the Dewin Mawr who held the allegiance of those magic mortals who so foolishly sought redemption rather than even greater power. Morcar would have been content to let their relationship continue, but Serafina had made it clear that she had no wish to simply be a mistress, not even to the one who ruled over the dark Families. Her ambitions were far more significant.

"What a pleasant, if unexpected, surprise," he said, surveying his visitors one by one, looking into each of their faces until they turned away. He came last to Serafina, who continued to smile up at him as sweetly as a child. She was dressed, in stark contrast to her companions and to Morcar himself, nearly all in white. Unlike most of those in the dark Families, Serafina had ever favored soft, light colors. They aided in the deception she played out among the *ton* and helped hide the truth of her immense powers. The gown she wore now, partly covered by a pink-trimmed redingote, was a flowing confection of lace and frills. Her blond curls were tied with pink satin ribbons, framing a sweet-looking, heart-shaped face of delicate beauty. Standing behind such an angelic apparition, the collection of sorcerers looked more like a flock of overbearing ravens.

"You are not in the least surprised, my lord," Serafina replied, and Morcar was struck by how perfectly her voice matched her appearance and demeanor. It was soft and high-pitched, filled with feminine music. "You were aware of our presence the moment we crossed Llew's borders."

"Oh, long before that," he said, waving one hand lazily

in the air. "So large a contingent of wizards can scarce move unnoticed, even many miles away. I could but wonder why you were coming to Llew when I had not called you. It must be a matter of grave import for so many of you to make the journey. Glasson, Hazelton, Moran, Craddick." Morcar looked at each as he said his name. "You even managed to persuade Thorne to come out of his hiding place in Northumberland, which is a feat not easily accomplished. I congratulate you, Serafina. I suppose I should be grateful that you weren't able to convince all of the Families to join you here. Or am I mistaken and can we expect Terrill and Collingsgate to arrive shortly? I know well that no Cadmaran would dare such a betrayal."

"Unfortunately," she said, folding her gloved hands in a demure manner, "they declined to accompany us. They retained faith in you, Morcar, just as your own family has done, foolish as that was. I'm sure you would be touched by their loyalty if such feelings were possible for our kind."

"I am lord over all our Families," Morcar said. "They owe me their loyalty, as you all do. Unless you wish to give your allegiance to the great Dewin Mawr." He smiled darkly.

"There are other choices available to us, Morcar," she said. "The Darays and many of the others"—she waved a hand at the men behind her—"have grown weary of having a lord who has done so little for our kind since he came into power. We have lost much and gained nothing, especially in the past two years."

Morcar's eyes narrowed. She was right, of course. He had made a great many mistakes of late. But he wasn't going to admit the truth of that or let her use those mistakes to pull him from his place of power.

"The Cadmarans have led the dark Families from the time of the exile," he said quietly. "The place of power is ours, and I will not give it up because of some mewling complaints."

An ugly expression briefly crossed Serafina's delicate features, transforming her beautiful face into something momentarily frightening. It passed as quickly as it came, and she mastered herself into mock innocence once more.

"You've done nothing to bring down the Seymours," she said softly, moving to stand at the very edge of the dais. "And you've failed in every attempt you've made to destroy the Great Sorcerer. You were even blinded by one attempt, punished by the Guardians for battling Niclas Seymour. But we accepted that, for your intention was to kill a Seymour, and we would have been glad if you had succeeded. But then, when you might have rightfully challenged the brother of Kian Seymour, you not only failed but gave way in a manner that brought shame to us all."

One of Malachi's hands curled into a fist. "I regained my sight by doing so," he said tightly. "The Guardians had blinded me for using my powers to try to kill Niclas Seymour. They plunged me into darkness and I was left alone to discover the way out again. None of you came to my aid," he said, fixing his dark gaze on those who stood behind Serafina. "Only the Cadmarans, my own clan, gave me their loyalty. The rest of you abandoned me—the lord to whom you had given allegiance. I had lived my life only to protect and serve all of the dark Families, yet when the curse fell upon me you waited and stayed away, hoping that it would bring me to an end. Unfortunately for you, my powers remained undimmed, and after two years passed I found the way to break the curse and regain my vision."

"By giving the Seymours a gift of tremendous value," Serafina charged. "You might have killed Dyfed Seymour without punishment, for he stole away the woman who had been given to you by solemn vow—an extraordinary sorceress possessed of immense powers who would have brought much to our Families with her dark magic. But you freely gave her to the Seymours!"

"Desdemona was in love with Dyfed Seymour," Morcar told Serafina, holding at bay the pain of the memory. He had come as close to loving Desdemona Caslin, daughter of the powerful American sorcerer Draceous Caslin, as he had ever come to loving a woman. She had been brought to Wales to be Morcar's bride and he had believed her to be his perfect mate, for her heart was as dark and cold as his own. "They were *unoliaeth*," he said. "Fated for each other. You know as well as I that the *unoliaeth* cannot be denied, even by a vow made before the Guardians. I could have held her captive forever, but she would have refused to become one of us. I believe she would have chosen death over being parted from Dyfed. By giving her to him freely I regained my vision—it would have been foolish to throw away such a chance in order to keep an unwilling sorceress beneath my hand."

"You gained much, aye," Serafina agreed, "but the rest of us gained nothing, and lost much. You were so fixed on your own troubles that you let Tauron slip away, beyond our reach. He turned to the Dewin Mawr for aid, and Malachi sent him to America, where Draceous Caslin has taken him beneath his protection. We might have borne the loss of a great sorceress like Desdemona Caslin, but the loss of Tauron has been the final blow. How can we continue to trust you after such a defeat at the hands of the Seymours?"

Morcar drew in a slow breath and forced himself to think clearly, to not let his features betray his emotions.

Aye, the loss of Tauron, coming so quickly on the heels of Desdemona's defection, had been a terrible thing. Worse, it had been a betrayal that Morcar should have foretold, but his pride had blinded him more fully than the Guardians had done.

His younger cousin, Tauron, had been born with the ability of transmutation and was capable of altering objects and substances into other forms. It was an uncommon gift, found among magic mortals perhaps once every thousand years, and, by good fortune, it had come to the Cadmarans.

Tauron had made the dark Families wealthy beyond all measure by changing common metals into gold and silver and had brought them foreboding power with his ability to make poisons out of mere water or to turn human flesh into stone. Aye, he'd been a valuable asset and Morcar had drained every bit of benefit possible from him, starting from the moment when Tauron could control his gift. He'd been but a child then, but that hadn't mattered in the least. It wasn't the way of the dark clans to care for anything beyond gaining power, for power was security and victory. Without it they would perish.

It hadn't occurred to Morcar that Tauron would long to be free of such a life, that he would even dare to escape the reach of his kind. But Malachi Seymour had known and had helped the lad to not only get out of England but also make it to the States, where Draceous Caslin had taken Tauron beneath his care. It would be impossible to wrest Tauron away and bring him back, for he had given Draceous his allegiance by making an oath before the Guardians, and such an oath could not be altered.

"So, now we are obliged to support ourselves as we once did before Tauron was born," Morcar told them. "Is that what you've come to complain about?"

Their silence was his answer. It was all he could do to keep from giving way to the scorn he felt.

"It needn't be a bad thing for our Families," he told them. "We had become lazy, depending upon Tauron for our wealth. Our lands have gone unused for far too long, and our skills in making our own way have become dull. Generations of Cadmarans and Darays and all the others once used to strive as hard as, aye, even harder than any Seymour or MacQueen or Bowdon in order to hold our place in the world."

Serafina looked at him as if he had lost his senses. She set one small booted foot upon the bottom stair of the dais and leaned forward, holding Morcar's gaze.

"This is precisely why you are no longer fit to be our lord. You speak of losing such power as if it could possibly be a good thing, when all it has done is weaken us. If we do not have power, then we become vulnerable to the world, and we die. Have you forgotten how our kind suffered at the hands of mere mortals because they were weak? How many spirits were sent to judgment through fire and water, by stones or knives or at the end of a rope? The Families banded together for protection, for survival, and only our great powers have kept us safe."

The words stung and Morcar stood, towering over them. "It is because of the might of the Cadmarans that our Families survived," he said angrily. "We have not been overlords in name only, but have ever been the first to fight, suffer, even die for the dark clans. I will *not* give way."

Serafina gave a single shake of her head, a movement that sent her silken curls bobbing. Her blue eyes glittered with unconcealed scorn.

"You may not be given the choice," she said.

"We come to it at last, then," he said slowly, gazing at the assembled. The wizards had lowered their heads once more, while Serafina's gaze remained bold. "Your true purpose in coming. Not to merely lay complaints at my feet, but to challenge me as head over our Families. And who will take my place? You, Serafina? A Daray?" Unpleasant laughter escaped his lips. He looked at those standing behind her. "I might have expected someone from almost any of the other clans, but can you truly mean to give your allegiance to a *Daray*?"

The wizards shifted uncomfortably beneath Morcar's derision; Serafina's delicate white skin turned a vivid red.

"The Darays are as powerful as the Cadmarans," she said hotly. "We are an ancient family, of noble descent—"

"Noble descent!" Morcar repeated, laughing more heartily. "The Darays? You have a gift for twisting a lie until it sounds true, Serafina, but that is far too great a stretch even for a master of deception. You are *animantis*, created by the One who made all as servants to your betters," he said, watching with satisfaction as fury distorted her features. "The Darays will *always* be creaturely, no matter how often your kind mixes with the *superum*, nor how closely you come to resemble humans."

"But we have strengthened our blood with such mixing, have we not, Morcar?" she asked angrily. "By the foolishness and weaknesses of the *superum*, and because we became the most beautiful of those cast out of the spirit realm. More beautiful even than the descendants of Mactus, who in time came to call themselves Seymour, and far more beautiful than Osor, the father of the Cadmarans. They used us for their pleasure, to fulfill their bidding, but we were wiser than any of the pure-blooded ones. We waited and watched and learned the power of beauty, how foolish it can make even the strongest of the *superum*." Serafina's pretty mouth curved into a mocking smile. "We drew them to our beds to steal their seed until the blood of the Darays was as powerful as any among the magical Families."

"Powerful, aye," Morcar said, "but you are still *animantis*. You can never be pure enough to rule over the dark Families. And your powers will never match mine, great though they may be. Not even all of you combined," he said, looking at those who stood behind her, "can overtake me. You should have tried it while I was blind, Serafina. You might have had a chance, then."

"Aye," she murmured, "we should. It was not for a lack of desire on my part, Morcar, I promise you. The others needed proof of your weakness before they would agree to come together. You provided it just as soon as Tauron departed our shores, and after, when you did nothing to return him to us."

Morcar gazed at her for a silent moment before saying, "We cannot have him back, Serafina. Draceous Caslin is my equal in power, and more than able to handle a sorceress of your skill. Tauron alone can decide whether he will return to us or not, and considering the manner in which we treated him, I very much doubt that he'll ever be eager to see us, or England, again."

"But he will, nonetheless," she said, the smile on her face widening. "And not even Draceous Caslin, powerful though he may be, will be able to hold him."

Morcar's eyes narrowed. "You have such a love of games, Serafina, but I've grown too weary for playing. Speak plainly."

A spark of excitement flared in her gaze.

"The *cythraul* is coming soon," she said. "Have you remembered it, Morcar? Have you even begun to prepare for it? The demon spirit comes but once every hundred years to test the mettle of our kind. Since the time of the exile the Cadmarans have failed to leash the great powers that the demon brings, to bring *us* that power." She lifted a small gloved hand and made a fist. "If they'd not failed it would have been our clans who held the greatest power among magic mortals, not the Seymours."

"I know the history of the demon," Morcar said in a low tone. "Indeed, I have thought of little else since regaining my sight. The *cythraul* will be my means of at last dealing with the Seymours. With its power I shall take Malachi's place as Dewin Mawr, and the Seymours will be ruined forever."

"Aye, they will be," she vowed, her voice softer now. "But you will not be the one to leash the power of the demon. It will be I who becomes its master, and I who takes the place of power over the Families. No magic mortal living will be able to gainsay me then, Morcar. Not you, not Malachi Seymour, and certainly not Draceous Caslin. Those who support me now will be the better for it. Those who are so foolish as to oppose me will be much the worse. I make this vow before the Guardians."

Morcar steadied himself. It was a formal challenge, then, declared before the Guardians. He could do nothing but accept, despite wanting, instead, to fling his uninvited guests into the far wall. He briefly envisioned Serafina's delicate body impaled upon a particularly large medieval spear that hung over the fireplace, but forced the thought aside.

"You're a fool, Serafina Daray," he told her. "You may be able to find a suitable mortal to offer up for the *cythraul*'s possession, but you'll have no way of knowing when or where it will arrive. The signs are given only to those who are in places of great power. It is a test of our mettle, just as you said."

"A test that the Cadmarans have always lost," she said

bitterly, "and the Seymours won. Malachi will send the demon back to its realm and the dark Families will remain second to the Dewin Mawr's powers for another hundred years."

"He'll not," Morcar vowed. "Not this time."

Serafina laughed, a high, chilling sound.

"You'll never best Malachi," she declared. "You never have and never will. But I can best the both of you, and when I have, the dark clans will at last have the power we've craved. The world will live beneath our sway, and no one, not even the Guardians, will be able to take such power from us."

Chapter 4

*W*ill there be anything else this evening, my lord?"

Malachi looked up from where he stood near the tall windows in his study. "No, Rhys. I'm content, thank you."

The butler made a long-practiced bow, giving Malachi a brief view of the white halo of hair atop the older man's head. Rhys had served the Seymour family nearly all of his life, just as his father had done, and had been born at Glain Tarran some seventy years ago. He was a mere mortal, one of the valuable sympathetics the Families depended upon to help them exist in a non-magic world. Rhys was also often the keeper of Malachi's sanity, the one he trusted to hold the world at bay when the Earl of Graymar sought peace and respite within the borders of his several estates. Especially at Glain Tarran.

The land was, and had been since before memory, a refuge for those possessed of magic. Even Mervaille, the Seymours' grand palace and place of safety in London, though Malachi loved it well, could never be what Glain Tarran was. This was the land that the children of Mactus had chosen as their home, where they had built their first dwellings, mimicking the native Celts, and had later

erected a medieval fortress in the time of William, then a
magnificent castle during the first Henry's reign, and finally, when Elizabeth ruled, the manor that made Glain
Tarran one of the most acclaimed estates in all of Great
Britain. Generations of Seymours had defended Glain Tarran and kept it safe from those who would scarce understand the secrets the land held. The land, in return, repaid
the favor.

Malachi wished he might remain longer, renewing his
mind and spirit with the aid of the elements. Each day and
night spent beside the wild sea, buffeted by salty winds and
chilled by thick fog, the rain pouring down as a sweet release of heaven, was surcease from life's pressures. After
so many weary months in London, serving in his position
as the Earl of Graymar as well as fulfilling the demands of
being Dewin-Mawr, he craved the succor that he found
only here. And needed it, too.

It was lonely at Glain Tarran, of course, despite the
presence of the servants and the occasional visits by
friends and relatives. But loneliness followed him everywhere he went, even to London. It was a part of his life that
Malachi had not yet found a remedy to. He'd long since
given up hope of finding a wife among his own kind, and
he'd not been blessed, as both his cousins Niclas and Kian
had been, with a wife from among sympathetic mere mortals. Malachi's mistress in London, Augusta, was one of
their sympathetics as well as a woman of excellent lineage.
He had considered her a suitable candidate to be his countess once upon a time, but when Malachi had broached the
subject of a more permanent union, Augusta had made it
clear that though she held him in great affection and
wished to keep him as a lover, she'd experienced enough
of marriage with her dearly departed husband to satisfy
her for all eternity. More than that, she had no desire to
bind herself to a magic mortal and take on all the difficulties that such a life required.

Malachi had tried to tell himself that he'd not been
too terribly disappointed, but that wasn't entirely true.

Augusta was an excellent companion and not given to a great deal of foolishness, as so many females were. He had thought that, perhaps, they might at least keep each other from feeling too solitary as the years passed. But it was not to be. He was now thirty-six and rapidly becoming an antiquity. There were no women near his own age whom he felt drawn to, and he no longer possessed the patience to deal with younger females for more than an hour or so at a time.

It was for the best, Malachi thought philosophically. He was too busy with his various duties to be a proper husband to anyone. God alone knew how often he was obliged to depart on but a moment's notice to handle some difficulty or other for one of the Families. What woman would want her husband disappearing in the middle of a ball or party, not knowing whether he'd reappear within an hour or perhaps not for several days? And such emergencies always seemed to happen far more regularly during the Season, when it was most difficult for Malachi to get away and when his frequent absences were so often noted. It was as if all the mischief makers among the Families suddenly sprang into action the moment Malachi set foot in London proper—which was another good reason for remaining at Glain Tarran.

But he could not stay in his private paradise much longer. Niclas had already returned to London and expected Malachi to follow soon. Parliament would begin meeting in a few weeks and the Earl of Graymar was a prominent member. There were several important matters to give attention to this year. France and Spain were on the verge of war, and the situation in Ireland was growing dire. Those members of the Families there who gave him their allegiance would expect Malachi to lend them his aid, and he was ready to do so, both outside of Parliament and in it, despite the unpopularity of his views. More important even than these were the prison reforms to be voted upon in the coming session. Malachi had longed to use magic to sway the obstinate mere mortals in Parliament to vote in the manner he thought best, but the Guardians would have punished him for using his powers to meddle in the governmental affairs of earth's true citizens. It was very frustrating. Now, however, enough of them had begun to see the rightness of such reforms, and he meant to be there to cast his vote and see them come about.

Fortunately, there were to be no come-outs among the Seymour family this Season, else he and Niclas would be obliged to keep a close eye on whichever young relative had been brought to Town to be presented. The young wizards and sorceresses of their kind were always so careless and unrestrained in controlling their magical powers; keeping them in line and out of trouble was an exhausting undertaking. And it was a miracle, truly, that none of them had so badly erred while out in Society that many mere mortals had become suspicious. Those few who did had been dealt with easily enough, though Malachi disliked altering memories, necessary as it was. It seemed unsporting to take people by surprise and change their thoughts to a previous place in time. They could never fight back and stop him, after all.

Malachi felt, rather than heard, the gust of wind coming before it struck the window, lightly rattling the pane. He set a hand against the cold glass to pull the sensation into himself and closed his eyes with pleasure. The wind blew fiercely tonight, as it had done so many nights in the past weeks. He longed to be out in the dark, cold air, to let the wind flow over him, caressing, lifting him into the sky to become one with its wildness. So high that he would only see Glain Tarran and the village some miles away as small specks of light, incomparable to the glittering stars and gleaming moon in tonight's crystalline sky. Aye, a few hours drifting in the heavens, transported beyond every care, that was what he wanted just now. He'd spent many such midnight hours since coming to Glain Tarran coursing over both land and lake, getting thoroughly soaked and cold and coming home at dawn to find a most unhappy and disapproving Rhys waiting for him with a hot bath and warm food at the ready.

But such pleasant evenings must come to an end, he told himself firmly, opening his eyes as yet another gust caused the pane to tremble. He would leave in but a few days' time, directly after Saint David's Day, which he could not miss celebrating with his people. Apart from Parliament, there was Miss Sarah Tamony to be dealt with and, above and beyond anything else, the *cythraul.* The former he didn't wish to think about until he was faced with her in person, but the latter . . . that was on his mind almost without respite. He even dreamed of the demon's coming, which made for an unpleasant night's sleep.

Malachi had always realized that he would very likely have to face the evil spirit. Only a youthful death—definitely not a desirable alternative—would have put the unpleasant task into the hands of the next Dewin Mawr.

His great-grandfather Hollace Seymour had been the last Great Sorcerer to face and defeat a *cythraul.* The tale of his courage and wisdom was still told to children in the Families, for Hollace had managed to stop the *cythraul* at its moment of arrival upon earth, not even allowing the demon the time to inhabit the body of a mere mortal before sending it back to the spirit realm. The Dewin Mawr who had dealt with the test a hundred years before that had not been so adroit, and the spirit had not only inhabited a mortal body but also been able to roam freely for three full days, wreaking terrible havoc in the small English villages it visited before at last being vanquished.

Despite the certainty he'd offered Niclas the night before, thoughts of the *cythraul* wrought an unfamiliar sense of unease in Malachi. He'd known, even as a child, how powerful he was in the way of magic and had been entirely comfortable with that knowledge. The mantle of Dewin Mawr, when it had come to him, had fit as easily as if he'd always worn it. And if he'd had the understandable moment or two of panic in his life, especially when faced with particularly trying circumstances—which was not to be wondered at considering the dangers their kind faced— those moments had passed so quickly that he could scarce recall them.

But the *cythraul* gave Malachi pause. He had faced demons before and overcome them with a measure of ease, though these, admittedly, had been far less powerful than the *cythraul* would be. His confidence had carried him through such times. But this visitation was a test, sent by the Guardians for a purpose, and Malachi was required not only to deal with the creature but to find it as well. Signs would be given to both himself and Morcar Cadmaran, and then it would be a race as to who could first divine the signs' meaning and reach the place where the *cythraul* would arrive, thereafter deciding the demon's fate. None of this concerned Malachi, either, for conceit apart, he knew himself to be far more clever than Morcar Cadmaran had ever been or could hope to be. What troubled Malachi was the fact that the *cythraul* was to arrive sometime during the spring and yet not one sign had thus far been given him.

He suspected that there was a reason behind the delay, just as there was a reason—even if not immediately evident—to everything that the Guardians did. If they wished to test him, this was certainly the way to go about it. His confidence was shaken . . . only a little, but shaken all the same. He didn't like the feeling at all.

"Oh dear, Sarah. I don't like this at all." Philistia paced nervously before the fireplace in the room that she shared with her cousin. "Julius is going to be so angry, to say nothing of Aunt Caroline and Uncle Alberic."

Sarah smiled reassuringly and put one last knot into the laces of her left boot. "It's no different than all of the other times when I've gone out on my own," she said. "Have you forgotten Vienna and Copenhagen? Or that night in Florence"—Sarah gave a happy sigh—"when that delightful stranger saved me from those assailants and then took me to visit the gypsies?"

Philistia's cheeks paled. "Don't speak of it," she begged. "It's precisely such incidents that give me nightmares. You were attacked that night, Sarah. You might have been"—she lowered her voice to a whisper—"ravished. Or even killed. Or both."

"That's true," Sarah admitted honestly, finishing with the other boot and standing to smooth the front of her boy's jacket. "But I wasn't, and the trouble was well worth the risk, for the gypsies told me such fascinating stories. I used all of them in my last book, remember?" She bent to pick up the heavy coat that lay across the bed. "I have a feeling tonight is going to be another such success. You can almost touch the magic here," she said, shrugging awkwardly into the warm garment. "The sense of it is so strong. I haven't felt anything this intense since that night when I met with the sorceress of Aberdeen who sold me so many enchantments."

Philistia hurried to help her. "I wish you wouldn't speak of magic," she said, tugging the sleeves up Sarah's arms. "You know how it distresses your brother and parents. They'll be so unhappy with me if they discover that I've let you go out alone in the middle of the night. Especially to Glain Tarran. Please, Sarah, wait until the morning. I'll go with you to Glain Tarran and we'll see if we can't speak with Lord Graymar." Another hard tug brought the coat up about Sarah's neck. "Surely we'll be able to find a way to hire a vehicle for a drive—we'll tell your parents we want to see something of the countryside. They'll believe us, for it is very beautiful, after all." Pulling on the laces, she began to tie the front of the garment. "And if we make certain to return in good time, no one will be suspicious that we've gone to Glain Tarran. Don't you think that's a far wiser plan than you going now, in the dark of night, all alone?"

"No, I don't," Sarah replied calmly, setting both hands on her delicate cousin's shoulders to force her into stillness. "You know full well that Mama and Papa and Julius are determined to keep me from Glain Tarran. I had the devil of a time simply getting them to journey this near the Earl of Graymar's estate."

"But it's still five miles away, Sarah," Philistia said with distress. "It's so terribly dark and cold outside, to say nothing of this awful wind. You'll take fever and fall ill, and how will I ever explain it to Aunt Caroline?"

"If I managed to live through that dreadful night in Martigny—do you recall that deluge of freezing rain?—I can certainly survive a windy night in Pembrokeshire."

"But what if Lord Graymar should discover that you've come to Glain Tarran uninvited? He's gone to such lengths to tell you that he doesn't wish to speak with you. He'll be furious."

Sarah took up the boy's cap that accompanied her on all her nightly adventures and began to push her hair up beneath it, taking care not to dislodge her spectacles.

"I'm only going to see whether the rumors of ancient ceremonial grounds on the property are true. Even the servants at the inn say they exist, and the women I met in the village this afternoon were able to give me an idea of their location. And if Lord Graymar should discover me there," she added with a smile as she reached for her gloves, "I shall simply do my utmost to charm him into giving me an interview this very night. Which would serve especially well since I could truthfully tell Papa that it wasn't planned and I hadn't broken my promise. What a wonderful boon it would be to have the earl's perspective before we achieve London. I could start the book right away."

Philistia shook her head. "The Earl of Graymar's not like the others you've swayed, Sarah. He's already proven to be immune to your appeals. He'll not give way so quickly."

"That's likely true," Sarah agreed, pushing her spectacles more firmly upon her small nose as she examined herself in the room's long mirror. "In which case," she went on, "I shall simply have to make certain that I'm not discovered." Satisfied, she gave a single nod and turned to pick up her battered knapsack. Moving to the rear open window, she lowered her voice. "Go to bed now, Philla, and don't worry. I'll be home before dawn, and no one will be the wiser. I promise."

"Oh dear," Philistia said fretfully, but Sarah had already hefted both legs out the window and lowered herself soundlessly to the tree branches below.

Chapter 5

$\mathcal{M}$alachi knew the moment the intruder crossed Glain
Tarran's boundaries. He felt the strange presence entering
his private retreat as if the person had walked into his study
and set a hand upon his arm—though the trespasser was
yet some miles away.

Looking up from the papers he'd been reading—a
lengthy report from Professor Harris Seabolt regarding
the *cythraul*—Malachi fixed his mind on the unexpected
visitor.

An extraordinary wizard could usually tell a great deal
about such individuals when they set foot upon that wizard's property: their exact location, their purpose, even
their identity. Malachi had been able to perceive all these
things even when he was a child. But there was a disturbing
blankness in this instance. He only knew that a stranger
had come to Glain Tarran on a cold, windy, moon-bright
night . . . seeking something. More than that he could not
discern.

He glanced at the bellpull near the wall and with a
thought caused it to lower once. A few moments later a soft
scratch fell upon the study's open door. Rhys's white head

appeared, his blue eyes solemn as he made his bow.

"My lord?"

"We have another unwelcome visitor, I fear, Rhys."

The older man's eyebrows rose slightly.

"One of the lads from the village, my lord?"

Malachi set his papers aside. "I don't believe so. There appears to be some magic at work, for this particular intruder is shielded from me. He does not possess magic himself, however. There may be a talisman of some kind."

"Shall I fetch Gwyllam, then?" The butler's tone was measured but expectant.

Malachi sighed. Involving Gwyllam, the head groundskeeper, meant involving the dogs, and the dogs meant terrifying an intruder—talisman or not—into never trespassing on Glain Tarran again. Generally, Malachi didn't hesitate to make use of the hounds for such work, but tonight . . . tonight he sensed it would be better not to.

"No, Rhys," he said quietly. "Fetch my coat. I'll find our trespasser far more quickly if I go myself."

The hedges were an unexpected problem, but not one that Sarah couldn't overcome. She'd faced more difficult prospects before, and nothing—not Philistia's warnings of doom nor the Earl of Graymar's wretched bushes—was going to stop her.

It was a cold night—Philistia had been correct on that point—made even colder by the biting wind, which, Sarah noted, increased as she made her way farther into Glain Tarran.

She was extraordinarily pleased by the phenomenon, for it gave credence to the tales she'd heard about certain lands being able to protect both themselves and their masters from invaders. If she hadn't been afraid of her precious journal being blown away, Sarah would have stopped to jot down a few quick notes, but that would have to wait until she achieved some kind of shelter. She only hoped the spirits there—if there were any—would be more hospitable than the elements. She'd had near escapes from unfriendly specters before, but never in so remote a location nor when she was so far from civilization. The horse she'd hired for the night's journey was a sturdy beast, but it wouldn't be able to outrun angry phantoms.

Sarah had a rough idea of where she was going, sketched out for her by one of the women she'd spoken with in the village earlier in the day. Once she cleared these ridiculous bushes, which appeared to go on forever, she was to head toward the sea. The cliffs were but a mile away, and there, surrounded by a small copse of trees, she would find the ancient ceremonial grounds that were her goal.

"Let me go," she told the low, grasping bushes as they increasingly clung to her. Lifting one trousered leg higher, she could actually see the long, leafy branches curling about her feet to slow her progress. With a sigh, she dragged the knapsack she carried off her shoulders and unbuttoned a small front flap. Pulling a thin vial from within, she held it over the offending sea of plants.

"These crystals," she said loudly, over the harsh cry of the wind, "were given to me by the sorceress of Aberdeen. I know very well that you understand who it is that I mean, for her potions are well-known in all of Europe. If you don't release me before I've counted to three, the stopper is coming off. I'm quite serious. One, two . . ."

The coiling branches began to withdraw, their leaves rustling with displeasure.

"That's better," Sarah said with relief, tucking the vial away once more and reshouldering the pack. "And although there's nothing I can do about the wind," she continued aloud, "you may inform any tree spirits on the premises that I don't wish to be grabbed at by them, either. I've something far more potent than crystals to make them behave, and won't hesitate to use it if I find my hat snatched away."

For once in his life, Malachi was lost on his own land. Or, rather, in the air above his land, as he flew over the length and breadth of Glain Tarran, searching.

And he didn't like it. At all.

"Where has he gone?"

The question, spoken aloud and with much aggravation, was carried away in the same furious wind that was making Malachi's flight a challenging task. The intruder was still somewhere within Glain Tarran's boundaries, but Malachi couldn't hold on to his exact location. His mind was confused by the conflicting emotions he received, each leading him in a different direction.

Intruders only came to Glain Tarran for two reasons: they had taken a dare from equally foolish friends to enter the fabled lands, or they thought they could steal something of value. But this intruder hadn't gone toward the house or vanished away into the woods. He'd simply disappeared.

The land was overset by this particular stranger . . . overset and yet . . . accepting, too. The elements were wary; even the wind couldn't make up its mind whether to continue blowing or not. It wasn't stopping the intruder's progress.

"Where?" Malachi murmured, coming to a sudden halt and whirling about, searching the ground below with the aid of the bright moonlight. *"Where?"*

"Sweet merciful day," Sarah murmured, pushing her spectacles up in her habitual manner and gazing in wonder at the massive stones hidden within the circle of trees. She moved farther into the center, turning about. "It's fantastic."

A fresh, chilling gust of wind lifted the corners of Sarah's heavy wool coat, sending shivers through her slender body. She must hurry, she told herself, before the land combined its various powers in order to get rid of her.

Sitting on the ground in the midst of the giant bluestone towers, Sarah took off her pack, laid it before her, and untied the main compartment. Pulling out her journal and pencil, she hurriedly began to make notes:

Glain Tarran, Pembrokeshire, Wales
The site is all that I could have hoped for, and far
more. There are twenty enormous monoliths, paired

together in a manner similar to those at Stonehenge, all of Welsh bluestone. I can only guess at the site's date of origin, though it is classically Druidic in arrangement. Unlike other such sites, no stones have yet fallen. It looks today as it might have when it was first completed hundreds of years ago. The forest of trees surrounding the stones was clearly grown in order to hide it from view, explaining the variety of rumors regarding the existence of sacred grounds on Glain Tarran. The main question [at this point the wind began to blow so heartily that she had to tether the edges of the page with her forearm] *is why this fantastic remnant of our historical past has been kept so secret from the government of England and the people at large. Why does the Seymour family so vigilantly hide it?*

The wind apparently had had enough. It finally succeeded in ridding Sarah of her hat, blowing so violently that writing became impossible.

"Oh, very well!" Sarah cried, stuffing her journal and pencil back into her pack. "If you must behave this way, I shall simply have to—oh!"

Somehow, her glasses had slipped far enough down her irritatingly small nose to be snatched off by the wind. Flinging her knapsack aside, Sarah grasped at the air, then went down on hands and knees to frantically search the ground, crawling in a desperate circle, praying to find them.

"That is the outside of enough!" she informed the element hotly. "I can do without the hat, but I *must* have my spectacles. It is entirely unjust of you to visit that manner of vengeance on me. I've touched nothing here, and have no intention of touching *or* taking anything!"

And that was how Malachi, the Earl of Graymar, came upon Miss Sarah Tamony.

To say that he was shocked would have been apt yet also something of an understatement. His intruder was female—accounting, he told himself, for at least part of his earlier confusion, since none of his previous intruders had ever been female—and also quite obviously out of her mind. She was crawling about in a frantic manner, running her hands over the grassy earth and angrily addressing herself to some unseen person in the middle of the night. In the midst of a violent windstorm. On Malachi's land.

He had no notion of why she'd come or how she'd ended up in the most sacred and secret place in Glain Tarran, but he did know that he had to get rid of her as soon as possible.

The vexing problem was how. If she'd been a man or even in her right senses, Malachi might have done his usual terrifying and been done with it. But could he use his powers in such a daunting manner on a madwoman? It might push her even further toward complete insanity.

However, he considered as he watched her continued bizarre behavior, she'd brought it on herself by trespassing on his lands.

By the time she'd finally circled his way and seen him, he'd decided upon a course halfway between terror and kindness. Extending one palm, he brought forth a small flame, only enough light to help the moon illuminate his face. Making his expression as foreboding as he dared—not very, considering how foreboding he could be when he wished—he said, over the wind, in a darkly stern tone, "What are you doing here?"

She pressed up to her knees and squinted at him, setting one hand over her windblown hair to hold it back from her forehead. "Well, at present," she replied loudly over the elements, "I'm trying to find my spectacles. The wind has knocked them off and taken them away. I'm usually very good about keeping them tied with a ribbon, but the last I had was accidentally torn when I was having my hair arranged for a dinner we attended three nights past at Clesington Hall and—well, to be brief, I haven't had a chance to replace it." She blinked up at him blindly and offered an apologetic smile.

It was hardly the response Malachi had expected or desired. Pulling himself up full height, he demanded more fiercely, *"What are you doing here?"*

Rather than becoming afraid, she merely looked affronted. "I apologize if you're angry, my lord," she said loudly, "but there's no need for such rudeness." Struggling to her feet, she pushed her flying hair from her face with both hands and approached him. "I suppose it's due, in part, to the fact that we've not yet been introduced, but that's easily remedied. I'm Sarah Tamony."

The flame floating over Malachi's palm died away, and he felt himself gaping. "Tamony?" He stared into her delicate, finely featured face, certain he'd misunderstood what she'd said, that the keening wind had twisted the words. *"Miss Sarah Tamony?"*

He expected the oddly dressed female standing before him to laugh at the mistake, to correct his misunderstanding. Instead, she smiled, shouted, "Yes, I am," and made a nimble curtsy.

"What the devil are *you* doing on my lands!" The words, impolite and furious, were out of his mouth before he could think on what he was saying. Not that it mattered, for rational thought at the moment was next to impossible.

Sarah Tamony. He could only stare and feel wrath course distressingly through his veins. What a horrid turn of events.

Miss Tamony, however, appeared to be perfectly at ease. She smiled and took a step closer, speaking very carefully against the wind so that he could hear her.

"As I said, I'm presently trying to find my spectacles. I don't suppose you might make it stop"—she motioned toward the wind with a wave of one hand—"so that I might discover where they've gone? It will be much easier to discuss our situation once I can see your face." She squinted. "Not that it's entirely necessary, of course, for you're so famous that I have an idea of what you look like. My Aunt Speakley is ever hoping to meet you so that she can invite you to one of her dinner parties. I've assured her it's useless"—her slender shoulders lifted in a shrug—"for it's well-known that you're terribly particular about the company you keep, but she continues hoping you'll somehow take a fancy to spending an evening with lesser members of Society. Now, about my spectacles . . ."

Malachi lifted a hand and commanded aloud, *"Peidio!"*

The wind died slowly and the attendant noise with it.

"Oh, that's much better!" Sarah Tamony said, looking about with approval. "If we could only—"

"Be silent!" Malachi told her angrily, then turned his attention back to the wind. *"Dwyn!"*

The wind began to blow along the ground, tumbling leaves and branches and, finally, a pair of battered spectacles, which landed near his feet.

Bending, Malachi picked the spectacles up and examined them in the moonlight.

"They're bent," he said curtly, holding them out to her. "I'll not apologize for that. Unwelcome intruders must expect some unpleasantness as recompense for their illegal activities."

She didn't answer him directly but spent a long time trying to set her spectacles to rights, then rubbing them as clean as she could with a bit of her shirt. When she finally put them on, the lenses, deeply scratched, tilted at a precarious angle. She smiled with satisfaction, nonetheless.

"Ah, that's better," she declared happily, gazing up at him, her face illuminated by the moonlight. "Much better. Oh, my heavens." She looked at him more closely. "The descriptions I've heard don't tell the half of it. You're shocking handsome, my lord. I confess I had no idea. But what a rude comment to make upon our first acquaintance. My parents and brother are ever reminding me of just how unruly my tongue is, but the fault is theirs, in part, for they're all quite as bad. We Tamonys do tend to speak our minds rather freely, as I'm sure you divined from my several letters."

Malachi gazed at her steadily, scarcely hearing a word she spoke. Niclas had been right. She was a beauty, despite the spectacles. An auburn beauty with large green eyes and fine, aristocratic features. A rare, famously intelligent beauty who knew how to charm her way into getting what she wanted.

And that made Miss Sarah Tamony a very dangerous female indeed.

She was doing it now, chattering up at him in so open and confident a manner, smiling in such a way that her eyes appeared to spark with a friendliness that she surely didn't—couldn't—feel, given the circumstances they found themselves in. He had no doubt she was wishing him to the devil just as he was her. But the pretense was well done, Malachi admitted, and obviously often practiced. He imagined that the beautiful Sarah Tamony had used such skills to fell any number of men. Unfortunately for her, he was a master in the art of beguilement, too, and immune to her feminine wiles. He hoped.

"Clearly you had none of *my* letters," he replied tersely, "or, if you have, failed to read them. If you'd done so you'd not be here now, trespassing on my land."

If the moon had been a little brighter, Malachi imagined he would have seen her blush. He could certainly see with what light there was her reaction to his words. The smile faded and the finely shaped chin lifted.

"I believe you mistake the matter, my lord," she retorted with equal sharpness. "If you had only granted me an interview, trespassing wouldn't have become necessary."

"Yes, I'm certain that your breaking the law is all my fault," he replied drily. "However, I'm not in any mood to discuss the particulars here. The wind is generous with its time, but won't cease blowing forever simply because I ask it to. I am not its master."

She blinked in momentary confusion, then looked immediately chagrined. "Oh no, of course not. Do you mean that we should go up to the main house? But of course you must if you wish to discuss—did you call it the particulars? I should like nothing better than to have the opportunity to speak with you about anything at all, Lord Graymar. Only let me gather my things and I'll go where you wish."

Her response made Malachi pause—for a woman so lovely she was remarkably uncaring of any danger he might choose to visit upon her. But perhaps she relied upon his being a gentleman—a plausible notion, if brainless. He was not, after all, his saintly cousin Niclas, though she had no way of knowing it.

And then something else occurred to Malachi—something that he chided himself for not realizing before. Sarah Tamony knew about magic—about him and what he was. She'd not turned a hair at the sight of his powers, in either creating light or holding back the wind or retrieving her spectacles. She'd shown no fear of the wild elements or shock at the discovery of the ceremonial grounds. She *knew* about his kind and wasn't afraid.

But of course, he thought with sudden clarity, watching as she knelt to gather her belongings and put them in order. Of course she knew about magic and those possessed of it. Her writings were alive with her belief in such things; if they'd not been, they would have been as dull and uninspired as all the books that had come before. Niclas had conjectured that Sarah Tamony might almost be one of their sympathetics, and if that was so, then . . . but he could take no chances, Malachi told himself firmly. She meant to write about the Seymours, to expose them to the world. No one who was sympathetic to their kind would do such a thing, knowing what the end might be.

She returned to stand before him, a boy's cap on her head and a small pack slung over her shoulder. "I'm ready. Are we walking?"

She almost sounded, at least to Malachi's ears, eager for such a venture.

"Miss Tamony," he said with waning patience, "it is well over two miles to the castle. I did not run here on foot to apprehend you, and I've no intention of using my feet to return." And he certainly wasn't going to take her up in the

air, though he could have, if he'd wished it. To carry her
aloft would require holding her very close, and although he
believed Sarah Tamony to be a fate worse than the plague,
there could be no denying that she was an extraordinarily
appealing female. The snug, boyish garments she wore—
though obviously practical for such outings—only served
to enhance her slender waist and generous curves. He
might be angry with Miss Tamony, but that didn't make
him capable of controlling his traitorous body when it was
pressed against an attractive woman.

He lifted his hand once more and gave a snap of his fingers. "Enoch, *dere!*"

Miss Tamony's eyes widened as Enoch, Malachi's powerful steed, suddenly appeared in the midst of the trees surrounding the ceremonial grounds. He was a magnificent
creature, possessed of his own peculiar magic and worthy
of the awe inspired in Miss Tamony's gaze.

"How marvelous!" she murmured. "Is it . . . I've heard
that such animals exist, but was never certain whether the
tales were more than rumors. Can he fly?"

Malachi frowned at her. "Is this how you conduct your
interviews, Miss Tamony? By asking impertinent questions of those upon whose land you've importuned?"

"Oh dear, it is rude of me, is it not?" she confessed, setting a hand over her cap to keep the wind from blowing it
away. "But if he can fly, then—"

"He cannot fly," Malachi stated, aware that the wind
was beginning to blow with increasing ferocity. "He can
travel great distances in short periods of time, but I've neither the time nor the desire to tell you how at the moment.
We will ride to the castle in the usual manner."

She smiled and nodded. "I do think that will be best, my
lord. As I was about to explain, I've a horse, too, tied just
outside your boundaries, sheltered within some trees. I really didn't mean to leave it this long. I'm sure it must be
growing weary of being out in the elements. Would it be
possible for me to fetch it, first, before accompanying you
to the castle?"

Enoch came near enough for Malachi to take hold of the horse's reins. He pulled the giant steed close. "The beast is no longer there," Malachi told her. "I sent it away, back to its barn, long before I found you. Come." He motioned for her to move forward. "There's a great deal I intend to make clear to you, Miss Tamony, before this night is done."

Chapter 6

*A*lthough she'd been born in England, Sarah had spent the better part of her life traveling through countries near and far and had seen many marvelous things—grand palaces, magnificent cathedrals, ancient ruins, astonishing pyramids. But as she crossed the threshold of Castle Glain Tarran, Sarah knew that she was entering a place like none she had ever experienced before. The power she'd felt from the land was nothing compared to the intensity in the castle. It must be centered here, she thought, and emanate out to the rest of the estate.

If any place was worthy of possessing such magic, it was Glain Tarran. It was truly a castle in every sense of the word, though even in the moonlight Sarah had been able to see that it had started life as a simple fortified keep and much later been finished as an elegant manor. In between the two, however, Glain Tarran had been built up as a tremendous medieval castle, and it was this part—still fronted by the keep and flanked from behind and on either side by the manor, that was the heart of the dwelling. By all accounts the estate should have looked like a confused jumble of mismatched architecture, yet the actual result was breathtakingly lovely. All of the ancient beauty of the castle had been perfectly retained—even the walls that comprised the inner and outer baileys—so that the gardens and trees preserved the image of far-gone times.

The elderly butler who opened the massive front doors for them seemed unperturbed by his master arriving with a strange woman in the middle of the night. Bowing low, the butler welcomed them and then proceeded to take Sarah's things—not so much as raising an eyebrow at the sight of her boyish garments—while a footman ably divested Lord Graymar of his own hat and heavy cloak. It was only at the sight of his master's very blond hair, which, being unfashionably long as well as currently unbound, fell tumbling to his shoulders once the hat came off, that the butler expressed a measure of unhappiness, and that only with his eyes. Lord Graymar sent his servant an answering look and said, "I know I look a fright, Rhys, but it can't be helped, and I've no intention of remedying my appearance just now. I wish to speak with our intruder first."

"Yes, my lord," the butler said obediently, though he was clearly pained at the idea of Lord Graymar being in any kind of company in so disorderly a manner. Sarah was aware that the Earl of Graymar was renowned in Society for the unfailing perfection of his attire, even in the simplest of gatherings. "Will you be in the study?"

"We will." Lord Graymar took Sarah's elbow in a firm grip. "Bring us some hot wine—the Burgundy, with plenty of spice—and whatever Cook may have at hand in the way of sustenance. Our guest will be the better for it, I believe."

"Oh, that's not necessary," Sarah assured him as Lord Graymar pulled her along. "I do hate to put you to any trouble."

The earl glanced at her, his gaze filled with irony. "It's scarcely more than what you've already put us to," he told her. "I confess, however, that I am not usually in the habit of entertaining trespassers."

"I'm sure that's so, my lord," Sarah replied meekly, walking quickly to keep up with his longer strides, scarcely able to take in the magnificence of the dwelling at their rapid pace, "but I am so grateful you've agreed to entertain me, even if only to vent your wrath."

He stopped before a large, ornately carved door. "You would be fortunate, Miss Tamony, if that was all that I wished to do. But come." The door swung open without being touched, revealing a large chamber beyond. "I'm cold and weary and want a drink."

Sarah preceded him into the room and immediately felt her jaw drop open in a very unladylike expression of instant awe.

"Oh," she murmured, her steps faltering as her gaze moved from one end of the room to the other. "How beautiful."

And it was. Having seen the castle's exterior, she had expected that the interior rooms would be built on a grand size as well and accordingly be rather cold and intimidating, as in other large castles she'd seen. But this room was nothing of the kind. It was certainly big, but not in the least uninviting.

"Those windows," she murmured, staring at the tall shining glass panes that rose from the floor all the way to the high ceiling. Deep red curtains were drawn back to the sides, allowing an unlimited view of the scenery beyond, which at this moment, illumined by the moonlight, was a wildly windblown garden and, beyond that, a darkness where the land dropped away to the sea.

"They are striking, are they not?" Lord Graymar remarked, closing the door behind him. Sarah could hear the touch of pride in his tone. "They're what newcomers always comment upon when first entering the study. The question that often follows is how is it possible that the room can stay so warm, exposed as it is by so much glass, and with but the one fireplace?"

Sarah glanced at her host as he moved nearer. "I find that hard to believe, my lord, unless you are much in the habit of allowing those who do not know you well into your home."

"I am not," he replied with polite brevity. "But I did say that it is what newcomers ask, not those who know me."

"Yes," she murmured, her gaze rising to the tall ceiling. "I imagine that those who know nothing of magic ask a great many questions when coming to such a place. I can only wonder at how you answer them."

"It can be trying," he confessed. "I perceive, however, that I shall be spared such difficulty with you, Miss Tamony."

She smiled. "I believe that is so, my lord. My faults are many—my presence at Glain Tarran gives full evidence of my lamentable lack of patience—but I am not so blind or foolish as to disbelieve the wondrous sights I've encountered in my research. I've written of them in my books."

"Ah yes," he murmured. "Your books. That is precisely the topic I wish to discuss with you, though I imagine you already knew that." With a light touch on Sarah's elbow, he led her toward a group of richly upholstered chairs. "Please be seated, Miss Tamony, and make yourself comfortable. Rhys will be here shortly with the wine. Forgive me if I drink before you." Turning, he strode toward a beautifully carved cupboard set in the midst of walls of dark bookcases that, like the windows, rose to the ceiling. Glass-paned doors opened at his approach, revealing numerous shining bottles and crystal glasses beyond.

He busied himself for a few moments, his back turned to her, and Sarah gave herself a moment to steady her nerves.

She was not, by nature or experience, given to moments of uncertainty or fear, but Malachi Seymour wasn't like any other man she'd ever before faced. Sarah had expected that he'd not be, of course, having heard so many rumors of his great powers—from sources as far away as Cairo—but she had been in the presence of other powerful wizards and sorceresses before and had assumed it wouldn't be so very different. It was.

She'd heard him called by several titles. Noble One, Son of Mactus, Great Wizard. In Wales, and among those who particularly knew him, Malachi Seymour was called Dewin Mawr, or Great Sorcerer. Now Sarah understood why he was spoken of with such deference and awe, even fear. He was . . . overwhelming.

Remembering what she'd said earlier, and that she'd been unable to halt the words that tumbled from her lips at setting sight upon him, made Sarah's cheeks hot with embarrassment. She was a woman well used to speaking her thoughts—within reason, of course—but to have told him to his face how handsome he was had been far beyond the pale. It had been an awful misstep. Lord Graymar would likely consign her in his consideration to the legions of females who were madly in love with him, who swooned when he entered a room and constantly sought his favors.

In all truth, the fellow wouldn't be far wrong. If she'd had the time or leisure, Sarah might have happily joined the man's admiring throngs. But she didn't have the time or leisure, nor the intention of letting her determination be turned aside by a good-looking man. Or a shockingly stunning one.

He was tall and perfectly proportioned. Slender in build—no, not precisely slender, she corrected mentally, for that bespoke a lack of strength, and Sarah knew firsthand from riding before him on that magnificent steed, his arms fast about her, that Malachi Seymour was powerful. No, she thought, tilting her head slightly as she watched his movements, he was sleek rather than slender, almost feline. If his eyes had been gold or brown, Sarah might have called him leonine, especially with his overlong mane of white-blond hair, which should have served to make the man look eccentric rather than even more attractive. But his eyes were blue. A light, clear, piercing blue that put Sarah in mind of a diamond that she had seen many years ago in a palace in India. As the memory flashed into her thoughts, Lord Graymar turned to face her, glass in hand, pinning her with those eyes as if he knew what she was thinking.

His face . . . Sarah struggled to ignore her host's amused gaze and to force her heart's increased pace into submission, giving herself permission to deliberately consider what it was that made the man's face such a shock to the senses. There was the obvious perfection of it—each part in ideal proportion and placement to the rest, from his aristocratic nose to the curve of his brows and cheeks, to say nothing of the alluring set of his mouth—and perfection generally drew attention and admiration from beholders. But there was more than simple alignment of features to account for such masculine beauty as the Earl of Graymar possessed. Sarah had seen it in the faces and figures of those she'd interviewed for her stories. There was an otherworldliness, a luminosity emanating from an unknown source. It sparked in the eyes and beneath the skin and could be heard even in their voices. Just as Sarah heard it in Lord Graymar's voice when he'd found her, even above the sound of the wind.

She had written in her first book about elves, fairies, and other such beings taking magic mortals as their mates, resulting in progeny possessed of unusual features. The Seymours, she'd been told, had inherited the beauty and fineness of the elves. If it was true, and Sarah had no reason to believe it was not, it would explain a great deal about Malachi Seymour's effortless ability to steal her breath away.

Lord Graymar's initial amusement at her scrutiny died as a long silence passed between them. Sarah knew she should lower her gaze and murmur an apology for her bold appraisal, but his reaction held her attention even more fully. His smile faded and his blue eyes grew troubled. He seemed to be—though she could scarce credit it—disconcerted. Lifting his unoccupied hand, he haltingly ran his fingers through his unbound hair, making a brief, and useless, attempt at combing it. Just as abruptly he straightened, dropped his hand, and looked away. "Rhys will be here soon," he said once more, a touch unsteadily.

He lifted the glass in his hand and drank deeply from the amber liquid within, then drew in and released a breath and looked at her once more, recovering the mask of control he wore.

"You know about magic," he stated, rather than asked. "And believe in it. You know that the castle is warm, regardless of windows or drafts, because I wish it to be. Because everything within Glain Tarran responds to the wishes of its master. You knew before you came tonight. Your books reveal that much about you, Miss Tamony."

Sarah nodded slowly. "Yes, my lord. But it isn't merely because of my writing, though that has certainly confirmed my suspicions. I've always known, since I was a child, that there were those who were very different from other mortals. From me."

Lord Graymar began to move slowly toward where she sat, gently swirling the contents in his glass. It seemed to Sarah that the temperature in the room rose a degree or two.

"We call those who know about our kind, either intuitively or by revelation, 'sympathetics,'" he said, "though I wouldn't precisely describe you by the name. Sympathetics"—he paused to seat himself in a comfortable chair opposite the couch—"help magic mortals survive in this world. They do not expose us to those who would bring us harm."

Sarah's eyes widened and she opened her mouth to speak, but Lord Graymar held up a staying hand.

"Come, Rhys," he said aloud, and the study's door opened to reveal the servant standing there, holding a tray in both hands.

"Thank you, my lord," the older man said as he entered the room, carrying the tray to a low table set within Sarah's reach. The alluring scent of spiced wine filled the room, mixed with the smell of warm pastry. "Would you care for a glass of wine, miss?" He indicated a steaming silver pitcher set beside a gleaming crystal goblet.

"Yes, thank you," Sarah said gratefully, proffering her widest smile.

"Rhys," Lord Graymar said casually, not turning his gaze from Sarah, "I believe you'll be pleased to be more formally introduced to our guest. This is Miss Sarah Tamony, whom we've had cause to speak of so often these past many weeks. She's been so good as to gift us with her company this evening. Or should I say 'morning,' as the hour is so advanced?"

The servant lifted his head to look with greater delight into Sarah's face. "Miss Tamony!" he declared, his blue eyes filled with happy surprise. "Miss Sarah Tamony, the authoress? Why, a great honor it is indeed." With deft skill he filled the goblet and held it out for Sarah to take. The crystal was thick and heavy, and the warmth of the wine was welcome against her ungloved fingers. "I have had the pleasure of reading your work, miss," he went on, bowing. "And my grandchildren, as well. They'll scarce agree to sleep at night without we read them a chapter or two, there is that much they love your stories."

His voice held the music of the Welsh that Sarah had heard so often in the past several days. It was there, even in the simplest words, whether spoken in English or Gaelic, from the lips of farmers, villagers, or gentry. Even Lord Graymar, though he spoke with the clear refinement of an English nobleman well used to moving in Society, couldn't keep the lilting rise and fall of certain words and syllables from his speech.

"I'm so glad," she said with sincere pleasure. "And how kind of you to tell me, especially when I've made such a nuisance of myself."

"Rhys has been among those who have pleaded your case to me," Lord Graymar told her, casting a wry glance at his servant. "You could not have had a better or more persistent advocate."

Rhys gave his employer an admonishing frown, as if Lord Graymar were a misbehaving boy rather than a man full grown, and an earl, at that. Then Rhys turned his attention back to Sarah. "I have merely assured His Lordship that the Seymour name would be safe in your keeping, Miss Tamony, seeing as how kindly and properly you've written of others. But you won't want to speak of that now, before you've had a chance to refresh yourself. Cook has warmed some lovely tarts, as you see. Here is a savory with leek and thyme, and here is one sweet with apples.

There are cheeses and a few slices of cold mutton." He looked at her with anticipation. "What may I give you, Miss Tamony?"

"Miss Tamony is perfectly capable of serving herself, Rhys," Lord Graymar said. "No, no, don't look at me as if I'd asked you to kick her," he added at the manservant's instant affront. "It's far too late for you to remain awake any longer on our behalf, and anyone with Miss Tamony's ability to cross the boundaries of even the most protected land is able to fill her own plate. You can retire for the night—or morning, as it may be—with a happy conscience."

"Oh yes," Sarah agreed. "I shouldn't want you to remain in service on my account. It was thoughtless of me not to think before now of how I've importuned you. I'm terribly sorry."

Rhys wasn't listening to her. He was occupied in scowling at the lord of Glain Tarran.

"My lord," Rhys began, to be stopped by His Lordship, who spoke to him in Welsh. Rhys responded in kind, though far more stiffly and with clear disapproval. Lord Graymar's reply was reassuring and calm but evidently very final, for the manservant bowed once more before turning back to Sarah.

"It was a pleasure to make your acquaintance, Miss Tamony," he said, the music absent from his voice now. "If you require anything at all, don't hesitate to ring. His Lordship's servants are *always* at the ready."

With another bow he turned and left. Sarah looked questioningly at Malachi Seymour, who was already watching her.

"Rhys served my father, and has known me from the cradle," he said. "He seems to think it's not safe for you to be left alone in my care." He lifted the glass and sipped slowly, his gaze held on Sarah. Lowering it, he went on, "I gave him my word of honor that you'd be returned to the village without harm before anyone awakes to discover you gone, and with your reputation untouched and unsullied."

"I'm certain my reputation will be safe in your keeping, Lord Graymar," Sarah told him, lifting the heavy goblet to breathe in the deliciously spicy scent of the warm liquid within. "Just as yours will be in mine—as your servant said—if you'd trust me with it."

The faint amusement was back in his face, and he leaned forward. "That's not the way in which to convince me, Miss Tamony. It is foolish to assume that you're safe with me at all. You are a remarkably beautiful woman, as you very well know, and I've been without female company since coming to Glain Tarran before Christmas—barring relatives of course, but that's hardly the same thing, is it? Rhys has good cause to be concerned, you see." His tone, low and meaningful, paired with his gaze, also quite meaningful, sent a shiver down Sarah's spine.

Well, this was unexpected. Sarah lowered her gaze to the goblet in her hands and wondered if the room's temperature had increased again. She wasn't unused to male attention; indeed, she'd had dozens of proposals of marriage from gentlemen in various corners of the world and had once even been kidnapped by a lovesick German prince who'd been determined upon making her his wife. But Sarah wasn't foolish enough to suppose that a man such as Lord Graymar—certainly not a man who looked like he did and who could have any and every female he desired— had any real interest in a bespectacled scribbler whose claim to the social niceties was limited, at best, and who presently looked like a complete harridan. Her hair was windblown, her clothes unseemly and dirty, and her spectacles scratched and bent. No man in his right senses could possibly find her attractive.

The Earl of Graymar was obviously toying with her or, worse, punishing her for her boldness in coming to Glain Tarran by pretending to make love to her. It would serve him a nice turn if she fell for such a trick, Sarah thought as she sipped the wine, finding it as delicious to the tongue as it was to the nose. But then he would only laugh and try to make her feel even more foolish. Apart from that, Sarah didn't have time to play games with a man who could best her with both eyes closed. She had a book to write. Summoning her best behavior to the fore, Sarah raised her eyes.

"You are kind to flatter me, my lord," she replied, pushing her spectacles a little higher up. "I had forgotten how chivalrous English gentlemen are in their compliments to ladies, no matter how false such words may be."

His brows lowered. "Let us forgo the niceties, Miss Tamony. A gentleman by birth I may be, but those who know me well will warn you that my temper cannot always be held to the fire. But despite the unfortunate weaknesses in my nature, I can at least lay claim to being honest. Or at least," he said, fingering the glass he held, "as honest as circumstance permits. Kindness, however, is not a virtue I feel compelled to expend on trespassers—most especially when they've been told that they're not welcome on my property. Your beauty is a fact, as is your temerity in coming to Glain Tarran in the dark of night. If you have any doubts as to my feelings on the matter, Miss Tamony, then let me be clear. I am not happy with you."

Sarah set aside the goblet, striving to maintain her composure. "I fear my own temper can be unruly at times as well, my lord," she told him. "But you have given me leave to dispense of formality, and I quite agree that such manners are of no use to us at present. I accept that I have misstepped by coming to Glain Tarran uninvited—"

"Misstepped?" he repeated with a laugh. "You've committed a criminal act, Miss Tamony. I could have you arrested for it, you know. Only think how exciting that bit of news would be among your legions of fans. London would talk of nothing else for weeks." For the first time that night, the Earl of Graymar actually began to sound cheerful.

Sarah felt herself blushing hotly and was furious at having such a reaction. It was ridiculous that he should so quickly be able to goad her into losing her calm. She'd always been very much in control of her dealings with others.

"Very well," she admitted tautly. "I have broken the law by coming tonight, and you have every right to be exceedingly angry. But I had to see Glain Tarran, especially if you continue in your refusals to give me an interview. I had heard so many legends and stories about the estate and didn't wish to write of such things without having a better understanding of them. Surely you wouldn't wish me to make inaccurate representations."

The room, in accord with the anger on His Lordship's features, decidedly grew much warmer. Sarah cast a glance at the fireplace, expecting the flames to be leaping almost out into the room, only to find that the fire was as it had earlier been, cheerful and perfectly controlled.

Sarah wished she might say the same of the earl. He sat forward again and said, "I do not wish for you to write about them *at all*. You cannot write as you do and be a simpleton, Miss Tamony, but you seem completely incapable of understanding me. You will not research my family, or any of the magical Families in Great Britain, unless you wish to be dealt with by me. As you appear to have an understanding of magic, I doubt that I need explain to you what I mean by such words."

"But why?" she asked. "You believe that I'm not among your sympathetics, yet I assure you upon my honor I am. I have always understood those who possess magic, and know full well the measures you must take to live safely among those without it."

"And yet you intend to expose us—by name and place, no less—to the examination of the public eye. For *profit*," he added scornfully.

The study grew even hotter. Sarah rose from her chair and moved toward the tall glass panes, fanning herself with a hand. She wondered if there was a way to open one of the windows to let the sea breeze in but decided against the idea when she saw that the wind was still blowing wildly out-of-doors, bending the trees and other plants that stood in the garden almost to the ground.

"If you think Society is unaware of the stories that have been told—for centuries—about certain families and places in this country, then you've been living in exile, my

lord. Forgive me for speaking so plain," she added when
she realized how rude the words sounded. "Only think of
the ghost stories that are told, emanating from every part
of Britain. Glain Tarran hasn't been spared, nor scarcely
any castle or ancient manor house. Apart from those who
are your sympathetics, the public at large treats such stories as mere entertainment. My own works are proof of
that." She turned to look at where he yet sat. "I have researched each incident that I've written of as carefully and
fully as possible, and presented them in as intriguing a
manner as I can, yet no one that I know of has taken them
as fact."

Lord Graymar drained his glass and set it aside.

"Tales of spectral visitations at Glain Tarran may be interesting enough for society at large to speak of," he said,
standing, "even for writers to write of. But they don't have
the power to draw hordes of inquisitive souls to my estate
in order to find evidence of whether they're real. I grant
you, Miss Tamony, that few mere mortals believe spirits
are real, much as they enjoy passing such tales along."
Slowly, he began to move toward her. "But such would not
be the case if you were to begin to write about the existence
of ancient ceremonial grounds that have been kept secret
on my lands lo these many centuries."

He came nearer, and Sarah drew herself up full height to
steady herself. But it did little good; she was a tall woman,
but somehow he made her feel insignificantly minuscule.

"I agree that such an outcome would be likely," she admitted. "Even probable. And although I've no notion of
why the Seymours have kept such a delightful treasure secret, I would, of course, not mention the ceremonial
grounds in the book if that was what you wished." She attempted to straighten her bent spectacles more levelly
upon her nose. "I promised in my letters that I would write
of nothing that would displease you. That is precisely why
the interview is so important—for both of us."

"That is very kind, Miss Tamony," he said tartly. "And
what if I say—as I believe I have been saying, endlessly, it

seems to me—that I don't want you to write anything about us? Not of the Seymours or the Cadmarans or whoever else you've contacted?"

She frowned. "But I don't see why you feel so strongly about the matter. How can I convince you that I mean neither you nor anyone else harm?"

His expression remained unchanged. Outside, a gust of wind rattled the panes of glass.

"If you've read my work," she said, moving a step nearer, gazing up at him, "then you know what my feelings are toward magic and those who possess it. My father—I imagine you've come across his many writings—says that to capture and hold a reader, the writer must first be captured and held by the subject he writes of. Since I was a child, from my earliest memories, I've been captured and held by the supernatural. When I began to write, I wanted to share that captivation."

His expression, and his stance, softened by degrees.

"Writing about ancient legends is very much like writing about ghosts," Lord Graymar said, his tone gentler. "It's easy to make others believe that such things, even if real, can never touch their lives. But to tell them that there are people who actually possess magic living as neighbors in their villages or standing beside them in a shop . . ."

"But I don't intend to do that," she countered. "I'm only going to write accounts of the most interesting historical figures from certain families, the Seymours among them. Sir Sigberct Seymour, perhaps, whose magic sword sparked with flames during battle, or the famous Lady Cynwise Seymour, who bravely faced the terrible dragon who roamed the Black Mountains and cast a spell to lock it forever within a hidden cave, where to this day it strives to find a way out, scratching and clawing and sometimes even causing the earth to shake." Sarah grew excited just thinking of how she would write the tales, of how wonderful her readers would find them. "And of a certainty I must tell the story of Mistress Helen Seymour, who was almost burned at the stake as a witch. I told my cousin and brother the tale but a few weeks past and they were fascinated. And although perhaps these stories aren't well-known to the public at large, they're certainly spoken of by those who live in the villages and counties where the events took place." She looked at him hopefully. "I would only be writing them down and presenting them to a wider audience."

Malachi gazed into her upturned face and tried to tell himself that she looked ridiculous. Her green eyes, touched with flecks of amber, gazed out from the most oddly twisted pair of spectacles he'd ever seen. How she could have seen him well enough past the scratches to declare him handsome was beyond all imagination. And her auburn hair, now uncovered from that hideous boy's cap, stuck out in all directions from the unfortunate arrangement she'd piled it into. Her face was smudged and dirty, her cheeks flushed, and her clothes far from being anything that a lady of fashion would attire herself with.

Yet she didn't look ridiculous. Not to him. Malachi could only look at Miss Sarah Tamony and see an extraordinary beauty that his rational mind told him wasn't, couldn't be, real.

He'd known any number of beautiful women in his life. Some he'd appreciated from afar; others he'd enjoyed in a far more intimate manner. Several could lay claim to possessing greater physical loveliness than Miss Tamony. But none had been able to steal Malachi's breath away. It was almost as if she had cast some kind of spell, impossible as such a thing was. She didn't possess magic; even if she had, he would be immune to it. He was the Dewin Mawr and very few lived on earth who could touch him with their powers.

Yet magic, somehow, was involved with Sarah Tamony. He recognized it. Felt it. And, worse, was utterly baffled as to what to do about it.

The sensations had started the moment he took Miss Tamony up before him on Enoch, when she'd settled her slim, feminine figure against him and sheltered beneath the circle of his arms. Malachi had expected to be aroused by the nearness of an attractive female—but he'd been taken aback by the rest of what he'd felt: heat and need and an intense surge of pleasure.

Intensity. Aye, that was what this strange woman's presence did to him. He'd struggled to press it down, to hide it behind coldness and anger, but now, as he stood so near her, with her face lifted to his, her emerald eyes gazing up at him . . . everything within him began to fill with want.

It had been prophesied before his birth that Malachi would take his father's place as Dewin Mawr, and even in his childhood the magic that would one day make him the most powerful wizard in Europe began to make itself known. He could not remember a time when he'd not had visions of things to come or heard the whisperings of spirits, revealing secrets, advising and guiding, showing Malachi which path to take. They were whispering to him now, telling him to take care, to be wise, that the magic she brought to Glain Tarran was far too powerful to take lightly. At the same time his mind was filled with visions—of him and her, touching, kissing, entwined in passion, with her glorious red-gold hair spread out on white sheets, her eyes shut with pleasure as he moved over her, touching, tasting. Her skin was white and pure, so soft, all of her, and he buried his face against that whiteness, in the perfumed silk of her neck and shoulders, pressing his lips beneath her ear as he pushed into the heat of her body. Her legs came about him and her eyes opened, and they began to move . . . not as he had done with other women, but almost as if they were flying. . . .

"My lord?"

Malachi struggled to bring himself back to the moment, to push the images away. His breathing had deepened and his body was so aroused that his clothing felt uncomfortably tight. He had another vision, more fleeting, of grasping one of her ungloved hands and pressing it against his body, of her strong fingers gripping him as he took her mouth with his own and with both hands began to frantically unravel her hair from its tenuous bonds. . . .

"Have I rendered you speechless with anger, my lord," she asked, clearly oblivious to his state, "or perhaps, I might hope, with approval?"

This was terrible, Malachi thought with real distress, blinking to focus his gaze on the woman before him. She looked ridiculous, he told himself again, firmly, pushing away the image of his hands and where they had proceeded in his vision after dealing with both her hair and clothes. She was a dirty, unkempt mess, and a dangerous interloper whose activities, if not stopped, would bring terrible harm not only to the Seymours, but to all magical beings. If his unruly thoughts and traitorous body couldn't remain in the present, then he would simply have to force them to do so.

His hands were clenched, he realized of a sudden, and damp. Drawing in a deep, slow breath, Malachi regained his composure.

"Not approval," he said, the inner shaking making his voice unsteady, but perhaps she would take that for displeasure. She was still gazing up at him with those glorious green eyes, marred only by the bent spectacles.

"But not entirely disapproval?" she asked. "Can there be no compromise reached between us, Lord Graymar? I feel certain that if we can only—"

"I think not, Miss Tamony," Malachi replied curtly. He didn't want her speaking of compromises or anything else that they could do together. He was already having trouble keeping the ongoing vision at bay. Flashes of them tumbling upon the nearby sofa weren't helping him maintain composure. "I fear there's nothing you can say that will cause me to change my mind." He tried to focus on the bent spectacles, rather than her disappointment, but they only made him more agitated.

"Forgive me," he said, and, careful not to touch her, snatched the glasses from her small nose. "I'm having difficulty concentrating with these making your eyes look skewed."

He felt her astonished stare upon him as he gave his attention to making repairs. It was quickly and simply done, requiring the most elementary sort of magic. Rubbing his thumbs gently over the oval glass pieces, he easily smoothed away the scratches, then ran his fingers across the metal nose and temple bars to make them straight. Beneath his hands the spectacles stretched and shifted until they had regained their original form. Lifting them with both hands, Malachi gently slid them back into place, using his fingers to fit them over her ears.

This time it was impossible for him to pull his hands away. The touch of the soft skin beneath her ears, the tickle of her hair on the tops of his hands, induced him to linger.

"That's better," he murmured, looking into her eyes once more, now much clearer beneath the shining glass. They were wide, gazing up at him with a mixture of alarm and confusion.

"Yes, thank you," she whispered hoarsely. "As good as new."

He had the ability to tell a great deal about others when he touched them. But this simple touch with her, just the tips of his fingers against her bare skin, was a revelation. He could feel the rapid pace of her heart, feel her heightened breathing as if it were his own.

Oh, aye, there was magic here. A powerful magic that was greatly unsettling. And with her, of all people, Malachi thought unhappily. The Guardians must be playing a trick on him and laughing merrily in their heaven as Malachi Seymour, the Earl of Graymar and the powerful Dewin Mawr, stood transfixed by Miss Sarah Tamony, a mere mortal, a scribbler of tales.

But if he was spellbound, then so was she. Miss Tamony should have slapped him for such impertinence, or at the very least stepped away. But whatever he was feeling seemed to be inside her, too. She was trembling, as he was, and stood before him so that their bodies nearly touched, equally captive.

"Your skin," he said, moving the tips of his fingers over her silken cheeks, "is very beautiful. Very soft."

It was among the stupidest things he'd ever said in his

life, Malachi knew, but impossible to take back now. His brain had clearly deserted him. Miss Tamony made no reply. Her mouth formed an "o" and, if possible, her eyes widened even further. She stood in silence, trembling as his fingertips slid into her hair, bringing his thumbs and palms to cup her face.

"Beautiful," he whispered, running his thumbs just beneath the rims of her eyeglasses. His hands moved downward, slowly, lightly tracing the curves of her lips, the delicate bones of her chin, and the slender length of her neck. He had no idea where he would have stopped if it hadn't been for the gold chain. It peeked out of the collar of her boy's shirt, and when his fingers encountered it he felt the distinct tingling of magic. The sensation helped to clear his senses.

"You've been to Aberdeen, I perceive," he said, scarcely recognizing the sound of his own voice, thick as it was with idiotic delirium. "And visited with Sorsha. I sensed that you had some of her potions and enchantments in your knapsack when I first came across you in the grove. She gave you a charm as well, did she?"

"Y-yes," Miss Tamony managed, her voice quavering. Malachi didn't wonder at it. A beauty she was, but likely never so boldly handled by a man before. He wished she would slap him. "It's supposed to protect me from . . . well, I'm not precisely sure from what." She drew in a shaking breath and released it. Her trembling lessened a degree.

Grasping the chain, Malachi pulled the amulet into the light. The sight was so surprising that it worked on him like a bucket of water. The erotic visions faded and his mind cleared.

"God help us," he said, then laughed, turning the tiny, misshapen amulet over in his palm. "What could Sorsha have been thinking?" He looked at her. "Did you buy this from her?"

She shook her head, still wide-eyed. "She gave it to me as a gift, insisting that I take it. I tried to pay her, but she would only let me pay for the other items—the crystals and potions. I know that some would find it rather odd and perhaps even ugly," she said, glancing down at the small golden object, "but I've come to love it. The little design on the band"—she touched the place where the amulet came together and was clasped by a ring of gold—"it's Celtic, is it not? I nearly showed it to my brother, for he's been researching Celtic history, but I didn't wish to explain about visiting a reputed sorceress."

"Aye, it's very old," Malachi said more soberly, "though the symbols are from the language spoken only by magic mortals in the ancient days. Your brother would not have recognized them. They tell of the enchantment that protects the wearer, along with the ashes that are held within the amulet itself."

"Ashes?" Miss Tamony repeated, looking up at him again. A mistake, for it made him feel instantly muddled. "She told me that only dried herbs were locked inside. I've tried to open it, but age seems to have sealed it forever."

He shook his head. "Not age, but magic. The amulet cannot be opened save by a powerful wizard or sorceress, and only one who is a complete fool would do so. The enchantment would be lost then, and the charm left powerless. Not that I expect you'll ever have any use for its protection, Miss Tamony."

"Why?" she asked. "What is it for? I thought perhaps it was a protection of some sort, something to ward off evil."

"Oh, it is that," he said. "But an evil that you are unlikely to come across. The ashes in this amulet—which has a name, though I doubt that will surprise you, knowing what you do about my kind and our penchant for giving names to everything—are from the remains of a mere mortal, one Guidric of Maghera, who was once possessed by demons, not one, but several, and yet lived to tell the tale. Ah, I can see by your expression that I've found a supernatural tale that you've not yet heard."

She looked immediately intrigued. "Demons! I know that they once roamed the earth freely. Even the Bible speaks of them."

"Exactly so," he said. "And they yet exist today, moving with far greater care among mere mortals, although very powerful demons have been banished and are only allowed to journey to earth for certain purposes. But when Guidric of Maghera lived, hundreds of years past, spirit possession was yet quite common. Guidric was taken hold of by five spirits, and no mortal man, either magic or mere, could free him. Not even the most powerful among my ancestors . . . at least not alone."

"Poor man," she said with sympathy. "But you said that he lived to tell the tale, so he must have been delivered from such an awful fate."

"He was," Malachi told her. "It was a time when magic mortals were beginning to learn that, when necessity required it, they must put their differences aside and combine their powers for a greater good. There were five spirits; thus five wizards and sorceresses were needed to overpower them. Together, they rid Guidric of the possession, and he lived a long and happy life." He gave a rueful shake of his head. "That is a lesson that my kind has not remembered well, I fear. A long time has passed since we have come together to help mankind."

"You are proud, it seems," Miss Tamony said, her voice unsteady. "Your kind is, I should say, my lord."

Malachi didn't dare look at her again. His heart was throbbing painfully in his chest and his body still hard with desire. Focusing on the amulet, he tilted his palm to roll the charm on its other side, exposing the remaining symbols. Miss Tamony, chained to the object, tentatively moved nearer.

"The amulet," he said, clearing his throat and setting his thoughts back to the matter at hand, "is called Donballa, which means, roughly, 'wall of protection.' The ashes within, infused with the memory of Guidric's survival of spirit possession, provide an immunity to the bearer."

"Do you mean to say," she said slowly, looking up at him, "that it protects me from being possessed by evil spirits?"

He allowed himself only a brief glance into the green eyes. "Yes, though only from the kind of spirits that possessed Guidric, not more powerful demons. But, as I said, any kind of possession is so rare these days that the amulet's value is questionable. The spirits have discovered that it's far easier to confound mortals through less invasive means, and the amulet cannot spare you from their ability to tempt and persuade. I can't imagine why Sorsha thought to give it to you, unless . . ." He thought of the coming of the *cythraul*. Sorsha, like all those possessed of great powers, knew that the demon would be coming soon. But surely she would realize that the Donballa would have no power over such a creature.

"It was beautiful, once, I believe," he said. "The craftsmanship is evident, as is the quality of the gold. Irish gold is as precious as diamonds, you know, though Welsh gold is more precious yet, and far finer, for that matter."

"Very proud," she murmured, and he could hear the smile in her voice. "The chain is new," she went on, "but of the plain English variety, I fear."

"Pity," he replied. "I shall have to see if I can't make the artful object outshine its poor English cousin." He lifted his other hand and set it over the amulet, pressing it tightly between his palms. Miss Tamony's auburn head bent nearer, teasing his nostrils with her sweet, feminine scent. Malachi closed his eyes to concentrate. This was harder work than merely straightening a pair of spectacles.

The amulet began to grow warm within his hands, then hot. The stinging sensation, which cleared his senses wonderfully, was more than a little welcome. And when rays of bright light began to escape from between his pressed flesh, Miss Tamony leaned back, putting a more comfortable distance between him and her alluring person. The chain about her neck strained, but Malachi held the amulet fast, waiting until the light died away before opening his hands.

"Oh," Miss Tamony remarked with delighted surprise.

The amulet lay upon his palm, still glowing faintly, renewed to its former glory. It looked, he thought with satisfaction, as bright and shining as the day it had been formed by the goldsmith's art.

"How lovely," she breathed, gingerly picking it up. "Thank you, Lord Graymar. How kind of you. I shall cherish it now far more than I did before. And thank you for telling me the story behind the Donballa, as well. I'll take very good care of it, I promise you."

She was smiling up at him again in a way that began to make him think of kisses—and other things—once more. He took a step away and fixed his stoniest expression on his face. It always worked wonders when he wished to make progress in Parliament.

"I hope that this small act will put you in some charity with me, Miss Tamony. I have acted unforgivably, touching you and speaking in a forward manner which I'm certain you must have found both alarming and disgusting. Rhys was quite right to distrust me in being alone with you. There is no excuse for such behavior, regardless how beautiful the woman or how ill-mannered the man. But I hope that you will forgive me, nonetheless, and strive to put the incident behind us. It is very likely that we will meet again in London during the Season, and I should not wish to think that my presence will distress you."

She was silent for a long moment, then said, "I can do no less than forgive, my lord, when I am the one who so boldly invited myself to Glain Tarran and placed myself beneath your unwilling, but very generous, hospitality. And you did repair my spectacles and restore the Donballa."

"You are very good." He steeled himself for the loss of this brief amity. "Perhaps, whenever you see the Donballa, it will lessen the sting of my refusal to allow you to write your proposed book."

As he had expected, her smile turned into a frown. She had a wonderful mouth, he thought. The lips were full and curving and extremely expressive. He had grazed them with his thumbs earlier and knew by touch how soft they were.

"I don't understand you, my lord," she said. "If you will

not give me an interview, I shall, of course, be disappointed. But it will not stop me from writing my book."

"You understand me," he replied curtly and firmly. "I shall make certain that you do not write your book. You know that I possess the means to do so. None of Sorsha's potions, nor any spells or enchantments you've purchased in your travels, will have the power to stop me. Find another topic to engage your pen, Miss Tamony. That would be best and easiest for us both. Don't persist in this matter," he advised when she tried to speak. "I can be vastly unpleasant when the situation warrants."

She fingered the now-shining amulet and regarded him somberly. He could almost read her angry thoughts, for her eyes were as expressive as her mouth.

"I'm sure that's true, my lord. But I can be as obstinate as you are, and I'm not afraid that you'll harm me. I have learned a great deal about those with magic, and know that you cannot harm mere mortals without fear of punishment. I may not understand precisely how and why, but you are obliged to live beneath certain rules. You can alter my memories, at best, but you cannot force me to do your bidding against my will."

"I'll not be obliged to do so," he said. "It would be easier to make your task impossible. And I can accomplish that, Miss Tamony, not as a sorcerer, but as the Earl of Graymar."

She gave a single shake of her head. "You are welcome to try, sir, but I will yet write my book. Truly, Lord Graymar, if it is ease you desire, then it would be far better if you agreed to help me. I am not a monster, nor as implacable as you seem to think. You will have far more power to affect the book if you work with me, rather than against me. Otherwise I must write as I see fit, not to please your delicate sensibilities."

Delicate sensibilities? Malachi thought angrily. What the devil did the woman mean by such a thing?

"There is clearly no purpose in us discussing the matter

further, Miss Tamony," he said sharply. "You refuse to understand what my objections are to the publication of your proposed undertaking. You will not see the danger of it, and blindly—and vainly, I might add—"

"Vainly!"

"Yes, vainly," he repeated furiously, throwing out a hand as he moved back toward the cabinet set in the bookcases, "assume that you can somehow make such an exposition of magic beings both right and safe from the meddling of mere mortals." The glass-paned doors slammed open at his approach. "History and the fact of human nature prove you wrong. Society hasn't changed so greatly that those who are different are so readily accepted. If you write of past Seymours, it will be logically concluded that present Seymours must have inherited some of their ancestors' powers."

"But no one will believe—"

"Yes, they will," he countered, pouring himself another drink. "I can safely say that I know human nature far better than you, Miss Tamony, despite your myriad travels. The survival of my kind has long depended upon our being able to understand and avoid the scrutiny of mere mortals. But none of us will be able to escape your interested readers once you've filled their minds with the facts of our lives." Lifting the glass, he drank deeply, aware that she was moving nearer. He turned and she fell still. "I am a member of Parliament," he told her. "There are a number of important matters coming before us soon. I do not wish to be distracted from those matters by having to constantly answer queries from my peers about whether the stories of my great-grandfather are true. The lives of my kind are already precarious enough, Miss Tamony, without being turned into a complete circus."

"I can find a way to keep that from happening," she vowed. "Only give me the chance to prove that to you."

"No," he said. Draining the glass, he set it down with a resounding thud. "I cannot take the risk. There is nothing more to discuss. I shall not change my mind."

Miss Tamony gazed at him from across the short distance that separated them, her lovely eyes slightly narrowed and her expressive mouth pursed. Her hands, he saw, were still toying with the amulet. She seemed to be considering whether she should continue to press her case or give way. After a long moment she tucked the amulet back beneath the collar of her shirt and then folded her hands primly before her.

"You are right, my lord. There is nothing else for us to discuss. Since I have come to Glain Tarran without invitation, I must be responsible for my return to the village. However, as you sent my horse away, I must necessarily borrow one of yours. Would you be so kind as to have one made ready for me?"

Her seeming capitulation should have calmed him, but Malachi only felt more aggravated. He knew full well that the accursed woman was going to attempt to write her book. She'd merely given up arguing about it.

"You would never reach the village in time to stop your absence from being discovered. Which would be just as you deserve for being so foolish as to have undertaken such a task in the first place. But if your parents haven't yet found the way to convince you to behave properly, I doubt any amount of humiliation and disapproval will cause you to do so. Nor will you be impressed by my speaking of the dangers that a young woman risks by riding about the countryside at such an hour."

"I am fully aware of the dangers," she told him, "and am prepared to answer both the anger of my family and the disgust of the villagers if my absence is discovered. This is not the first time I've ventured out for the sake of my work."

He uttered an unpleasant laugh. "I had the idea that it was not. What you need, Miss Tamony, is a firm hand to keep you from such foolishness. If you ever marry, I shall pray that your husband is capable of managing you."

For the first time since she'd come to Glain Tarran, Sarah Tamony looked truly angry. Her green eyes flashed beneath her spectacles and her mouth thinned into a small, straight line. Malachi had the most shocking urge to cross the distance between them, grab her up in his arms, and kiss her until her passion changed from fury to something altogether different.

"I am six and twenty years of age, my lord," she said coldly. "I have managed my own life full well for most of those years, and my family will tell you the same. I grant you that they've had moments of despair on my account, but if I had listened to their dire predictions of doom I never should have had the courage to put pen to paper. Please tell Rhys that I have absolved you of the promise you gave him. I do not think it wise that we should be in company any longer this evening. Or morning, rather. If you will give me the loan of a horse, Lord Graymar, I shall have it returned to you come daylight. If not, I shall walk back to the village."

Malachi's eyebrows rose. She clearly meant what she said, and he had no doubt that her current temper had her within but minutes of striding out of the castle and onto the road that led toward the gates. What a remarkable female she was, despite being so troublesome.

"You know very well that I'd not let you, or any woman, make such a journey in either the wind or the darkness, certainly not alone. I shall have Enoch saddled and—"

But she was already moving toward the door. Malachi was so surprised that he neglected to make it impossible for her to open, and the next moment she was out of the room entirely. Muttering a curse, Malachi followed.

"Miss Tamony," he said, catching up to her in the hall. "I really cannot let you . . . Miss Tamony, please stop. There's no need for such behavior."

She ignored him, deftly retracing their earlier path toward the castle's entry. A footman appeared at the end of the hall and looked at his master inquiringly. Malachi waved him away.

"Miss Tamony, will you please stop and allow me to—"

She whirled about, the motion causing her already-precarious hair arrangement to become partly undone.

Several auburn curls slipped from the top of her head past her shoulder and almost to her waist. Malachi was so enchanted by the sight that he nearly missed the heated glare she had set upon him.

"Allow you to do what, my lord?" she demanded. "Insult me once more? I may have trespassed uninvited upon your lands and forced myself into your company, but at least I have not been discourteous. I suppose I cannot be entirely surprised by your behavior, for you did warn me that you are not always a proper gentleman." Lifting a finger, she poked him in the chest. "You may take some comfort, my lord, in the knowledge that you're at least honest." Turning on her heel, she walked away again.

Malachi followed. "Insulted you?" he repeated with some affront. "By speaking the truth?" It occurred to him that she'd been more offended by his remark about needing a man's firm hand than by his earlier, far more outrageously improper behavior. Women could be so confoundedly bewildering. "Is this how you writers behave when matters don't fall your way? If so, it's a miracle that anything ever gets written."

She cast him a gaze so filled with scorn that Malachi was surprised it didn't burn a hole in his head.

"I'll write my book," she said hotly. "And I don't need any man telling me how or why or whether I should do it." They had reached the vestibule, and she began searching for her things.

"Rhys is coming with your belongings," Malachi told her. "Be still a moment, Miss Tamony, and collect yourself." To Rhys, who appeared a moment later bearing Miss Tamony's coat, hat, gloves, and knapsack, he said, "I told you to go to bed."

"Yes, my lord, and so you did." Rhys walked past him to help Miss Tamony with her garments. "I hope you found the refreshments to your liking, Miss Tamony."

"Oh dear," she said as she took the cap from the older man. "I only managed a sip of the wine, and had none of the tarts. They did look delicious, and the wine was excellent. I'm afraid my discussion with His Lordship made eating impossible."

Rhys cast a disapproving look at his master. "Yes, miss," he said. "I fear that's all too common. I do hope you'll come again, when we can welcome you more properly."

"You are very kind, thank you," she said, taking his hands in both of hers and squeezing them. "But I'll not be coming to Glain Tarran again. Perhaps I shall see you in London? I'll be giving a lecture at the Society for the Study of the Mystical and Supernatural, and I should be gratified if you'd come."

Malachi couldn't stop the groan that escaped his lips, which earned him glares from both Miss Tamony and Rhys.

"Thank you, miss," the butler said with clear pleasure. "I shall indeed come and hear you, if His Lordship will allow."

"Oh, does he believe you require a firm hand, as well?" she asked. "I'm so sorry."

"His Lordship won't be required to have any kind of hand," Malachi said, "for you'll not be giving any such speech. I have already warned you, Miss Tamony, that I shall put a stop to—"

"Yes, yes, I know," she put in angrily, tugging a glove onto one hand. "You'll not allow me to write my book or expose your family or do anything that you don't want me to do. I am not deaf, my lord. I heard every word you said." The other glove was on, and the hat as well. Taking up her knapsack, she slung it over her shoulder. "Good-bye, Rhys," she said. "It was wonderful meeting you, and thank you for the lovely things you said about my books. I hope that you and your grandchildren will enjoy the next one. It will be published sometime next year."

Rhys looked from Miss Tamony to Malachi and back to Miss Tamony again. "Thank you, miss; I'm sure I shall. But surely you don't mean to go out without His Lordship?"

"Of course she doesn't," Malachi stated flatly. "Fetch my coat, Rhys, and have Enoch made ready. I'll be escorting Miss Tamony back to the village."

"No, he won't," she said. "Little though you may credit

it, I am perfectly capable of walking five miles. And I am well armed for any kind of attack, be it from man or beast. But you know that, do you not, my lord? You knew what I carried in my pack from the moment you found me."

He did, Malachi admitted. She had packed a number of useful powders and potions in her knapsack. Sorsha's mixtures were among the best and most powerful to be had. Miss Tamony would be able to blind, confound, or paralyze anyone who attempted to touch her . . . save magic mortals, who would be immune.

"My coat, Rhys," he repeated. "Miss Tamony is eager to be away."

Rhys obediently turned, and in the same moment Sarah Tamony strode to the great castle doors and, with an effort, pulled one open. The howling wind made the task more difficult, but she managed to get out, shutting the door firmly behind her.

Both Malachi and Rhys stared at the door in astonishment.

"But why did you not stop her, my lord?" the servant asked. "Why did you not make the door hold fast?"

"I did," Malachi murmured faintly, disbelieving what he had seen. "I willed it not to open, but she . . ." He looked at Rhys. "It didn't stop her."

"But you can't have," Rhys said. "You must be mistaken. The doors of Glain Tarran cannot be opened if you do not wish them to."

"I willed them not to," Malachi repeated, much stunned. He was the most powerful sorcerer in all of Europe. Not even those who possessed great magic could avoid being affected by his spells. No mortal had ever done so. "I locked the doors before she touched them. They *must* be locked."

Rhys hurried forward and tested each door, pulling hard. They were locked tight. He turned, and the two men stared in stunned silence. It was magic, as the whispers had warned. A strong and terrible magic that was wrapped about Miss Sarah Tamony. It had held Malachi spellbound when they were in the study and somehow made her immune to his powers. The implication filled him with dread.

"Fetch my coat," he said again. "Quickly, Rhys."

"And Enoch?"

Malachi gave a shake of his head. "She'll be halfway to Glain Tarran's boundaries by the time he's ready. I shall have to take her the other way."

"Oh dear," said Rhys, "I cannot think that wise, my lord. Miss Tamony seems full angry with you."

Malachi cast him a wry smile. "She is a woman who needs a firm hand, Rhys," he said. "I'll be more than happy to oblige."

Chapter 7

"A firm hand," Sarah muttered as she strode along, her long legs eating up the road. "A *man's* firm hand," she went on, pulling her cap down more tightly as the wind threatened to whip it off. She stuffed several loose strands of hair up beneath the hat, wishing that her arrangement hadn't come undone. Her hair was far too thick and long to stay up without being pinned, and she didn't have the time just now to deal with it properly.

"I need a husband to manage me, do I?" she asked no one in particular, pushing her spectacles up with one finger. "I suppose he thinks I researched and wrote my books by the merest chance. Perhaps he thinks that my father actually wrote them, or my brother, and that they let me put my name to the work as a gift. Ha!"

He would be coming after her, of course. Not because he was a gentleman, but because he was a man, with a man's misguided sense of what a woman needed—which at the moment was a man to take charge and make her decisions for her. Sarah wanted to walk off as much of her fury as possible before he arrived. If she'd thought there was any chance of outdistancing him or avoiding his discovery, she might have been tempted to veer off-course and into the trees. But he was not a mere mortal, nor limited by a mere mortal's senses. And she wouldn't be able to make him go away and let her walk to the village in freezing peace, for he was bigger and stronger and at least as stubborn as she was. He would throw her on his magnificent horse and carry her home and see that she was safely deposited in the village. Then he would ride away with a "good riddance" and very likely pray that he never set eyes on her again. Sarah would sneak back into her room, make herself ready for sleep, and lie in her bed and cry until the sun came up.

It would be foolish to pretend that she wouldn't cry, because she knew very well that she would, and if there was one thing that Sarah was, it was honest. Especially with herself.

But it was all right. A good cry was just what she needed, especially after being in company with the Earl of Graymar for the past hour. He had completely upended her emotions; had made Sarah feel things that no man had ever done before, had even made her imagine things—God help her, such things—that would stay in her thoughts forever.

She was six and twenty and not ignorant of what passed between men and women. Indeed, she'd been held and groped and kissed and even fondled before—not always because she wished to be, either, though some of those embraces had been rather pleasant. She had especially fond memories of the handsome, magical stranger who had rescued her in Florence, who had parted from her with a kiss that still had the power, after three years, to make her skin tingle.

But men, she had discovered, could often be quite insistent when aroused, and she'd been obliged to deal forcefully with particularly determined males in the past. A knee here, a slap there, an elbow in the stomach. She'd learned how to deal with unruly admirers.

But never before had *she* been the unruly one. Never before had it been her desire that had driven Sarah to want a

man to do things to her that were surely, surely sinful. Just
thinking on the visions that had come to her mind when
Malachi Seymour touched her made Sarah hot with embarrassment. Where had such ideas come from? She'd
seen them in her mind's eye, herself and Lord Graymar in
a bed, completely unclothed and . . . oh, heavens, doing
such things. And then, when he'd told her that she was
beautiful, that her skin was warm and soft, Sarah had felt
something deep within her that had been frightening. Her
body had become infused with an ardent, intense, desperate need. If Lord Graymar had led her to the couch and
laid her down upon it, she would have gladly gone and
done whatever he wished.

And then . . . then he'd done the most enchanting thing
that any man had ever done for her. Or, rather, that any man
who was not her father had done.

He'd told her a story, a wonderful story about the supernatural, one she'd not yet heard, and had made it so delightfully real. It had been a precious gift, far more
valuable to her than any other kind of present could be,
though Sarah suspected the Earl of Graymar didn't realize
that. Her father had often teased that none of her many
suitors would be able to win Sarah's heart until one of
them had mastered the ability to enchant her with a good
tale. The man who could do that would be the man Sarah
could love.

"He's a wretched, ignorant brute," she muttered, trying
to push away the memory of Malachi Seymour's handsome face, so near her own, as he'd gazed down at the
amulet, and the sound of his voice, so perfectly measured,
as he'd told its tale.

It had all been a trick. It must have been. Another attempt to make her heart vulnerable so that he might wreak
vengeance. For just as her heart had indeed begun to
soften, he'd changed again, becoming cold and hard and
implacable. And insulting. She might have deserved all the
rest for coming to Glain Tarran uninvited, but not the last.

And the thought hurt. Badly. He had captured a tiny

piece of her heart with his storytelling, and Sarah wasn't at all certain whether she'd ever have it back again. After all these years, after being so careful with the men she'd met, after telling herself that she wasn't vulnerable to masculine wiles and tricks, not even those of wizards, because she understood them so well . . . Sarah had fallen prey to the simplest possible ploy. A story. God help her. A mere story had let him sneak past all her defenses.

"I suppose I should be grateful that he didn't regale me with his entire family history," she muttered, pulling her cap down tighter upon her lowered head during a particularly strong gust of wind. "There'd be nothing left of me after that. He'd have devoured me whole, and I probably never would have even realized what—oh!"

She thought for a moment, as her feet lost their balance, that she'd accidentally run into a tree. But trees, she realized at once, didn't emanate warmth or wear heavy wool.

"If I had wished to devour you, Miss Tamony," said the Earl of Graymar above the wind's roar, "I would have done so." With strong, deft movements he righted Sarah and steadied her. "For a woman so determined to have her own way," he went on, "you certainly have a knack for importuning others."

She looked up at him from beneath the rim of her cap. He looked just as aggravated as he sounded, which from what she'd seen thus far appeared to be the Earl of Graymar's most common state of mind. He had come after her in a hurry, for although he wore his heavy cloak he had taken no hat, with the result that his lengthy blond hair was flying in every direction. He looked like a windswept Viking lord at the helm of his ship.

"I am no longer importuning you, my lord," she told him with matching displeasure. "If you will move aside, I shall shortly be off your land and then we can be done with each other. You have my permission to treat me as a complete stranger in London, and if we do have the misfortune to be introduced, I give my solemn oath that I shall make the acquaintance as distant as possible at every event that we both happen to attend."

She tried to move around him; he stepped in front of her.

"My lord," she began between gritted teeth.

"Be quiet a moment," he commanded, setting a steely hand on her arm to keep her still. "I can scarce make sense of what you're saying over all this noise." Lifting a hand, he shouted, "Peidio!" and the wind, as it had done earlier, began to quiet. "That's better," he said, and with a gloved finger tilted Sarah's gaze up to meet his own. "Now, Miss Tamony, listen well, for we've not much time left in which to safely return you to the inn, and I would rather not be forced to use magic on any of the villagers—all of whom know me well—or your family. This means that we must travel quickly, and do not have the luxury of arguing any further this night."

"I—"

"Please," he cut her off firmly. "I should not have spoken to you as I did about requiring a man to guide you. You clearly found the words to be particularly insulting, in part, I should imagine, because of the independent life you've been encouraged by your free-minded parents to live. And I do not," he added quickly when Sarah opened her mouth once more, "mean any insult to your good family by making such a statement. I simply meant that you have been raised with the notion that you do not need a man to have a successful life. It is an odd idea, which I'm sure you would acknowledge, but it is yours, and I must therefore respect it. In any event, I apologize, fully and sincerely."

"That," Sarah replied, pulling free of his touch, "was the most graceless apology I have ever heard. I should think a nobleman of your rank and breeding could do far better with even a small amount of effort. I suppose you would not be insulted if I were to tell you that you needed a woman to manage you? Or be quite thrilled if I then apologized by saying that your thought of self-sufficiency was merely a 'notion' bred into you by parents who, though you may call them 'free minded,' you truthfully believe to be eccentric?"

"Miss Tamony," he said, sighing. "If you were to tell me that I require a woman's managing, I would agree wholeheartedly and then proceed to inform you that there are no women in existence who would be willing to take on the task. As to your parents, they are decidedly eccentric, else they'd not have a daughter who makes a habit of roaming about the countryside in the wee hours of the morning, trespassing on the lands of strangers and exposing herself to any and every manner of danger. As to my parents, I would also readily agree that they were just as odd, probably more so, but they, at least, had the excuse of not being mere mortals. All of my people are strange from birth, and there is nothing that can be done to change them. I can only assume that you are strange because of your upbringing. Now, can we please make peace and tend to the matter of getting you back to the village?"

Sarah's temper was scarcely mollified by his words, but she had to admit that, sparing that bit about no woman on earth being willing to take him on, he had spoken honestly and openly. Apart from that, why should she be so angry that he thought her odd when it was what so many others believed, too?

"I suppose it's the least I can do after coming to Glain Tarran as I did," she said. "Very well, Lord Graymar. All is forgiven." She extended a gloved hand. He looked at it for a bewildered moment before lifting his own. Sarah grasped it and gave it a firm shake. "There." She released him. "We can now meet in Society and be perfectly polite."

"You're yet angry," he said, just as the wind grew impatient with being still and began to blow again.

"I'm freezing," she said loudly, huddling into her coat. "It's enough to make anyone ill-tempered. I had not intended to stay at Glain Tarran so long, and thought to have a warm horse to ride back to the village." She looked about and felt a stark sense of disappointment at not seeing Enoch. "Are we to walk, then?" she asked, unable to keep the lack of enthusiasm for such an undertaking from her tone.

He smiled. "Were you not planning on walking back?"

Her spirits dampened even more fully. "Yes," she admitted. "I was. It's kind of you to keep me company. I'm sure it will make the miles pass more quickly."

He stepped in front of her again when she tried to move around him. This time he set both hands on her arms.

"I believe that you are a brave soul, Miss Tamony. Are you afraid of heights?"

Sarah gave him a curious look. "No, not in the least. I can't abide complete darkness, but heights have never bothered me. Why?"

"Because you're about to experience a certain kind of magic that I've never shared with a mere mortal before, and I wished to make certain that you'd not faint or scream or react with terror. Otherwise I might drop you."

Her eyes widened. "Drop me?"

"I'd better take these," he said, pulling her spectacles from her face. "Without a ribbon, they might fall off."

"Fall off?" she repeated. "But—"

"Make certain your knapsack is secured on your back and your cap fixed on your head," he instructed, safely tucking the folded spectacles into an inner pocket. "Now, put your arms about me very tightly. About my neck. You will have to go up on your toes."

Sarah, in the midst of pulling the cap down a bit more, stopped and stared at him. He gazed back calmly.

"Hurry, Miss Tamony. The wind isn't going to hold back its full force for much longer."

"But I—" She gave a shake of her head. "My lord, I can't simply put my arms about you as if I . . . as if we . . ." She flung her hands into the air. "I don't know you that well."

The smile that touched his lips was more than a little amused. "I'm pleased to know that you possess some sense of propriety, Miss Tamony, despite the penchant for trespassing. But I'm afraid there's nothing for it. We must hold on to each other quite closely if I'm to carry you into the sky. In fact, I fear I must give you a complete disgust of myself before we arrive at the village, for I do find you very attractive, as I made clear to you before."

Sarah's heart gave a thump as she remembered the caress of his warm hands on her skin. But the memory was easily overpowered by what he'd said before.

"Lord Graymar," she asked, taking a step nearer so that he could hear her over the wind, "did you say that you intend to carry me into the sky?"

He nodded. "If you're willing for such an adventure, Miss Tamony. We can fly to the village very quickly, and I can keep you warm on the journey."

A rush of excitement filled Sarah, pushing all other thoughts aside. To fly, like a bird, up into the air . . . it was a dream come true.

"Oh, my lord," she said happily. "I'm certainly willing. How wonderful!"

She stepped even nearer and put her arms about his neck, smiling up into his face. His own expression was more sober, but he gave his attention to setting his cloak about her, being careful to envelop the knapsack as well. He murmured a single word, far too low for her to make out, and the heavy garment wrapped itself close to Sarah's body, cocooning her inside with Lord Graymar and imparting a comforting warmth. Then she felt his arms slide carefully around her waist, pulling her flush against his hard body.

"Oh," Sarah said, suddenly understanding what he'd meant by giving her a disgust of himself. Not that she was disgusted, but perhaps a bit alarmed. She was not unfamiliar with the sensation of being held against an aroused man, though always before it had been unwillingly and she'd been engaged in pushing said man away. But she'd never before stood like this, of her own volition, and actually felt that arousal for more than a brief moment. "Oh dear."

"I apologize," he said somewhat grimly. "I'm afraid there's nothing I can do to spare you. If it's of any help, you might think upon the fact that I find it as irritating as you do. If you feel that you cannot bear such intimacy, we can return to Glain Tarran and saddle Enoch. He is very swift, but I cannot promise that we'll achieve the village in time to avoid notice."

"Oh no," she said at once. "I promise you I don't mind. Please, Lord Graymar. Please take me into the sky."

She was like a child being offered a marvelous treat, Malachi thought, gazing into her upturned face. Her eyes sparkled beneath the moonlight, filled with an anticipation that only made his body harden further. Then, to make matters worse, she snuggled closer and wrapped her arms even more tightly about his neck. He stifled a tormented groan.

It took an effort to set his mind to the task at hand. He had never actually held a person while flying before, but he believed the attempt would be successful. Sarah Tamony was not a tiny or delicate female, but she was slender and, he discovered as they began to rise, light to carry.

She uttered a sound when she felt their upward motion, similar to a squeal, and when her feet left the ground her arms squeezed about Malachi so tightly that they nearly cut off his intake of air.

"I have you securely, Miss Tamony," he promised as they went higher. "You may trust that I'll keep you safe. Are you warm enough?" The wind, as they rose, blew harder, colder.

"Oh yes," she assured him, looking from side to side, a wide smile on her lips. "Very warm, thank you." Then she laughed and gave a shake of her head. "We're *flying!*" she cried happily. "I can scarce believe it, but we are!"

Malachi found himself smiling, too. Sarah Tamony was an easy female to please, at least when it came to magic. He wondered what she would do if he performed a truly difficult feat. The idea was a mistake, for it filled his brain with forbidden images again. Having her pressed so intimately against him didn't help.

He took her up even higher, as he liked to do himself when flying, so that she could see the landscape far off into the moonlit distance, the wild, vast sea to one side and the rolling countryside to the other. She was speechless with wonder, gazing all about and then upward, to the endless stars above.

"Are you all right, Miss Tamony?" Malachi asked, filled with an unusual satisfaction at her reaction. Any other mere mortal female of his acquaintance would likely have been screaming to get down by now.

Sarah looked at him, her expression filled with open happiness. "Can we go higher?" she asked. "Up to the stars?"

"No," he murmured, thinking that if she truly wished to make the attempt, he'd be willing. "There is a way to get there, but it requires a different kind of magic. If you wish it, we can let the wind blow us to the village." He hesitated, wondering if she was that brave. "It can be frighteningly wild," he warned, "but we'll not be harmed."

"Yes, let's!" she cried eagerly. "Please, my lord."

"Very well, then," he said. "Hold tight." To the wind, he shouted, "Chwythu!"

The wind obeyed and sent them twirling in the direction of the village. Sarah Tamony shrieked with delight as they were lifted and dropped and then lifted again, spinning wildly, even tumbling head over feet in great circles. Her hat blew off, falling away unnoticed and uncared for, and her long auburn hair flew free of all bonds. She tilted her head back and closed her eyes, letting her hair make a banner behind her, shouting out as freely and unashamedly as Malachi had never heard another female do. He laughed, too, feeling foolishly giddy. They were like two children and, indeed, Malachi couldn't remember being this abandoned since he was a boy. He could scarce open his own eyes for the force of the wind's play, but enough so that he could look at her, with her head thrown back and her mouth opened, joy exuding from every pore.

He wanted it to go on for hours, to keep her body next to his, so close that they might almost be making love, and not return to the ground or reality until the sun rose and took the choice away. But they neared the village within minutes, and the wind gradually ceased amusing them.

Slowly, carefully, Malachi brought them to earth behind a copse of trees near the village inn, experiencing the usual momentary unsteadiness of being on solid ground again. It passed quickly and they stood grinning at each other and swaying to gain balance.

She was still laughing, and Malachi lifted a finger to touch her lips, warning her to be quiet. Which only made both of them laugh again.

"Shhhhh," he said, still grinning foolishly. "We can't be heard."

"Oh, that was *wonderful*!" she declared, her voice low but no less excited. "I wish it had never stopped. Thank you, my lord, a thousand times over. I shall never be able to repay you for such a boon."

He wanted to kiss her. Desperately. He wanted to pull her down to the ground and continue what they'd begun in the air. For it had been a seductive intimacy, flying together. It had been passionate and pleasurable and intense, and he knew, with a sense of painful clarity, that he'd never know that same pleasure with another woman.

Sarah came to her senses more quickly than he did, and began to withdraw. Malachi fought the urge to hold her fast, to keep her sheltered within the folds of his cloak. But if he didn't let her go he would give her that kiss, and nothing would stop him thereafter. And if someone from the village, perhaps the baker or dairyman, happened to step out-of-doors to begin his early day, all of Malachi's good intentions in sparing Miss Tamony embarrassment would be lost.

Pulling his cloak apart, he let her step back, and the coldness swept in once more. Her arms slid from his neck and her warmth departed, but as she stood away she yet smiled up at him in that enchanting, well-pleased manner. Her unbound hair, he saw, was thick and lovely and hung to the small of her back. She looked like one of his ancestors from the ancient days, a wild, pagan woman far closer to nature and far freer in spirit.

But she was not a pagan woman. She was a lady of good birth, and he was a gentleman by name and the Earl of Graymar, as well. They were no longer tumbling unconstrained by earth's decrees, high in the cold night sky and unfettered from life's cares, but standing on the ground and bound by all that such a thing meant. He had always been starkly aware of the difference. Sarah Tamony, by her subtly changing expression, was, too.

"Thank you," she said again, straightening her coat and running her hands over her hair. "For all that you've done, my lord. I'm quite all right now." She cast a glance at the nearby inn. "I'll just go and make certain that the horse made its way safely back to the stable and—"

"I'll take care of it," he offered quietly. "I can move more silently than you, and will see that the horse is unsaddled and properly stalled. I hope its return woke no one, else there'll be a search party out looking for you. But I'll take care of that, as well, if necessary. You need only worry about how to return to the inn without being discovered. Shall I go with you to make certain of it?"

"No." She shook her head. "I climbed down a tree near the window and can easily scale it again. My cousin, Philistia, is well used to my adventures and will have left it unlatched."

"Poor Philistia," Malachi murmured. He reached into his coat and pulled out her spectacles. "Here. They appear to be unharmed from our journey. I'm sorry that your hat was lost. There are some things that the wind will give back, some it will not. I fear the hat is one of its amusements, now."

"I don't regret it," she told him, slipping the eyeglasses over her ears and upon her nose with the skill of long practice. She gazed at him for a moment, blinking as her vision cleared, and smiled. "I would have given away all my hats to have such an experience. I shall never forget it, to the end of my days."

"I'm glad, if it gave you pleasure."

"Very much," she assured him. "I fear my stubbornness in the matter of the book is a poor way to repay such a gift."

"There is no need to repay," he said honestly, thinking that she had already given him a far greater gift, one that he would equally treasure. "But I don't wish to be at enmity with you, Miss Tamony. Can you not reconsider and choose another subject? You are a writer of great skill, after all. Any topic you embark upon is certain to be welcome to your readers."

"That is good of you to say, my lord," she replied, "but my heart has fixed upon telling these wonderful stories. I don't think I can unfix it."

He took her hand and bowed over it. "I shall hope that you will at least make the attempt." Rising full height, he released her. "But if not, I beg you to believe that I meant what I said earlier. I shall stop you from writing about the Seymours and any of those families who have given me their trust. It is my duty to them as their guardian, and I can do no less."

She nodded. "I understand, my lord. But I will write the book, and it will be wonderful. I'll send you an inscribed copy—or two, perhaps. One to give to Rhys."

"Then it appears we're still at cross-purposes," Malachi said, sighing wearily.

"Yes," she agreed. "But I trust that we won't have to think of each other as enemies, my lord."

"I hope not, Miss Tamony," Malachi said, but the whispers at the edges of his thoughts told him that it would be otherwise. She would hate him soon.

With another beguiling smile she bid him good night, then hurried through the darkness toward the inn. Malachi stood behind the trees, watching as she nimbly scaled the tree that grew by the old stone building. A time or two he nearly flew—literally—to catch her, certain she was about to fall, but she was as adept at climbing as she was at crossing stubborn boundaries. Sitting on the ledge of the open window, she turned to wave at him. Malachi lifted a hand, as well, though he knew she couldn't see it.

The next moment she was gone, and Malachi's heart gave an unexpected lurch of pain. He drew in a breath of cold night air and wondered at what he was feeling. Loss. Sorrow. Longing. And something else that was deeply familiar: a stark aloneness.

Chapter 8

LONDON, MID-MARCH

*B*ut, Sarah, you can't possibly go out today," Philistia said unhappily. "Madame Duget will be coming soon to do fittings for the gowns we ordered, and to discuss the other garments we want made. You'll wish to choose your own cloth, I'm sure, for you're always so particular about the colors you wear."

Sarah set aside the book she'd been examining with some regret—it was the most recent addition to her new collection—and gave her attention to her cousin.

"With hair like mine, it's a necessity," she replied. "But I do think that you and Mama have had enough experience ordering garments for me that I might leave the task to you." She pushed her spectacles higher on her nose. "I have an appointment with Professor Seabolt this afternoon and don't mean to abandon it because of a few new gowns."

"I don't mind taking charge of your wardrobe, Sarah," her mother said, not looking up from the numerous cards and letters that lay before her upon a small writing desk, "but you must promise not to complain if you end up with a dress made in a color not of your liking. You can be most particular, at times."

"Avoid yellows and pinks and any shade too pale and we shall all be in charity with one another at the end of the day," Sarah advised. "And I can't think that Madame Duget will have any trouble adorning me with suitable shades, for she did remark upon my hair when we were at her shop."

"But the fitting," Philistia said worriedly. "Surely you must stay for that."

Sarah smiled at the younger woman reassuringly. "I'll stay for that, I promise. The rest I'll leave to the two of you, and to Madame Duget, of course. From the samples we saw in her shop, I believe we're in very capable hands."

Philistia's face lit with excitement, and she scooted forward so quickly to the edge of her chair that Sarah thought for an alarming moment she might fall off.

"The gowns in her shop were beautiful, weren't they?" Philistia said. "Aunt Speakley was perfectly right in sending us there. And how fortunate that Madame Duget and her assistants have all read your books, Sarah! They seemed almost overcome at meeting you. All of London is overcome, just as Aunt Speakley said they would be. We can scarce step out-of-doors without meeting one of your readers. And the invitations we've received!" She pressed her hands together and held them to her breast. "It's far more wonderful than I'd hoped."

Sarah was glad that her cousin found the attention they'd received since reaching Town to be so pleasant. For her own part, Sarah found it tiresome. She could scarce go about London, doing research or conducting interviews, without being approached by someone who'd read one of her books and had myriad questions or comments. She was glad, of course, that so many people enjoyed reading her work, but she did wish that she weren't so confoundedly identifiable. It was due to the spectacles and hair color, Sarah knew, for the combination was rare enough in Englishwomen to cause her to stand out in public.

Not that it mattered, she supposed, for many of the interviews she'd planned on while in London had been canceled by the individuals she'd contacted, all of whom had suddenly lost their previous enthusiasm for speaking with Sarah. She'd also discovered that other research sources were mysteriously closed to her, certain bookstores and shops, for instance, where items dealing in the supernatural were secretly sold and private libraries that had been collected and maintained by those who might be considered sympathetics to magic mortals.

Lord Graymar had worked quickly in keeping his promise, much to Sarah's displeasure. But he'd not yet managed to close every avenue that had been opened to her, and foremost among her few remaining contacts was Professor Harris Seabolt. Nothing—certainly not a dress fitting—was going to stop her from keeping her appointment with him this afternoon. Especially not now that she needed his opinion on a certain baffling occurrence.

"We do seem to be desirable company," Lady Tamony remarked, setting aside one piece of paper and picking up another. "The Season hasn't even truly started yet and we've received so many invitations that we can't possibly accept them all. Yet they keep coming." She gave a bemused shake of her head. "I scarcely know how to respond, and your father isn't any help."

"Papa wants to go to everything," Sarah said with a laugh. "He's the most social member of the entire family, next to Philla. If it was up to the two of them," she went on, casting a teasing smile at her cousin, "we'd spend all of our time dancing and eating and none of it sleeping."

Lady Tamony sighed. "I don't recall half these names. Sir Alberic and I never could have had so many acquaintances in England. Here's an invitation to a musical evening at Lady Pettenborough's on Friday next, and this one, for the same evening, is for dinner and cards at Mrs. Silverby's. She's a friend of your aunt's, isn't she?" She looked at her daughter and niece. "Do either of these interest you girls? If not, there are four other invitations for gatherings on the same night, all of the same variety."

Sarah exchanged glances with Philistia, who looked as nonplussed as Sarah, herself, felt.

"Will there be dancing, do you think, Aunt Caroline?" Philistia asked.

"Not at these sorts of gatherings, dear," her aunt replied. "But a few evenings engaged in quieter pursuits might make a nice change. Sir Alberic enjoys cards and conversation and Julius will find nothing but balls and dances most trying."

"Dinner and cards, then," Sarah said. "Especially if Mrs. Silverby is one of Aunt Speakley's friends. She's set her heart on introducing us to her particular acquaintances, after all."

"Very well," Lady Tamony said, placing the invitation in a small pile upon the desk and shoving several others aside. "Now, the ball being given by Lady Madden is to be held the following week—"

Philistia uttered an ecstatic trill, causing her aunt to give her a patient look before going on.

"—and your Aunt Speakley declares that we cannot, on any account, miss it. Fortunately, we've been granted tickets to attend Almack's two evenings previous so that Philistia can be given permission to waltz."

"Oh, Mama, how foolish," Sarah declared. "It's 1823, after all. The waltz is no longer such a shocking dance that one must ask permission to participate."

"Nevertheless," her mother said, "we will observe the proprieties for Philistia's sake. You're old enough to waltz without permission, but Philistia is scarcely past twenty. We'll take no chances that unpleasant talk will spring up."

Sarah had a good deal to say about the rumors that London society thrived on, but as Philistia's eyes had begun to glimmer with happiness at the thought of being given permission to waltz—a dance she'd already enjoyed in nearly every country on the Continent—she wisely held her peace.

"However," Lady Tamony went on, "there is one function that takes precedent over all others, and that is the Herold ball. Invitations have already been sent and we were fortunate enough to receive an additional invitation to join Lord and Lady Herold for dinner before the ball along with a select few other guests. Your aunt informs me that one of those expected to attend is someone of particular interest to you, Sarah."

Sarah, whose mind had wandered to her coming appointment with Professor Seabolt, pretended to look interested. "Oh?"

Her mother gave her a knowing look. "Yes, my dear. He is the Earl of Graymar, who you spoke of so often as we journeyed to London. I've not heard you mention him of late, but I supposed that was because you didn't wish to displease Julius. If, however, you still desire an opportunity to speak with the man, a dinner party would be an ideal opportunity, and there's nothing Julius could do to stop the meeting."

At the sound of the earl's name, Sarah's heart gave a thump. She straightened in her chair and made her tone purposefully light.

"Lord Graymar? How interesting. Of course I should like nothing better than meeting him. How odd that we should be invited to the same gathering as someone of his stature."

And now her heart began to do something altogether different, racing at the thought of seeing him again. She had relived their hours together over and again since leaving Pembrokeshire and had wondered if, or when, she might see him once more. She'd listened for any hint that the Earl of Graymar had returned to London, for surely Aunt Speakley would know of it the moment he came to Town. If he had agreed to attend the Herold ball, along with the dinner beforehand, then surely he must be at Mervaille.

"Shall I reply that we'll attend, then?" Lady Tamony inquired.

"It sounds as if it would be terribly entertaining," Sarah said. "Perhaps you should, Mama."

"But you'll not overset His Lordship, will you, Sarah?" Philistia asked, looking at her with a worried expression. "Someone at the table will be sure to bring up the subject of your books, and considering all the letters you've exchanged with Lord Graymar and the feelings he's expressed . . ."

Sarah had been careful not to tell her cousin about her adventures in Lord Graymar's company on the night when she'd gone to Glain Tarran. She'd told Philistia, when she'd asked the following morning, that nothing had happened and that her journey to the Earl of Graymar's ancestral estate had been entirely uneventful. They'd not spoken of the matter since.

"I feel certain that nothing I do could surprise the Earl of Graymar," Sarah replied truthfully, "but I give you my promise that I'll be on my best behavior when meeting him."

A scratch came at the door and Annie, the downstairs maid they'd hired after arriving in London, entered the parlor bearing a small silver tray. Lady Tamony looked at her askance, clearly expecting another invitation, but the maid curtsied and hurried to Sarah, instead.

"This was just delivered for you, miss," Annie said, bobbing another quick curtsy as Sarah took the sealed note.

"Thank you, Annie," she said, and the maid departed. Frowning, Sarah examined the inelegantly scrawled address on the missive before breaking the seal. The words within had been just as hastily written.

Miss Tamony, it began. *Forgive, please, this late notice regarding our intended meeting of this afternoon. I'm afraid that matters have arisen which make it impossible for me to keep this appointment with you, and I find that my calendar is such that I shall also be unable to reschedule it for another time in either the near or distant future. I also regret to inform you that the meeting of the Society for the Study of the Mystical and Supernatural at which you were scheduled to speak has been canceled. I believe there may, in fact, be no meetings of the Society at all this Season, and thus we must permanently postpone the lecture to which you had so kindly offered to treat us. Please accept my deepest regrets for this unfortunate turn of events, and my sincerest thanks for your understanding. I remain, your servant, Harris Seabolt.*

"What is it, Sarah?" Philistia asked. "You look as if you've received some bad news."

"No, not at all," Sarah said quickly, folding the missive and stuffing it inside her sleeve. "It's merely from my publisher, Mr. Stafford, regarding our meeting tomorrow afternoon. He wished to remind me to bring the notes I've made for the next book." She smiled at both her cousin and mother. "That's all. Is Aunt Speakley coming today, Mama? I thought she had promised to help you sort out our many invitations."

"Yes, she should be here soon," Lady Tamony said, her attention diverted to the piles on her desk.

"Excellent," Sarah murmured, though her thoughts weren't really on her beloved aunt at all. They were firmly fixed on a certain diabolical earl who was beginning to make Sarah very angry indeed.

He must be in London, then, she thought silently. And he must have visited with Professor Seabolt quite recently, for the professor had undergone a rapid change of heart to have written to her in such a manner.

The parlor door opened once more and Julius entered, looking very handsome in the new dark green jacket that Weston had only just made for him. He was dressed for riding and shook his head when Philistia offered to pour him a cup of tea.

"No, thank you, Phil," he said. "I'm just going out to try the new mare Father bought at Tattersalls. I only stepped in to find out whether Sarah still means to visit with Professor Seabolt this afternoon."

"Yes, I do," Sarah told him. "I've only to wait for Madame Duget's arrival and stand still for a few measurements. Then I'll be off."

Julius nodded. "I'll take you, then, if you don't mind. One of the curators at the museum told me that the professor keeps a collection of fine Celtic artifacts that he allows visitors to view upon request. I should like to make an appointment for a viewing; then I'll leave you to your interview."

"I'm sure that would be fine," she said. "It would be nice to have your company, Jules." And helpful, as well, she thought as he departed. Professor Seabolt would find it difficult to send her away if her large and compelling brother was with her, and he'd certainly not be able to explain that he'd canceled their arranged meeting because Lord Graymar had asked him to. Julius's interest in Celtic history would give Sarah the time she needed to charm the good professor into at least answering a few of her inquiries. And far more important, he would be able to give her an opinion on her journal and the strange writing that had appeared within. She only needed a few moments of the professor's time, and she would have them.

"Surely you jest, Malachi," Niclas said in disbelief, gaping at his cousin. In one hand, held above a small table bearing two piles of various cards and papers, was an elegantly addressed invitation. "Dinner and cards at Mrs. Silverby's? You?"

Malachi, sitting behind a much larger desk, finished signing the last of the papers that Niclas had earlier put before him before replying, "Yes, me. And why not? I spend a great many evenings with such entertainment."

"I know you do," Niclas said, "but usually in far more exalted company. You must have some acquaintance to receive invitations from her, but do you know who Mrs. Silverby is?"

"The widowed sister of Sir Benjamin Lott," Malachi said. "Her father was Squire Lott and her mother was the third daughter of Sir John Talfrest, who was known for brewing an excellent beer in his cellar, thereby endearing himself to every neighbor within riding distance of his otherwise humble manor. I can only pray that Mrs. Silverby has managed to get her hands on the recipe and serves some of it at her party."

Niclas stared at him in silence, causing Malachi to add, "Don't be a snob, dear cousin."

"Me?" Niclas's tone was filled with insult and disbelief.

"Well, it doesn't sound as if you approve of me having dinner at Mrs. Silverby's," Malachi said, standing from the desk and surveying the neat piles he'd left. "There, that's everything, I think. Gad, what a lot of business there is to attend to when one has been away from Town so many weeks. I don't know how I'd manage it without your excellent aid, Niclas. But, then, organization is one of your gifts."

"I don't mind you having dinner at Mrs. Silverby's," Niclas insisted, slowly placing the invitation in the "accept" pile. "I'm simply surprised, because—well, you'd be the last to deny that you've always been particular about the company you keep."

With a sigh, Malachi strode around the massive desk. "So I've been told of late," he said, sitting in a chair opposite Niclas's. "Are there many other invitations to reply to?"

Niclas shuffled through the items on his lap. "About ten, but you've already filled your calendar for the next several weeks, almost up until the Herold ball."

"Yes, the Herold ball," Malachi murmured, tenting his fingers together thoughtfully. "And the dinner beforehand. It should make for an interesting evening."

"And that's another thing that's not like you, Cousin," Niclas said, eyeing Lord Graymar with suspicion. "I went to great lengths, at your insistence, to dissuade Miss Tamony from continuing in her quest to meet with you or anyone in our family, and yet you accept the Herold dinner invitation knowing full well that she'll be there."

Malachi lifted one shoulder in a light shrug. "You and Julia will be there as well, and also our cousin Dyfed and his sweet, darling wife. Perhaps I merely wished to spend an evening in the company of my loved ones."

The words only served to make Niclas look more curious. "You've been in company with us part of nearly each day since returning to London, and with Dyfed and Desdemona, as well, though that isn't quite the same thing."

"Heavens, no," Malachi agreed with a laugh.

"I grant you," Niclas continued thoughtfully, "that it's because of your nieces and nephews that you've come to see Julia and me, on the main, but you've had enough of their parents' society to be growing weary of it."

"I believe it would be impossible to grow weary of being in company with your beautiful wife," Malachi countered. "Now, you, *cfender,* are quite another matter. . . ."

Niclas's enormous intellect, famous among both mere and magic mortals, was working so perfectly that Malachi could almost see the wheels turning behind his cousin's eyes.

"You're already well acquainted with the other guests, most especially Lord Herold," he went on, "but you've gone to such lengths to avoid being in company with Miss Tamony, despite your admiration for Sir Alberic . . ." He fell silent for a moment before at last focusing his blue-eyed gaze on Lord Graymar.

"You accepted the invitation specifically because of the Tamonys," Niclas stated. "Why?"

Malachi shifted uncomfortably beneath his cousin's basilisk stare. He'd not told anyone about the night when Sarah Tamony had trespassed on his lands, and had forbidden Rhys to do so. Malachi hadn't yet come to any understanding about what had happened that night and didn't want to suffer anyone else's opinion until he did. Certainly not Niclas's. Some Seymours were far too prescient for their own good.

She had been constantly in Malachi's thoughts since they parted ways in the early-morning hours near the village inn. He'd not been able to escape her even in his dreams, which were so vivid that his body reacted when he simply thought of them. He had followed on her family's heels as they'd made their way to London, shortly after Saint David's Day. And once he'd achieved Mervaille, Malachi had used every bit of influence and power he possessed to know all that both she and her family did. Every outing undertaken, shop visited, order given, conversation held, and invitation received—he knew all of it.

His actions—and his obvious obsession—both surprised and alarmed Malachi. Never before had he been so bedeviled by a female. But this was magic, as he was constantly forced to remind himself, and could be neither avoided nor denied. Whatever the fates had in store for him regarding Sarah Tamony, Malachi could only accept and prepare for it. At the moment, most of his waking hours were occupied in finding a way to see her again without making too much of a spectacle of himself. Thus far he'd managed to secure invitations to nearly every event that the famous Miss Tamony had also been invited to, and now had only to decide which to accept or reject.

"I wished to meet the famous Miss Tamony," he said at last, offering a meager half lie. Niclas would see even through that but would likely make something entirely different out of it. "I've heard of little else since coming to Town, and well before that, as you know. But it's far worse now, with one and all speaking of having had a glimpse of her. She's yet to attend a single evening's amusement, yet every shop she's entered has become a shrine, and every street she's walked down a pilgrimage that must be taken. Helen of Troy appearing stark naked in the middle of St. James's could scarcely have caused such a fuss."

Niclas should have laughed at that last bit, at the very least, Malachi thought with a measure of discomfit. But he was still staring at Malachi in that direct and penetrating manner.

"I know you haven't had a change of heart about her book," Niclas murmured. "You've managed to put a stop to every interview the woman had. Even Professor Seabolt agreed to put her off, and if anyone loves to speak of the supernatural, it's him. Perhaps—" He pursed his lips and was thoughtful. "Perhaps it's because Dyfed and Desdemona will be present at the dinner as well, and you wish to make certain Miss Tamony doesn't interrogate them there? You don't wish to harm Miss Tamony, I know, or put her beneath a spell. You've already said you don't."

"It's not for that," Malachi answered honestly. "I haven't any fears regarding Dyfed or his lovely bride. Desdemona and I are in complete accord regarding the dangerous nature of Miss Tamony's writings." In point of fact, Desdemona, having been born a Caslin, was closer in nature to the dark Families than those aligned with the Seymours.

Her ideas about how to deal with troublesome mere mortals were much more forceful than Malachi's. Fortunately, she had given him her allegiance when she'd married his cousin Dyfed and was bound to obey Malachi's strictures about not using magic to deal with Sarah Tamony.

"It can't be to incite Miss Tamony's hopes in order to dash them or to meet Sir Alberic. You could arrange an introduction far more easily through one of your men's clubs and forgo being in Sarah Tamony's presence, which, if I recall correctly," Niclas said, tapping a long, well-manicured finger against the line of his jaw, "was of great importance but a few weeks past. Your exact words, I believe, were that you wanted her to leave you in peace while in London."

"I've changed my mind," Malachi replied as carelessly as he could. "I've decided that the best way to defend against Miss Tamony is to become acquainted with her. I'll better be able to counter any attempts she makes at gaining access to our family history if I'm in her confidence."

Niclas looked slightly alarmed. "In her confidence?" he repeated. "I dislike the sound of that, Malachi. Be careful, I beg you. People will begin to speculate if they should see you in company too often with Miss Tamony, and you know how readily women fall in love with you."

Malachi smiled at the words. "You make too much of it," he said. "Women fall just as easily in love with you, or used to, rather, before Julia took you in hand. It's common for mere mortals to be attracted to our kind. We are so very unusual, after all." The smile broadened.

Niclas didn't appear amused in the least. He sat in silence, frowning.

"Don't worry so," Malachi said reassuringly. "I'll be on my best behavior, and you and Julia will be there to make certain that everything goes as it should. I imagine you're both looking forward to meeting Miss Tamony, being such admirers of hers."

Clearly unsatisfied still, Niclas replied stiffly, "Yes, we

are. It's quite a boon to be among those invited to any gathering she's to be at. Every member of the *ton* is scrambling for invitations. The dinner to be held before the Herold ball is foremost among them."

"Poor Miss Tamony," Malachi murmured, thinking of the windblown beauty he'd spent two very interesting hours with at Glain Tarran. She was a brave woman with a formidable will, but her heart was with her writing, not Society.

"Are you aware that the Seymours won't be the only magic mortals present at the Herold dinner?" Niclas asked. "Serafina Daray managed to secure an invitation, as well."

"Yes, I know," Malachi said grimly. "Serafina and her malformed minions usually remain unseen during the winter months, but not this year. She's up to something, I fear."

"She's always up to something," Niclas muttered. "The Darays are as dangerous as the Cadmarans, but far more clever."

Malachi nodded. "I believe Serafina may be trying to form an alliance among the dark Families to overthrow the Earl of Llew. She's been doing a great deal of traveling among the heads of each clan, and led a delegation to visit with Morcar not too many weeks ago."

Niclas's eyebrows rose. "You said nothing of this to me."

"What transpires within the dark Families is Morcar Cadmaran's business, unless it begins to affect those who've given me their allegiance. It's of little consequence to me if Serafina bests the Earl of Llew—heaven knows he's foolish enough to let such a thing happen—and I could do nothing to stop her if that's her plan. You know the rules of our kind. If she succeeds I'll deal with her as firmly as I have with Morcar."

"Serafina is a clever sorceress," Niclas said. "She'd likely be a great deal more trouble than Morcar."

"I'm keeping a watch over her," Malachi assured him. "Just as I keep an eye on all the dark Families. Speaking of which, Morcar will be in London shortly. He left Llew yesterday."

Niclas was clearly unsurprised by the news. "I thought he'd be coming to Town soon," he said. "He's ever loved the Season and the admiration he enjoys among his mere mortal peers."

"It's not entirely for that," Malachi said soberly. "He's coming because of the *cythraul,* to seek out clues about its arrival and to select a mere mortal for its possession."

"It's odd that the Guardians would allow such a thing without punishment," Niclas said. "Our kind has been charged with the care and guidance of mere mortals. To bring them harm is to break the most strident rules by which we live."

"Which you know far better than I, *cfender,*" Malachi said. Niclas had once used his single magical power, the ability to feel the emotions of mere mortals, to reveal a secret that led to the death of his dearest friend. The Guardians punished Niclas with a blood curse, making it impossible for him to sleep until he found a way to remedy his crime. Three years of suffering had passed before the way had been found, and in making everything right Niclas had gained far more than sweet slumber. He had also found his *unoliaeth,* the one who had been fated to him, and he and Julia had now been married for five blissful years. "But this is a test, and tests are held to far different standards. Apart from that, if Morcar manages to leash the power of the *cythraul,* there's little the Guardians, or anyone else, could do to touch him."

"And you, Cousin," Niclas said. "Have you had any signs yet? Any hints at all from the spirits?"

Only about Sarah Tamony, Malachi thought wryly, saying, "No, not yet. It will be soon, however. Even today, perhaps. I woke with a feeling about it. But, now," he said more firmly, sitting forward in his chair, "before we continue with the invitations, there are two important matters that I wish to speak to you about."

Niclas set the invitations aside and looked at him expectantly.

"First," Malachi said, "I want you to make some financial preparations for Lady Whiteley. I'm thinking of ending our arrangement and want to make an appropriate settlement on her."

"Augusta?" Niclas said with faint surprise. "You wish to break things off after so many years? I always thought the two of you were comfortable with each other."

"Perfectly comfortable," Malachi agreed. "But I believe it would be best to break things off now, before we begin to treat each other like a favorite pair of shoes. I'll pick out something more personal, of course, but I should like to present her with the papers when I make my visit. Be generous."

Niclas nodded. "Of course. Lady Whiteley will be well pleased, though doubtless rather bewildered. But I imagine you'll be your usual charming self."

"I shall do my best," Malachi vowed. "The second task will require your lovely wife's help."

This time Niclas looked fully surprised. "Julia? How so?"

"There's someone particular I wish to be introduced to and would appreciate Julia making the arrangements. I believe she already claims an acquaintance with the woman."

"Who is it?" Niclas asked curiously.

"A widowed lady of gentle birth," Malachi said. "Mrs. William Speakley."

Chapter 9

*A*re you sure you're expected, Sarah?" Julius asked, lifting one gloved hand to the heavy door knocker again. "Where are the man's servants?" Turning on the step, he looked up and down the street. "This is a ramshackle spot for a fellow to house Celtic artifacts. Any number of thieves are probably lurking about, waiting for an opportunity to steal them. Such invaluable antiquities ought to be kept in safer surroundings."

Sarah arranged the large purse that was her usual companion during interviews more comfortably on her forearm and pushed her spectacles up. "Most thieves are hoping to find jewels and silver, Jules, not ancient relics that they wouldn't know how to pawn. I must say, however, that I hadn't expected a scholar of Professor Seabolt's authority to live in such a place. And he clearly needs a better gardener."

The professor's overbuilt home, located just outside the city, was a converted Elizabethan inn, fenced in by black iron gates. A small courtyard in front of the dwelling had been left to grow wild, giving the premises a dark and foreboding aspect.

Impatient, Julius turned about and grasped the knocker again, just as the door was opened.

They both took an involuntary step back at the sight before them; a slender, bent youth in ill-fitting garments peered at them from beneath a thick curtain of unkempt black hair. His face was misshapen on one side and he had but one eye on the remaining side. That eye, however, was abnormally large, putting Sarah in mind of drawings she'd seen of Cyclops, the one-eyed monster. The boy's thin, tilted mouth, when it opened to speak, revealed small, sharp teeth, not dissimilar to a wolf's.

"May I help you?" the boy said in a voice that sent shivers down Sarah's back. She felt Julius's comforting fingers curl about her arm, drawing her nearer to his solid warmth.

"We are seeking Professor Harris Seabolt," he said. "Do we have the correct address?"

Sarah could scarce blame her brother for sounding so hopeful that they might be mistaken. The boy's one eye, as black as his hair, stared at them in an unfriendly, piercing manner.

"This is the professor's home," he replied, markedly hissing each "s." The dark eye moved from Julius to Sarah, where it lingered. "May I ask who is calling?"

Sarah felt it then: the whispering sensation that told her magic was present. She had expected to have the feeling while visiting Professor Seabolt, for she knew he was deeply involved in the supernatural, but this feeling was coming from quite another, very unexpected source.

The boy was not mere mortal—or even fully human. She knew that the same magical beings that had long ago bred with magic mortals had also taken mere mortals as mates, but with a far less pleasing outcome. Those creatures who retained enough of their faint human heritage could pass for human, or near enough, and move in the world of men, as this one did, if Sarah's suspicions about him were correct. Whatever he was, he most certainly possessed magic and, unlike the magic that Sarah had felt at Glain Tarran, it was of the dark variety.

Julius had removed a card from his pocket and placed it in the boy's remarkably long-fingered hand. His nails, Sarah noted, were as pointed as his teeth.

"I am Julius Tamony, and this is my sister, Miss Sarah Tamony. She has an appointment with Professor Seabolt."

The servant eyed the card and made a soft hissing sound.

"Please be so good as to come in," he said, slipping the card into the pocket of his grimy shirt. The black eye gleamed as it focused on them once more. He limped back, one leg being shorter than the other, and with the talonlike fingers indicated that they should enter.

Sarah both felt and heard Julius draw in a deep breath before he guided her forward. The interior of the house, far different from the exterior, was comfortingly clean and well-ordered. The floors and furniture in the entryway shone with fresh polish and the lamps overhead put off a cheerful light.

"If you'll wait a moment," the boy said, managing a slight bow, "I'll inform the professor of your presence."

He limped away and Julius at last released his grip on Sarah's arm.

"What the devil is Seabolt doing letting a servant like that open his door? My God, it's enough to frighten Wellington into heart palpitations. Only imagine some unsuspecting female arriving to have that creature facing her down. The screams would be heard all the way to Whitechapel."

Sarah couldn't help but laugh at her elder brother's fierce—and shaken—affront. He was normally so calm and unflappable, usually to the point of aggravation.

"It's not as bad as all that," she countered soothingly, patting his arm.

"It's worse," Julius muttered angrily. "Such unfortunates shouldn't be allowed out where they might be seen by the general public. Surely there are sufficient sanitariums for the likes of that boy. I shall say something about it to Seabolt."

"Oh no, Jules, please don't," Sarah pleaded, knowing

what a mistake it would be. That boy, or creature, shouldn't be contended with by a mere mortal. Why Professor Seabolt kept a dark servant in his employ was a mystery, but she supposed he was sympathetic to the sorrows and difficulties of all magic beings and had taken the creature in out of kindness. "For all that his appearance is frightening, it's obvious the boy is intelligent." As all magic beings were, she thought wryly. "His manner of speech was refined, if a bit odd. It would be unfair to judge him merely by his outer form. He must be capable of serving Professor Seabolt quite ably."

Julius wasn't swayed. "He should *not* be answering the door," he stated flatly.

"Yes, that's so," she agreed in placating tones. "But it's Professor Seabolt's home, and his decision as to who he has in his employ and what their tasks are. And you're not even an invited guest," she reminded her glowering brother. "It would be rude beyond reason to lecture him about his choice of servants."

The words appeared to calm Julius; his stiff posture relaxed a fraction. "Very well. There's sense in that. I'll say nothing. But my estimation of Seabolt as a man of reason and intelligence has slipped somewhat."

"That's because you're a terrible snob, dear," Sarah said, pushing her spectacles up and smiling up at him.

A door opened at the far end of the hall and a short, round, bespectacled gentleman emerged, rapidly making his way toward them. He was covered by a large apron, which in turn was covered by a great deal of dust, and his round face, framed by untrimmed side-whiskers, was filled with a mixture of chagrin, alarm, and exasperation.

"Please forgive me, Miss Tamony," said the man as he hurried onward. "What a fright Tego must have given you. I do apologize. And Mr. Tamony, how delightful that you've come as well. I'm terribly sorry that you should arrive at my home and be received in such a manner. Tego is never to answer the door." Extending an arm, he grasped Julius's hand and gave it a firm shake. To Sarah he made a quick bow. To Tego, who had shuffled behind him, he cast a stern glance and repeated, "Never."

"I apologize, Professor," Tego said contritely. His head was lowered so that the black hair fell over his misshapen face, hiding his expression. "Mrs. Keller wasn't expecting visitors and was engaged directing Cook about dinner, and none of the others seemed to hear the knocker. I didn't know what else to do. I'll not do it again, I promise."

Sarah managed to keep her smile from wavering. She had a good idea what, or who, had stopped anyone else from hearing them at the door but had little time to consider the matter. Professor Seabolt must be dealt with before he said anything to make Julius suspicious.

"I'm sorry to have come upon you so unexpectedly, Professor," she said cheerfully. "I realize I'm a bit early, but I was so eager to speak with you that I couldn't delay coming. If there's any fault in this matter, it's mine."

Professor Seabolt gazed at her with dismay. "I'm afraid there's been a mis—"

"Oh dear, and I should have more formally introduced my brother." Sarah waved a hand at Julius, who had removed his hat and was making a bow. "He wished to speak to you about your collection of Celtic artifacts. Professor Seabolt, my brother, Mr. Julius Tamony. Julius, Professor Seabolt."

"A pleasure, sir," Julius said with polite correctness. "I shall not interrupt your interview with my sister, I promise."

"But, Miss Tamony," the professor said, looking from one to the other, "I sent you a missive—"

"Regarding our meeting. Yes, I received it." Sarah moved forward and tucked her hand under the professor's arm, forcibly moving him back down the hall. "It was good of you to go to the trouble to send me a reminder. I don't know if you're familiar with my brother's work"—she cast a glance at Julius, who was following behind with Tego trailing, "but he's extensively researched Celtic history and has written a fascinating treatise on the subject. It's to be published at the end of the summer."

"Well, yes, I had heard something about his work," the professor said, his voice thick with confusion. "Indeed, I was only just speaking with Professor Price about it the other day—"

"Professor Oswald Price?" Julius asked, catching up to them just as Sarah, who had no idea where she was going, brought Professor Seabolt to a halt. "Of the Antiquities Society?"

"Just so," said Professor Seabolt. "The publisher asked him to read your manuscript before they agreed to publish it. He was extraordinarily enthusiastic about your work, Mr. Tamony. I must say, I've never heard him speak in such glowing terms. I was quite taken aback, for he is the most reserved of gentleman."

"Sir!" was the only word Julius could manage to say.

Beneath the younger man's stunned awe, the professor warmed to the topic. "And I can tell you this, Mr. Tamony: Professor Price gave you the highest compliment I have ever heard from him. He said that your manuscript is work equal to your father's best, and that, as I need not tell you, is high praise indeed."

Julius was bereft of speech. He set a hand over his heart and stared.

"It's quite true," the professor assured him. "He's made me all eagerness to read this wondrous work of yours. Indeed he has." He looked at Sarah and nodded. "He has."

"I can well imagine," she replied. "And so you understand, Professor, why my brother is so eager to see the collection of Celtic artifacts that you have in your possession, and how grateful he would be if you would allow him the privilege."

"Of a certainty I shall," Professor Seabolt assured the still-speechless Julius. "I'd be honored if he would take a look at the lot and give me his opinion. I can't think you'll be disappointed, sir," he said, leaning closer to Julius and speaking in confiding tones, "for I've been most fortunate in securing some very fine and well-preserved examples of Celtic pottery and adornments, also some weapons, which you'll doubtless find most interesting."

"I—" Julius began, then fell speechless once more.

"Come!" the professor said with sudden eagerness. "We'll go have a look at them now."

He led them down another hall, to a pair of double doors. Pulling a key chain from a pocket behind the apron, he unlocked these and opened them wide.

"Tego, the lamps," the professor said. "Quick, lad!"

The servant moved with a speed and agility that belied his limp, and Sarah felt a growing certainty in her assumptions about him. Magical beings could move at speeds that mere mortals couldn't perceive. Very little limited them.

As each lamp was lit, the room beyond was revealed, and Julius drew in an audible breath.

"Oh, my," Sarah murmured, equally awed by what she saw.

It was as if they'd stepped into a museum, not merely a private collector's array of antiquities. Professor Seabolt had filled the room with beautifully crafted cases, all lined with shimmering gold and red velvet, displaying each piece of his collection in a unique and elegant setting. Even the lamps were set in such a way as to shower each piece of pottery or jewelry with the most attractive amount of light.

"I've never . . . dreamed," Julius whispered, moving forward.

Professor Seabolt was clearly pleased by their reaction. He was beaming with pride. "It's lovely, isn't it?" he said. "I've been years collecting it all, though many were gifts from friends. I can't think you'll find so many unique pieces in all of England, or so well preserved."

Julius wasn't listening. He began to walk about the large chamber in a daze.

Professor Seabolt started to follow, but Sarah set a hand on his arm.

"I must speak with you privately," she whispered. "It's very important."

She could feel Tego's black eye staring at her from

across the room, not missing a moment of her interaction with the professor.

"Miss Tamony, you shouldn't have come," Professor Seabolt said, his voice equally hushed. "I cannot speak with you, as I said in my note. I'm sorry you've traveled so far, but it's impossible."

"I understand that the Earl of Graymar has forbidden you or anyone involved with the Seymours to accept an interview with me, but I must speak with you, nonetheless," she pressed. "The matter does not involve the Dewin Mawr or any magic mortals."

Professor Seabolt's eyes widened. "You *know?*" he murmured.

"About magic?" she asked. "Yes. And what's more, though I doubt His Lordship told you, I've been to Glain Tarran and seen the ceremonial grounds."

The professor took her arm and led her toward the door, farther away from Julius—who appeared to be completely ignorant of their presence—and Tego, who was still watching them.

"You saw the ceremonial grounds?" the professor repeated. "Lord Graymar granted you such a boon?" His voice was filled with disbelief.

"It's rather a long tale," she confessed, "and one which I would happily relate at another time. Suffice it to say that His Lordship was obliged to speak to me, and we—"

"*Obliged* to speak with you?" the professor repeated faintly. "Malachi?"

"Yes, he was, for he thought to convince me to give up my work, which of course I have no intention of doing, but we—"

Sarah stopped chattering and straightened. The warnings were whispering again. Tego could hear what they were saying, despite his distance. She turned her head and met his dark gaze and knew the moment he realized that she understood what he was. The single eye narrowed, and his lips parted to show the sharp, unpleasant teeth.

"Can we speak somewhere else, sir?" Sarah turned back to the professor. "It must be completely private, for I must show you something that's happened. Something that has to do with magic."

Professor Seabolt nodded, then looked questioningly at her brother, who had wandered even farther into the room.

"Julius," she called. He didn't look up from his contemplations. "The professor and I will go and have our interview now. I'll come to fetch you when we're done."

Julius made a grunting sound. Tego began to limp toward the doors, clearly meaning to accompany the professor, but Sarah said, "Oh, would it be all right if Tego stayed here, in case Julius suddenly realizes we've gone?"

"An excellent notion," Professor Seabolt said. "Tego, remain with Mr. Tamony and don't bother him. If he should ask where we are, escort him to my study."

Tego nodded obediently and said nothing. When the professor turned to lead Sarah from the room, the creature caught her eye, flashing a look of fury. Sarah returned a level gaze and slowly pushed her spectacles up. The single eye widened in surprise, and Sarah, pleased, followed Professor Seabolt out the door.

"I *knew* you were one of our sympathetics," Professor Seabolt said as soon as they'd reached his study and he'd shut the doors behind them. "I knew it immediately upon reading your work. Malachi would hear none of it, but I told him that surely you were." He began to remove the dusty apron he wore.

"I'm not surprised that His Lordship was immune to your words," Sarah said as he hung the garment on a mirrored clothing tree. "He is a very stubborn man, which I know firsthand."

"And your brother?" he asked, waving her farther in. "Is he one of our sympathetics, as well?"

"No," Sarah replied. "None of my family is. In fact,

quite the opposite. They believe all the stories I write are nothing more than lovely fairy tales."

"Now there's a pity," said the professor, looking about the messy room, trying to decide where best to seat his guest. "I'm a great admirer of your father's work. I've always thought he might be one of us. I shall be attending his lecture at the Antiquities Society, of course."

Professor Seabolt's study showed the first signs of disorganization that she'd seen since entering the residence. It looked very much like the sort of study a scholarly man would have: Papers sat everywhere in piles and were scattered about his large desk; books were left lying all about, some half-open. A fireplace, currently glowing with a small fire, put warmth into the room. Sarah couldn't help but think of the Earl of Graymar's magnificent study by comparison. But that was rather unfair. It was unlikely that anyone else, anywhere, possessed such a private retreat as that.

"I wish you might be able to say the same of the lecture I was to give," Sarah said, moving along a cabinet where many small, interesting objects lay. With tentative care she touched the top of a unique stone box, rapidly pulling her hand away when it emitted a growling sound.

"I did argue about that in particular when the earl visited this morning," the professor said as he cleared a chair near the room's fireplace of its mountain of books, "but he was most insistent. I hope you'll believe me when I say that I was deeply disappointed to have to cancel the lecture. Deeply disappointed." Dusting the seat with his hand, he said more cheerfully, "Please be seated, Miss Tamony. Shall I call for tea? I should have thought of it sooner, but I—"

"No, thank you, Professor," she said, settling herself into the chair and putting her purse upon her lap. "The fault is mine for coming upon you without warning. But I had to see you, as I said. And I shouldn't wish to serve your staff any further surprises." She chose her next words with care. "Tego seems to be especially vigilant about watching over you."

"Oh, Tego's something of a nuisance," the professor said with a wave of his hand, clearing the chair beside her for his own use. "He's not been with me long. Only a few weeks, in fact. But he's very much underfoot, trying to lend me aid. He's really an intelligent lad, despite his appearance."

"Professor," Sarah said delicately, fingering her purse, "you do realize that he possesses magic, do you not?"

Professor Seabolt's eyebrows rose as he took his chair and looked at her. "You divined that, did you?" he said admiringly. "You must be very sensitive to the presence of magic, as I have so often wished I were. But some sympathetics are, while others of us are not so blessed." He sighed. "Malachi told me that you possess no magic yourself, for I did wonder if it was possible. Now I understand how it is that he was so sure, as you were in company with him at Glain Tarran. You must tell me all about your visit there," he said with renewed enthusiasm.

"I shall be glad to do so," Sarah said. "But, before we speak of it, or of what I've come to discuss with you, tell me what Tego is. Do you feel safe having him in your employ?"

"Oh yes, indeed," he assured her at once. "Do you ask the question because he's a crossbreed? Rest assured, Miss Tamony, for there's seldom any harm in the creatures, bless them. I have several in my employ, though none will show themselves so boldly as Tego. They're often shunned by magic mortals, you know," he said more soberly, "and need a secure haven where they'll be safe. Tego has more human blood than most, and could have survived in the world of men as a common laborer or low-ranking servant, so long as he wasn't often seen. Or he might have become a circus freak, as some of his kind have done."

"But what is he? Apart from his human blood?"

"Goblin, I should think," the professor replied. "I never ask when they come to me for safety. It seems so intrusive." He leaned a bit nearer and said more confidentially,

"Magic beings can be so sensitive, you know. We mere mortals must be careful not to overset them."

Sarah nodded with a sigh of resignation. "Very true, sir. The Earl of Graymar appears to be a perfect example. And I must say, it's terribly distressing to see how everyone he speaks with is ready to do his bidding. What have any of you to fear by meeting with me? He cannot harm you."

The professor paled. "It is not for that reason that I agreed to do what he asked of me regarding you, Miss Tamony. It was a matter of respect and friendship. Lord Graymar and all of his family, most especially his father, who was my very dear friend, have been exceedingly good to me these many years. Almost all of those artifacts that your brother is currently viewing were given to me by the Seymours as tokens of thanks. They have always trusted me, as well, you see, to help keep them safe. If you're a sympathetic, then surely you understand this."

"Lord Graymar doesn't believe me to be one," she said unhappily, "though I promise you I don't mean to bring the least harm or trouble upon any of the magic mortals beneath his care. If he would only help rather than hinder me, that task would be far easier. I'm tempted to risk going to Mervaille to speak with him, save that I'm quite sure it would avail me nothing."

Professor Seabolt shook his head, causing the hairs on the side of his head to wave back and forth. "You could not go to Mervaille without Lord Graymar taking you inside the gates himself. No mere mortal, not even a sympathetic, is allowed on the grounds without his express permission. There is a powerful magic that protects the estate."

"Indeed?" said Sarah, much intrigued by this. The temptation to try became an entirely more enticing prospect. "I did not know. How interesting." She gave herself a mental shake. "But we really must speak of what I've brought to show you. My brother will be coming to look for me soon, no doubt, and I should like to have your advice on what's occurred."

"What is it, my dear?"

Sarah opened the bag on her lap and pulled out her battered journal.

"I had this with me when I was at Glain Tarran," she told him, deftly untying and opening the book. "I take it with me while doing research to jot down notes, just as I was doing in the ceremonial grounds when the earl came upon me."

"He came upon you *there*?" the professor asked, much surprised by this. "I must have misunderstood earlier, for I assumed the earl showed you the grounds himself. Do you mean to say you didn't have his permission first?"

"Certainly not," she said, pushing up her spectacles to peer at him. "He wouldn't answer any of my letters, so I had to sneak onto the estate in the dead of night to see whether rumors of the existence of such grounds were true. And they were, of course, but you already know that. His Lordship came upon me just as I was jotting down notes, and—"

He put a staying hand on her arm and gazed at her, wide-eyed. "But you couldn't have," he said faintly. "Not without Malachi's permission. I grant you might have been able to cross the boundaries—foolish lads from the village are always making the attempt in order to boast of their bravery—but you could never have seen the ceremonial grounds without the Dewin Mawr's express knowledge and permission. No one can."

"I most certainly did," Sarah said with a measure of affront.

"But you *couldn't* have," he said more insistently. "The grounds are kept hidden from mere mortals by magic. That's why there are only rumors of them. No one, save magic mortals, has ever seen the ancient places on Glain Tarran."

"Places?" Sarah was instantly diverted. "You mean to say there are more? I should love to hear of them."

The professor looked deeply troubled. "Perhaps later,"

he murmured. "I must speak with Malachi of the matter again. What have you come to show me, Miss Tamony?"

With a pang of disappointment Sarah returned her attention to the journal on her lap. "Well, as I was saying, I wrote a description of the ceremonial grounds in my journal. It's brief, which I'm sure you'll understand, as the earl quite distracted me upon his arrival. What you are going to see below the entry is what I found there this morning. I did not write it, and no one else has access to this journal. My belief—and my sense—is that it appeared through some kind of magic."

Turning the book upon her lap, she pointed to the page in question. Just beneath the notes she'd made that windy night at Glain Tarran was a series of symbols—or letters; Sarah wasn't quite sure—written in a script much larger than Sarah's, created by an ink or dye that put her in mind of a red-orange sunset.

The professor bent his head to look at it and then, after a moment of silence, uttered an odd, almost frightened sound.

"Do you understand what the words mean, sir?" Sarah asked. "I speak Latin, French, and Italian and cannot make it out in the least. It doesn't appear to be any language that I've yet come across in my travels, and I have been exposed to many. The closest approximation I can find is the language found here, on this little amulet that I wear."

Sarah pulled the Donballa out from beneath the neckline of her dress and showed it to the professor. If it was possible, he went a shade paler. His hands shook slightly as he examined the small, shining gold ball.

"God's mercy," he whispered. "The Donballa. But how is this possible?" He looked up at her. "How do you come to have it?"

"It was a gift from a sorceress in Aberdeen," Sarah replied. "Sorsha is her name. Perhaps you know her?"

Silent, he nodded.

"His Lordship was surprised, as well," Sarah told him. "But he very kindly repaired it for me, and made it look new again. Is it not beautiful?"

"Repaired it?" Professor Seabolt seemed unable to either understand or believe what she was saying. "Malachi? Did he?"

"Professor Seabolt, are you feeling unwell?" Sarah asked with concern, looking at him more closely. "You're terribly pale. Shall I ring for that tea? Or something a bit stronger?"

"No, I'm fine," he assured her, though both his voice and hands shook so that Sarah wasn't convinced. "It's all just so . . . difficult to believe. So surprising. And Malachi said nothing of this to me."

"I suppose he wouldn't think it necessary," Sarah said. "His only object was to keep you from speaking with me, and knowing of the Donballa wouldn't have made a difference. But do you not agree, Professor, that the writing on the Donballa and the writing here are rather similar? The shapes of the characters—I believe one is even exactly alike."

"It's the ancient tongue," the professor said hoarsely. "I have seen it many times." He looked up at her. "It was their language before they were cast to earth. The ones who were exiled."

A memory drifted into Sarah's thoughts. A memory of a low voice speaking close beside her, of the warmth of his body as they gazed at the Donballa on the palm of his hand.

The symbols are from the language spoken only by magic mortals in the ancient days. Your brother would not have recognized them. . . .

"Can you read it, sir? I can't imagine why the words appeared in my journal, for surely whoever wrote them would know that I can't decipher the meaning."

"I'm sorry to say that I cannot," Professor Seabolt admitted. "It's not possible for mere mortals to understand the symbols, no matter how devotedly they might study them. And there are few among magic mortals who have been gifted with the knowledge. But I believe this message must be vitally important, Miss Tamony, regardless of where it has appeared. The Earl of Graymar must see it at once. He'll be able to decipher and understand it. Will you trust me with your journal for a little while so that I can take it to him?"

"My journal?" Sarah said with dismay, instinctively gathering the book up and holding it close. "I couldn't possibly take the risk, Professor. I don't mean to suggest you'd not take every care with it, but surely you understand that it contains the most valuable information—all of the notes I've made during my research. I should be lost if anything happened to it, and, to be perfectly honest, Lord Graymar would likely think it a very good thing if it should somehow be misplaced."

"Oh no, my dear," the professor countered. "You can't think that a man of Lord Graymar's rank and birth would do such a thing. A nobleman, Miss Tamony. A gentleman."

"A magic mortal who is also the Dewin Mawr," she replied. "Yes, I do think it. He's vowed to stop me from writing my book, and the loss of my journal would make that a fait accompli. Can I not be the one to take it to him?"

"Miss Tamony," Professor Seabolt said reasonably, "I spoke with Malachi just this morning, and I can assure you that it's very unlikely he'll allow you entrance to Mervaille. If only for the sake of not giving you further interesting information for your book. It is an extraordinary place."

"I've already seen Glain Tarran," she said, "and can't possibly be more deeply impressed."

Professor Seabolt gazed at her with ill-concealed impatience.

"Oh, very well," Sarah said irately. "I see you don't trust me any more than he does, despite knowing that my intentions are honorable. I shall tear the page out and let you take it to him, but you must give me your word as a gentleman that you'll return it to me, regardless what the Dewin Mawr says."

"I do not distrust you, Miss Tamony," said the professor. "Quite the contrary."

"Ha," Sarah muttered, giving her attention to carefully tearing the thick page from the journal's excellent binding.

"I ought to insist that you give me an interview in exchange for this, you know. Although I suppose, as you've been so good to allow my brother to view your private collection, we could consider ourselves even. Oh dear, I'm tearing it. I don't suppose you've a pair of scissors at hand?"

The professor rose from his chair just as the door to the study opened. Tego stepped in with Julius behind him. They stopped when both Sarah and Professor Seabolt gave an exclamation of dismay.

"Forgive me, Professor," Tego said in his hissing voice. "I did not mean to take you by surprise. You did not hear my knock, I think." His black eye settled on Sarah, then the book she held. "Mr. Tamony has finished examining your collection, sir. I've brought him to the study, as you instructed."

Sarah closed the journal slightly, hiding the page from the creature's view, and realized the mistake the moment she made it. The action only caused his gaze to sharpen.

She exchanged glances with the professor before saying, "A moment if you please, Julius. Professor Seabolt and I are nearly finished."

The door closed once more, but not before Tego had given Sarah an unpleasant smile.

"That creature," she said. "I don't know that you should trust him, Professor. I'm surprised that the Earl of Graymar would allow you to keep such a being in your employ."

"But why?" the professor asked with genuine surprise, handing her a small pair of scissors. "Tego's an excellent servant, despite his appearance. Very quiet and helpful, which are necessary qualities to me as an employer. Has he done something to offend you, Miss Tamony?"

"Does His Lordship know about him being here?" she pressed, opening the journal once more and setting to the task of carefully cutting the page away.

"He must," the professor replied. "He senses all magical beings wherever he goes. Although, come to think upon it," he added more thoughtfully, "Tego was gone from the dwelling when Malachi arrived this morning. I'd intended to introduce them, for it is a great honor among those with magic to speak to the Dewin Mawr. I had meant it as a treat for the lad."

"Then you must be very certain," she advised, "to make that introduction when His Lordship next comes."

"Indeed I shall."

"There," Sarah said with satisfaction when the page at last gave way. She closed the journal and put it into her purse. "I'll fix it back in with a bit of glue when you return it to me. And please, sir," she said as she stood and passed the page over to him, "bring it to me yourself when Lord Graymar has finished reading it. I shouldn't want it to be waylaid."

"I promise that I shall bring it myself," he vowed, blind to Sarah's expression of dismay as he folded the page twice and slid it into a coat pocket. By the time he looked at her again she had composed herself. "Thank you, Miss Tamony. I believe this may go a long way toward softening Lord Graymar's heart toward you and your project."

Sarah offered Professor Seabolt her hand in parting. "I shouldn't wish you to be disappointed on my account, Professor. It would likely be best not to raise your hopes where Lord Graymar is concerned." She smiled. "I certainly don't intend to."

Chapter 10

$\mathcal{T}$here was not a mere mortal alive who could describe the interior of Miss Serafina Daray's town house. Many mere mortals had been in her domicile, almost all of them men, but none could ever after remember why, what had transpired, or what the place had looked like. Even those men who had served as her lovers for more than a few days or weeks could not say with any clarity what her home was like inside. The memories of their visits there were so dreamlike as to almost be imagined.

The mystery was but a part of what made Serafina Daray such a sensation among the *ton*. Other particulars included but were not limited to her delicate and stunning beauty, her exquisite sense of style, and her delightful charm and wit. Anyone you asked would tell you so, and believe it. Serafina made certain of it and put herself on display as often as possible in order to prove how right her admirers were.

Her home, however, was Serafina's private refuge and not open to public speculation. Mere mortals wouldn't understand, even if she did let those who had been allowed within her sanctuary to remember it.

She needed darkness. Craved it. Especially after being in sunlight, which hurt her delicate eyes. Her home gave her the darkness Serafina required and sweet surcease from the misery of being in company with mere mortals. They were tiresome and stupid and thoroughly exhausting and Serafina longed for the day when she'd at last possess the power to put such beings in their proper place—as servants to their magical betters.

Being in company with mere mortals day and night, having to converse and laugh and pretend to be interested or amused by their ignorant, small-minded utterances, was what Serafina hated most about the farce she was required to live. But soon everything would change. All she had to do was watch the great wizards and place her minions in ideal locations to spy as well, and the clues to finding the *cythraul* would fall into her capable hands.

Tego, the best and brightest among Serafina's servants, was the first to bring his mistress intriguing information.

" 'Mr. Julius Tamony,' " she read from the little card, reclining on a black velvet lounge and stroking her fingers gently over Tego's long, silky hair as he rested his head in her lap. "How interesting. The brother of the famous Sarah Tamony, and soon to be known in his own right. Is he handsome, my dear?"

Tego, who lay in ecstasy beneath his mistress's caress, made a sound of disdain. "He is handsome, my lady, in the way of mere mortals, and does not possess the horrible red hair, as the sister does. But his eyes are weak, for he wears spectacles."

"He is a scholar," she told Tego, "and reads a great deal. A man of intellect, in the limited manner of mere mortals. And handsome, you say?"

"Aye, mistress. He is just what you like best." The fact seemed to displease Tego a great deal, for he added, "I should enjoy killing him very much."

"Not yet, my darling," Serafina murmured. "Not until we've done with him and the sister. Did he know about the journal?"

Tego gave a slight shake of his head, the motion moving the silky cloth on her lap back and forth. "She was cunning, my lady, and played the brother for a fool. He believed all that she said of interviewing the professor, though Professor Seabolt had already broken their appointed meeting."

"Only at the Dewin Mawr's insistence," Serafina reminded. "I've no doubt the old fool was eager to speak with her, despite that. He must have been disappointed when Malachi put a stop to the connection. It's clear that the woman is a source of fear to Lord Graymar, else he'd never go to so much trouble. Yet she possesses no magic."

At this Tego lifted his head. "But she knows of magic, mistress. She recognized it in me almost at once. I saw the understanding in her eyes."

"She's one of our sympathetics, then," she said softly, tracing the tip of his sharp chin with a single finger. "A dangerous woman for us. And this journal—you say that the professor insisted upon taking it to the Dewin Mawr at once?"

Tego nodded. "But the woman said it was too valuable to let out of her possession and took it away with her, giving him only a page to take to the Great Sorcerer. She made the professor give his vow that he'd return the page to her on the morrow."

"Are you quite certain, Tego?"

"I heard all they said once I had the brother out of the artifact room. The study doors were no hindrance to my ears. And it must have been very important, for the professor left for Mervaille immediately after the woman and her brother had gone."

Serafina nodded slowly, thoughtfully, before at last focusing on his misshapen face.

"I must have that journal, Tego," she said in gentle tones, stroking his cheek. "We must find a way to obtain it."

"Yes, my lady."

"I shall think of a way, and perhaps allow you to help in stealing it, my most faithful servant. But before then, you must bring me the page that was torn from it. It should be a simple matter to get it away from Seabolt, so careless as he is."

"It will be in your hands before midnight," Tego vowed. "But I must return it to the professor's possession before daybreak. If he discovers it missing he'll likely call for the Dewin Mawr's aid."

"Excellent," she murmured, well pleased, and leaned to kiss him on the forehead, just above his single eye. "My faithful Tego." She began to stroke his hair again. "You are the only one I can truly trust. I'd not be able to continue in the world of men without you. One day soon, you'll be well rewarded for your loyalty to me."

His expression grew hopeful. "You know what it is that I desire, mistress."

"And you will have it," she promised. "When I've come into my rightful place I shall at last possess the power to make you the handsomest being on earth. And then, my dearest, no woman, mortal or magic, will be able to resist you. Not even me."

The Earl of Llew's journey to London was not turning out to be a pleasant one. It was plagued by rain and muddy roads, and he had been obliged time and again since departing Castle Llew to exit his carriage when one of the wheels had gotten stuck in a rut. He'd used magic in order to get it unstuck, for his servants were all mere mortals and he had neither the time nor patience nor desire to stand in the rain waiting for them to lift the heavy carriage free. This only proved to him more fully how inferior mere mortals were, and the knowledge that he was surrounded by such feckless beings made him irate.

He might have employed magic mortals as servants, as clans like the Seymours sometimes did, but Cadmarans had always felt it wrong to place their magical peers in servitude when either mere mortals or *animantis* were available. But Morcar particularly disliked being in company with *animantis*. There were none left now who were pure-

blooded and therefore few who, like Serafina, had retained
their ancient beauty. Cadmarans had rules about ugly and
inferior creatures, first and foremost that they should be
drowned at birth. After two days of standing in the rain because his idiotic coachman couldn't avoid ruts, Morcar was
ready to consign all mere mortals to the same fate.

He wasn't in any particular hurry to reach London,
knowing what awaited him with Serafina's challenge at
hand. But he'd been warned in a dream that he would receive no signs regarding the *cythraul* while he remained at
Llew and had departed for London the following day.

The Season this year would be remarkable. Numerous
magic mortals would be in Town, many who claimed allegiance to the Dewin Mawr and an almost equal number
who had, at least until recently, given their allegiance to
Morcar. He found the thought supremely depressing.

With a sigh he turned to the window, gazing at the rain-
splattered pane—beyond which he could see nothing—
with a feeling of both loneliness and despair.

He was thirty-seven years of age and his life, so far as
he could tell, had been useless. From his birth he had been
made fully aware of what was expected of him—to destroy
the Seymours and take on the mantle of Dewin Mawr. His
father, a wise and powerful wizard, had been his mentor,
and Morcar had tried fervently to please him. He had
vowed upon his father's death to be the Cadmaran who at
last would find the way to best the Seymours.

Not only had Morcar not bested them; he'd utterly
failed at each attempt. He'd tried to comfort himself with
the thought that he'd been unfortunate to come against
Malachi—a wizard of such power as only came along once
every thousand years—but he'd at last had to accept the
truth. It wasn't that Malachi was a superior wizard but that
he, Morcar, was inferior. Proof, he knew, was that he'd not
been able to make a woman love him. At least not of her
own free will, and the other kind of love, forced by magic,
had soon grown dull.

But he had loved. Not deeply, perhaps, but enough so

that when she had been taken from him, he'd felt the loss. And she would be in London this Season. Desdemona.

He closed his eyes as the memory washed over him, unsure of what it would be like to see her again. She had been his perfect mate, and he had greatly desired to have her as his wife. With Desdemona at his side, Morcar might have conquered anyone or anything that stood in his path, not merely because she, herself, was so powerful a sorceress, but because she would have completed him. Or so he had dreamed. But it had not been fated and thus had not come to be.

She was a Seymour now. Desdemona Seymour, wife of Dyfed Seymour, brother to Kian, Baron Tylluan, who would one day be the Dewin Mawr in Malachi's place. Unless Morcar became Dewin Mawr, first.

Dyfed was not an extraordinary wizard, as Morcar was. Nor was Dyfed a greater wizard. The truth, more insulting than any other fact, was that Desdemona had chosen a lesser wizard for her husband, and not merely a lesser wizard, but one possessed of such a minor gift as to nearly make him mere mortal. The only magic Dyfed Seymour held was that of silent speech, of being able to speak into the minds of listeners, rather than into their ears. From what Morcar had heard, Dyfed wasn't even capable of levitating small objects, which was a simple magic that nearly all wizards and sorceresses, regardless of whether they were lesser, greater, or extraordinary, could perform by the age of three. How Desdemona, the daughter of the famed wizard Draceous Caslin, as well as an extraordinary sorceress possessed of incredible powers, could choose such a husband when she might have had Morcar was beyond all comprehension.

Equally unpleasant to contemplate was the Seymours Morcar would have to contend with during the Season and the game that Cadmarans and Seymours had been playing in public almost from the beginning of the exile. For if they didn't smile and speak pleasantries while among mere mortals, rumors would begin to spread that there was some argument between the two families. Rumors would lead to close observation by outsiders, curious to know what the truth was, and questions would soon begin to be asked. Neither family could afford such inspection, and so they had agreed to ever behave with perfect amity when in Society.

It had become difficult to continue the farce over the past several years, however. Five years ago Morcar had kidnapped Niclas Seymour's beloved, Julia, with the intention of making her his mistress and then had tried to kill Niclas when he'd come to rescue her. The Guardians had blinded him for the attempt, and it had taken the loss of Desdemona to restore Morcar's sight. He supposed that the beings who ruled over magic mortals had realized he'd been sufficiently punished for his misdeed. Apart from that, no lasting harm had come to Niclas. He and Julia had married and lived happily thereafter, producing two daughters and two sons in the years that had passed. But it was always awkward to see them during the Season; Morcar couldn't look at the happy pair without feeling a pang of jealousy.

The carriage gave a sudden familiar thump and lurched to one side, flinging Morcar toward the door so that he nearly struck his head. With a curse he righted himself, then shut his eyes and prayed for patience. He was close to abandoning the carriage altogether in favor of the fast traveling extraordinary wizards could employ when they wished. But it was his due as the Earl of Llew to arrive in London in his grand carriage for one and all to see and admire. If one couldn't make a grand entrance, there was scarcely any point in going to Town at all.

The carriage door opened and one of the footmen, ashen faced, said, "My lord, I'm afraid we've—"

"Struck another rut," Morcar finished for him. "Yes, Fulham, I've realized."

With a loud sigh he heaved his tall, muscular person out of the elegant equipage and put his expensive, now-ruined, boots once more into the mud. Heavy rain splattered on his face, hair, and shoulders as he stood full height, wetting again the clothes that were still damp from the last rut.

"Stand aside, you fool," he commanded irately, shoving the footman back. "Let me have a look at it."

He peered through the rain to see that it was one of the front wheels this time and that the rut was indeed quite deep.

He shouted up to the coachman over the pouring rain. "When I give the word, drive the horses forward. Just get the front out and I'll repair the hole before we—"

A sudden flash stopped the rest of his speech, blinding all of them and terrifying the horses into bolting forward. The carriage wheel cracked, then with an explosion of sound burst into pieces, sending the entire carriage hurtling to one side.

Morcar had spent three years of his life living in darkness, and not even the sudden onset of blindness had the power to overset him. All of his senses reacted as they would have done during those three years, and he reached out a hand, calling forth his supernatural strength to push the carriage upward. With a few spoken words the wheel was magically repaired and replaced upon the shaft. By the time his men had hurried to fix it firmly on, Morcar's vision had returned.

He blinked, feeling the same relief that he did upon waking each morning to know that he had his sight. Drawing in a deep breath, he steadied himself. And then he heard it. A voice calling to him from above, though he couldn't make out the words. He looked up to find the source. Rain poured on his face, into his eyes and mouth, but that did not distract him from the sight he saw, floating directly above him.

"My lord?" It was Fulham.

"Do you see that, Fulham?" the Earl of Llew asked. "Right there above us? Did you hear the voice?"

Fulham looked and neither saw nor heard anything. He decided that the earl had likely hit his very hard head.

"No, my lord. There's nothing."

Morcar smiled, his spirits lifted as nothing else could

have done. "Yes, Fulham. There is. A flower. I can see it very clearly."

Fulham looked again, only to get his face even more thoroughly wet than it already was. Still there was nothing. But he had learned that it was impossible to naysay the Earl of Llew, even when one wished to.

"A flower, my lord? As you say, my lord."

Morcar laughed aloud and along with his delight knew a deep sense of relief. It was the first sign, and he'd wager that he'd been given it even before the Dewin Mawr.

"Let's get to London," he said, laughing once more and looking at his befuddled servant. "I want to be there by tomorrow, and no later. We've a great deal to do before the Season starts."

"Can you read it, Malachi? The symbols are ill written, I fear."

Malachi frowned at the thick paper in his hand, far more displeased by the knowledge of where it had come from than he was cheered by the message it related.

"Yes, I can read it," he replied somberly. "There are two lines. The first says, 'This is not the place.' The second is 'All become one or all will fail.'"

Professor Seabolt leaned nearer, peering at the paper more closely. "'This is not the place'?" he repeated curiously. "Whatever can that mean?"

"It's a sign regarding the *cythraul*," Malachi told him. "I believe it means that it will not be arriving at Glain Tarran. Which only leaves the rest of England."

"Oh, surely it's more specific than that," the professor said. "I can't believe the Guardians would go to the trouble to send a useless sign. What do you think the second part means?"

"It sounds like an exhortation of sorts, doesn't it?" Malachi said thoughtfully. "'All become one or all will fail.'"

"Or that all of the clues must be put together else you'll fail to find the *cythraul*," Professor Seabolt suggested. "Why would they appear in Miss Tamony's journal? How could the Guardians have known that the page would find its way to you?"

The Earl of Graymar had been wondering the same thing. Aye, the Guardians were having a fine time toying with him by way of the confounding Miss Sarah Tamony.

"The spirit world is mysterious," he said. "And Sarah Tamony understands magic. I'm sure they knew she would seek out the advice of someone more knowledgeable. Perhaps they even caused her to do so. I'm more astonished that you managed to persuade her to part with a page of her journal. I'm sure she wished to bring it herself."

"She did, my lord," Professor Seabolt said, straightening. "But I assured her it would be impossible to gain entrance to Mervaille without your permission, and considering that you've been so decidedly set against her proposed book, I was able to convince her that it would be best for me to bring the page."

"Ha," Malachi retorted. "That wouldn't have stopped her. She would have found scaling the walls a marvelous adventure, I've no doubt." And if she had, he realized with dismay, he would have been glad, so long as she wasn't harmed. He had wondered, in the past several days, whether she would display as much delight in Mervaille as she had in Glain Tarran.

He shook the thought aside. "Thank you, Harris, for bringing me this so quickly. The meaning of the words will make itself clear to me very shortly, especially as additional clues arrive." He began to fold the page with the intention of pocketing it. "I'll take care of returning this to Miss Tamony, and to thank her for the loan of it."

"I apologize, my lord," the professor said at once, lifting a hand to stop him from secreting the page away. "I gave Miss Tamony my word as a gentleman that I would return the page to her personally. I fear I cannot do otherwise." With a delicate tug and a reddened face he pulled the paper from Malachi's grip.

Malachi smiled, wanting to ease his friend's discomfort.

"Of course," he said mildly, greatly at odds with the dis-

appointment he felt at not having an excuse to visit the
Tamony residence. "I'm sure that would be best." He
waved a hand dismissively as he moved to pour each of
them a drink. "Miss Tamony doubtless is quite angry with
me at the moment. I shouldn't want to overset her. But do
thank her for me, will you? Tell her that I . . . I am in her
debt." Oh, gad, he thought with an inward grimace. That
sounded mawkish.

Turning, a glass in each hand, he changed the subject.

"Tell me about the brother." He offered Professor Seabolt
a glass. "He's something of a scholar, is he not, as his father
is? Celtic history, rather than Roman, I understand. He must
have found your collection of artifacts intriguing."

Professor Seabolt, thus diverted, plunged into a detailed
and enthusiastic account of the Tamony siblings' visit.
Malachi listened politely, nodding and murmuring when
appropriate. His mind, however, was far from the conversation. It was occupied, as it had so often been since that
night at Glain Tarran, with visions of a lovely, smiling face
and bright green eyes, bent spectacles, and deliciously unkempt red hair. He wondered what she looked like in a day
dress, all prim and proper, gloved and hatted. Or a silk ball
gown, with her glorious hair piled in some fashionable
arrangement, her throat and shoulders bare, and dancing.
With him. Just as they had danced in the cold night sky,
whirling around and around and . . . he brought himself
back to reality just in time to give another nod and murmur.

Soon he must see her. Speak with her. And find a way to
conquer the spell she had placed him under.

Chapter 11

$\mathcal{I}$t amused Sarah to think that her first encounter in London with the Earl of Graymar was to be at her Aunt Speakley's modest town house. But she was deeply pleased, as well, for he had clearly remembered what she'd said at Glain Tarran about her aunt's ardent desire to be able to claim him as a guest and must have decided that this would be a fitting way in which to repay her for giving him the page in her journal.

Aunt Speakley had arrived unexpectedly at the Tamony household three days ago in a state of near hysteria, declaring that she'd had the *most astonishing* day of her life.

It had begun with an invitation from Mrs. Niclas Seymour to go driving in the park at the fashionable hour—an honor of no small significance, for it was well-known that Julia Seymour rarely took acquaintances up in her private phaeton during her daily drive—most especially not acquaintances of such a passing nature as she and Aunt Speakley were. That boon alone would have been sufficient to keep Aunt Speakley in raptures for a month, but something *even more remarkable* had taken place.

They had met Mrs. Seymour's cousin by marriage, the

Earl of Graymar, during their drive, and Mrs. Seymour had *actually made an introduction*. It had been more than Aunt Speakley could bear, for she'd lost her senses entirely and found herself inviting Lord Graymar to a small gathering at her home ... *and His Lordship had accepted*. With delight!

Aunt Speakley had grown short of breath just relating the tale. In the hours since, she had been a whirlwind of activity, desperate to make certain that, first, all her acquaintances knew that the Earl of Graymar was to honor her with his presence and, second, everything was absolutely perfect for his coming. Lady Tamony, Sarah, and Philistia had helped, and Sir Alberic had insisted that Aunt Speakley accept the loan of some of their servants for the great event. Aunt Speakley's house had been cleaned and organized from rafters to cellar, the dinner prepared with the finest ingredients, and the wines, again thanks to Sir Alberic, were the best that could be found.

Yes, it was all rather amusing, Sarah thought as she watched her aunt nervously converse with the first guests to arrive. She tried to tell herself that all this fuss was Lord Graymar's due as a high-ranking nobleman, also as one of the wealthiest and most politically powerful men in England. But when Sarah thought of him, all she could see in her mind's eye was an alarmingly handsome, alternately irate and charming gentleman, rather unkempt, with windswept hair and brilliant blue eyes. Who also happened to be a powerful wizard.

She couldn't fix him in her imagination as merely the Earl of Graymar. He was the man who'd turned her world upside down, then taken her up into the air and out of the world entirely. And he was also the man who, once they'd come back to earth, had set himself up as her adversary. Sarah had anticipated seeing him again from the moment they'd parted ways; now she wondered what he would see when they met—the woman he'd called beautiful or the troublesome scribbler who'd trespassed on his lands.

Apart from the Tamonys, several of Aunt Speakley's

particular friends were present: Major John Skutley, late of His Majesty's army, Sir Timothy Wilbay and his wife, Lady Wilbay, the widowed Lady Bawstone, and her gentleman friend, Mr. Charles Winston. An even number of guests to make up sets for cards after dinner—if Lord Graymar ever made his appearance.

"I'm certain the earl is merely arriving fashionably late," Sarah assured her aunt later as they sat side by side in the parlor, where drinks were served. Aunt Speakley cast a glance at her guests, all of whom had disbelieved her insistence that such a lofty individual as the Earl of Graymar had truly deigned to attend such a modest event. Lady Bawstone and Lady Wilbay had even wagered Aunt Speakley that despite what he'd told her in the park, Lord Graymar would not appear. Those two ladies, at the moment, were exchanging satisfied looks.

Sarah patted her aunt's hand. "You told me yourself that Lord Graymar is famed for making a grand entrance, which necessitates a late arrival. And he's a gentleman as well as a nobleman. If he accepted your invitation, he'll come."

Philistia, who was sitting nearby, leaned close to whisper, "But do you really think so, Sarah? It's almost too incredible to believe that he'd want to have dinner with our family, especially after refusing your appeals for a meeting. Julius said it's all a complete farce, for His Lordship would likely far rather be at the end of the earth than in a room with you."

Sarah frowned darkly at her brother from across the parlor, where he was conversing with Major Skutley, and declared to her cousin, "Julius is a fool." To her aunt, who had made a sound of despair at Philistia's words, she repeated, "He'll come."

Aunt Speakley looked as if she'd rather be at the other end of the earth, at the moment, but just then the sound of carriage wheels and many horses drifted up from the street below. Everyone in the room fell silent, and Philistia, unable to contain herself, stood and hurried to the nearest window.

"It's him!" she cried, pressing her hands together. "Oh, my heavens, such a grand carriage! And so many horses—and the footmen in elegant costume—you never saw such a sight!"

"Philistia," Lady Tamony murmured disapprovingly. Philistia came away from the window at once.

Aunt Speakley, who had looked so miserable only moments earlier, now appeared ready to faint. Sarah gave her hand a brief squeeze and helped her rise from the settee—no small task, as Aunt Speakley was a short woman of formidable proportions, very different from her younger sister, Sarah's mother, who in middle age was slender and still stood straight and tall.

Everyone in the room rose and stared at the door, waiting, so that when it was opened a few moments later and Lord Graymar was announced, he stepped into a parlor of pale, fixed, gaping faces. With the exception of Sarah and her mother. Sarah was trying hard not to smile at Lord Graymar's expression—he looked as if he were entering a torture chamber—and her mother was the sort of person who was seldom perturbed by anything or anyone.

If the Earl of Graymar had looked handsome to Sarah on that wild night at Glain Tarran, then he was equally so now, save in a far more refined manner. He looked every part the Earl of Graymar, with his overlong hair tied back in a neat tail at his neck and his elegant evening clothes in the deep black and gleaming white colors that she had heard he preferred. He was far more beautifully and expensively attired than any other person in the room, and knew it. Rhys must have been exceedingly pleased with his master's appearance on this particular evening.

The earl's gaze swept the parlor, stopping and lingering on Sarah long enough to return her amused smile with a flash of stern reproach, then took in the remainder of those assembled. He bowed with perfected elegance at Aunt Speakley's approach.

"My lord," she greeted in ecstatic tones. "Welcome to my home. It's so kind of you to grace us with your company."

"Mrs. Speakley," he replied as solemnly as if he were addressing the queen, a detail that Sarah was certain thrilled Aunt Speakley no end. He accepted her hand and bowed over it. "I'm delighted. I've looked forward to this evening since we last spoke in the park. It was very good of you to invite me."

Introductions were made. The earl lingered for a few brief moments with each guest, pausing when he came to Sir Alberic.

"Sir Alberic, what a special pleasure it is to make your acquaintance," the earl said. "I am a great admirer of your work, and have been since my days at university. One of my professors taught extensively from your first few publications. I often thought that you should have been lecturing in his place, instead. And wished it, as well."

Sir Alberic had spent the better part of his life being feted and admired by the most powerful and noble figures in Europe, but even so he was not proof against such praise. Sarah could see a faint flush spread over her father's face.

Lord Graymar continued down the line of guests, declaring himself charmed by Lady Tamony and Philistia and sending Julius into nearly speechless rapture by telling him how greatly he was looking forward to reading his soon-to-be published manifest, for as he said, "It should make excellent reading, considering the influence your father has likely had upon you, and the topic of Celtic history is of particular interest to me." He cast a brief glance at Sarah, who stood at the end of the line, and she could almost feel the Celtic amulet on its chain growing warm beneath the satin of her gown.

Sarah waited, striving for patience, as His Lordship made his way, greeting each guest in a formal but genial manner. Finally, after what seemed an eternity, he stepped in front of her. Sarah discovered that her smile had suddenly deserted her.

"And this is my niece, Lord Graymar," Aunt Speakley said warmly. "Miss Sarah Tamony. You may have heard of her before now, for she's another writer in the family, and her books have been very popular."

Sarah gazed up at him, into the piercing blue eyes and the unsmiling mouth. He gave no evidence of knowing her, but she'd not expected that he would. She had to be careful to play the same game, else her family would learn that she'd sneaked out of their inn in Pembrokeshire and trespassed at Glain Tarran. And then they'd want details.

Good breeding came to her rescue, and Sarah sank into a proper curtsy, bowing her head and murmuring, "My lord."

"Well, well, Miss Sarah Tamony," was his reply. "You do clean up nicely, I must say. I thought you might, but your appearance is even more greatly improved than what I expected."

Sarah's head snapped up.

"Not that there was anything wrong with your manner of dress when you visited with me at Glain Tarran, of course. I found your masculine attire to be quite . . . charming." He smiled in a meaningful way. "But I did wonder what you might look like in something more feminine. I'm not in the least disappointed."

She rose full height and looked back down the line of guests. They were all frozen in place, utterly still and silent, like statues. Even her parents.

"Good heavens," she said, turning back to him with wide eyes. "You've put them beneath a spell. Without so much as saying a word or lifting a finger."

"Only for a moment or two," he admitted. "They'll not be harmed. We must be careful not to move, however, for when I release them they'll expect to see us exactly in the manner and place we were in. It can be disconcerting, or so I've been told, to come back into the moment and find something changed."

Sarah looked at the others once more, discomfited by the sight. It was especially difficult to see her parents frozen in time, utterly helpless.

"They'll be perfectly fine," Lord Graymar repeated

more gently, and reached for her hand. "I only wanted a moment to thank you properly for the page from your journal"—bowing, he brushed his lips against her bare knuckles, causing Sarah to draw in a sharp breath—"also to warn you not to smile at me as you did when I first arrived." He straightened and released her. "If you do, I shall very likely lose my own composure and everyone present will wonder at us."

"Yes, of course," she replied, flushing. "I shall strive to control myself. I don't wish you to think my amusement a sign of ingratitude. I'm terribly thankful to you for making my Aunt Speakley so happy, especially as I'm certain this isn't the sort of evening you care for. It's very good of you to come."

He tilted his head, considering her. "I was glad to do so. And I assure you, in all honesty, that there is no other place I would rather be tonight. Or any other company I would prefer to be with."

"That is a pretty thing to say, my lord," she told him, smiling. "I wish you could be so amenable at all times. Apart from your coming tonight, I'm vastly displeased with you."

"I know," he said. "But I did warn you how matters must stand between us regarding your book. We agreed, however, that it must not necessarily make us enemies."

"Certainly not," she agreed. "But it also doesn't mean I have to pretend happiness at having my interviews and appointments canceled. Still, I shall find a way to write my book. You'll see."

"I'll be watching very closely," he promised. "In the meantime, can we agree to be civil in Society? I do not know why, but the spirits who guard over my kind have involved you in something of great importance to me, and I have no way of knowing whether they may choose to involve you further."

"The message, do you mean?" she asked, her interest piqued. "Professor Seabolt told me what was written, but

I could make no sense of either of the sentences, and he would tell me nothing else. And it's disappeared since he returned it to me. The symbols faded away just as they appeared."

He nodded. "I thought perhaps they would."

"But what did it mean?" she asked. "And why should any spirits use my journal to communicate with you?"

"I don't know," he said once more. "But we haven't the time to discuss the matter more fully just now. Your aunt has a small garden at the back of the house, does she not?"

Sarah looked at him curiously. "Very small, my lord. It's not really suitable for strolling in the evening. And it's quite chilly outside, as well."

He made a "tetching" sound. "Small inconveniences and easily dealt with," he replied. "I shall invite you for a breath of air after the first few rounds of cards, and would be grateful if you'd be ready to agree."

"My parents will be displeased," she warned. "Despite your being an earl and a gentleman."

"Then perhaps we'll invite your brother and charming cousin to accompany us. I won't mind the company."

"My lord, I really can't like you putting spells on my relatives."

He nearly rolled his eyes heavenward. "You mere mortals are always so delicate about such simple matters. Leave it to me, Miss Tamony, and all will be well. Now, curtsy, if you please."

"What?"

"Curtsy," he advised, "just as you did before, and pretend not to know me. Or that you find me so irresistibly handsome. I shall pretend that you're not devastatingly beautiful."

Sarah flushed. "What impudence, my lord," she muttered as she lowered herself into a curtsy.

He chuckled before becoming the regal Earl of Graymar once again, making a slight bow and saying, in formidable tones that nearly had Sarah smiling again, "Miss

Tamony. A pleasure. May I say how greatly I've enjoyed receiving your many letters?"

"Oh, has Sarah written to you, my lord?" Aunt Speakley said with surprise, looking from one to the other. At the other end of the room, Julius gave an uncomfortable cough.

"Yes, Aunt," Sarah replied. "I've asked His Lordship for an interview for my proposed work regarding supernatural events among England's older families. The Seymours, you see"—she paused long enough to make him stiffen— "are a very, very old family." She smiled at him innocently and saw the blue eyes spark, though he relaxed. "I had hoped His Lordship might share any peculiar events that his forebears had documented in journals or records. But thus far," she added sweetly, "I've been unsuccessful in securing his aid."

"Regrettably true," said Lord Graymar, addressing Aunt Speakley, "but I hope that Miss Tamony and I may come to some agreement on the matter soon. I am an admirer of her work, as well as Sir Alberic's, and shouldn't wish to be at enmity with any author possessed of so great a talent. Perhaps you might act as mediator for us, Mrs. Speakley. I'm sure your niece will be obliged to listen to the wisdom of her dear relative. I know that I should be gratified to do so."

Miss Tamony had spoken the truth, Malachi thought later as he led her into the yard behind the house. It was but a small, unilluminated patch of grass, accompanied by a few rosebushes and a single tree. Sufficient for a widowed lady to sit on sunny afternoons and enjoy tea but utterly unsuitable for private conversations when others were present. It was cold, as well, as she'd warned, and the sky covered in thick, threatening clouds, but that was easily dealt with. Malachi had waited long enough to speak with her in private and didn't wish to wait further.

He'd sat through a richly prepared and quite enjoyable dinner, during which he'd undertaken to charm his hostess and her guests to the best of his ability—a talent that, he accepted without too much pride, was considerable—all the while striving to ignore Miss Tamony's mocking glances. Afterward, the company undertook to enjoy several hands of whist. Malachi had allowed himself to be paired with Mrs. Speakley but made certain they were seated at the same table as Miss Tamony and her cousin, Philistia. He had discovered, not surprisingly, that Sarah Tamony was a serious competitor. She wasn't going to lose easily at anything she undertook. Her sweet and rather timid cousin had nearly been driven to tears by Miss Tamony's impatience over a poorly played card, so that Malachi had made certain the younger girl always held the winning hand. After the third such hand Miss Tamony looked at him sharply and commented that her cousin was having an uncommonly lucky evening. Philistia Tamony's delight, however, repaid him for the small deceit.

At the end of the fifth set, Malachi had declared himself in need of a bit of fresh air. The objections that would have normally followed were easily silenced, and the cousin and brother agreed to attend without so much as a pause to reflect. Now Malachi had to make certain they were far too fully occupied to pay any attention to Miss Tamony and himself.

"Come and sit," he instructed the pair following behind just as soon as they had cleared the house. "Here." He indicated a place, and an iron bench suddenly appeared.

Miss Tamony watched, her mouth opening slightly, as her brother and cousin obediently seated themselves.

"Miss Philistia," Malachi said, "you'll wish to discuss the latest fashions. And the upcoming balls you've accepted invitations to. Oh, and Almack's, I should imagine." He glanced at Miss Tamony, whose hand was upon his arm. "Young ladies do love to talk of Almack's, though I vow you'll find it something of a disappointment." She gave no reply but merely continued to stare. He turned back to the bench. "Mr. Tamony, you'll enjoy discussing the latest politics as well as the books you've recently read on Celtic history. You might also wish to regale your cousin yet again about the artifacts you examined in Professor Seabolt's home. Please proceed."

The pair on the bench each turned to the other and began to speak in low tones, oblivious to the others in the garden.

"Can they not hear each other?" Miss Tamony asked, her voice touched by worry. "Or do they imagine that they're actually having a conversation? And I thought it impossible, even for a great wizard, to create something out of nothing."

"There's not truly a bench there," he told her. "It's a deception. They're floating in a seated position, but quite comfortable. If anyone should happen to see them, however, it will appear that they're seated on a bench. You and I will sit here, opposite them."

With a flick of a finger he created another bench, exactly the same, and led her toward it. When she hesitated, he said reassuringly, "It will feel exactly as it should. Touch it."

She did, running her hands over the length of ornately curving iron. When she straightened, she said, "My lord, you have my permission to be seated first."

He smiled. "Miss Tamony, I would never ask a lady to sit upon an unworthy seat." To prove the matter, he sat, crossed one leg over the other, and patted the bench. The false iron gave off a satisfyingly solid sound.

She looked unconvinced but gingerly sat, stiffly, until she had leaned back and discovered that nothing gave way. Nodding to where her brother and cousin appeared to be lost in profound discussion, she asked, "What are they hearing from each other?"

"What they wish to," Malachi said easily. "They'll come away from the garden perfectly satisfied with their conversation, despite not being entirely able to recall what it was about. In a day or so, the memory of having accompanied us out-of-doors on a cold evening will have faded altogether."

"But it's warmer now," she said, lowering the wrap she'd brought, having assured her mother and aunt that she'd be warm enough. "You did that, as well."

He gave a single nod. "I've placed a shield of protection about the yard and it will keep us safe from the elements for as long as I wish it to. Even if rain should begin to fall, we'd not feel it. And now for a bit of light, so that I can see your lovely face when you become angered and wish to rail at me."

"Dear me," she said with a laugh. "Am I going to lose my temper? And we were having such a pleasant evening."

Malachi lifted one hand, palm up, and a flame appeared. With a slight push he sent the light into the air where it dispersed until the area was bathed in a gentle glow. The light was natural enough and so fully diffused that any onlooker might suppose it came from a nearby street lamp or lit window.

"Marvelous," Miss Tamony murmured, looking all about as if she could now see the protective shield. He wished it weren't invisible, if only to have her delighted reaction. Her love of magic pleased Malachi almost as much as she, herself, did.

He had longed to be with her again, perhaps because he had instinctively known what it would mean to him. Contentment. Happiness. A quietness and certainty that he'd never before known. The only thought that distressed him was of the moment when they must part: it would be hours before he would see her again.

He'd meant what he'd said about her cleaning up nicely, though that wasn't close to half the truth. He'd seen her beauty in wildness and now when it was tamed. Both states had much to recommend them, the wilder being the more sensual of the two. But the tamed Miss Tamony was equally stunning to the senses. Her glorious hair had been artfully arranged atop her head, with soft red-gold curls framing her face. Her figure was encased in a fashionable gown of rich plum, which enhanced her feminine curves to perfection and revealed the shoulders and neck just exactly as he'd imagined. Those naughty visions that he'd suffered at Glain Tarran had come to life the moment he'd set sight on her in Mrs. Speakley's parlor, and it had taken a great deal of willpower to push them aside for later contemplation. And when he'd stood before her and held her hand, he'd caught the scent of her perfume, rich and soft, delicately applied in order to gently tease those close enough to smell the fragrance. Just as he was close enough now, and breathed deeply.

"I know now where you inherited your beauty," he said, glad when the comment caused her to look at him inquiringly. "Your mother is exceedingly lovely."

The compliment pleased her, for she smiled widely. "Yes, she is, isn't she? She has been much admired in Europe."

"I can well imagine," he murmured. "As you have been, I should think."

The blush again. It was good to know that she was as unnerved by him as he was by her.

"And your father is just as interesting as I imagined he would be," Malachi went on. "I hope I shall have the honor of speaking with him often during the Season."

"He would like nothing better," she said. "My father is excessively fond of socializing. Far more than the rest of us."

"Not more than your cousin, I'd wager," he said, glancing to where Philistia Tamony sat cheerfully conversing with her oblivious cousin. She was a sweet-natured creature, vivacious and feminine in a dainty way, but she paled when set beside her far more handsome cousins. "Her mind is fixed on the coming Season, is it not?"

Miss Tamony gazed at her cousin fondly. "Very much so. We've always been out in Society during our travels, for my father's fame has made us desirable guests."

"And your fame of late, as well," Malachi said.

"Yes," she confessed. "Mine, too. We've been spoilt beyond measure, and the sad truth is that we've enjoyed it a great deal. Especially Philistia. She has had the pleasure of dancing with kings and princes and noblemen throughout much of the Continent. She has a great love of dancing, as you might expect in a young woman." She looked back at Malachi. "But she has longed to dance in England, with her own countrymen. She was only eleven when we last visited home, and not yet old enough to partake in parties and balls."

"Her heart has been untouched by love," Malachi said, sensing the longing that lived inside the younger woman. He glanced at his companion and wondered whether her heart had ever been captured. The answer, which he could have divined from any other mere mortal, was hidden by the same spirits who made her impervious to his magic. It was very frustrating.

"Your brother would prefer reading to dancing," Malachi remarked.

"Entirely," Miss Tamony said. "And discussing Celtic history with like-minded scholars to reading. Some young men dream of gaining entrance to London's most elegant clubs, but Julius would be glad to spend every waking moment at the Antiquities Society. Unfortunately for him, Mama insists that he accompany us to social functions. She thinks it's good for him, but Julius finds being in company tedious. He appeared to enjoy his brief discussion with you, however."

"We spoke of his visit to Professor Seabolt's home. Your brother was deeply impressed by the professor's collection."

"He's talked of almost nothing else," she said with a sigh. "It was a blessing, really, for he asked nothing of my supposed interview"—she looked at him pointedly—"nor made mention of its brevity. My interviews generally last two or more hours."

"Indeed?" Malachi said, raising his eyebrows. "You are very thorough, then."

"Very. When I'm able to conduct an interview, of course."

Her gaze had narrowed, and Malachi shifted slightly.

"You might take some comfort in the fact that Professor Seabolt wasn't pleased with me, either. Especially after having met you. He wants very much to pursue an acquaintance with the various Tamony authors."

"Then perhaps he shall," she said. "If he is both wise and bold and realizes how foolish it is to obey you in this matter."

Malachi rose to his feet, pacing away from her a few steps.

"Miss Tamony, I've come to make peace with you. To offer a temporary truce."

She gazed at him warily. "Does it involve me giving up my planned work?"

"Temporarily," he said, adding when she scowled, "in return for something that I believe any student of the supernatural would greatly desire."

Sarah Tamony's interest, as Malachi had thought it would be, was clearly aroused. The scowl died away to be replaced by quick attention.

"Yes?" She sat up a bit straighter and looked at him expectantly. "Would this something be as wonderful as flying?"

Malachi moved back toward her, his hands folded behind his back. "That is something only you can decide, but I believe it would be. In return for this boon, you must agree to set aside all discussion of your book until the end of the Season. You must also agree, without debate, to completely obey me if your involvement in this supernatural event might prove dangerous."

By her expression he could tell that she didn't like either of his conditions.

"What, precisely, is this supernatural something?"

"I should have phrased it more clearly," Malachi said. "It's an event which occurs but rarely in the lives of magic mortals. Only once every hundred years, in fact." He smiled. "This will be your only opportunity to witness it, unless your family is given to extremely long lives."

Miss Tamony gazed at him thoughtfully.

"This event," she said. "Did the writing that appeared in my journal have anything to do with it?"

"It did."

"I see." Lifting a hand, she began to finger the chain about her neck. "This event, then, is what you were referring to when you said that the spirits had involved me in something of importance. And if that is so, my lord, it would seem that you need my help far more than I need yours."

Malachi had always admired intelligent, quick-thinking

females, but he'd never liked being outwitted by them. With a light shrug, he sat once more.

"I'm certain the spirits will find another way in which to communicate with me if you don't wish to become involved. I merely thought we might help each other. I should like to focus my attention on the event without having to spend a great deal of time and energy in keeping you from writing your book, and you would be exposed to a magical occurrence that few mere mortals have ever been privy to. If you find that you cannot put your work off for a few months, however, or bear to be in company with me, then perhaps we shouldn't speak of it further."

"No, please," Miss Tamony replied quickly. "I didn't say we couldn't come to some understanding, Lord Graymar. If you would agree to freely allow me to conduct interviews at the end of our bargain, I'd be ready to agree at once."

Malachi shook his head. "I can't make such a promise," he said honestly. "But perhaps, by the time the Season has come to a close, you'll have found the way to convince me that I can trust you in writing about my family's history."

She looked skeptical. "I know from experience that you're remarkably stubborn, my lord. It's just as likely that I'll not change your mind and my efforts will have been in vain. And I'll have lost valuable time, as well."

"But you'll have gained a remarkable experience," he countered. "And if you do nothing, my determination will certainly remain unchanged. This is likely the only chance I'll give you to make the attempt."

She bit her bottom lip and was thoughtful. At last she murmured, "I don't mean to speak rudely, Lord Graymar, but somehow this feels like a trick."

There was something in her tone—a touch of sadness, almost—that made him reach for her hand.

"There's neither trick nor treachery involved, Miss Tamony. But I must be completely honest with you about what accepting my proposal would mean. If the spirits have chosen to use you as a means of communication, we may find it necessary to meet with some frequency, and if we are to avoid the rumors that might arise from such constant companionship, we must keep the wagging tongues of gossips busy with talk of our own choosing."

"Of our own choosing?" she repeated, tilting her head with confusion. "What can you mean, my lord?"

"There must be some excuse for us to be in company with each other," he said. "And if we don't wish to excite opinion that we're having a torrid affair, then we must pretend to a more acceptable relationship. We must undertake a formal courtship. Or, rather, I must," he clarified. "You must pretend to be agreeable to my advances."

"C-courtship?" Miss Tamony stammered. He could see her cheeks blooming with color even in the dim light. "With *me*? My lord, have you lost your senses?" She tried to pull her hand free.

Malachi held her fast. "I don't believe so. Can you devise a better plan to allow us to be in company when necessary without endangering your reputation?"

"Yes, I can," she told him. "You might agree to let me interview you for my book. That would require numerous meetings. Or at least we can tell anyone who asks that it does."

"No one would believe it. One or two meetings, perhaps. Not several. And I shall need to be able to seek you out at social events, to have cause to take you driving in the afternoons, to be able to speak to you whenever we meet without doing more than causing the *ton* to speculate upon when an announcement will be made. At the end of the Season, if all goes well, you can tell your particular friends that we've quarreled and I shall cease being in company with you so often. If we continue to treat each other kindly, without evident malice, we should come out of the entire escapade without damage to either of our reputations."

"But we'll be at odds once more about the book," she said.

"Unless you manage to change my mind," he acknowledged.

Pulling her hand free at last, Sarah Tamony stood. "No one will fall for such a deception," she said. "I've seen your mistress, you know. Lady Whiteley. Aunt Speakley pointed her out to me when we were in Piccadilly one afternoon. I realize I shouldn't discuss such things with you, but the fact of the matter—which of course you already know—is that she is very beautiful. No one could possibly think that the Earl of Graymar would leave a woman like that in order to court a bespectacled lady author possessed of an honorable but by no means exalted lineage."

She strove to keep the sound of jealousy from her tone, but Malachi could hear it. Just faintly, but it was there all the same. Strangely, the knowledge gave him pleasure. He wouldn't be so cruel as to linger over it.

"Lady Whiteley is indeed very handsome," he agreed. "But if you believe, Miss Tamony, that you are not her equal, perhaps more than that, then you clearly don't spend enough time looking into a mirror. I don't wish to waste time discussing such matters, which are, quite rightly, private. Suffice it to say that Society doesn't consider a man's relationship with his mistress as having any bearing at all on his relationship with his wife, and that Lady Whiteley herself will be neither overset nor harmed by any pretense we undertake. In point of fact, she's planning on leaving London before the Season begins in order to travel. She has always wished to see Italy in the spring."

Malachi had been surprised, pleasantly so, when he'd visited Augusta to make a settlement on her for her years of devoted and affectionate service. He'd offered to give her whatever she desired, and she'd replied at once that she wished to travel. Not just to Italy, though it was a start. She wished to see the entire Continent. Malachi had promised that he would make it possible, and they had parted as friends.

"Oh," Miss Tamony said, sitting beside him once more and looking into his face. Her expression, he saw, had cleared of whatever emotion had been troubling her. "I see. How fortunate for her. I'm sure she'll have a marvelous time. Italy is especially lovely in the late spring and early summer. We've spent a great deal of time there, as you might imagine."

"Given your father's love of Roman history," he said, "I would be surprised if you had not. But you haven't yet given me an answer, Miss Tamony, regarding my proposal."

She gazed at him for a long, silent moment, her lips slightly pursed in consideration.

"I'll agree," she finally said, "on one condition."

"What is it?"

She leaned slightly nearer, her green eyes alight with excitement.

"I'll agree to your proposal, Lord Graymar, if you'll promise that, at the end of the Season and before we part ways, you'll take me flying again."

The request made him smile. If she only knew how he wanted to fly with her in his arms again, she'd realize it was a boon he'd grant regardless of her agreement.

"If that is what you wish, Miss Tamony."

"More than anything."

He lifted his hand, then, and stroked a single finger down her cheek. "What an amazing woman you are, Miss Tamony. Is there nothing you fear?"

The smile on her face faltered beneath his touch, and now, he knew, it was her heart's turn to race. Her eyes widened and he felt a shiver coursing through her.

"Many things," she murmured. "But I believe that I can trust you, even with my life."

"I hope that's so," he said, thinking of the *cythraul* and praying that he wasn't exposing her to a graver danger than he could keep her safe from. With a sigh he dropped his hand and grew serious. "I mean for it to be. Remember, Miss Tamony, that you must obey me in the matter to come—without question—especially if danger arises."

The smile lifted the corners of her lips again, creating the most charming dimples. "I can scarcely agree to that without knowing what the supernatural event is. Perhaps when you tell me, you'd best exaggerate and make it as frightening as possible in order to instill a proper fear in me."

"Exaggeration won't be necessary," he assured her. "And powerful demons always instill fear in those who become involved with them. It's part of their peculiar magic."

"A demon," she repeated breathlessly, looking utterly thrilled. "Oh, please. Tell me everything at once."

Most women, even some who were magic mortals, would have pleaded with him to stop speaking of such awful things. Sarah Tamony only looked as if Malachi was the next best thing to Father Christmas. The pleasure her reaction gave him was frighteningly addictive.

"They'll be expecting us inside soon," he said. "I must explain quickly. If you have any questions, they shall have to wait until we're able to speak privately again."

And with that, he told her about the *cythraul,* his plans for finding it, and the spirits who, for completely unknown reasons, had involved her in the matter. With every word he spoke her excitement grew, causing her eyes to sparkle and her lovely features to fill with anticipation. By the time he had finished, Sarah Tamony was already making plans for helping him to capture the demon, and that was exactly what Malachi had hoped for.

Chapter 12

*M*alachi arrived at the Tamony household the next morning to pay a visit, which, as he had at last been formally introduced to the family, was now socially acceptable. All of the ladies were at home and he enjoyed their genuine pleasure at his appearance, though Sarah Tamony again did little to temper her teasing looks. Malachi managed to remain composed and, following social dictates, took his leave after fifteen minutes of conversation. He then made his way to Mrs. Speakley's less fashionable dwelling to tender his gratitude for the previous night's amusements and found her in company with her friends Lady Wilbay and Lady Bawstone. He politely endured twenty minutes of their ecstatic admiration and then made his escape, returning to Mervaille to consider his next move.

The fact of the matter was that he was thirty and six and had never attempted making a siege upon a woman's heart. Indeed, it had usually been quite the opposite, and he'd been obliged to avoid the traps that young ladies and their mamas had laid for him—some of them quite elaborate and cunning, too. His mistresses and briefer dalliances had come to him easily and willingly and, with the exception of Augusta, had never birthed any desire for a more permanent union.

But he had vast experience in the art of courtship, nonetheless. From the moment he'd gained his majority it had been one of Malachi's tasks each Season to oversee the romances of not only the Seymours but the other magical Families who gave him their allegiance as well. He had become so proficient at keeping love-sickened youths in line that he might almost have made an occupation of it.

He knew all of the rules and dictates of proper courtship. For example, to keep rumors from springing up and making all those concerned uncomfortable, especially the parents, it was vital that the couple involved not be seen in company too often or attend the same social events each evening until a formal betrothal had been announced. This particular rule had been the bane of all the young lovers Malachi had chaperoned, for as they had often assured him, being parted from their loved one for even a few brief hours was agony. Malachi had been sympathetic with their plight but had firmly maintained his resolve. Magic had sometimes been necessary to keep the lovers from sneaking out and meeting in private, and then it had been Malachi who'd had to endure agony as they'd poured their tears and misery into his ears. Once they were wed this same couple came to their senses and thanked him for keeping their names and reputations free from harm. They realized, just as he did, that honoring expected standards was not only good but also necessary.

Which was why, later that evening as he was ushered into Lady Kendall's drawing room in anticipation of a poetry reading, Malachi could only wonder at his lack of self-control. Perhaps he needed someone to chaperone him, now.

He found her at once in the crowded room, standing with her cousin and mother and surrounded by too many male admirers. A few were addressing Miss Philistia and two older gentlemen were speaking to Lady Tamony, but the majority were fixed on the beautiful authoress, who wasn't even wearing her spectacles to frighten them away. The gown she wore, composed of a soft gold material that almost appeared to glow, clung to her curves in a manner designed to entrance every man who set sight on her. The color caused the highlights in her hair to shimmer and made the glorious green eyes even more astonishing. Malachi had no doubt that every man in the room wanted to be near her, for what could be more alluring than a beautiful, unmarried, famous, and wealthy woman of good birth? If her scribbling and travels made her something of an oddity, so much the better. Everyone knew that a desirable object only became more valuable if it was unique.

But Malachi could tell, as he approached, that Sarah Tamony was bored. She stood with a polite smile upon her lips, nodding every now and then as the men around her chattered on, but her gaze was unfocused, filled with disinterest.

His arrival caused the sea of men to part. Many of them were acquaintances, and these he nodded at with the correct reserve that was expected of the Earl of Graymar. Then he moved forward, giving them the option of either moving aside or being walked over. They moved aside.

Sarah Tamony's eyes lit with pleasure when he came close enough for her to recognize him, and the smile she gifted him with filled Malachi with satisfaction.

"My lord, how marvelous," she said, then realized that she'd spoken out of turn. Propriety declared that he must greet her mother first.

Lady Tamony was cordial and Miss Philistia was openly delighted. The same could not be said of the group of admirers, who suddenly seemed to realize that they'd somehow been outdone in being able to claim prior familiarity with the Tamony ladies. One by one they began to wander away.

"Sir Alberic and Mr. Tamony haven't accompanied you?" Malachi asked Lady Tamony politely.

"Papa would have come," Sarah replied before her

mother could speak, "but he wished to work on his speech for the Antiquities Society. Julius would rather be shot in the foot than attend a poetry recital."

"Sarah," her mother reproved. To Malachi she said, "You must forgive my daughter's plain manner of speaking, my lord. I fear her upbringing has been rather too lax."

"Not at all, my lady," Malachi assured her. "Miss Tamony is refreshingly frank. I prefer it to the practiced conversation one so often must endure in Society. I would wager you find the English to be more deeply entrenched in such behavior than citizens on the Continent."

He was very good, Sarah thought as she watched the Earl of Graymar lead her mother into exactly the sort of philosophical and political conversation she liked best. Lady Tamony was never pleased to be treated by men as if she were intellectually inferior, and His Lordship clearly understood that. With Philla, however, his tactics changed. He complimented her on her dress and jewels and admired the arrangement of her hair. He asked whether she was to attend Almack's and related a few small pieces of gossip about the famous patronesses that made her laugh.

At last he turned his attention to Sarah, and she could see that he was satisfied with himself.

"I hope I find you well, Miss Tamony," he said politely. "Are you a devotee of poetry?"

"If it is good, yes," she replied. "If it's not, I fear I will probably begin to laugh and embarrass my poor mother and cousin." She leaned slightly nearer, confiding, "It's one of my particular failings, you see. Inappropriate laughter. I daresay the idea is foreign to you."

"Of course it is," he replied without so much as a change in tone. "The Seymours never laugh out of turn. Or step a toe out of line. We are a very exacting sort."

She laughed at that, but not inappropriately. The evening, which moments before had been deadly dull, suddenly became pleasant. "I fear I must disagree with you, my lord, though it pains me to contradict you in regards to your own family. I could tell you stories about your fore-bears that would—"

"Sarah." Her mother's voice broke in. "You're not to speak of your writing tonight, dear."

"Why not? I'm sure His Lordship doesn't mind."

Lord Graymar cleared his throat and addressed her mother. "Perhaps I might divert your daughter's mind, madam, with a short parade about the room. I understand the recital is to be rather lengthy. Some exercise before-hand might prove beneficial."

"An excellent thought, my lord," Lady Tamony said with approval. "Perhaps it will help Sarah to sit still for the space of an hour."

Sarah rolled her eyes. Lord Graymar held out his arm and led her away.

"Is this the beginning of our pretend courtship?" she asked the moment they were out of her parent's hearing. "I should like to be certain so that I can smile at you a great deal and nod worshipfully at everything you say."

He laughed. "Worshipfully *and* adoringly, Miss Tam-ony. Be certain not to confuse the two. Tell me, pray, what's become of your charming spectacles. I hadn't thought you would ever be so vain as to leave them off."

"I wouldn't have," she said, sighing. "I'm perfectly blind without my eyeglasses. Everything and everyone is a blur unless I get quite close. But although my mother hasn't any trouble letting me wear them during the day, she refuses to allow it on particularly fine occasions."

"Ladies don't often wear their spectacles in public," Lord Graymar admitted. "Even when they should. It's but one of the details I find so refreshing about you, Miss Tamony. And your looks don't suffer from wearing them. Quite the oppo-site. I find them vastly attractive. Perhaps I should tell your mother so."

"You are very kind," she told him with sincere grati-tude, warmed by his compliments. "But I fear it wouldn't do any good. You'll note that she's not wearing her spectacles, either, and she's quite as blind as I am. There's only this, you see?" She lifted one wrist to show him the lorgnette dangling there by a silk ribbon.

"God help us," he murmured. "Do you intend to use it?"

"Absolutely," she vowed. "You'd best take care never to wear a quizzing glass, my lord, else it might well be war between us. I've been told I'm a deft hand with my lorgnette."

"I shall take every care, Miss Tamony, not to engage you in such a battle. Perhaps we had better find our seats. I believe the recital is about to begin."

They sat side by side during the recitation, which proved to be nearly disastrous, for the poetry was indeed quite bad. Though Sarah tried valiantly to contain her amused reaction, His Lordship's quiet remarks, heard only by Sarah, nearly undid her.

"That was unjust," she told him later as they stood on the terrace overlooking Lady Kendall's garden while the other guests partook of refreshments. "I might have made the most dreadful scene if my mother hadn't been poking me on the other side."

"It's a pity she was," he remarked evenly. "One good shout of laughter would have broken the monotony. What the devil possessed that fellow to go on about flowers so unceasingly?"

"Flowers are considered very romantic," she told him. "Which you clearly have not yet realized, my lord."

"I happen to know a good deal about flowers, Miss Tamony. And one thing I've realized in particular is that they needn't be compared to everything from a woman's lips to the moon above. It's repulsive."

"The poor young man," she said. "He was remarkably repetitive, was he not? When he compared the heavens to a cluster of bluebells I was certain I should lose all countenance. And then you made that sound—"

"I?" he said, looking at her with feigned bewilderment. "Made a sound? Impossible. You must have imagined it."

"You made that 'hmmm' sound, just as if you couldn't

make out whether the fellow was mad or simply a fool," she said. "You know you did, and I'll not have you deny it."

"I'm the Earl of Graymar, Miss Tamony," he replied. "No one would believe such a thing possible."

She sighed. "I know. You are the perfect gentleman, after all, as well as the ideal nobleman. You have no faults."

"I have many faults," he said, "but it's true that I don't wish to make them known. It's helpful in my position to be held in awe."

Sarah smiled. "I know that, too. Now tell me the truth, please. You dislike poetry recitals as greatly as I do. Surely you don't mean to force yourself into such engagements simply to beget the idea that you've an interest in me?"

"You make it sound like a tedious chore, Miss Tamony," he said. "Your company will more than make recompense for any unpleasantness I might suffer."

She made a face at him. "If you're going to begin to spout such silly nonsense, Lord Graymar, I'll return indoors and plead with the poet to make his recitation all over again."

"Your modesty is refreshing," he told her, "but I wasn't making a pretty speech. Despite our differences regarding your work, I find you to be a nearly ideal companion. You're intelligent, witty, beautiful to gaze upon—"

"My lord," she said, blushing hotly.

"—and, most important, you have no fear of magic. More than that, the spirits who oversee my kind have clearly found you to be a suitable conduit for their communications. I truly doubt I could find another such woman in all of England whose company would be more pleasant."

"Your mistress, perhaps," Sarah suggested, then immediately wished she hadn't, for his expression, which had been open and relaxed, instantly shuttered. "Forgive me," she said at once. "That was inexcusably rude."

"Yes," he agreed coolly. "It was. I certainly don't compare you to Lady Whiteley, or any other woman of my acquaintance."

She had truly offended him, Sarah realized, and was deeply chagrined.

"I am sorry, my lord." Reaching out, she touched his gloved hand. "Please pretend that I never said such a stupid thing. My unruly tongue, just as my mother warned you."

His gaze had fixed upon her hand. She made to pull it away, but his fingers curled about her own, stopping her.

"It's forgotten," he said, lifting his eyes to hers. "But there is still the matter of your disbelief in my sincerity, Miss Tamony. Perhaps you might be assuaged if you consider that our charade might be of use to you, apart from witnessing the advent of the *cythraul*."

"Of use to me?" she repeated faintly, very aware of how strong and warm his fingers were as they pressed against her own. "In what way?"

He rubbed a thumb lightly over the back of her hand. "I'm a powerful man, Miss Tamony, with powerful connections."

"I know that well enough, my lord. You've done a splendid job of using that power to stop all my interviews."

"True," he admitted with a nod, "but I can also use it to open doors for you, if you wish. Not in the way of interviews, but to other supernatural interests. There are numerous private collections in Town—my own among them—that few mere mortal eyes have seen. And I can arrange personal viewings for you at various museums, during hours when the curiosity of the public won't act as an impediment. We can speak freely when alone. I can relate histories to you that don't involve magic mortals, but which I daresay will fascinate you, nonetheless. There are a great many things you know about magic, but likely just as many that you don't."

Sarah felt as if she suddenly couldn't breathe. "You would take me to Mervaille?"

"Perhaps," he murmured. "In time. There are any number of fascinating objects there that you would find interesting. But there are other places I can take you, as well." He bent his head nearer and lowered his voice. "What is it that you truly wish to see and do in London,

Miss Tamony? Is it poetry readings and card parties?" He nodded toward the gathering indoors. "Or the opera and ballet? The theater? What of lectures on the supernatural? You cannot enter half the halls in London on account of being a woman, but I can disguise you so that no one, save myself, would see you as anything other than a man. Or at all, if I chose to make you invisible. You could attend the highest scholarly functions that your sex has always kept you from and no one would be the wiser."

Sarah's heart beat painfully in her chest. Everything he said, every word he spoke, were the things she had dreamed of.

"Don't tease me, my lord," she murmured. "It would be too cruel."

"You're going to help me with the *cythraul*, Miss Tamony. I wish to make the effort worth your while. I mean precisely what I say. Put me to the test and see."

"My father's going to speak at the Antiquities Society on Monday. Could you make it possible for me to attend?"

"Easily," he said. "I had planned to go, myself. I shall take you and make you—which would you prefer? To be a man, or to be invisible?"

"Oh, invisible, please," she said, laughing with delight. "I've already spent far too much time dressed in boys' clothing to care for that. But to be invisible!" She felt giddy. "It would be as wonderful as flying."

"It's settled, then. Apart from your father's lecture, are there not other, more usual places you would wish to go? I realize you've traveled the world and seen a great deal, but surely you've a preference in amusements. We must be seen in company, recall. I don't wish to bore you."

Sarah eyed him consideringly. "I suppose," she said, "that you have your own box at the theater, my lord?"

He smiled. "Yes, Miss Tamony. With an excellent view of the stage. Do you suppose if I speak to Lady Tamony your family might accept an invitation to join me there in the near future?"

"Indeed I do, my lord," she replied. "In fact, I believe I could assure you of it."

Malachi had never enjoyed himself during a London Season as he did now. When he woke each day it was not to lie in bed and consider with resignation the duties that lay before him, though they certainly remained, Parliament foremost among them. But he knew that at some point during the day or coming night he would be seeing Sarah, and even if the event lasted but a few minutes, it was enough to fill him with anticipation.

She made him smile and laugh with her infectious sense of humor, but she also had the gift of serious well-reasoned conversation that readily complimented his own. They often spoke of magic but just as often discussed history, philosophy, and politics. She was interested in the Prison Reform Act, which gratified Malachi no end. The only other person apart from fellow members of Parliament who wished to discuss the matter with him was Niclas, and though Malachi loved his cousin dearly, it was a far more enchanting experience to sit beside a green-eyed, red-haired, bespectacled beauty possessed of a curvaceous figure that made Malachi's mouth dry and who smelled faintly of lily of the valley discussing any and every topic under the sun.

He discovered something new about Sarah each time they were together. When he invited Julius Tamony to go riding in the park one morning, Sarah came along, demonstrating a proficiency at horsemanship that had surprised him. Though why it had, Malachi couldn't guess. Her nature was competitive; he should have known that she would strive to excel at anything she set her hand to.

She was also capable of handling a carriage, which she proved on two occasions when they'd gone driving. On the first of these, the day following their attendance at the Antiquities Society, they had come across his cousin Julia, who was enjoying her daily drive in the pretty high-perch phaeton Niclas had bought her. It was her favorite time of day, Malachi knew, for it was the only hour she had to herself. Julia was delighted to make Sarah's acquaintance but clearly baffled at seeing Malachi in company with the authoress. Niclas appeared at Mervaille some hours later to demand an explanation.

"I cannot explain my actions to you," Malachi told him, "for I don't understand them myself. When I do, you'll be the first to know."

Niclas had not been amused, but it was often thus. Some Seymours lacked a sense of humor. Some had far too much of it.

"You asked Julia to arrange a chance meeting with Mrs. Speakley because she's Sarah Tamony's aunt, didn't you?"

"Yes," Malachi admitted.

Niclas began to pace. "Since then, from what I've been able to gather, you've been in company either with Miss Tamony alone or with her family as well. It's also become evident that the presence of Sarah Tamony was your reason for having accepted Mrs. Silverby's invitation."

"I'm afraid that's true."

Niclas stopped pacing and stared at him. "You've gone out riding with both Miss Tamony and her brother," he said, "and invited the Tamonys to your box at the theater—"

"I expected that you'd hear of that particular event and come to speak to me far sooner," Malachi said. "You've no idea how people stare at the famous Miss Tamony. And whisper behind their hands. It's quite distracting."

Niclas ignored this. "Yesterday you attended Sir Alberic's speech at the Antiquities Society," he continued, "and today you took Miss Tamony driving in the park. Alone."

Malachi held his hands out wide. "All true," he confessed.

"Tell me why," Niclas demanded. "After everything I went through to put the fear of God into Miss Tamony, after all of the letters I wrote, after endlessly listening to you rant about how dangerous Miss Tamony's works are—"

"I did not rant," Malachi countered with faint insult.

"Endlessly," Niclas insisted. "All the time I was at Glain Tarran, when I did my utmost to get you to simply speak to the woman—and now!" He threw his hands up. "Behind my back, almost, you not only speak to her, you're with her every moment—"

"Now you're becoming irrational, *cfender*," Malachi said. "I am not with her every moment. That would be impossible until we've wed."

"*What!*"

"I meant to say 'unless,'" Malachi said quickly. "*Unless* we were wed. Niclas, please sit down. I'm sorry that I haven't taken you into my confidence before now, especially as I've always been able to trust you so completely."

"Then tell me what's happened."

Malachi did, beginning with Sarah Tamony's intrusion at Glain Tarran and the magic that appeared to protect her. He related the facts of how she'd come to have the Donballa, of how the Guardians had used her journal to communicate the clue regarding the *cythraul*. He said nothing of the intense desire he felt for her, but Niclas must have heard it in his voice.

"Malachi Seymour," he said with wonder when Malachi had finished speaking. "You've fallen in love. After all these years. And with Sarah Tamony, of all women."

"I don't know that it's love," Malachi told him honestly. "I don't know what it is at all, save some kind of madness. But, God help me, if this charade of courtship should lead to a permanent union, I cannot say that I'd be displeased."

Niclas's fury had faded, to be replaced with wonderment.

"It must be love. You not only took her flying; you made her invisible—at the Antiquities Society. Nothing but love could have made you so incautious." He considered the matter for a moment. "Are you *unoliaeth* with Miss Tamony? Can it be?"

"I don't know," Malachi said. "Such a union was never foretold for me, just as yours with Julia was not. But the ways of the Guardians are peculiar. It would be a fine jest to bind me to a woman whose writings will be the end of us all."

"But if you wed her," Niclas said thoughtfully, "you

would have the power to control what she writes. She would be your wife, and as her husband you could stop the publication of her work."

Malachi gave him a surprised look. "I don't recall Julia bending to your wishes when she doesn't desire to. But that's neither here nor there. Miss Tamony has agreed to put aside writing her book until the *cythraul* has been dealt with. I shall set my mind to the matter then."

"And until then?"

"I intend to make Society believe I'm courting Sarah Tamony, and keep her near in case the Guardians should give her another clue."

Niclas sighed. "You had best let us help you, then," he said. "Julia will be invaluable as a chaperone and in gaining helpful introductions, quite apart from the fact that she adores Miss Tamony's writings and will never forgive you if you keep her to yourself. And I can lend a hand with the parents and brother and even the little cousin, if necessary."

Malachi smiled at him warmly. "That is good of you, *cfender*. I'd be grateful for your excellent help. I don't suppose you might work up the courage to attend Almack's on the morrow and help me keep the wolves at bay? Between the father and brother and the two of us, we might contrive to keep the Tamony ladies dancing much of the night."

"God help us all," Niclas murmured, gazing at him with a knowing smile. "You're already jealous of other men paying court to the famous authoress. Only tell me, Cousin, if the stories I've heard of her beauty are true?"

"They are," Malachi said. "But you'll see for yourself tomorrow night."

And he did.

Sarah had never been to Almack's assembly rooms before. Her parents had tried to obtain tickets for them when they'd briefly visited London ten years earlier, only to be denied. Apparently the patron ladies who oversaw the assembly rooms didn't read Sir Alberic's works and had been put off by the incessant amount of traveling the Tamonys undertook. Now, however, they were all eagerness to allow the family into Almack's sacred halls. Her parents, brother, and cousin believed it was due to Sarah's fame; Sarah believed otherwise.

"You forced them to let us in, didn't you?" she whispered to the Earl of Graymar, who, having finished greeting her family, had taken her on his arm to parade her about the room and introduce her to his particular friends. Every eye in Almack's was upon them as they made their way, and audible whispers accompanied their progress.

"I would have done so," he replied in soft tones, smiling and nodding at acquaintances as they passed, "if it had been necessary. I hardly need tell you that your fame has made both you and your family desirable guests."

"You sound truly jealous, my lord," she murmured with a smile. "You are not often cast into the shade, I believe, being so notorious a figure."

"My cousin Niclas tells me that it's good for my soul," he said. "He believes I'm too conceited."

"You?" she remarked with feigned disbelief. "Because you are handsome, powerful, and wealthy? I don't know how he could ever have come to think such a thing."

"I'm sure he'll be glad to tell you," Malachi said, "for here is my cousin and his good lady Julia now."

Meeting Niclas Seymour was an unexpected pleasure. He was different from his powerful cousin in every way, different, in fact, from most Seymours. He was much taller and more muscular than the Seymours who'd inherited elvish blood and far more serious in nature. He was known to be a man possessed of a great intellect, skillful in debate, and a devotee of philosophical discussion. He was also a practiced gentleman who knew how to put others at ease—especially mere mortals. He charmed Lady Tamony by speaking to her as an equal, made fast friends with Sir Alberic and Julius by speaking to them as fellow intellectuals, and caused Philistia to blush and giggle by speaking to her as an admirer. He was so handsome that Sarah could scarce blame her cousin; she nearly blushed and giggled, too. His wife, Julia, was a fitting mate for such a man. Equal in beauty, she matched him in intellect and poise.

"Don't let my husband fool you, Miss Tamony," Julia murmured when the two men briefly excused themselves. "He's just as upended as I am to meet you. We adore your writing."

"You're very kind," Sarah said. "Thank you. And thank you, as well, for going out of your way to arrange a meeting between my aunt, Mrs. Speakley, and the earl. She's scarce stopped talking of his attendance at her gathering, or of the visit he made the next day. She is the envy of all her friends."

"It was my pleasure," Julia assured her. "Mrs. Speakley is a delightful woman. Of course now I understand Lord Graymar's reason for making the request."

It took Sarah a moment to understand what Julia meant and why she was smiling just so.

"Oh, dear me, no," she said quickly. "I'm afraid you have the wrong notion, Mrs. Seymour. He undertook the meeting as a way of repaying me for aid rendered."

"For the messages in the journal?" she asked, keeping her voice low so that no one could overhear her. "My dear Miss Tamony, it wasn't for that. Believe me."

Sarah blushed hotly. "I'm sure you must be wrong. His attentions are merely a ruse, a way for us to be together in case we need to discuss the . . . if by chance there should be another clue."

"If it's a ruse," Julia murmured, nodding toward two approaching figures, "then the Earl of Graymar is certainly playing it to perfection."

Sarah had told her mother and cousin that it was foolish for a woman to be given permission to waltz. She'd said it, perhaps, because she knew that no woman of her advanced years would be expected to be given permission and had wanted to make it clear that she didn't care. But when Sarah found herself facing Lady Emily Cowper and being invited to waltz with a sober-faced Lord Graymar, she was stunned into an uncustomary speechlessness—and filled with an unexpected jolt of delight.

"I would be honored if you would consent, Miss Tamony," Lord Graymar said, holding out his arm.

Sarah let him lead her to the dance floor. She gazed into his face as he set his hand on her waist and lifted her other hand high.

"It will be like flying again, my lord," she murmured.

"Yes, Miss Tamony," he replied softly, his strong fingers pressing against her in such a manner that she moved a little nearer. "It will."

Chapter 13

Serafina Daray leaned forward on the seat within her elegant carriage, peering more closely through the glass window. "That's the brother, then?" she asked Tego, who sat opposite her, looking out as well. "Mr. Julius Tamony?"

Tego gave a single nod and looked at the tall, finely dressed man with displeasure. "That's him. The young woman is his cousin, Miss Philistia Tamony. She's of no worry to us."

"I should think not," Serafina murmured. "What a drab little creature. Nothing at all like the famous Miss Tamony. But the brother is . . . perfect."

The tone of her voice drew Tego's sharp attention, and he silenced the words that wanted to tumble from his lips. He knew what that tone meant. His mistress was intrigued by a particular man . . . again. And now she'd not rest until she had him. Which was a damned lot of inconvenience for Tego.

"I'm already busy with the professor," he reminded her. "Send Artus or Callidus if you want him snatched."

"How foolish you are, Tego," she said softly, her gaze held on Julius Tamony's muscular frame. "Mr. Tamony is a well-bred gentleman, not a common laborer. I shall go after him myself. Where do you think they're going to?"

"Hookham's," Tego replied, wishing that she'd not made him come out in the daytime, where the light hurt his eyes and mere mortals gazed at him with contempt. "They're all bookish in that family, even the cousin, though she favors romantic novels. The brother spends more time in libraries and bookstores than in Society. The Dewin Mawr has attempted to introduce him to some of the gentlemen's clubs, with little success."

Serafina made a purring sound. "A man who can resist the Dewin Mawr's persuasions is a man worth possessing. I like his manner of walking. He moves with such lordly confidence."

Tego preferred to call it swaggering and to believe that it was pride that made the man stride along in so haughty a manner, but didn't say so to his mistress. She was foolish when it came to handsome men. One day, Tego prayed, she would be foolish over him. It was the only wish he had in life.

"The Earl of Graymar has spent a great deal of time with the sister," Serafina continued thoughtfully. "I heard he even deigned to ask permission to lead Miss Tamony out in her first London waltz. And each day since, he's been in company with her. Is he truly smitten?" she wondered aloud. "Or does he merely want the journal, as we do?"

"Does it matter?" Tego asked. "If you control the brother you control the sister. She'll do whatever you wish in order to keep him safe."

Serafina shook her head. "She'll run to Malachi. And if the Dewin Mawr discovers what I've done, we'll all suffer for it. It would be far better, I think, to let him focus his energies on Miss Tamony while we engage to have Mr. Julius Tamony do our work for us in fetching the journal. Apart from being safer," she said with obvious anticipation, "it will be far more pleasant."

"Don't wander this time, Phil," Julius said firmly as his cousin peered up at him from beneath her wide-brimmed bonnet. "We can't spend more than an hour this afternoon. Mother expects us home in time for tea."

"I'll stay in the romances this time, Jules, I promise." Philistia set a gloved hand over her heart.

Satisfied, Julius left his cousin perusing the latest arrivals and made his way to the history section. He'd already read most of the books on Celtic history that Hookham's library possessed but had noted an interesting text on prehistorical tribal migrations across Europe during his last visit, and there had been a slender volume on the stringent techniques of the Masorites in the preservation and documentation of Scripture that had caught his eye. He hoped neither had been taken yet.

The door to the library opened just as Julius reached the aisle he intended to traverse, and a moment later everything in the place seemed to stir.

A clerk hurried to greet the new arrival, his voice loud above the chatter of other customers and filled with deference. About him, Julius both saw and heard some of the other customers stiffen with recognition and delight. Their expressions almost made him think that the king had entered, but the sound that next greeted his ears caused that idea to dissolve.

It was the sweetest voice he'd ever heard. Beautiful, bell-like, and utterly feminine—there was nothing in his experience to compare it to. He knew, even before he turned to look at her, that the one who possessed it would be equally lovely.

But he was wrong. "Lovely" was a foolish, insignificant word to use. She was . . . magnificent. Incredible. Fantastic. Like no other woman on earth. It was impossible to stop staring.

She was small and delicate yet had a woman's curves and possessed a heart-shaped face that was utter perfection. Her eyes were an unearthly shade of blue, large and shining, and her curls were a bright gold that put all other colors to shame by comparison. When she spoke, the music of her voice filled the air with life and sparkling beauty. She was dressed all in white, like an angel, touched only here and there—about her waist, on her skirt and sleeves— by falls of delicate white lace and bows of blue silk ribbon.

Her bonnet, a wide-brimmed confection of that same lace and blue silk, framed her face in a manner that, if possible, only made her more enchanting.

Julius was captivated, as were all the other fortunate beings near enough to see and hear this heavenly vision. The clerk, when she smiled at him, looked as if he might faint. Julius understood how he felt. His heart pounded furiously in his chest, and when the angel sent her blue-eyed gaze about the library, coming at last to rest upon him, he thought he might faint, too. She paused, and then her bow-shaped lips curved into a shy smile. Julius's hands began to tremble so greatly that he had to curl them into fists to make them stop. Then she looked away and his heart fell to his feet, filled with despair.

The angel murmured something to the enrapt clerk, and they both glanced at Julius. With a nod the clerk made a reply, and then, almost beyond Julius's belief, they began to walk in his direction. All those in the library who were near enough watched as she made her way, their eyes fixed on her just as Julius's were. As she neared, the glorious creature looked up at him from beneath the brim of her bonnet, the shy smile yet upon her lips, and Julius forgot how to breathe. Or think. His mind went completely blank in the presence of such beauty.

"Mr. Tamony," the clerk said, his voice shaking badly, "may I introduce you to Miss Daray? She wishes to speak with you."

Julius's mouth was dry, but somehow he managed to make a bow and say, "Miss Daray."

"Mr. Tamony," she replied in the sweet, bell-like voice. "I'm so pleased to meet you. I'm an admirer of your sister's work. I understand that you are a scholar, as well, and hoped you might recommend a book to me. I enjoy history, you see, but can never seem to find a book that truly interests me." She moved a step nearer, and the smile widened. "Men are so much better at these things. It's terribly rude of me to ask upon such short acquaintance, but would you be so charitable as to lend me your most excellent aid in recommending a book suitable for a woman to read?"

◆ ◆ ◆

Philistia Tamony had never been considered a particularly clever female, certainly not when compared to her aunt Caroline or cousin Sarah. But Philistia was educated and well-read, for all that, and enjoyed settling down to a good novel while her scholarly relatives busied themselves with far duller historical tomes.

The trouble she always encountered, however, when faced with shelves filled with possibilities, was making a decision. This was, unfortunately, a general failing in her character, not limited to the choosing of reading material. It made itself evident from the start of Philistia's day to the end, causing even the simplest decision, from which dress to wear to whether she should drink chocolate or tea with her breakfast, to become something of a chore.

Currently, she was trying to decide whether to select *Adventures on the High Seas: My Life Among Pyrates,* written by "A Young Man Kidnapped from the Bosom of his Family," or *Dark Castle of Intrigue,* by "A Lady." Philistia tended to enjoy novels written by authors defined as "A Lady," for they were usually far more romantic than those penned by unfortunate youths or men. She had just closed the volume about the young man and the pyrates with the intention of returning it to the shelf when an odd tremor shook the air around her, causing the book to drop from her fingers. Someone very large bumped her from behind, knocking Philistia off-balance and sending her flying forward, but a strong pair of arms came about her at once, pulling her back just before her head struck the bookcase.

"Oh!" she cried, looking down to see two masculine hands encased in black gloves planted directly beneath her breasts. "Oh!" She shoved the hands away and whirled about, finding herself looking into a man's broad, elegantly attired chest.

A quiver of fright washed over her and she shuffled back until she came up against the bookcase. Then she looked up—way up—into the face of the man before her.

Her first impression—apart from the fact that he was

very tall and muscular—was that he was the devil. His hair
and eyes were as black as coal and his expression was
sharp and cunning and . . . very angry. Philistia's slight
frame began to tremble, for his every aspect was terrifying. He looked as if he hated her, as if she were an inconvenience that he wished to knock aside and be rid of.
Pressing more fully against the bookcase, she looked both
up and down the aisle, but there was no one else nearby.
They were alone. She opened her mouth to cry out for
Julius, but the stranger divined her purpose before she
could make a sound and, with movements so quick that
Philistia didn't even know he'd made them, he had her
tight against his body, one arm about her waist, actually
lifting her off the ground, and one hand covering her
mouth, stopping all sound.

What a damnable mistake, the Earl of Llew thought as the
girl in his grip squirmed and whimpered. He'd intended to
transport into an aisle where none of Hookham's customers
were present, and since he, himself, avoided the romance
section like the plague, it had seemed a likely choice. Serafina Daray was occupied with Julius Tamony in the history
aisles, far enough away that Morcar knew he could secret
himself into the library without her recognizing his presence. The magic he'd used had been performed several
blocks away, and she'd not sensed it. But if he used magic
now, within the library's confines, in order to silence the
stupid, squirming girl, Serafina would immediately know
that a powerful magic mortal was present and would act accordingly. And that was something Lord Llew couldn't risk.
Not if he wanted to find out what Serafina was up to.

One of his footmen had disappeared—the one whom
he'd foolishly related his vision to—and he had a good
idea that Serafina had been behind the disappearance. She
hadn't killed the man, of course, for that would have enraged the Guardians. She'd merely gotten whatever information she needed through the use of her exceedingly
great charms, then sent the fellow on his way, likely disre-

membering his entire life. That she'd done it didn't surprise Morcar; she had warned him, after all, that she would do whatever she must to find the clues to the *cythraul*'s arrival. It was how she'd done it that bothered him. All of his servants were mere mortals and all of them held in servitude by powerful enchantments that he had placed upon them. He had not thought himself vulnerable in such a way, and the fact of it made him exceedingly irate.

Now she had fixed her mind on the Tamonys, a family that Morcar had had only a fleeting interest in until he'd achieved London. Indeed, he would have no interest in them at all if he'd not agreed to give Sarah Tamony, the authoress, an interview during the Season—an agreement he'd forgotten about almost the moment he'd had his secretary reply in the affirmative to the request Miss Tamony sent to Castle Llew some months earlier.

But once he'd arrived in London he'd taken note of two fascinating facts: that Malachi Seymour had openly begun to court Miss Tamony and that Serafina had likewise begun to stalk the remainder of the family, at last honing in on the brother. Morcar had set out to discover why the odd family of scholars was suddenly of such great import to two powerful magic mortals. And fate, in all its strange humor, had seen fit to throw the little dowd of a cousin, Philistia Tamony, literally into his arms. He would have far preferred the famous authoress, whose beauty, when he'd first seen her, had been a pleasant surprise.

Morcar had assumed that Sarah Tamony would possess the same plain sturdiness as all the bookish females he'd known before, but, excepting the spectacles, she was far and away something altogether different. Unfortunately, Malachi was neither blind nor foolish and had snapped her up for himself. The two were in such constant company that Morcar was obliged to be patient until Miss Tamony came to him for the proposed interview. If he made the first move, Malachi would know at once and probably interfere, just as rumor had it he'd been interfering in the woman's writing since they'd both come to Town.

Which in itself was an intriguing mystery. Why would the woman allow the Earl of Graymar to court her when he was the very source of frustration in her research? It was common knowledge among the Families that the Dewin Mawr meant to put a stop to Sarah Tamony's proposed work. If she understood that, as well, then either she was secretly hoping to land a titled husband, not knowing what the Earl of Graymar truly was, or Malachi was using some kind of enchantment to keep her on a short tether and beneath his watch.

The question was why?

Miss Philistia Tamony's struggles lessened, and Morcar realized that she was about to either faint or suffocate—or do both. A number of ideas rushed through his mind, but each seemed a poor solution to his current troubles. If she fainted, he might leave her lying in the aisle and disappear in the same manner that he'd come, but that would require magic and Serafina would feel it and be alerted to his presence. Or he could simply walk through the library and out the front doors. It was unlikely that Serafina would see him, focused as her attention was on the scholarly Mr. Tamony. But someone else might find the girl before Morcar could depart, and if he was seen walking out of the aisle . . . no, it wasn't worth trying. And if she should suffocate and die, the Guardians would punish him, and he didn't have the time for such nonsense just now.

There was nothing for it but to charm the girl, and do so without the use of magic. He was somewhat out of practice, for it had been a number of years since he'd bothered to be attractive to a mere mortal woman without using his powers. But Morcar wasn't blind to the fact of his supernatural beauty, and mere mortals, particularly dull little peahens like this particular chit, were notoriously easy to charm. It might even be amusing to make her fall a little in love with him.

Moderating his grip, Morcar bent his head near her own and murmured, "I mean you no harm, miss. I only wished to stop you from screaming and disturbing the entire library. I know that my sudden appearance gave you a terrible shock, and I apologize profusely. Please believe me. I'll let you go now, but please, don't alarm the other patrons. There's no need, truly, and it would be most upsetting to everyone present."

The gentle tone did its work. Her movements began to still. When he loosened the hand on her mouth she drew in a gasping breath but didn't make any desperate sounds.

"I do apologize most sincerely, miss," he went on, not lowering his hand completely, in case she needed silencing again. They'd been fortunate not to have been seen by anyone else yet and fortunate, too, that the bookcases were so high. Still, someone might come along at any moment. He had to hurry. "It was foolish of me—quite unforgivably stupid, really—to have come upon you without warning. I should have known better. Women do tend to be frightened of me. The black hair and eyes, you see, as well as the height. But I vow that I mean you no harm. I was looking at the titles, I'm afraid, instead of where I was going, though I saw when I came down the aisle that someone was here."

She'd relaxed further, and her shaking lessened. Morcar lowered his hand a bit more so that she could lift her face to look up at him. Her lips were parted, drawing in much-needed breath, and her brown eyes were wide as she met his gaze. He smiled in the manner that he knew most women found appealing—partly boyish, partly chagrined. It never failed to charm.

"Will you forgive me? Can we cry friends and start over?"

Silent, she nodded, and he released her altogether, setting her back on the floor and holding her lightly about the waist until her unsteady feet had become firmer.

"Are you all right?" he asked gently. "Can I get you anything? A glass of water, perhaps? I'm sure one of the clerks can bring you one."

She shook her head, yet striving to catch her breath. The frightened look was still on her face and she was pale, but it appeared that she was no longer on the verge of screaming.

Morcar smiled again, more beguilingly than before, and

made as formal a bow as the small space would allow. "Please allow me to introduce myself," he said. "I'm Morcar Cadmaran."

"Oh," she said, and Morcar silently thought with amusement that it appeared to be the only word the foolish chit knew how to say. But her eyes widened, and he realized, with a surge of pride, that she recognized the Earl of Llew's Christian name without having to be told his title. Sinking into a slight, unsteady curtsy, she said, "My lord." When she looked up at him, her cheeks had bloomed with pleasant color.

"And you are . . . ?"

"Oh," she said again, and he nearly laughed aloud. How foolish mere mortals could be. "Forgive me, Lord Llew. You *are* the Earl of Llew, are you not? I know because my cousin has corresponded with you. My cousin Sarah, that is. Miss Sarah Tamony. Perhaps you recall her name? She is quite famous. Oh dear, what an impudent thing to have said. Aunt Caroline will be so disappointed. And we haven't even been properly introduced yet, for I've not told you my name." Her tiny hands fluttered nervously and the color in her cheeks deepened. "I'm Philistia Tamony, my lord." She made another curtsy. "I'm . . . my cousin Julius is here as well . . . I mean to say, Mr. Julius Tamony. He's in the h-history section." She seemed to realize at last how silly she sounded and fell silent.

"I'm delighted to meet you, Miss Tamony," Morcar replied, forcing every bit of sarcasm from his tone. He always found conversing with mere mortals trying. The females, when they were pretty, made pleasant companions for the short while that they warmed his bed, but he had no use for them otherwise. And this one—she had a charming figure but was far too stupid and plain even for that much effort. Still, she was a Tamony and the only one left of use to him now that Malachi had the authoress in thrall and Serafina had claimed the brother. "Though I might wish our meeting had been under different circumstances. I do indeed know of your cousin, the famous Sarah Tamony. I look forward to the interview I'm to undertake with her, and hope it may be in the near future.

Have you and your family been in London long? Do you intend to remain for the Season?"

"Yes," she replied, smiling tentatively. "We're to stay
until the end of summer."

"I hope I shall have the pleasure of seeing you about
Town, then, Miss Tamony. Is this your book?" Bending, he
retrieved the volume she'd dropped. Reading the title, he
frowned before holding it out to her. What a ridiculous
thing for a young woman, or anyone, to read. Morcar was
by no means given to much reading, but he knew a good
book when he saw one.

Philistia Tamony took note of his brief disapproval.

"No, not at all," she said quickly. "I hadn't really decided." She slid the volume back into its place. "I don't
suppose, my lord, that you might recommend something to
me? I have such difficulty making a choice with so many
before me."

As it happened, Morcar had just finished a novel that he
had found quite acceptable, and as it was located closer to the
history section, he held out his arm and replied, "I do, Miss
Tamony, and would be pleased to escort you to its location.
Unless you've read it already? *The Fortunes of Nigel*, by
Scott?"

She looked at his arm as if it might bite her and gingerly
set her tiny gloved hand upon it.

"N-no, my lord, I haven't. But if you recommend it, I'm
certain that I shall like it very much."

Julius Tamony was everything Serafina had hoped for.
They stood very close between the bookcases in the history
section, so close that their bodies almost touched, and she
gazed into his handsome face, half-listening as he spoke,
envisioning how pleasant it would be when they first lay together. She'd never had a man who wore spectacles before.
Thinking of how she would take them off made her feel
even more aroused. She'd never had a scholar, either, come
to that. Perhaps he would speak Latin as he made love to
her. Perhaps she would make him.

He was enchanted by her, of course, and utterly beneath her spell. But every man was. Serafina made it thus. Julius Tamony had fallen harder than most, but that was because he was somewhat inexperienced with women, also because he dreamed, as so many did, of someday finding his one true love. This dream woman would be a female who needed him, who would make him feel powerful and masculine. Mere mortals always seemed to long for that feeling, to be needed, to be vital to someone else's happiness. Perhaps it was because they didn't possess other powers, as magic mortals did. Serafina was more than happy to fulfill their foolish desires, so long as they fulfilled hers, though she found playing the part of a childish, helpless female trying at times. It was only the knowledge that she would soon be able to put all such pretense behind that made it bearable.

He'd been shaking so hard when she'd first approached that Serafina had nearly thought he'd be incapable of speech, but when she'd cast him the comforting safety line of history, he'd readily grasped it. And had kept clinging throughout their conversation, so that she'd heard more of the Celts and Druids than she'd ever cared to.

"A simpler approach," Julius Tamony was saying, "might be to begin with the history of Britain—there are a number of excellent works which you'll not find too taxing—and thereafter move on to more challenging subjects, such as a concentrated treatise on the Roman occupation or, perhaps more suitable than that, the Viking incursions. Those are particularly interesting, I believe, and more readily engage the mind. If these prove too difficult or seem to weary you too quickly, I might recommend starting with something by Gibbon—"

"Everything you speak of sounds so wonderful, Mr. Tamony," Serafina said, careful to make the voice as silly and adoring as possible. "I wish I could understand such matters as easily as you do. When I listen to you, I know just how foolish I am in wanting to learn about matters that are so far above my limited understanding." She drew nearer, gazing up at him worshipfully. "If only I had someone like you to answer all my questions, I should be very happy. I do want to broaden my knowledge, but it can be so difficult."

He looked at her with the kind of helplessness that Serafina found particularly attractive in a man.

"I should be glad to do anything that you asked of me, Miss Daray," he vowed. "Anything at all to relieve your worries."

"Would you, Mr. Tamony?" she asked. She had to make certain that he gave her his agreement of his own free will. Only then would she be able to make the spells she placed upon him binding. "You're such a kind gentleman that I think perhaps you only mean to be polite."

"Not at all," he countered firmly. "Only tell me what you desire, Miss Daray, and I shall do it. I swear upon my honor that I speak the truth."

She smiled. That was perfect. He had said the words aloud and had meant them. The Guardians would have no argument about what happened to him at her hands. How delightfully chivalrous Englishmen were, she thought with pleasure. It was bred in them from centuries past, an unfortunate part of their heritage that made them terribly vulnerable to the likes of her.

"Would you come home with me, Mr. Tamony?" she asked, reaching out to slip a hand into his own much larger one. "Now? Without question? Without a moment's hesitation?" She could feel it there within him—a sense of stubbornness that she would have to overcome. Surely he wouldn't worry about the cousin now? The girl was old enough to find her own way home. But that was part of that damnable chivalry. Serafina hated to place a spell upon him so soon, here in Hookham's, but it seemed impossible to avoid. "I have so many questions to ask of you," she went on, putting a particularly helpless note into her tone. "So many matters I must have explained to me by someone of your greater knowledge. I know that you can help me to understand, if only you will."

Serafina looked at him longingly, willing him to go

away with her. She pressed her free hand against his elegantly crafted coat, at the same time squeezing the other hand lightly.

"Come with me now, Julius," she murmured in her own voice, far lower and more seductive than the childish tone she used in public. "Empty your thoughts of everything and everyone but me. Think only of how greatly I need you, and of how you must take care of me above all others." Her hand slid upward, curling about his neck to draw his ear to her lips. "*Pareome*, Julius," she whispered, then released him.

He straightened, and Serafina saw with satisfaction that the spell had worked.

"We must go now, Julius," she told him. "Give me your arm and escort me from the premises. I have a carriage waiting just across the street. We will go to it and enter, and then you will do as I say and give no trouble."

He did exactly as she willed and offered her his arm. There was no mention of his cousin or the tea that he had promised his mother to attend. When they walked out of Hookham's Lending Library they were watched by several patrons, many of them envious of Julius Tamony, and were escorted, as well, by eager-to-please clerks. But only one individual in the library who watched as they left knew and understood precisely what was transpiring. And that individual, the Earl of Llew, didn't care about the fate of Miss Philistia Tamony, either.

He had left her to her own devices much earlier, having escorted her to the location of the book he had recommended. Then, bowing and stating that he hoped they would meet again soon, he had taken himself off to a location of the library ideal for listening, with his exceptionally keen ears, to what Serafina had to say to Mr. Julius Tamony.

There had been little of interest. Serafina had displayed the usual lustful behavior that Morcar had known when they'd been lovers. She'd nearly thrown the object of her desire upon the floor and taken him then and there but had restrained herself enough to wisely use a bit of magic and usher the fellow out of the establishment. What she intended to do with him afterward Morcar had no doubt. Julius Tamony would eventually arrive home exhausted but well pleased, also living in blissful ignorance beneath a spell of Serafina's choosing.

Setting aside the book he'd been pretending to look at, the Earl of Llew decided that it was time to depart. He walked to the doors and bid the clerk there to signal his coachman. A few moments later His Lordship's elegant equipage pulled up to the curb and he was being ushered out to the pavement.

Just as the door to his carriage was opened, Lord Llew heard his name being called. He recognized the pleading voice at once and, though he would have far preferred scowling, fixed a polite smile on his face before he turned.

"Miss Tamony," he said as she hurried up to him. "What a pleasant surprise."

She clearly found nothing to be pleased about. Her plain face was stricken with concern and her large brown eyes were filled with fear. She set a hand in his and gripped it tightly.

"My lord, please, will you help me?"

"Of course, Miss Tamony. Whatever is the matter?"

She cast searching glances down either side of the street, then gazed back at him pleadingly. Her voice, when she spoke, was a quavering whisper.

"My cousin has left without me," she said, so faintly that Morcar was obliged to lean closer to hear what she said. The words, once he understood, were spoken in such a way that he was left in no doubt about her terror of abandonment.

"Are you quite certain, Miss Tamony?"

She nodded and looked as if she might start weeping in earnest. "Yes, my lord. The clerk told me so."

It required an effort on Morcar's part not to smile. Serafina had known about the little cousin and had purposefully allowed Mr. Tamony to play the cad in abandoning his helpless relative. It would serve the fellow right if Morcar took the girl home and ruined her, but that was likely what

Serafina had hoped for. Not that it would be the Earl of Llew, of course, but that Miss Tamony would find herself forced into the care of strangers. Or at least suffer a terrible fright. There was always a measure of amusement to be had in the misery of mere mortals. He and Serafina had understood that, even if the sainted Seymours didn't.

Morcar was torn about what to do. He'd not had a woman in several days, and though he didn't find the girl appealing, Morcar had no doubt that once she was lying naked on his bed he'd discover her attractions sufficient for his needs.

There was a pressure on his fingers that drew him back to attention. Miss Philistia Tamony was squeezing his hand, gazing up at him. He could feel her slender fingers hard against his own, a silent tension and pleading . . . and something else.

He knew about fear and loss. And loneliness. He'd held his own personal grief close, seldom sharing it, never caring about anyone else's. But there was something in Philistia Tamony's touch that spoke to what he knew.

She recognized it, too.

He looked into her eyes and saw his own hidden fears reflected back at him.

"I'll take you home," he said, oddly displeased with the faint uncertainty in his tone. "To your home," he clarified, which made him even angrier, because of course he meant her home and shouldn't have had to explain. "Perhaps your cousin will be there. I believe scholars can be somewhat forgetful at times."

The relief that filled her features gave him a curious sense of comfort.

"Yes, I'm sure you're right," she said. "Julius has been so preoccupied of late with his book—he's a writer as well, you see, like my uncle Alberic and cousin Sarah— and his mind does tend to wander. That must be why he forgot me."

"I'm certain that's the cause," Morcar told her. "But

there's nothing to fear, Miss Tamony. I'll see you safely to your door."

"I knew you'd not leave me," she murmured, gazing at him with gratitude. "I knew you'd help me."

Of course she did, he thought as he helped her into his carriage. He was a gentleman, after all, and a nobleman. It was his duty to give aid to a lady of gentle birth. If he had other designs on Philistia Tamony and her kin, that had nothing to do with it. And if he had been moved by what he'd felt when she'd appealed to him, that was meaningless, as well.

"My aunt Caroline—Lady Tamony—will be serving tea, my lord," Philistia said after the carriage began to move. "Would you like to join us? I'm sure it's not what you're used to, but my cousin Sarah will be there and I'm sure my aunt would be pleased. And Sarah will be so glad to have an opportunity to speak with someone she so dearly wishes to interview."

Morcar had been playing the part of an English noble from his birth. It was required of his kind to fit into the world of mere mortals as best they could. He didn't particularly enjoy taking tea, but he'd done it with élan countless times.

But to take tea with Miss Sarah Tamony would accomplish something that Morcar had only ever dreamed so simple a task could accomplish. It would make Malachi Seymour angry. Very angry.

"How kind of you to invite me, Miss Tamony," Morcar said with honest pleasure. "I should be delighted."

Chapter 14

$\mathscr{I}$ can't tell you how greatly you've brightened my day, Lord Llew," Sarah said to the man sitting beside her cousin on the nearby sofa. He was such a large and muscular man that he took up most of the room, squishing the tiny Philistia into the corner. Sarah had never seen her cousin look so happy. "I've had rather a difficult time convincing certain individuals to let me interview them. Your willingness is very welcome."

The Earl of Llew put his teacup aside. "I can't imagine why anyone would decline to lend you their aid, Miss Tamony. Your books have proven your talent as a writer, and nearly every family in England has an interesting character or two in their history. The Cadmarans aren't too proud to let others know something of our past. Indeed, quite the opposite."

Sarah gazed at him approvingly. "It's refreshing to hear you say so, my lord. I look forward with great anticipation to hearing about your family's history, and to writing of it. I've already done a bit of research. Do you recall me telling you about Prothinus Cadmaran, Philla?"

Philistia's eyes lit with the same excitement that she'd shown when Sarah had told her the fascinating story.

"Ah yes, Prothinus," said the earl. "The disappearing and reappearing exorcist. Of course you know there's an explanation for his reappearance." Lord Llew sat forward. "He never actually fell down the well. There had been a great deal of celebration in the village that night—a wedding or some such. Prothinus was drunk, aye, but so were the rest of the villagers. When he disappeared, the rumors began that he'd fallen into the well, but the truth makes a far more interesting tale."

"You intrigue me, Lord Llew," Lady Tamony said from her chair near the fire. "Tell us, if you please."

The earl appeared delighted to do so. He was, Sarah noted, a man who enjoyed being the center of attention. And he was certainly that at present, having utterly charmed not only Sarah and her cousin but also Lady Tamony and Aunt Speakley.

"I should be pleased," he said. "The truth, then, is this. Old Prothinus became so drunk that he couldn't find his way to his own dwelling. He wandered, instead, for hours through the dark night, at last coming upon a shelter that he took for his own. Stumbling in, he found what he thought was his bed and lay down upon it, falling fast asleep. In the morning he discovered that he was not in his own home, but had unwittingly gone into a goat shed. Unfortunately for him, the shed was on the property of an elderly witch who didn't take kindly to trespassers."

Sarah made a "hmphing" sound, thinking that there was a dismal lack of compassion for trespassers among magic mortals.

"When she found Prothinus there, she was so angry that she turned him into a goat."

"How dreadful," Philistia murmured.

"Not at all," Lord Llew assured her. "For he made a very fine goat, and sired so many kids that he increased the witch's flock by a goodly number. After three years, she rewarded him by turning him back into a man. And although perhaps I shouldn't say such a thing among ladies," His Lordship said with a touch of naughtiness in his tone, "he wasn't at all happy about it, for he much preferred the company of the goats."

Sarah and her mother laughed, Aunt Speakley and Philistia blushed hotly, and the Earl of Llew looked well pleased.

He wasn't what Sarah had expected. She knew that the Cadmarans were a dark Family—and indeed could feel the immense, dark power emanating from him—and had assumed that the head of that clan would be nasty and unpleasant. But Lord Llew was a man of practiced charm, perfectly refined in manner and speech. And he told a good story. The one about Prothinus was but the latest in the past hour since he'd arrived with Philistia in tow. He had regaled them with stories of famous members of the *ton* and had them laughing nearly to tears with accounts of various noble scandals. He had a gift for leaving out just enough shocking parts and exaggerating the humorous ones to make the stories delightful, even for the ears of ladies.

Sarah was grateful to Lord Llew as well for being so kind as to bring Philistia home. But Julius's disappearance, and his inexplicable abandonment of his helpless cousin, baffled her. If he'd left Sarah alone in a shop it would have been a different matter. She was used to taking care of herself without anyone's aid, but Philistia couldn't be let out of the house without an escort, else she'd panic, and Julius knew that full well.

"Will you have more tea, Lord Llew?" Sarah offered politely, rising to fill everyone's cup.

"No, thank you, Miss Tamony," he said. "I believe I shall be leaving shortly." He looked toward the door and rose to his feet even as it was opened to admit the Earl of Graymar.

Sarah's heart gave its familiar leap at the sight of him, and she smiled in happy welcome. He scowled back with a thunderously angry look, then mastered his expression into something less severe as he moved farther into the room.

"Lord Graymar, what a pleasant surprise," Lady Tamony said, rising and offering him her hand. "We didn't expect you today, sir, but I'm glad you've come."

"Lady Tamony," he replied with rigid politeness. "Mrs. Speakley." He bowed to the beaming woman who was still seated. Turning, he pinned Sarah with an angry glare. "Miss Tamony, and Miss Philistia. I hope I find you all well?"

Sarah gave an inward sigh and strove to maintain her calm. She knew he was angry to find her having tea with the Earl of Llew, especially in light of the fact that they were both seeking information about the *cythraul*. When he'd told her about the demon, Lord Graymar had been completely forthcoming about everything, and everyone, involved in the matter. And perhaps he assumed that she was reneging on her promise regarding her book. But that wasn't the case at all, as she would explain when the chance arose. She would gladly put off her interview with Lord Llew until the *cythraul* had been dealt with. But that didn't mean she couldn't further the man's acquaintance.

All of this she would tell Lord Graymar. At the moment, however, she only wished to diffuse his fury and preserve her goodwill with the Earl of Llew.

"We are very well, thank you, my lord," she said, setting the teapot down and moving toward him. "I believe you are already acquainted with our guest, Lord Llew?"

Lord Graymar's eyes glittered in a frightening manner as he turned his gaze upon the Earl of Llew.

"Yes," he murmured. "We know each other well."

Lord Llew smiled so widely that Sarah almost thought he might laugh. "Very well indeed, Miss Tamony. Since we were but young lads. We used to go fishing together. It's good to see you again, Malachi. You've been busy since coming to Town, I hear."

"As have you," Lord Graymar replied icily. "Enough so that it should have been perfectly clear to you that you were not to involve yourself with Miss Tamony and her family."

Sarah gave a start at the words, inappropriate as they were for a social gathering, and glanced to where her mother and Aunt Speakley sat, expecting to find them aghast.

"Oh, Lord Graymar, you've done it again," Sarah said with dismay, seeing that her parent and relatives were frozen in place. "I wish you wouldn't. You know that I can't like it."

He ignored her. "What are you doing here, Morcar?"

"Enjoying a cup of tea and the pleasant company of these lovely ladies," Lord Llew replied easily. "And lest you think I forced my way in through magic, allow me to set your mind at ease. I was invited in the usual mere mortal fashion."

"Yes, that's true," Sarah put in quickly. "Indeed, we owe Lord Llew a debt of gratitude. He escorted Philistia safely home after Julius left her alone at Hookham's Lending Library. We don't know where Julius is or why he did such a thing, but we're terribly grateful to His Lordship for rescuing her."

Malachi's eyes narrowed. "How convenient that you should happen to be present, my lord. What did you do to send Julius out of the way so that Philistia would require your aid?"

"Really, Lord Graymar," Sarah said reproachfully. "What a terrible thing to insinuate, as if Lord Llew should do such a thing. We were very fortunate that he did happen to be there."

"Be quiet, Sarah," he ordered, surprising her. It was the first time he'd spoken her Christian name, though he didn't seem to realize it. "You don't know this devil as I do." To the Earl of Llew he said, "What did you do with Julius Tamony?"

But Lord Llew wasn't paying him any attention. He was gazing at Sarah with discomforting deliberation. Slowly he began to move, making a circle about the pair standing in the middle of the room, looking at her. She felt Lord Graymar's hand press against the small of her back, both a warning and a comfort.

"Well, well," Lord Llew said at last. "So Miss Sarah Tamony is one of our sympathetics, is she? I should have realized it before now. I suppose you've placed her beneath your protection, have you, Malachi?"

"I have," Lord Graymar stated flatly, his hand sliding until his fingers curled around her waist.

"Pity," the Earl of Llew said, and gave Sarah a flashing smile. "I had hoped to try my charms on her when we met for our interview, but I suppose I shall have to forgo such pleasure."

Sarah frowned, wondering what he could possibly mean, for surely he wasn't so foolish as to think she'd let him ravish her. But his meaning was evidently clear to Lord Graymar, for the hand moved from her waist to take hold of her forearm and draw her up against his side.

"She is protected by magic beyond my own," he said in warning tones. "The spirits have given her immunity for reasons of their own. But if any of our kind should make an attempt to use their powers on her, that wizard or sorceress will answer to me, and the Guardians will judge me accordingly."

Lord Llew's eyebrows rose in surprise. "I see," he said. "You've declared it openly, then? I confess to being surprised." His gaze ran over Sarah once more, consideringly, from top to toe. "She's lovely, of course, and the Seymours have never seen the impropriety of mixing with mere mortals, but for you, Malachi, the Dewin Mawr, I would have thought—"

"I don't wish to hear what your thoughts are," Lord Graymar snapped furiously. "You're going to depart just as soon as I've released the others, and thereafter leave the Tamony family alone. *Completely* alone."

"That's impossible," Lord Llew replied. "I'm engaged to take Miss Tamony and her delightful cousin driving tomorrow afternoon. And it's more than likely that we'll be in attendance at several of the same gatherings during the

Season. Surely you wouldn't wish me to ignore the Tamony ladies? How would I explain such behavior to Lady Tamony? To Miss Philistia?"

"He speaks with a measure of sense, my lord," Sarah said calmly. "I don't think it's necessary for Lord Llew to have to avoid us. There's no harm to be done by the acquaintance, after all, and just because there's been such a lengthy enmity between the Seymours and Cadmarans doesn't mean that my family need be involved on one side or the other."

"You must trust me in this matter, Sarah," Lord Graymar told her, his tone allowing no argument. "To believe a Cadmaran is to believe a snake. He'd destroy you if it furthered his purposes. He'd use anyone—Julius or Philistia, even your parents—to get what he wants. And then he'd destroy them. Because he despises mere mortals, don't you, Morcar? You'd love nothing better than to rid the world of every one of them. Save that you can't, for then you'd have no one left to serve you."

The Earl of Llew made a scoffing sound. "What rot," he said. "You've grown fanciful in your dotage, Malachi. I hope you'll pay him no mind, Miss Tamony. Jealousy has clearly sent his sense of reason fleeing. If I bore hatred for your kind, I scarcely would have bothered bringing your cousin home. I certainly wouldn't have agreed to give you an interview. In truth, Miss Tamony, he wants to frighten you away so that you'll not wish to speak with me of my family's history. Isn't that what truly worries you, Malachi? We all know that you've put a stop to Miss Tamony's research, with a few exceptions like myself, and you'd be pleased to put an end to those, too."

A frisson of emotion ran through Lord Graymar's body, so intense that Sarah felt it through the fingers gripping her arm. The room shook slightly, rattling the windowpanes and whatever small objects were set about the room. When he spoke, she scarcely recognized the dark, dangerous voice as his own.

"You will leave, Morcar, and stay as far from the Tamonys as you can. I vow before the Guardians that if you ever bring harm to any of them, I shall exact repayment in kind."

The Earl of Llew gave him a look of such hatred that it took Sarah aback. He was a different man from the one who had so fully charmed them over the past hour. As he moved back to stand in the spot he'd been in earlier, before the others had fallen beneath Lord Graymar's spell, he said, "You're a fool, Malachi. You're so captivated by the woman—a mere mortal—that you've become blind to what's taking place around you."

His tone made Sarah shiver. "What does he mean?" she asked. "Surely not the *cythraul*?"

"No," Lord Graymar said, glancing at her before returning his gaze to the Earl of Llew. "He refers to someone else."

"You told her about the demon?" Lord Llew replied with disbelief. Then he laughed. "Have you lost your senses, telling a mere mortal—telling *her*—about such a thing?"

"Why shouldn't he tell me?" Sarah said, fully insulted. "Why does everyone suppose I'm not trustworthy? And you said that you were willing to give me an interview."

"That's an entirely different matter, Miss Tamony," said Lord Llew. "The history of our kind is nothing compared to the importance of the *cythraul*. No mere mortal could possibly understand it. But Lord Graymar seems to have forgotten just how vital the demon visitation is. Have you received any signs yet, Malachi? Or have you been too busy squiring a beautiful woman about London to even look for them?" He leaned forward, taunting, "Nothing has been allowed to cloud my vision, for which I've been well rewarded by the spirits."

"Hush, Sarah," Lord Graymar said when Sarah opened her mouth to retort that they'd had a clue from the spirits as well. She scowled, but he ignored her and asked, "Where is Julius Tamony, Morcar?"

Lord Llew smiled in an unpleasant manner. "You'll find

out easily enough. Don't be alarmed, Miss Tamony. Your brother will be home soon, unharmed. Believe me when I tell you that he's far too useful to be mistreated. At least for now. When you wish to speak with me, send word. Lord Graymar won't be able to stop me from speaking to you, so long as you're brave enough to do so."

"We shall see," Lord Graymar said tightly. He released Sarah and turned her to face him, then gave a wave of one hand. Addressing Lord Llew, he said, in more pleasant tones, "Yes, very busy. Have you only just arrived in London, then, Llew?"

"A few days past, actually," Lord Llew replied, his own manner perfectly pleasant. "I wished to be here in time to attend the Herold ball. It's always proved to be one of the Season's better events."

Sarah stood staring at them, trying to find her place in the conversation. It was easy for the two men, obviously, for they must have performed the task any number of times in their lives, but Sarah found it difficult to recall what they'd been discussing earlier, much less participate. Her cousin, mother, and aunt were awake and aware once more and watching the two men converse with smiles on their faces, completely unaware of what had taken place only moments earlier.

"I'll look forward to seeing you there, then," Lord Graymar said, and turned away. To Lady Tamony he said, "I apologize for coming upon you so unexpectedly, ma'am. I had hoped to secure an appointment to take Miss Sarah and Miss Philistia driving in the park tomorrow afternoon."

"Oh, but we can't," Philistia said, blushing when Lord Graymar looked at her. "I mean to say, it's very kind of you, my lord, but we're already promised to go driving with Lord Llew."

"Are you?" Lord Graymar looked at the other man, raising one eyebrow. Sarah could see Lord Llew's jaw clench, but he was polite when he spoke.

"Forgive me, Miss Tamony," he said. "I'd forgotten

that I'm already engaged for tomorrow day. Another time, perhaps?"

Philistia's disappointment was clear to all those present. "Of course, my lord," she said sadly. "Another time."

He took his leave, then, bowing grandly and thanking them for the enjoyable afternoon. He declared that he couldn't have imagined a more fortuitous occurrence than meeting Miss Philistia and being invited to tea with her lovely mother and charming aunt and engaging cousin.

"And, of course, the final prize was so unexpectedly seeing my dear friend Graymar. If you're leaving, as well, my lord, we might walk out together?"

Lord Graymar gave him a scorching look. "I wish to speak with Miss Tamony for a few moments, first. But we must have dinner at White's soon, Llew, and catch up on old times."

Lord Llew smiled with cherubic agreement and confessed himself filled with anticipation. Then he bowed once more and quit the room, leaving behind at least two sighing ladies.

"Such a charming gentleman," Aunt Speakley declared.

"Oh, indeed he is, Aunt," Philistia agreed. "He was so kind to me at Hookham's. I should have been so frightened if he'd not been present to help me. And even before that he was kind enough to recommend a wonderful book to me."

"He was most charming," Lady Tamony agreed, accepting another cup of tea from her daughter. "But there was something in his manner that seemed a touch insincere. But I shouldn't say such things in front of you, my lord," she said to Lord Graymar, who shook his head when Sarah offered him a cup. "He's a close friend of yours, it seems."

"An old acquaintance, Lady Tamony," His Lordship corrected rather stiffly. "Our families met infrequently."

She gazed at him for a long moment, then murmured, "I see," and changed the subject to the weather.

The Earl of Graymar conversed politely for a few minutes more, then with a quick movement made the women in the room, save Sarah, frozen once more.

Sarah set her teacup aside and stood. "My lord, I must insist that you stop doing that. I know you wish to speak to me, but I can't have you putting spells on my family because you can't wait a few more moments to—"

"Your brother is coming," he said curtly. "He's hurrying down the street on foot. He'll be at the door in but moments."

"Julius? Is he all right?"

"I can't tell yet," Lord Graymar said. "Believe whatever he tells you and don't press for details. I'll take my leave shortly after he arrives and try to discover the truth of where he's been." The Earl stopped for a moment, lifting his head as if he could hear something. "Your brother is weary," he said after a moment. "Cancel your plans for this evening so that he'll have the chance to retire early. It's the best remedy if magic has been used on him."

"Magic!" Sarah said. "Who would use magic on Julius?"

"Hush!" He waved her toward the chair she'd vacated. "I'll try to come tonight. We must speak. Sit down now—quickly—and I'll release them. He's at the door."

Sarah sat. The next moment Lord Graymar undid the spell and her family came back to awareness just as the parlor doors burst open and Julius flew in. His expression, fraught with worry, filled with relief at the sight of Philistia, who, like Sarah and Lord Graymar, had quickly stood.

"Phil! Thank God!" Julius cried, hurrying forward to catch her up into his arms. "Thank God you're all right."

"Julius Tamony," his mother said reprovingly, "whatever has come over you? Put your cousin down and let her breathe."

He did as his mother bade but held Philistia's face between both hands and kissed her forehead and cheeks. "Are you all right, dear?" he asked worriedly. "I went back to Hookham's and they said you'd gone off with the Earl of Llew. I was in such a state, though they swore he was a gentleman and fully trustworthy. I'm so sorry, Phil. You must have been terrified. I swear upon my life it will never happen again."

"I'm fine, Julius," Philistia assured him. "Perfectly fine. And the Earl of Llew was a complete gentleman. He brought me home and stayed for tea, and was most charming and kind. But what happened to you? Where did you go?"

"I scarce know," he said wretchedly. Lord Graymar was right, Sarah thought as she watched her brother. Julius did look weary. As if he'd run ten miles. His hat was covered in dust and his spectacles were askew. "I was introduced to a lady at Hookham's who desired my opinion on a book of history. One moment we were speaking on Viking incursions, and the next we were . . . we were . . ." His voice trailed away and he began to fall to one side.

By the time Sarah realized that her brother was about to faint, Lord Graymar already had him by the shoulders and was easing him down to the sofa.

"That's all right, old man," Lord Graymar said gently, pulling the hat from Julius's head and tossing it aside. "You're safe. Rest easy."

Lady Tamony was instantly across the room, sitting beside her son and feeling his forehead.

"Bring him a cup of tea, Sarah," she commanded. "Hurry. Philistia, sit and calm yourself. There's nothing to cry about. Julius is fine." Of Lord Graymar, who was leaning over her son, examining him, she asked, with admirable calm, "Is he ill, my lord? I don't detect a fever. Should we fetch a doctor?"

"He's had a bit of a shock, I believe," Lord Graymar replied. "Nothing more serious, ma'am. It's likely he's overextended himself with research, or perhaps he's been worried about the publication of his book. Having lost his cousin, who was in his care, clearly added to the strain. He'll be the better for some sleep. Here, let me." He took the cup of tea and lifted it to the younger man's lips. Julius, who was beginning to come around, sipped when Lord Graymar told him to. Handing the cup back to Lady Tamony, the earl said, "I'll help him to his bed if you'll show me the way."

"I'll help him, Mama," Sarah said quickly, hurrying to

open the parlor doors. "Perhaps Aunt Speakley wishes to go home now. We'll get Julius to bed and you can see Aunt Speakley to her carriage, then come and check on him. Philistia, run ahead of us and get Julius's bed ready."

Philistia ran out of the room just as Lord Graymar helped Julius to his feet. Sarah got on her brother's other side and helped guide him up the stairs.

"What's happened to him?" she whispered.

"I don't know, precisely," Lord Graymar whispered back. "But I'll find out. Remember what I told you. Don't press him to remember anything. Keep the others away from him for now."

"Is he—is it a spell?" she asked.

Lord Graymar looked grim. "Yes," he said. "There's nothing I can do for him now save protect his physical body."

"Can't you just undo it?"

"I'm the Dewin Mawr, sweetheart," he said, settling Julius's large, heavy body a bit higher on his shoulder, "not God. Some enchantments can only be dispelled in very precise ways. Until I know exactly what's happened there's nothing I can do, save bid him sleep for as long as possible and let him recover as best he can. But keep a sharp eye on him. Regardless of what may happen, don't let him sneak out of the house until I've come. Feed him laudanum, wine, anything to keep him insensible." They neared the landing and saw Philistia's anxious face peering down at them.

"But why?" Sarah demanded in a low voice. "Surely he'd not wish to go out again tonight."

"The magic will call to him, and he'll have no choice but to respond. He'll be drawn to the one who cast the spell. Irrevocably drawn, until she's done with him."

"She?" Sarah repeated, but he gave no further reply, for they'd gotten near enough for Philistia to overhear them.

With the help of one of the footmen, Lord Graymar assisted Julius out of his clothes, then remained long enough to see him tucked into bed.

Leaving the others to care for her brother, Sarah escorted His Lordship to the door.

"Where's your father?" he asked as a footman handed him his hat and walking stick.

"At the Travellers Club, I think."

"Fetch him home," Lord Graymar said. "I don't want your mother worrying alone. I quite like your mother." He put his hat on. "I have a feeling she might be one of our sympathetics."

"My mother?" Sarah said, her mind whirling. "A sympathetic? What?"

"Don't worry so, sweet." He touched her cheek briefly, a reassuring caress. "I'll be back." He looked over her head, then bent and, without warning, set his mouth lightly against her own. It was the briefest possible kiss but so stunned Sarah that when he lifted his head, she was speechless.

"Sorry," he said, sounding somewhat stunned, himself, as he backed toward the entryway where the footman— out of view—waited. "No one was watching and I couldn't resist."

She lifted her fingers to touch her lips, staring at him.

Lord Graymar looked abashed. "I'll strive to improve on the performance at another time. I hope you won't mind if I make the attempt?"

Dropping her hand, she shook her head. "Not in the least."

He smiled and Sarah could have sworn that his cheeks darkened with a bit of color.

"Then I'll be certain to hurry back," he said, and, making an elegant bow, departed.

Chapter 15

She was asleep by the time Malachi returned to the Tamony home, though, fortunately enough, it was in a chair near the small fireplace in her brother's room.

Malachi tended to Julius Tamony first, removing a small vial that he'd brought from Mervaille from an inner pocket and unstopping the cork. The younger man slept fitfully but made no struggle as Malachi spoke to him through his dreams in a low murmur, lifting his head and telling him to drink. The contents of the vial disappeared down the man's throat, and in a few moments he was asleep again, except now it was fully and deeply. He'd suffer no dreams and would not wake until daylight.

Malachi wished he could do the same. Wearily he dropped into the chair opposite the one Sarah sat in and welcomed the warmth of the fire. He hated the thought of waking her, for he knew she was as tired as he was. She must have offered to stay with her brother through the night, sending the rest of the family to their beds. A book, still open, lay upon her lap, one hand lying lax upon it, while her head had drifted to one side, pushing her spectacles askew.

"Sarah."

She stirred. Her eyes fluttered, then closed, until he spoke her name once more. Then she made a sound of aggravation—clearly realizing that she had to truly come awake and that he was the cause—and began to stretch, lifting the back of one hand to her lips to stifle a yawn. Her face pressed into the high back of the cushioned chair, pushing her glasses more fully from their moorings. With a movement of long practice she grasped and set them aright, at last sliding upward into a sitting position.

"My lord?" she murmured sleepily as the book slid off her lap to the floor. "You've come."

"Yes," he said simply, bending to retrieve the book and set it on a nearby table. "I'm sorry to wake you."

"No, it's fine," she mumbled, rubbing her face with both hands so that the spectacles bobbed up and down. "I thought perhaps you'd come earlier, but this is—" She blinked at him. "What time is it?"

"Late," he said. "I'm afraid we haven't much time before we must go."

She blinked a few more times, then swallowed and forced her eyes open wide. "Go?"

"I wish I could spare you, Sarah. Truly I do. But the spirits are pleased to carry out matters in ways that are difficult for lesser beings to understand. Like forcing us out into the night to discover something more about the *cythraul*. It doesn't make any apparent sense to the rational mortal mind, but in time we'll discover why it had to be."

"But what about Julius?" She glanced to where her brother slept. "I can't leave him without someone to guard over him. You told me not to."

"I told you not to let him leave the house," Malachi countered. "I've given him a potion that will cause him to sleep for hours. We'll be back long before then. But to ease your mind, I'll set a spell of protection over the dwelling. No one will be able to leave or enter until we return. It will be completely secure."

She gazed at him, troubled, then stood and moved to sit on the bed beside her brother.

"What happened to Julius today?" she asked. Malachi watched as she gently touched her brother's hair, pushing a few strands into place. "Were you able to find out?"

"He was enchanted by a sorceress who wishes to use him for her own purposes," Malachi said. "Are you familiar with the name of Daray?"

She lifted her head and gazed at him. "Yes, of course. They're among my research subjects. Stories about the Darays have long been told in . . . in Cornwall, if I remember correctly." She rubbed her forehead and said, with exasperation, "I'm so weary that my mind isn't working as it should. Please, my lord, tell me what's happened without making me think."

He understood what she was feeling. He longed to make this easier for her, too. But there was no simple way. She would be hurt, disgusted, very likely enraged, when the truth was told.

"You've remembered it correctly, Sarah. The Darays have long hailed from Cornwall. After the exile, the various Families went their separate ways, and the Darays chose that part of the earth as their home. They were not precisely like the other beings exiled, but were created to be servants to my kind. Their lowly status didn't mean they were without powers, only that those powers were limited to pleasing their masters. But after the exile, they saw a way to become equal by mixing their blood with magic mortals until they at last produced a sorceress of great and cunning power. Serafina Daray."

Sarah rose from the bed. "I had hoped to approach Miss Daray for one of my interviews," she said, moving back toward him. "Are you saying that she's responsible for what happened to Julius?"

He nodded, watching her closely. "She wants to possess the power of the *cythraul,* and discovered that the spirits had sent a message through your journal."

"How? No one apart from you and Professor Seabolt knew."

"I don't have the answer to that yet," he told her. "We all have spies, some more gifted than others. I was able to discern what happened to Julius because as Dewin Mawr I've been gifted with unique powers. One of these is the ability to disguise myself from my own kind. I made myself invisible and entered Serafina's dwelling. In this manner—and by aiming a few simple spells at her servants—I discovered what transpired. Serafina knew about your journal and believes that your brother is the key to discovering more about the *cythraul.* To this end, she met him at Hookham's and lured him back to her dwelling, where she placed him beneath an enchantment."

"What kind of enchantment?" Sarah asked, her brows drawing together with suspicion.

Malachi sighed. "She's made him her slave, invoking an ancient magic that even I cannot break. She's stolen part of his life . . . how can I say this?" He cast about for the right words. "Serafina seduced him," he said bluntly, looking at Sarah for understanding. "Not once, but several times. She . . . it's why he's so exhausted, you see . . . she stole that part of him that gives life. His seed." The words acted on Sarah just as he knew they would. Her mouth dropped open and her expression filled with shock.

Malachi hurried on to get it over with. "It's a fearsomely binding magic. And as Julius went with her willingly and let desire rule his better senses, I can't very well go before the Guardians and argue that he was a helpless victim. Serafina was particularly clever about that aspect, gaining his agreement at every step, even if he doesn't recall it now. The result is that she controls his thoughts and memories, and has the power to call him to her side whenever she wishes. He'll do whatever she asks, without regard for family or friendship."

"Sweet merciful day," Sarah murmured, casting her gaze about the room, anywhere but at him. "Julius will be so distressed if he should ever learn of it. It's not that he's ignorant of women—we've been through most of Europe after all, and he is nearly thirty. But he's just so . . . circumspect about such things. A very correct and proper Englishman, despite our travels."

"I understand," Malachi said. "He need not know the full of what's transpired once the magic has been broken. Unfortunately, unless I keep him drugged, we'll be unable to keep him from going to her when he's waked. Each time Serafina has him in her thrall, the more difficult it will be to free him."

"But if you can't break the spell, my lord," she asked, "how can it be done?"

"Serafina alone can set him free," he said. "And I doubt she'll do that unless we can find a way to make her do so."

She looked at him more closely. "Would she let him go if I give her my journal?"

"It's the power of the *cythraul* she desires," he replied. "She believes the journal may help her gain that power. If she should discover it contains no further clues—"

"I understand," she murmured. "She'll have no reason to release Julius."

Malachi nodded. "We must on all accounts keep Serafina from learning that truth, and use her belief in the journal's mysteries to keep her distracted and buy time to find the way to force her hand and gain your brother's freedom."

Her eyes lost their look of despair and instead lit with a new fire. "What must we do to discover the way, my lord?" she asked, sitting forward.

He sighed, feeling weary all over again. "First and foremost, we must keep her from gaining the power of the *cythraul*. And to that end, we must leave," he told her. "Now, I'm afraid."

"To where?"

"Consider it a surprise," Malachi said, rising. "You'll want to fetch your warmest cloak, Sarah. This manner of traveling isn't as exposed as flying, but it will be cold when we arrive."

• • •

Fast traveling, Sarah discovered, was just as thrilling as flying, only much quicker and more bewildering. Lord Graymar had folded her into his cloak as he'd done before and instructed her to hold on to him, and the next moment everything around them began to spin. Julius's room whirled away in a flash of colors, and then, as Lord Graymar's arms tightened, all color faded and they were standing in a swirling darkness. It was an odd sensation, for they didn't move at all, only stood very still, warm against each other, while everything about them tumbled violently. It was like being caught up in the midst of a terrible storm yet left completely untouched by the elements. Not even Sarah's hair lifted from the motion.

"We're almost there," she heard him murmur against her ear.

The motion slowed and color began to seep back into the whirlwind, though darkness yet remained. Coldness crept through the layers of cloth and a damp breeze touched her cheeks. Colors settled into distinguishable objects, becoming trees and large rocks and, beyond this, dimly visible beneath a dark and partly cloudy sky, a large, slow-moving river that filled the air with the sound of movement and the musky smells of water and fish.

"Are you all right?" Lord Graymar asked, looking down at her. "Steady on your feet?"

"Yes, completely," she assured him, pushing her spectacles up so that she could peer about. "What a marvelous way to travel! Can you go anywhere in the world so quickly?"

"Regrettably not," he said, unfolding his cloak so that she could step back. "One can only journey over land or small bodies of water. Large oceans cannot be crossed by fast traveling, although I've often crossed to Ireland with ease."

"Where are we now?" she asked, shivering in the sudden cold. "Is this still England?"

"The English would like to think so," he said. "But it is Wales. North Wales, I should say, and not too far from the border. That"—he nodded toward the river—"is the River Dee."

"Beautiful," she said, watching as the water shimmered even beneath such a dark sky. Its motion sent a sweet burbling music into the air, covered only by a sudden gust of cold wind rattling the trees. Shivering, Sarah pulled her cloak more tightly about her. "And why have we come here, to this particular spot in Wales, my lord?"

"To be given a sign," he said. "Or, rather, for you to be given a sign, as the spirits evidently don't wish to communicate with me directly. But come, Sarah. We're fortunate that it hasn't begun to rain yet." He cast a glance toward the sky. "But it will," he said, sighing. "And soon. We must hurry and finish our business." Lifting one hand, he created a flame that illuminated their path. Reaching out with the other, he took her hand and began to lead her along the riverbank.

"Is it far?" she asked, careful not to trip on any rocks or fallen branches.

"No. We'll be there shortly. In the course of your research, have you learned anything about the varieties of coloring among Seymours?"

"Do you mean the hair color?" she asked. "That blond Seymours tend to be powerful wizards while those with darker hair usually possess gifts more common to mere mortals."

"Exactly," Lord Graymar said with approval. "My cousin Niclas, as an example, is a skilled communicator, and his two sons, both dark haired, are gifted musicians. There's enough of a difference from what mere mortals are capable of to cause remark, perhaps to declare genius, but not so much that anyone becomes suspicious of magic. Are you familiar with the powers that redheaded Seymours generally possess?"

"No, I'm afraid not."

He slowed his stride as they neared a fire-lit clearing, where a number of men stood.

"You're about to learn," he told her.

"You make it sound ominous," Sarah said.

"Not ominous, particularly," he replied, pulling her out into the clearing. "They're often born mystics, with powers both immense and rare, and mystics can be a damnable nuisance at times. The one you're about to meet certainly is. But as he's a Seymour, I'm sure that won't surprise you."

A Seymour? Sarah thought with disbelief as she surveyed the ragged collection of men standing before her. The Seymours were wealthy, highborn members of the *ton*. These fellows looked far more like dangerous highwaymen.

But if they were, at least some of them were possessed of magic, for Sarah could feel it. And one in particular was emanating the sort of strong sensations that only wizards with great powers had ever before engendered.

The one standing at the forefront moved toward them. He was tall and slender and, she saw as he came nearer, possessed of a mane of red hair so lengthy that it fell halfway down his back. He was also, Sarah noted, very handsome. In that respect he was certainly a true Seymour. And then, when he was quite close, she realized with something of a shock that he was blind. He moved with great certainty, as a seeing man would, but his gaze was fixed somewhere off to the left, toward the trees. The man cried in glad greeting, raising his arms to set them on Lord Graymar's shoulders. Then he kissed the earl on both cheeks in the Continental manner and proceeded to speak rapidly in Welsh.

"*Na, na,* Steffan, you must use the English," Lord Graymar reprimanded. "Our guest doesn't understand Cymraeg."

Steffan Seymour turned toward Sarah, smiling widely and reaching out both hands. "Are you quite certain, *cfender*? I thought I felt magic in her. And kinship. And the spirits named her the one who has understanding, so I assumed, of course, that she must be one of us." Grasping Sarah's hands, he bent to kiss each in turn. "But welcome to you, my lady. Welcome to our humble dwelling place. My men and I are honored that you've come." To Lord

Graymar he said, "Introduce us at once, Malachi. I perceive that she's remarkably beautiful."

"Watch your manners, Steffan," Lord Graymar said in a dark voice. "And tell your men to behave themselves, as well, else they'll be sorrier for it."

"God's mercy, you've no need to lecture us, *cfender*," the other man said. "We see so few ladies that we find them precious as gold. Now an introduction, if it pleases you, my fine lord."

Lord Graymar scowled, then looked at Sarah, who gazed back with intense interest. What a lovely surprise this was turning out to be—first the fast traveling and now meeting an actual mystic. She'd never have thought the evening could turn out so well, considering how ill it had started.

"Miss Sarah Tamony, this is my cousin Steffan Seymour, who is the sorriest excuse for a Seymour that ever was, excepting our great-great-uncle Cornelius, whose amorous exploits nearly destroyed the family entirely. Steffan and his men are scoundrels and thieves and live like animals in caves, robbing the rich to line their own pockets."

"Oh, come," Steffan interjected. "That's hardly fair."

"Very well, then," Lord Graymar amended. "They rob the rich and line their pockets and give what's left over to the impoverished. When they're not otherwise employed in robbery, they go to the local villages and wreak havoc. Last year alone I was called upon to—"

"Cousin, please," Steffan said with a touch of embarrassment. "I'm sure Miss Tamony doesn't wish to hear of such dull, ancient matters."

Lord Graymar sighed. "Very well. Miss Tamony, I should like to make you known to my cousin Steffan. Steffan, this is Miss Sarah Tamony, of the famous writing Tamonys."

"Miss Tamony." Steffan repeated the words with open pleasure, slowly, as if they had a delicious taste that should be savored. "Miss Sarah Tamony." He swept a perfect bow, causing his long, unbound hair to fall forward. "A great pleasure. I speak for my men as well." Those standing behind him murmured and nodded. They looked, to Sarah, to be struck at having a woman in their presence. Or perhaps they were simply in awe of Lord Graymar, knowing him as their Dewin Mawr.

Standing full height, Steffan waved toward the area beyond. "Welcome to our camp, Miss Tamony. It's crude compared to my fine cousin's excellent dwellings, but *castell pawb, ei dŷ*, as the saying goes."

Lord Graymar bent near and whispered a translation: " 'A man's home is his castle.' "

"It looks very fine," Sarah assured the other man. "Thank you for allowing His Lordship to bring me. It's especially wonderful because I've always wished to meet a true mystic. You're my first."

The men standing by the fire laughed, and Sarah blushed when she realized what the words had sounded like. But Lord Graymar made a sound of grave displeasure that brought the laughter to an immediate halt, and Steffan Seymour responded with gentlemanly delight.

"In truth?" Steffan said, his blind gaze lifting up to the trees as he made a grand show of offering Sarah his arm. "If that is the case, dear Miss Tamony, then I can only be thankful that the spirits have chosen to bless me with so singular an honor. Let me bring you nearer to the fire. We've not much time before the spirits will visit us, now that you've come."

"Visit us?" She looked at Lord Graymar, who walked on her other side. "This is going to be rather different from discovering a sign in my journal, I take it."

"It would be impossible for you to see or communicate with the spirits who speak to our kind," he told her. "They would have to inhabit a human body to make it possible. But you can hear them, if you will listen and if they allow it."

"Are you certain you've no magic, Miss Tamony?" Steffan asked as they reached the leaping fire. "My blindness does not limit me in such matters, and I feel it quite strongly."

"She bears the Donballa," Lord Graymar said. "Will it make a difference?"

"The Donballa!" Steffan said with surprise, and the men about him murmured. "How in the name of Mactus did Miss Tamony come to bear the Donballa? I thought it had been long lost."

"It was given to me as a gift," Sarah said. "By a sorceress in Aberdeen."

Steffan's eyebrows rose. "Sorsha? How did she come by it, I wonder?" To his cousin he said, "The spirits must have been at work, *cfender.* 'Tis clear they have plans for Miss Tamony."

"How so?" Sarah asked, fascinated.

"I'm not certain," he said. "They commanded that the woman who possesses understanding be brought to the fire in order to be given a sign regarding the *cythraul.* They told me the Dewin Mawr would know your identity and be able to bring you quickly. That they should involve a mere mortal in such important matters speaks very well of you, Miss Tamony, and of your usefulness to our kind. I hope you don't find the idea alarming?"

"Not in the least," she said sincerely as Lord Graymar uttered a snort of laughter.

"Don't worry over that, Steffan," he said. "She finds everything about the supernatural fascinating. I doubt you've read any of her works, living so far from civilization, but Miss Tamony writes about magic mortals. Indeed, she intends for her next book to reveal the history of our kind, even the Seymours, to the mere mortal world."

"Do you?" Steffan asked, clearly intrigued. "That sounds as if it would be most interesting."

"I'm gratified that you think so, Mr. Seymour," Sarah said. "There are some who don't quite understand what my intentions are"—she cast a glare at Lord Graymar—"but my hope is to relate some of the older and more unusual tales of supernatural mortals. I imagine a mystic would have any number of interesting stories to tell. I don't suppose you might consider—"

"Sarah," Lord Graymar said in a dark tone. "You gave me your promise."

"Oh, very well," she said, tamping down a surge of aggravation. "But only until the *cythraul* has been dealt with."

Steffan chuckled and patted the hand tucked through his arm. "I have little idea what the two of you are speaking of," he said, "but I should be pleased to commune with you at any time, Miss Tamony. No matter what my cousin may say."

The flames before them suddenly came alive with color and began to grow unnaturally tall.

"Ah, they're coming," Steffan said, gently removing Sarah's hand and stepping nearer—dangerously close, Sarah thought—to the towering flames. "Marvelous." Lifting his hands toward the fire, he began to murmur in an indistinguishable language.

Lord Graymar took Sarah's arm and pulled her back a few paces, and the other men surrounding the fire did the same.

"He'll speak to the spirits for a few moments," Lord Graymar whispered near her ear. "And then he'll ask you to accompany him into the flames."

"What!"

"Shhh," Lord Graymar uttered calmly, setting a hand about her waist and pulling her nearer. The strength of his body was dearly comforting. "You'll not be burned, Sarah, I promise you. But the spirits will not be able to speak to you unless you enter one of the earthly elements, and it's far better than having to go swimming in the river in the dead of night, which was what I feared. We'll come out of the flames dry, at least."

"We?"

He looked into her eyes. "I'll be with you, Sarah."

She smiled tremulously, greatly relieved.

"I'll be all right then," she murmured. "Thank you."

"Come!" Steffan called. "Hold my hand, Miss Tamony, and have no fear. All will be well. I have you safe and the spirits have made the flames harmless. Are you coming as well, Malachi? I suppose they'd not mind, seeing as you're the Great Dewin. Come, then, and take her other hand."

Sarah could feel Steffan's hand holding her own as her feet moved—unwillingly, she had to admit—toward the fire. But she was squeezing Malachi's fingers so hard that she knew it had to hurt him. He gave no sign of displeasure, however, and murmured to her encouragingly as they went.

"It's not unpleasant, in all actuality," he said. "Rather like the welcome heat of an open oven on a cold day. Close your eyes if it helps. Or perhaps fix your mind on the knowledge that you're likely the only mere mortal to experience such magic."

Sarah had shut her eyes. "I think perhaps this is one supernatural event I shouldn't mind simply seeing from a safe distance."

They walked on until the sound of the crackling flames was about her ears. Any moment Sarah expected to feel the fierce heat licking at her hair and clothes, but it never came. Instead, it was as if they'd walked into the midst of a hot desert windstorm, save that there was no sand to scratch her skin or cause her eyes to burn. She'd experienced just such a storm when her family had journeyed to Morocco, but this was far more pleasant.

"Open your eyes, Sarah," Lord Graymar said. "We're inside."

She did and found to her great surprise that they weren't in Steffan Seymour's camp any longer. They were in the midst of an unending place of swirling color—not only orange and yellow and white but also blue, purple, and red. She could feel the hands of the two men holding her but couldn't see them.

"My lord?"

"I'm here." He gave her hand a gentle squeeze.

"Where are we?"

"We're still on earth," Steffan answered. "There are dimensions hidden from the eyes of mere mortals, yet they exist. You've been given the gift of seeing one. Now you must be quiet, Miss Tamony, and listen. The spirits will communicate to you."

Sarah fell still. She felt Lord Graymar enfolding her

hand within both of his. Slowly, he ran a thumb over the back of it, filling her with an immeasurable calm.

The words didn't come in sound. They were more of a sensation, a feeling that lit her thoughts.

"They . . . I think they're showing me something. I can see it in my mind."

"What is it?" Steffan asked.

Sarah concentrated on the vivid picture that filled her senses. "It seems to be a bell of some kind. A large bell. There's a figure on it . . . of a man, I think . . . yes, it's a man, but he's . . . rather oddly attired. . . ."

"Can you make him out more clearly?" Lord Graymar pressed.

Sarah concentrated, but the picture began to fade.

"I'm sorry," she said. "It's gone now. I'm certain that if I could see a depiction of it I'd recognize it. Or perhaps a portrait of the man. He must be of some import to be on a bell."

Lord Graymar sighed. "There must be hundreds of such memorial bells in England."

Sarah could hear the frustration in his tone. "I'm sorry," she said. "Perhaps if we wait, they'll tell me something more."

"They've done with the sign," Steffan said from the multicolored swirl on her other side. "Now they want you to remove the Donballa and give it to them."

Sarah released his hand and set it over the place where the golden amulet lay beneath her layers of clothes. The fingers of her other hand curled into a fist within Lord Graymar's palms.

"But why?" she asked. "I've taken very good care of it. It means a great deal to me."

When Steffan spoke, she could hear the smile in his voice. "They don't mean to keep it, Miss Tamony. The Donballa is yours forever. It was the Guardians who made certain that it was put in your care, for Sorsha never would have given it to a mere mortal. They only wish to borrow it for a few moments." When Sarah hesitated, he said, "They quite insist, Miss Tamony."

"It's all right, Sarah," Lord Graymar told her. Opening his hands, he released her. "Remove the Donballa and give it to the spirits. They have a purpose."

She wished he hadn't let go and left her standing untethered in the whirling mass. With trembling hands she pulled the gold chain out from beneath the rim of her neckline until the little amulet slid free. Then she lifted the chain from her neck and over her head.

"Do I just . . . hold it out to them?" she asked.

"Aye, Miss Tamony. Hold it out and let go. The spirits will do the rest."

She did as Steffan instructed and held the chain into the hot whirlwind. It glittered with all the colors in the mist, and the amulet shone with the same bright, gleaming light as it had on that night when Lord Graymar had made it new again. She opened her fingers. The necklace floated where it was for a few brief seconds, then disappeared.

"It's gone," she murmured.

"Only for a moment," Steffan murmured. "Wait, and watch."

Sarah groped about toward where she knew Lord Graymar was and with relief felt his fingers on her arm.

"Watch," Steffan whispered once more.

Sarah did. The colors about them began to move with greater intensity, swirling into myriad circles, large and small. The wind blew harder, more hotly, buffeting her skirts and sending tendrils of her uncovered hair flying about her face. In the distance—it seemed so far away—there was an explosion of movement and sound, as if a firework had gone off. Lord Graymar's fingers curled more surely about her arm as the event caused the sphere about them to quiver and shake. Then the realm calmed once more, returning to its more usual swirling and flow. The air cooled a degree or two and blew less fiercely.

Sarah felt something warm about her neck just as Steffan said, "Has the necklace been returned to you, Miss Tamony?"

She lifted a shaking hand and touched the place where the amulet should be.

"Yes. It's there, just as if I'd never removed it."

"Excellent. You should find it far more useful to you now. You are never to remove it until the *cythraul* has been dealt with. The Guardians also send you on your way with all blessings for the future. Malachi, there is something else—"

"They've spoken to me already," Lord Graymar said quickly. "There's no need to say more."

"Very well," Steffan said, his tone curiously amused. "Now we must depart. Miss Tamony, give me your hand, please."

Sarah lifted her hand in the general direction of his voice and felt him take hold of it.

"It will feel rather colder than usual for a few minutes once we're on the other side," Steffan warned, "but my men will have a cup of wine and some blankets ready. We simply walk forward, just as we walked in."

It seemed to Sarah that if they merely walked forward they would walk forever, for her eyes told her that the place they were in was endless. But Steffan had the right of it, as she had assumed he would. They moved but four or five steps and were suddenly standing in the cold night air on the other side of the fire, surrounded by Steffan's men.

"Are you all right, Sarah?" Lord Graymar asked, pulling her even farther from the flames, which she supposed were capable of burning once more.

She turned to smile up at him, exhilaration rushing from head to toe. "My lord, it was wonderful! I vow I've enjoyed myself far more than I had ever believed possible since making your acquaintance. Nothing I've experienced before can possibly compare. Not even the pyramids in Egypt."

Behind her, Steffan murmured, "It's fortunate you feel that way, Miss Tamony."

Before she could wonder at the words, someone was placing a blanket about her shivering body.

"I'm gratified to know that I've been able to entertain you so well," Lord Graymar said, putting up a hand to ward away the man who attempted to put a blanket on him. "And the Donballa?"

"Oh, I'd quite forgotten." Sarah quickly pulled the chain from beneath her clothes and examined the shining gold ball. "It's unharmed. Indeed, it appears to be unchanged in any way."

"But it has been," he said. "Where it was once nearly useless to you, to anyone, it has now become exceedingly powerful. It will ward off any powerful demon, even one as mighty as the *cythraul*. And that makes the Donballa not only very valuable, but also dangerous. There are some who will wish to take it from you. At any cost."

"Don't frighten her so," Steffan said, pressing a cup of wine into Sarah's hands. "Drink this, Miss Tamony. It's been enchanted to warm you quickly. And there's nothing to fear in my cousin's warnings, dire as they may be."

"I don't want her taking chances, Steffan," Lord Graymar said sternly.

"I'm sure Miss Tamony would never do such a thing," Steffan replied, ignoring the "ha!" his cousin uttered. "In any case, there's no need to terrify her. Now listen to me, Miss Tamony. The Donballa cannot be taken from you even in death. It can only be removed by you and given to another of your own free will."

Sarah held Lord Graymar's gaze as she lifted the cup and drank, wondering if the amulet would save Julius from Serafina Daray's spell.

"It will only shield you from demons, Sarah," he said, as if reading her thoughts. "It cannot protect from spells. But we should delay no longer in returning to your brother's side." He pushed his cup of wine back toward Steffan. "Come." He held his hands out to her. "We'll be back in London in but a few minutes and make certain that all is well."

Chapter 16

The brother was still sleeping soundly when they returned to the dwelling, as Malachi knew he would be, and there was no one in the room, which was fortunate, for he wasn't obliged to alter any memories. He hoped that no one had entered the room while they'd been absent or, if they had, hadn't also gone to Sarah's room to discover her missing. But Malachi sensed that there was neither panic nor movement in the house, save for the kitchen cat and the mouse it was hunting. Her family had known Sarah was watching over her brother and had known, too, that she could be trusted to wake them if he required attention.

"He's all right," Sarah said, rising from where she'd been bent over her brother's sleeping form. She moved about the bed, toward the fire, but Malachi said, "I'll take care of it," and with the lift of a finger caused the blaze to stir and renew.

The greater warmth was welcome, and the greater light as well. He watched as Sarah held her hands to the heat, warming them. Tendrils of curling hair fell loose from her arrangement, gleaming in the firelight. Her face, the side of it he could see, was relaxed and happy. She was think-

ing, he could tell, of her latest adventure. The smile that
tilted her mouth upward gave evidence of her pleasure
and contentment.

His gaze wandered down, over her tall, elegant figure
and the feminine curves. One of her hands drifted upward
to touch the place where the Donballa lay, and her smile
widened. The spectacles, which had slid partly down her
tiny nose, shone in the firelight. As if sensing his gaze, she
looked at him.

"I still can't believe it happened," she said. "Not just
standing in the fire, but the spirits and the fast traveling.
You're so fortunate to live every day of your life with such
wonderful things."

He might have said the same of her life, he thought rue-
fully, gazing into the depths of her sparkling green eyes.
How often had he wished—prayed, even—that he could
cast aside the responsibilities of being Dewin Mawr? She
wouldn't know what that was like, living each day as the
Earl of Graymar, always watching, always moving and
speaking with care, never able to be what he truly was. At
least not in London. Glain Tarran was the only place where
he was free, and yet even there she had broken in, gotten
past every defense, and turned his life upside down.

"Sarah," he murmured. "Come here to me."

Her eyes widened a fraction and her lips parted, but he
saw that she understood his intent very well. Better yet, her
own expression softened with a matching desire.

Women had desired him before. Many women, actually, which was a truth he could state without fear of exaggeration. He wasn't blind to the beauty magic mortals
possessed or unaware that he had been especially fortunate in face and form. Some of his admirers hoped to lure
him into marriage, but just as many wanted something entirely different. Niclas liked to joke that Malachi, from the
day he'd attained his majority, had had more lures cast at
him than all the fish in the sea. Malachi had been happy to
satisfy those who were sympathetics and had avoided
those who weren't as graciously as he could. When Au-

gusta had signaled her availability he'd been content to embrace a form of monogamy and found that it suited him. But no woman he'd known before, either magic or mortal, had been able to look at him as Sarah Tamony was now and have him trembling with such need.

She moved toward him, clearly unafraid of what he might do. But that was foolish, he thought. She believed that because she was in her own home, in the room where her brother lay sleeping, that the most Malachi could do was kiss her. Or perhaps she thought that, as a gentleman and a nobleman, he'd control himself. If she'd known about the visions that haunted his every moment, sleeping or waking, she'd run from the room screaming.

Or perhaps not. Sarah Tamony was a lady by birth, but she was neither frail nor fearful. She'd been close enough to him on two occasions—during their flight and the fast traveling—to realize what his reaction to her was. And yet she came without hesitation, and she looked—or at least he prayed it was so—as if she wanted this intimacy as greatly as he did.

She stopped before him, her face lifted to his. He realized with a sudden flash of hot jealousy that she had been kissed before. Not in the way that he had kissed her earlier, but truly kissed. By another man.

"I'll drive the memory of him away forever." He said the words aloud before he could think to stop them.

That smile of hers made him feel dangerous. Rather than looking affronted, her expression softened with a measure of confident amusement. It was maddening.

"Drive whose memory away?"

"The man who kissed you."

"You've already done that," she told him. "I am nearly twenty and seven, my lord, and have known many things that my peers can only dream of. In but a few weeks you've managed to make me forget almost everything and everyone I've known before. But I truly doubt that, from here forward, anyone else will be able to make me forget you."

Lifting a hand, he stroked a single finger down her cheek.

"You speak as if this will come to an end."

She tilted her head slightly. "If I don't take care, Lord Graymar, you'll break my heart. That experience I yet remember from my foolish youth. I have no desire to repeat it."

"I'll make you forget that, too," he vowed. Lifting the other hand, he gently removed her spectacles, and with slow care set them aside. Then he put his fingers on either side of her face, caressing, drawing her closer until they stood with their bodies nearly touching.

"Say my name, Sarah," he murmured.

"It's improper," she told him, her eyes closing from the pleasure of his touch. "I shouldn't."

Malachi lowered his head. "Just tonight, then. Just once. I promise I'll never tell a soul."

"Very well," she whispered. "If you promise, Malachi."

"Yes," he said, touching the sides of her mouth with his thumbs. "Malachi. Will you let me kiss you, Sarah?"

Her answer was to raise her arms and slip them about his neck, drawing him down to her.

Malachi lightly touched her lips with his own, the barest of caresses, murmuring her name, then covered them more fully. One of his hands slid to the back of her head, into her soft hair, holding her, while the other moved downward, his fingers spread wide as he pulled her flush against himself. She made a sound of surprise as their bodies met, then relaxed and willingly pressed into his warmth.

He took his time, savoring the taste and softness of her lips and her acquiescence as he angled her body to fit more readily into his embrace, turning her head to fully meet his kiss. Sarah sighed with pleasure, and her hands began to roam, caressing his face and neck, then slipping upward to his hair. The black ribbon that held the lengthy mane in place came undone beneath her clever fingers and fell to the floor. He groaned against her mouth as her hands stroked upward, against his scalp, her fingers coursing through his hair.

"It's so soft," she whispered when he lifted his head to

better enjoy her petting. "Like silk. I've longed to touch it from the first moment I met you."

"I wish you'd said so earlier," he said with a groan. "I would have let you do whatever you desired. Anything at all."

She uttered a husky laugh and rose up on her toes to press her lips against his chin. Malachi took her mouth again, touching her with his tongue. Her reaction surprised and pleased him, for the sudden stiffening of her body had nothing to do with the desire that had taken possession of them both. She'd been kissed before, but never like this. With a surge of delight, Malachi realized that, in this, he was the first.

"Don't be frightened," he said, setting his forehead against hers. His heightened breathing caused the words to be pelted against her cheek. "I know it's strange at first—"

"Is it *done*?" she asked, uttering an embarrassed laugh. "I didn't know. It never occurred to me—"

"I'll show you," he murmured, covering her face with soft, rapid kisses. "Follow my lead. I'll stop if you don't like it. But you will like it, Sarah. You will. . . ."

And she did. She liked it so much and became so quickly proficient that Malachi didn't know how much time had passed before he heard the warning bells ringing wildly in his brain.

Someone in the house was waking.

Malachi pulled away and, breathing harshly, tried to make sense of his surroundings. Sarah gave a murmur of protest and tried to pull him back, but he managed to say, "Wait," and she sighed and rested her head against his chest. Her hands had wandered under his cloak. One had pulled his shirt from his trousers while the other had burrowed up to stroke his back. Malachi's own hands were in places they shouldn't be, one fondling her bottom and the other in the midst of unbuttoning buttons.

He lifted his head a bit higher to see where they were. They had staggered into the room's farthest corner and were wedged between the two walls. He supposed his intention had been to next drag her down to the floor.

"Your mother is stirring," he said thickly, his senses clearing. He had a fleeting thought that next time he would place all those in the house into a deep slumber, making it impossible for them to rise. "We've got to—" What? He couldn't think. He could transport her to a safer place . . . to Mervaille . . . but the hour was late, and if she was discovered missing . . .

"I've got to go." He began to pull his hands from her body.

"Go?" she murmured, her voice thick with desire. She turned her head and began nuzzling the base of his throat—which she had earlier bared by unwinding his cravat and tossing it to the floor. Malachi had a vague memory of telling her at the time what a clever girl she was. "Don't leave me."

He kissed her, quickly, and then began the unhappy task of bringing her back to her senses.

"I'm sorry, sweetheart, but we've only a few minutes before your mother walks through the door. If you don't want me erasing her memory, then you'd better let me go." Stepping back, he began to look for his hat and gloves.

"But Malachi—"

The confusion in her tone brought him back to her. "We'll finish this soon, love," he promised, taking her head between his hands and kissing her soundly.

"But what about Julius?"

"He'll sleep until morning, and then you'll have to let him do as he wishes. We can't keep him sedated forever. I'll come tomorrow to take you driving, and we'll speak of it more. *If*," he added sternly, "you'll promise not to look at me the way you're looking at me now. Otherwise I'll consign the park to the devil and take you to Mervaille for the remainder of the day."

"Mervaille?" Her eyes widened with the interest that he'd seen spark so often, which had far more to do with her passion for magic than anything else. "Truly?"

With a sigh he held out a hand, calling both his hat and gloves to come to him. "You make me crazed, Sarah Tamony," he told her, reaching out to catch the flying objects and take them in a firm grip. "I wish I didn't enjoy it so much."

He disappeared, then, just as the door opened. Sarah only had enough time to whirl about, hiding her undone buttons, before her mother entered the room. Snatching up her glasses from the table where Lord Graymar had set them, she put them on and said, "Oh, it's you, Mama. Hello."

"Hello, Sarah." Her mother's gaze went first to the bed. "Is Julius awake? I thought I heard him speaking."

"No, no," Sarah assured her at once. "He's sound asleep, just as you see. He's been resting peacefully. I'm sure he'll be himself again in the morning."

Lady Tamony looked at her curiously in the dim firelight. "Sarah, dear, what on earth happened to you?" Closing the door, she made a closer inspection. "You look as if you've been rolling down a hillside. What's become of your hair?"

Sarah reached up a hand and realized, with a sinking heart, that Lord Graymar had completely relieved her hair arrangement of its moorings. Hairpins were scattered all over the floor.

"I had a dream," she said. "I fell asleep in the chair and . . . well, it was quite a dream, as you might imagine."

"Indeed," her mother replied, gazing at her with disbelief. Bending, she picked something off the floor—a gentleman's rumpled neckcloth. Holding it up to her daughter, Lady Tamony asked, "And was this part of your dream as well, dear?"

Sarah blushed hotly as she remembered unwinding the cloth from Lord Graymar's neck and the things he'd said—in a particularly naughty tone of voice—as she'd done it.

"It must be one of Julius's." She snatched the cloth from her mother's hand. Backing toward the door, Sarah said, "I'm terribly tired, and Julius should sleep comfortably through the remainder of the night. Or day. It must be morning by now." Blindly she fumbled for the doorknob, finding it at last with tremendous relief. All the while her mother watched her with a steady expression. "I'll just go to bed, then. Good night, Mama."

"Good night, dear," her mother said calmly.

Sarah backed out and closed the door, catching just a glimpse of her mother's smile before it shut entirely.

Chapter 17

Sarah slept late into the morning the following day, something that had only occurred in her life on those rare occasions when she'd been ill. The Tamonys were early risers, even following late nights, and she felt guilty for having wasted so many precious hours that might have been productive.

Despite that guilt, Sarah lay quietly in her bed for a few minutes, staring at the bed curtains and reliving the night before. It had been among the most terrible, considering Julius, and yet magical of her life. The fast traveling, meeting a real mystic, the journey into the fire, and the transformation of the Donballa had all been quite amazing. But far more wonderful even than these had been Lord Graymar's kiss.

The memory made her feel heated all the way through. If her mother hadn't come to check on Julius, Sarah couldn't say how, or if, the embrace would have stopped. Neither she nor Lord Graymar had shown any sign of bringing it to an end. In truth, she had to admit, she hadn't wanted it to end. Nor was she relieved, as any decent maiden should be, that it had.

Sarah supposed that was partly due to her advanced age and her increasingly slim prospects of ever marrying, as well as her experience of the wider world. Not every unmarried woman had the advantage of seeing how other peoples viewed such affairs. But perhaps that was unjust to the English, who readily endured both men and women taking lovers outside of marriage, and men, especially, setting up mistresses. The problem was that she wasn't married and if she pursued a union with Lord Graymar, no matter how fleeting, she would be ruined if it became known, and her books might suffer for it.

"Or perhaps not," she said aloud, thoughtfully. "A good scandal might make them seem more appealing."

Not that she would ever give herself to Lord Graymar, or any man, with the hope of monetary gain. But it would at least be one less thing to feel guilty about.

For she did intend to take him as a lover. Her first and only lover, for as long as he was willing to play the part. At least until the end of the Season, when they would go their separate ways. She wasn't foolish enough to think that more would come of it. He was not only the Earl of Graymar but the Dewin Mawr as well, and she was a writer who was the daughter of a writer and the sister of a writer. It scarcely mattered that her father was a baronet and possessed lands and wealth. A nobleman of Lord Graymar's power and prestige didn't marry so far beneath him, especially not a woman who was already believed by one and all to be so firmly on the shelf and perhaps incapable of providing him with an heir. From her research she knew that wizards of great standing seldom took mere mortals for mates. Lord Graymar's own parents had been powerful magic mortals. His father had been the previous Dewin Mawr and his mother descended from ancient Dewin Mawrs. Faced with such facts, Sarah knew that she must guard her heart against hoping for more than a brief dalliance. It would have to be enough, she told herself. But she wouldn't dwell on the ending before the beginning even arrived.

A soft knock came at the door, and Sarah sat.

"Yes, come in," she called. "I'm awake."

Irene, one of the youngest of the maids, peered into the room, smiling.

"Good morning, miss," she greeted cheerfully, pushing the door wide to carry in a tray. "Her Ladyship thought it best if breakfast was brought to you this morning. She said you were up with Master Julius all night and likely to be too weary to come down to eat."

"Thank you," Sarah said as the tray was placed upon her lap. "I confess to having slept very well, and to being hungry." She grinned. "How is my brother this morning? Has he waked yet?"

"Oh yes, miss," Irene told her, uncovering a plate of sausages and egg tarts. "He was up and on his way quite early. And looked fit as could be, so there's no need to worry."

Sarah had already picked up a sausage with her fingers and taken a large bite and had to chew quickly in order to speak.

" '*On his way*'?" she repeated. "But surely not. Do you mean to say that Sir Alberic and Lady Tamony *let* him go?"

Irene looked bewildered. "Why, yes, miss. They thought the fresh air would do him good, and he did seem much recovered after a night of sleep."

"Sweet merciful day." Sarah pushed the tray aside and swung her legs over the side of the bed, hurrying across the room to fling open her closet door. Her purse hung on the peg where she'd put it last night. A frantic examination showed that her precious journal was still safely inside. Uttering a sigh of relief, Sarah turned back to the bewildered maid.

"Where did Master Julius go? What time did he leave?"

"To the Antiquities Society," Irene answered. "He left three hours ago."

"Three hours!" Sarah cried. "Run and fetch Charlotte. Tell her I wish to dress at once. Quickly now." Going back into the closet, she grasped the first suitable gown—a light blue day dress—and threw it on the bed. "And please ask

Henry to send a lad around to Lord Graymar with a note asking him to come at once. No, better yet, tell the lad to wait for the earl and bring him back. Or perhaps I'd better go myself," Sarah said with indecision. "Yes, come to think of it, that would be—"

"But miss," said Irene, carrying the tray to the door, "Lord Graymar's manservant is already waiting in the parlor to speak with you. I told him that you might not be awake yet, and that you'd wish to eat, but he said he'd wait. He has a note for you from the earl."

"Oh, bother," Sarah said irately, certain this wasn't good news. She began to unbutton her nightgown. "Are my parents and cousin at home?"

"No, miss," Irene replied. "Sir Alberic and Lady Tamony have gone visiting, and Miss Philistia and her maid left shortly afterward to do some shopping."

That was odd, Sarah thought as she began to unbraid her long hair. Philistia never went out with just a maid.

"Hurry and fetch Charlotte, then," Sarah told the maid. "And tell His Lordship's manservant that I'll be with him right away."

Twenty minutes later, with her hair not entirely anchored in its arrangement, Sarah hurried down the stairs, pushing up her spectacles and buttoning the last few buttons of one sleeve. She entered the parlor without announcement to find Lord Graymar's manservant standing near the fire. He turned as she entered the room and smiled in greeting.

"Rhys!" she cried with gladness, hurrying toward him with outstretched hands. "What a wonderful surprise! How are you?"

His smile widened. "Very well, Miss Tamony. And you?"

"I'm having such a grand time in Town," she assured him. "Despite His Lordship interfering in the writing of my book. He's proved to be just as great a nuisance as he said he would, but he's more than made up for it. He took me to Wales last night," she told Rhys, "by the use of fast traveling. And then we stood right in the middle of a fire. It was extraordinary!"

"He told me some of what transpired with Master Steffan and his men," Rhys said. "And explained that the Guardians have seen fit to involve you in the mystery of the *cythraul*. I only wish your brother hadn't been drawn into magic, and by a sorceress the likes of Serafina Daray." He visibly shuddered. "I pray all will be well for him. I was sorry to hear that he'd already left the house when I arrived, though His Lordship warned me it might be the case."

"But where is the earl?" she asked.

Rhys glanced beyond her to the still-open parlor door and lowered his voice. "He was called away," he murmured. "It's an unfortunate aspect of being Dewin Mawr, but when a situation arises among the Families he is bound to go at once. This particular incident was most urgent, for it involved one of the sons of The MacQueen and the daughter of a mere mortal laird who wants nothing to do with magic. The daughter is of a different mind, however. She and The MacQueen's son were handfasted in secret, though the daughter had been promised to another."

"Oh dear."

"Aye." Rhys gave a woeful shake of his head. "Just so. His Lordship will be hard-pressed to keep them from shooting one another. He took two of his cousins who were near at hand, Master Niclas and Master Dyfed, in order to make the task quicker. The earl is determined to return this evening, if possible, and certainly no later than tomorrow."

"He's already gone, then?" she asked, her spirits plunging. "But my brother has left the house, and very likely gone to . . . well, to that woman's house again." She blushed just to speak of it. "I can't let him remain there as he did yesterday. She might do him an injury if . . ." Sarah could scarce think of the way to say it. "If she keeps using him that way."

"Very true, miss." Rhys's gaze was sympathetic. "I came just as soon as His Lordship was away." He put a hand into a pocket inside his coat. "He bade me to bring you this"—he set a small vial into her hand—"and said that you must give your brother a few drops every few hours until His Lordship has made his return. Unfortunately, as I said, Mr. Tamony had gone before I arrived." He pulled out a slender sealed missive as well. "Lord Graymar also asked me to give you this, and said you're to read it three times before doing anything else today."

Sarah stepped back and opened the missive, reading the brief contents in but a moment.

My dearest Sarah, it said. *Rhys will have explained to you why I've gone. Do nothing until I've returned, no matter what may transpire. I shall be very angry if you do anything dangerous.*

Sarah obediently read it through twice more, then folded the page and put it in her pocket. Looking at Rhys, she said, "I must go and fetch my brother back at once. Will you help me?"

Rhys's eyebrows rose. "You can't mean to go to Serafina Daray's home, Miss Tamony. His Lordship would be extremely displeased if I were to let you undertake so bold an action."

"Nevertheless," Sarah replied, "I must make the attempt. Surely she'd not dare harm two members of the same family. I can't believe she'd risk the rumors. Apart from that, she'd be far too frightened of what the Dewin Mawr would do to her."

Rhys shook his head. "No, miss, I can't allow it. I gave Lord Graymar my solemn promise."

"I see," she said more gently, reaching out to touch his hand. "I understand, of course. But you must excuse me, please, if I take my leave. I don't know how long it will take me to discover where Miss Daray lives."

"It's a rash and foolish task, miss," Rhys countered forcefully. "You'd not even be able to get beyond the gates of her town house, for the dwelling is enchanted. No mere mortal could manage the task without the help of an extraordinary *dewin*."

"Then I shall stand out front and shout until someone comes to stop me. I must do something, Rhys. Surely you understand, for I can't think you'd sit on your hands while one of your loved ones was suffering beneath a terrible spell."

"No, I'd not," he admitted, and was thoughtful for a moment. "There is one powerful *dewin* among the Seymours remaining in London, and as she was once allied with the dark Families, she will readily understand the likes of Miss Daray."

"She?" Sarah repeated.

He nodded and said, "She."

Desdemona Seymour was not in the best of moods. She was seven months pregnant and what her husband politely called large with child. It was not a description she liked, but she couldn't deny that it was apt. Her back ached, her feet were swollen, and she'd not enjoyed a good night's slumber in the past week. Worse than all this, the Dewin Mawr had appeared without warning early in the day and taken her husband off to Scotland, where some ridiculous feud between magic and mere mortals was about to erupt.

Desdemona didn't care about such things. She thought the Great Dewin far too kind and long-suffering toward both mere and magic mortals. In her opinion he needed to utilize less patience and diplomacy and more power and discipline. It would be a simple matter for Malachi to arrive at the place of trouble and knock enough heads together—so to speak—until everyone involved did what he told them to do. But no, he refused to use his powers in the manner that her father, Draceous Caslin, the Great Sorcerer of her native America, so efficiently employed.

And so Malachi had taken along not only Dyfed, whom Desdemona hated being parted from even for a brief time, but also Niclas Seymour, the family's skilled communicator. Julia, Niclas's wife, wasn't bound to be any happier about the matter than Desdemona, but at least she wasn't suffering an advanced pregnancy or being visited by the mere mortal scribbler Malachi had inconceivably set his sights upon and who presently stood before her insisting that Desdemona must help her rescue her stupid brother, who'd managed to get himself placed under an unbreakable spell. By Serafina Daray, no less, whom Desdemona passionately hated. Serafina had set herself as an adversary shortly after Desdemona and Dyfed had arrived in London. She'd laughed at Desdemona's American accent and made endless jests at the dinners and parties they'd attended together about the inferiority of anyone from the former Colonies. Desdemona was sensitive about her heritage, especially as she'd been raised to feel a similar disdain for all things English. But Dyfed had found ways to smooth away the fury that had risen up at the other woman's words. At least until Serafina made the mistake of insinuating that Desdemona's child would be a useless creature, having been sired by a lesser wizard and birthed by an American.

Desdemona had nearly killed her. Dyfed, unfortunately, had stepped in the way and made Desdemona stop. But at least she'd had a few moments of pleasure in seeing the shock of the other woman as she'd discovered just how powerful and cunning an American could be. Serafina Daray's alarm had been a beautiful thing, for she'd also learned that she wasn't the most powerful sorceress in England any longer, and it had left her shaken.

"To be frank, Miss Tamony," Desdemona said, lowering herself with care into a comfortable chair, "I don't see why I should lend you my aid. Your brother means nothing to me, and as you and I aren't related yet, I owe you nothing. Apart from that, Malachi wouldn't like it, and although that wouldn't stop me if I wished to deal with Serafina, it's sufficient to sway me when I'm feeling as weary and unpleasant as I currently am. If you've not yet noticed, Miss Tamony, I am expecting."

"I do apologize, Mrs. Seymour," Sarah said with feeling. "I didn't realize."

"The fault is mine," Rhys put in. "I failed to mention your condition, madam."

Desdemona sent him a heated look. Her back ached like the very devil. She wished Dyfed were there to rub it. It would serve Malachi right if she did help his woman. Desdemona had asked him—nicely, even, which hadn't been easy for her—not to take her husband for this foolish purpose. But Malachi wanted to be done with it quickly so that he could return to Miss Tamony and had insisted that his cousins accompany him. Just thinking of it made Desdemona angry all over again.

"Of course I couldn't ask you to leave your home," Sarah said. "Not in your condition. You have every right to be angry with me for intruding on your privacy during so delicate a time."

Desdemona was trying to move into a more comfortable position but stopped at Sarah's words and looked at her sharply. "Why shouldn't I leave the house if I wish?"

Sarah flushed with embarrassment; Rhys looked at the floor as if it suddenly fascinated him.

"Because of your condition, Mrs. Seymour," Sarah explained. "I'm sure your husband wouldn't wish you to leave the safety of your dwelling."

That was true enough, Desdemona thought unhappily. Dyfed refused to let her leave the house unless he was with her, and he'd given strict instructions that she was to remain home until he returned from his journey with Malachi. It irked her to be treated like a child; more irksome still was the idea of others thinking she was the kind of woman who was ruled by a man. Any man. No matter that it was true.

"I do as I please," Desdemona declared irritably, shifting on the chair. "And my husband is not here to bid me stay or go, due to the Dewin Mawr's determination to take him from my side."

"It's shocking that Lord Graymar should have done such a thing," Sarah agreed with sympathy. "Your husband had a far greater duty to remain with you than hare off with his cousin."

"There's no use speaking of it," Desdemona said, though she was a little mollified. "Malachi is given to doing as he pleases, which is his right as the Great Sorcerer."

"That's true," Sarah said with a nod. "Still, I'm sure you'll be grateful when your husband has come home. I am sorry for bothering you, Mrs. Seymour," she said again, and began to back toward the door. "We'll leave you in peace."

Desdemona eyed her knowingly. "You still mean to make a try at gaining entrance to Serafina's dwelling, do you not? It's impossible for a mere mortal."

"I must at least try," Sarah told her. "It seems unsisterly to let my brother languish beneath her spell, even if I can't break it. Julius would do everything in his power to rescue me if our positions were reversed."

Desdemona sighed. Mere mortals were so foolish about such things. "I'd better go with you, then," she said, sounding very put-upon. She struggled to lift her girth from the chair.

Sarah hurried across the room to help her. "Oh no, Mrs. Seymour, I really don't think it a good idea. I never should have asked you to help us, and certainly not to face a sorceress of Serafina Daray's powers."

With an effort Desdemona gained her feet, swaying until both Sarah and Rhys, who had joined them, steadied her.

"And why not?" she asked, her tone filled with immediate insult. "Do you imagine, by some unfathomable chance, that her powers could possibly exceed my own?" The measure of her wrath made the room shake and the windowpanes rattle.

"Not at all," Sarah assured her quickly. "I know that they do not."

"Good," Desdemona said, her anger fading as quickly as it had begun. The room about them settled. "As it happens, you've come just as I decided that I want to take some air. I've been in the house all day, and some exercise will do me good. But we'll take my carriage. It's been enchanted for comfort, and I won't sit in some wretchedly unpleasant hack."

Morcar Cadmaran lowered the paper he'd been reading and stared at his butler, who stood at the doorway of the breakfast parlor.

"What did you say, Stoton?"

"A Miss Philistia Tamony to see you, my lord," the butler repeated. "She says it's urgent that she speak with you."

"God in heaven," Morcar muttered. "Was she accompanied by another woman?" he asked, hoping that the lovely cousin might have come, as well. Or even Lady Tamony, who was not only still very attractive, despite her years, but also disarmingly witty.

"No, my lord. There was a maid, but she bid her wait in the hall. She wishes to speak with you alone. I've taken her to the blue parlor."

Morcar felt a surge of irritation. What did the silly chit think she was about, visiting a man of his standing in broad daylight with no one more than a maid to accompany her? Anyone seeing her might suppose they were carrying on an affair—and would disapprove, as she was a virginal unmarried female and he a nobleman who would know better than to meet her when anyone might see. If and when Morcar did relieve the little fool of her maidenhead it would be in a far more private setting.

"Hellfire and damnation," he muttered, pushing aside the late breakfast he'd been eating and rising from his chair. "I'll have to get rid of her as quickly as I can. What a tiresome way to start the day."

Morcar had composed himself by the time Stoton opened the parlor doors for him. Philistia Tamony gave a start at his appearance, jumping up from the chair in which she'd been sitting and staring at him as if he were a wolf come to eat her.

Entering the room, Morcar forced a smile upon his lips and said, "Miss Tamony, what a delightful and unlooked-for surprise. You look very fine today. I hope you've not come because something is amiss? Shall I have Stoton bring tea?"

She looked rather more charming than she had the day before, Morcar thought as he moved toward her. She was wearing a gown made in the latest style, composed of various shades of purple and coupled with a bonnet of pale violet. It suited her well and gave her plain face a dose of much-needed color. She put him in mind of a tiny, delicate flower that needed picking.

"No, thank you," she said in a small voice, still staring at him from large brown eyes. "I only just finished my breakfast before coming. I'm sorry to have arrived without an invitation, but something's happened and I didn't know what else to do."

"Indeed?" he remarked curiously.

She nodded and looked past him to where Stoton yet stood, awaiting instructions. Morcar made a dismissive motion and the servant bowed and departed, shutting the doors behind him.

"Please sit and be comfortable, Miss Tamony," Morcar invited pleasantly. "You know it's very true that you shouldn't have come without a proper escort. Your cousin or Lady Tamony at the least. Society can be cruel to young ladies who step across certain invisible boundaries, though perhaps, having been out of England so often, you were not aware."

Her cheeks flushed and she looked so painfully contrite that even Morcar's wicked heart softened a bit.

"I do know, my lord, which makes my coming even more unforgivable. I'm sure you think me a terrible creature for doing anything so bold and unseemly. But please believe me when I say, Lord Llew, that I should never wish to give you a disgust or . . . or a dislike of me."

"That would be impossible," he said reassuringly, amused at her concern over losing his good opinion. She clearly held him in awe, perhaps had even fallen a little in love with him. But he was used to such emotion from young maidens enjoying their first Seasons in London, especially those who were plain and in want of a rich, titled husband. "I hope you consider me a friend, for I certainly regard you as one. It was only as a friend that I spoke of the matter to you. Now we must put it behind us and be comfortable. Shall we?"

The blush deepened and the look in the eyes changed from fear to pleasure. Yes, he thought, she had certainly become infatuated with him. The thought of taking her maidenhead was growing more appealing by the moment. And, really, she looked very pretty with that sparkle in her gaze.

"Thank you, my lord," she said. "It would be an honor to have you as a friend."

"Then it's settled. Now, what is it that's brought you to me this morning, when so charming a young lady ought to be out shopping and enjoying the sights of London?"

"Oh," she said, as if just remembering the cause of her visit. Turning, she picked up a drawstring purse and began to open it. "It's the strangest thing, my lord. I suppose it has to do with the supernatural, and I really should have shown it to my cousin Sarah, for she's an expert on such matters. But something told me that it was better to bring it to you. Is this not odd?" She pulled something solid and rectangular from the purse and held it out to him. "It's the book you recommended to me yesterday at Hookham's, my lord. Do you remember? *The Fortunes of Nigel*, volume one, by Sir Walter Scott. But look." She pointed to the cover. "The title on the cover has changed, but the book within is still *The Fortunes of Nigel*. Is that not odd? And look at the little symbols at the bottom. They don't make any sense at all."

Morcar leaned forward to take the book, frowning as he read the title. *The Life of St. Justin.* There was no author listed, but beneath the English words was a line written in the ancient text, which translated to read, *All become one or all will fail.* Flipping the book open, he saw that what the girl said was true. It was still *The Fortunes of Nigel*, by Scott.

"Very odd," he murmured, looking at the cover once more. "*The Life of St. Justin.* I wonder how that could have come to be there. Perhaps it and the symbols were a mistake of the printer, and we simply didn't look closely enough at the cover to make certain of it. On the spine, as you see, the title remains *The Fortunes of Nigel,* volume one. It would be a simple mistake to make."

The rate of his heartbeat had increased, and his thoughts begun to race. It was a sign from the Guardians. The use of the ancient tongue made it certain. But why had they sent it through a mere mortal? Especially one such as Philistia Tamony, who had no magic or any real understanding of it, as the cousin did?

But perhaps, he thought suddenly, she did understand. Perhaps she was a sympathetic. Her cousin was, and Malachi was likely making the most of Sarah Tamony's knowledge in his quest for the *cythraul.* Perhaps Morcar could do the same with the young woman sitting before him.

"What do you make of this occurrence, Miss Tamony?" he asked slowly, looking up at her.

Her expression grew shy again, and she hesitated before she spoke. "I think that, perhaps"—her gloved hands folded and unfolded nervously—"there's a bit of magic involved, my lord. And that, perhaps, you might think so, too."

"And why would you think such things?" he asked, considering her with interest.

If it was possible, she turned more brightly red. "Because I think you may possess magic, my lord," she whispered. "Sarah says you do, and if I didn't believe her before, I do now."

Morcar set the book aside on a nearby table and settled more comfortably into his chair. Tenting his fingers beneath his chin, he regarded her soberly.

"And if that were true," he asked, "what would you think of it? Of me? Would you not be quite afraid?"

"Oh, not at all, my lord," she said at once, shaking her head so that the soft ringlets of her hair quivered with movement. "I could never be afraid of you, or believe anything save that you're the most wonderful . . . I mean to say, the kindest and most honorable gentleman of my acquaintance. If you're truly a wizard, as Sarah says, then you must be a very good one. I know that I can trust you completely."

"You are very kind," he said. "I hope that you will always feel that way. I hope even more that I shall not give you cause to cease doing so. I am, just as your cousin has told you, a magic mortal."

Rather than appear alarmed, a little smile touched her lips, and her nervous hands pressed together as if the knowledge delighted her.

"I *knew* it must be so. I knew that you were different from other men. Unique," she clarified, "and remarkable."

It was odd, Morcar thought, but the way she said the words filled him with an unfamiliar warmth. Perhaps that was because it sounded as if she truly meant them.

"May I dare to hope that I can trust you to keep my secret? You can well understand how vital secrecy is to my kind."

"Of course, my lord," she said fervently, leaning toward him as if to convince him of her sincerity. "Sarah has told me how dangerous the lives of magic mortals would be if the world should discover and believe in their powers. She doesn't think anyone ever would believe it, apart from a few sympathizers, but I would never take the risk of exposing you to harm, Lord Llew. You can trust me completely."

"I believe that I can, Miss Tamony," he said, surprised to discover that he meant it. "You used the word 'sympathizers.' We call those mere mortals who aid us our sympathetics. You are clearly among these."

She blushed again and sat more primly in her seat. "I hope that I am, my lord."

"You are," he told her, smiling. "I thought you might be when we met at Hookham's. I had a feeling about you, you see."

Her brown eyes widened. "I had a feeling, too," she said. "About you."

She really was rather charming, he thought.

"But what does the changing of the title on the book mean?" she asked. "Does it make any sense to you?"

"Not yet." He unfolded his long legs and rose from his chair. Approaching her, he held out a hand. She placed hers in it. "But it will, in time." With a gentle tug he pulled her to her feet. "I wonder, Miss Tamony, if fortune hasn't brought you to me for another purpose altogether. The plans I'd made for this afternoon have fallen through, and I was left to contemplate a long and lonely day, made all the worse at the knowledge that I might have been in company with you after all."

She stared at him as if he were a god. Morcar liked the expression. He gave her fingers a gentle, sensual squeeze.

"Now that you've come, would it be too much for me to hope that you might rescue me?"

"I should be honored to do anything you ask, my lord," she answered faintly.

He smiled. "You must be careful what you say to me, Philistia. May I call you Philistia? It's shocking, I know, but now that you know my deepest secret I feel that we can be more than mere acquaintances. You must call me Morcar."

She nodded. "Yes, my lord."

"Morcar," he prompted.

"Morcar," she repeated rather breathlessly.

"You make it sound almost attractive, Philistia," he told her. "I hate my name, you see. Or have, before hearing it on your lips. But you must be careful of what you say to me, just as I told you, for I do find you a charming lady, and I'm sure you wouldn't wish to excite false hopes in me."

"Oh, my lord. Morcar. I'll be most careful, I promise."

"If you believe your aunt will not mind, then, would you be willing to spend the remainder of the day in my company? I would enjoy showing you some of the sights of London, and then we shall go driving in the park. Perhaps we might even enjoy a picnic. I know a pleasant spot and my cook can prepare something for us quickly. We'll be accompanied by my servants and your maid at all times, so there will be no chance of whispers. And I'll return you to your family in good time to make ready for any outings you intend for the evening."

"It sounds wonderful," she breathed, her eyes lighting with pleasure. "I should love it above all things, Morcar."

He squeezed her hand once more. Normally he would find such an outing with a mere mortal female deadly dull, but the prospect of spending just such a day with Philistia Tamony actually seemed pleasant.

"I'll send a note to your town house, then," he said, "and let them know where you'll be. Why don't you sit and make yourself comfortable while I have Stoton bring us some tea? I'll show you my library and recommend some excellent books for your pleasure while we wait for Cook to prepare our lunch."

Chapter 18

"Will you please relax?" Desdemona Seymour insisted. "You're behaving as though you've never been in an unusual dwelling before now."

Sarah glanced about the room they'd been brought to. It was painted in shades of black and red and had been hung with heavy black curtains that kept out all light. Dimly lit lamps provided a small measure of light but cast the parlor in a gloomy yellow glow. And the furniture—it was large and excessively ornate, as if it belonged in a cathedral rather than a home. The chair Sarah sat in, with its high back and vivid red cushions, put her in mind of a throne— yet it was among the smallest seats in the room. She could understand why Rhys was so relieved when the servant who'd admitted herself and Desdemona Seymour refused to let "another mere mortal" enter.

"I apologize," Sarah murmured. "It's just so dark. Like a dungeon, or the deepest recesses of a pyramid."

Desdemona was reclining comfortably on a black velvet settee, her feet resting on an ornately tasseled pillow, indifferently amusing herself by floating little flames from her hand into the air and arranging them in various patterns. She looked as innocent as a child, trying to stave off boredom. Sarah knew better than to believe such outward appearances.

She'd never before been afraid of magic mortals. Indeed, she usually found them far more fascinating than fearsome. Desdemona Seymour was the first to give her pause.

She was a powerful sorceress—Sarah had felt that the moment they'd arrived at the woman's home—and one born from within the dark Families. That she had married into the Seymours clearly meant little in altering her personality. Her advanced pregnancy had made her fitful and short-tempered, with the result that her scarcely contained emotions threatened to come flying out at any and every moment.

Like the rest of her kind, Desdemona Seymour was an extraordinary beauty, with raven black hair and violet eyes. She put Sarah in mind of the Earl of Llew's dark beauty, save that Desdemona was tiny and birdlike in form, her daintiness much at odds with her enormous belly.

"My child is a daughter," Desdemona said suddenly, as if divining Sarah's thoughts. "Adona is her name." She smiled in a manner that softened her starkly beautiful features. "She will be a powerful sorceress, like her mother, and very wise, like her father. It has been prophesied."

"I'm so glad for you," Sarah murmured, feeling an unbidden pang of jealousy. She would likely never know what it was to carry a child. "You must be filled with anticipation."

"More than I thought I would be," Desdemona confessed. "I didn't want children before I knew Dyfed, but the thought of carrying his daughter fills me with great pleasure. You've not met him and so cannot know why. I believe you'll have the chance at the Herold ball, if Malachi brings him back before then."

"I look forward to meeting him," Sarah replied sincerely. She shivered and looked about the room once more. It was oppressively chilling. "Why would anyone wish to live in such a place?" she asked.

"Serafina's kind thrives in darkness," Desdemona said.

"She's a creature of the night. She'll go out in daylight if she must—to meet your brother, as an example. But she and her servants usually avoid it at all costs. The sun hurts their eyes and burns their skin."

"Her servants," Sarah murmured with a shiver. "They're all so odd. Yet she manages to keep them from Society's eyes."

"Well, she has to, doesn't she?" Desdemona said, beginning to sound not only bored but also weary. "They'd all be murdered, otherwise. And what an alarm it would cause among mere mortals. Malachi would be hard-pressed to contain it, even with magic."

Sarah knew that Desdemona spoke the truth. Serafina Daray's servants were frightening, misshapen creatures that the mere mortal world would never understand. Sarah had been more than a little thankful to have a magic mortal of Desdemona's powers at her side, for the creatures not only had allowed them entrance but had also bowed in marked deference to the presence of a dark and powerful sorceress.

"But why does she keep them? Why doesn't she have more normal servants? Some from among her own kind?"

Desdemona laughed, a malevolent sound that raised the hairs on Sarah's arms.

"These *are* Serafina's kind, my dear Miss Tamony. Don't you know about the Darays and what they are?"

"Lord Graymar explained that they'd been created as servants for magic mortals. That's all I know."

Desdemona left off toying with the flames above and turned to look at Sarah. "That's only part of the truth," Desdemona said. "I suppose Malachi didn't want you knowing. Mere mortals can be so foolish about such things."

"What do you mean?"

"The One who created all made many different beings, some greater than others, some lower. Our kind—magic and mortal—are called *superum*. Superior, do you understand? There are others made as we are—elves, as an example—with whom we can mix our blood. We are high beings, though not so high as others. And then there were those created lesser. Serafina's kind were among these, called *animantis.* They are creaturely, and made to serve the *superum.*"

"Animantis?" Sarah repeated. "It sounds similar to 'animal,' but surely that can't be what it means." It was impossible.

Desdemona sighed. "This is why Malachi didn't tell you. The sensibilities of mere mortals are far too delicate."

"Sweet merciful day," Sarah murmured, standing as the truth of what Desdemona said struck her. "She's not even human and she's been . . . *with my brother?*"

"She is not *fully* human," Desdemona corrected. "But she is partly so. The Darays mixed their blood with enough magic mortals to inherit some of their features. Serafina would look far more like her servants, otherwise."

"God's mercy," Sarah said with dismay, little mollified by this. "If she's not fully human, is she an animal, then?"

"Not as you think of animals," Desdemona said reassuringly. "She is creaturely, as I told you. And the Darays are really quite attractive among those who are *animantis.* Similar to faeries, but with sharper teeth. I understand they once had tails, hundreds of years ago, before they mixed with *superum,* and long ears and noses that—where the devil are you going?"

Sarah had started for the door. "I have to find Julius and get him out of here. *Now.*"

"I'd stop if I were you," Desdemona advised, still reclining comfortably on the settee.

"Why should I?" Sarah shot back.

"Because the door is about to open."

And it did, just as Sarah reached for the knob. Stepping back, she was greeted by the sight of a diminutive, delicate and beautiful young woman, or creature, as Sarah wasn't entirely sure what Serafina Daray was, garbed in nothing more than a thin silk robe, whose flowing blond curls fell to her hips. She was exquisite in every feature, and if not for the fact that her large blue eyes were filled with fury she would have even seemed childlike. Sarah had once owned a porcelain doll with precisely the same tiny pink rosebud mouth and glowing white skin.

"What do you mean by coming here?" Serafina demanded, pushing past Sarah as if she were inconsequential and marching toward Desdemona. "How dare you come into my dwelling without invitation? I don't *want* you here. I won't *have* you here."

Desdemona laughed again, that same frightening sound, and looked at Serafina with disdain. "You forget yourself, Serafina. You may be able to insult me among mere mortals, but you don't possess the power to bid me stay or go. I am your better, and always will be."

"I am an extraordinary sorceress, just as you are," Serafina said hotly, stamping one foot. "I don't have to tolerate you intruding upon my private refuge."

"You might be able to bid me leave," Desdemona admitted, "if you had only me to deal with. But the child within me is a powerful sorceress as well, and you cannot match our magic combined. You'd do far better to attend to the matter before us and give me every reason to leave, for I dislike being in this slovenly pit far more than you dislike having me here."

"What is it then?"

Desdemona looked beyond Serafina to where Sarah yet stood. "I don't believe you've had the pleasure of meeting Miss Sarah Tamony yet. She wants her brother back."

Serafina whirled about, pinning Sarah with an angry glare. "You brought a mere mortal here?" she cried. "You'd force me to erase the memory of the Dewin Mawr's woman?"

"Miss Daray," Sarah said calmly. "I realize you're displeased by our coming, but there's no need to speak of altering memories. I know that you possess magic and that you've used it on my brother. I only wish to take him home."

"You cannot touch Miss Tamony with magic," Desdemona said. "She's protected from all of us, even Malachi."

Serafina's eyes narrowed until her delicate features took on an ugly mien. "He's given her a talisman to protect her," she said. "I can feel its power. He's made the woman who would destroy us with her words invulnerable. That is how your lauded Dewin Mawr protects those who give him their allegiance."

"I haven't come to debate you about my work, Miss Daray," Sarah said impatiently. "And you may be quite certain that I no longer have any intention of bothering you with my requests for an interview. I only wish to remove my brother from the premises and take him home. Nothing more."

Serafina's demeanor changed quickly. Mastering her fury, she calmed into a scornful satisfaction. Wrapping her robe more carefully about her slender waist, she said, "I've not finished with him yet. There's still a great deal of pleasure I can have of him before he's spent." She smiled at Sarah's heated blush. "You should be grateful that I mean to send him home each night, else your parents might begin to become suspicious."

"You can have no notion of how quiet a life my brother has led if you believe his coming home late night after night won't excite my parents' concern," Sarah told her. "Tell me plainly what you want in return for his freedom."

"Surely you already know, Miss Tamony."

"I do," Sarah replied, forcing her voice to remain steady. "And surely you know that the *cythraul* is beyond my power to give you."

"I don't need anyone to procure the demon," Serafina said scornfully. "I intend to do that myself. But I want the clues the Guardians have given to the Dewin Mawr. Give me your journal and if it proves useful I'll be far more amenable to the idea of setting Julius free."

"I'd do anything for my brother," Sarah said honestly, "but you must release him first, wholly and completely. Then the journal will be yours. I swear it upon my life."

Serafina dismissed Sarah with a wave of her hand. "I'm not such a fool as to believe anything that a mere mortal says. You'd give me blank paper as soon as part with the real thing."

"I'll not," Sarah vowed.

Serafina looked at her with disgust. "As long as I have Julius, I hold the upper hand, and I'll not part with him save for something of equal value. When you're ready to give me the journal, Miss Tamony, I'll be willing to see you again. Until that time, don't bother me." She began to stride toward the door. "And I wouldn't give Julius any more of Malachi's potions," she advised as she passed Sarah. "I've instructed him to eat and drink nothing unless he's in company with me. You needn't worry that he'll waste away, for I'll take very good care of him." To Desdemona she said, in a particularly nasty tone, "Don't invade my private refuge again, or it will be war between us."

Smiling, Desdemona rose to her feet with a grace and ease that belied her pregnancy. She seemed to be far taller of a sudden, and the power that emanated from her was so fierce it made Sarah's head hurt.

"We *are* at war, Serafina," Desdemona said, her smile as wicked and frightening a thing as Sarah had ever seen. "And have been from the day you chose to insult my unborn child. You'll soon learn that there's little mercy to be found among the Caslins, regardless how we marry."

Serafina's face pinked beneath the dim light, and her mouth thinned. She began to appear taller, too.

"When I've gained the power of the *cythraul*," she vowed in a low voice, moving back toward the center of the room, "you'll be the first one to die. I swear it before the Guardians."

Desdemona's smile didn't change in the least. Her eyes narrowed.

"And I shall take pleasure in watching you suffer beneath my hands," she said. "Once my daughter has been born I shall be free to—"

Sarah knew from her research that when two magic

mortals began threatening each other, it could take a great deal of time before they had at last vented their mutual wrath. She didn't have time to waste on such nonsense. Moving to the door before either of the sorceresses could react, Sarah walked out of the room and hurried down the hall to the foot of the stairs.

"Julius!" she shouted as loudly as she could, striding quickly. *"Julius!"*

Two of Serafina Daray's odd-looking servants appeared out of thin air—literally—and said, "May we help you, miss?"

"Stop her!" Serafina screeched behind them. "Stop her!"

The servants moved to do their mistress's bidding, but as they attempted to wrap their clawed hands about Sarah's arms they were somehow repelled. They fell back as if she'd struck them, pressing their hands together in pain and staring at Sarah with shock. She pushed past them and started up the stairs.

"Julius!" she shouted once more, and heard a door opening somewhere on the landing.

"Damn you!" Serafina cried furiously.

"Sarah, come back!" Desdemona shouted with equal wrath.

Sarah kept climbing. She felt little shocks striking the length of her back, as if someone was slapping her bare skin, and knew that Serafina Daray was sending spells at her. She had expected to be felled by the woman's magic almost at once, but it was as Desdemona had said: Sarah was protected from magic.

"Julius Tamony!" she called out, racing quickly now. "Julius!" Breathless, she reached the landing and looked about. Should she go higher, to the next floor?

"Sarah."

Whirling about, she saw him, standing completely naked at the open doorway of what must have been Serafina's bedroom.

"My God," Sarah said before she could think not to. She'd seen her brother bereft of clothes when he was a boy, but certainly not since either one of them had passed childhood. He would be embarrassed beyond all measure when he at last came to his senses. If he remembered anything at all, which she fervently hoped he didn't. "Julius," she said, moving toward him with her hands held out. "Yes, it's me, dear. You know me?"

His gaze was confused and unfocused, but he held a hand out to meet her own and said, slowly, "I know you, Sarah."

"Thank heaven," she murmured. Her fingers wrapped about his own, finding them cold as ice. "Julius, you must—"

"Julius!" Serafina Daray had gained the landing as well. Julius stiffened at the sound of her voice, and his eyes clouded. "Strike her, Julius," Serafina demanded. *"Punish her."*

"Julius, no," Sarah said fervently. "It's me, Julius. It's Sarah. Please, listen to me—"

His expression remained passive, but he pulled free and lifted his fisted hand high. Sarah tried to step away but knew she'd never move quickly enough to avoid the punishing blow.

"Cesso!"

Desdemona's raven head appeared at the top of the stairs, one hand holding her belly as if to protect it, the other lifted toward Julius, who had frozen at the fierce command.

Serafina emitted a wrathful high-pitched sound that made the dwelling, and everything in it, shake, just as Desdemona's had done earlier.

"You cannot overcome my powers," Desdemona shouted over the noise. "Not while the child is within me. Send him away and we'll leave you in peace." She halted the spell of constraint. Julius's fist relaxed and fell to his side.

Serafina released a harsh breath; the house still trembled from her ill-contained fury.

"Go into the room and await me, Julius," she commanded.

He immediately obeyed, turning and walking back into the room. Sarah watched him go in silence.

"Leave," Serafina demanded. *"Now."*

Sarah moved toward the stairs in defeat. She didn't look at Serafina as she passed her.

Rhys hurried out of the carriage the moment the door to the Daray dwelling was firmly closed behind them. Sarah blinked up into the bright afternoon sky, thankful for the light of the sun after being in such a tomblike enclosure. Desdemona released a harsh breath and whirled about, grasping Sarah by the arms and, despite being so much shorter, giving her a furious shake.

"Don't *ever* do such a thing again," Desdemona said. "If Malachi hears of it, and he *will* hear of it, for he knows everything that occurs among our kind, he'll kill me. Directly after he's killed you, you *foolish* mortal. It's all well and good for one of my power to challenge a sorceress like Serafina Daray, but you're powerless, Sarah. It scarce matters that you've been protected from her magic. She has innumerable ways to harm you, and one of our kind won't always be about to save you."

"God help us," Rhys said, looking from one woman to the other. "Never tell me—Miss Tamony, you promised me quite faithfully that you'd do nothing dangerous if I made it possible for you to gain entry into Miss Daray's dwelling."

"I'm sorry," Sarah said, wincing as Desdemona's sharp fingernails dug painfully into her flesh. "But I had to make an attempt at speaking to Julius, didn't I? And did you see?" she added more hopefully. "He knew me for a moment. He said my name, and responded to my question."

"Yes, that's wonderful," Desdemona said drily, dragging Sarah in the direction of the carriage. "It will be a memory to cheer you when Serafina kills one or both of you as a measure of repayment. Come, Sarah. I'm taking you to your home, where you are to remain until Malachi returns. After that, you're his problem. Poor man."

Chapter 19

Sarah thought that she'd never be able to sleep after such a distressing afternoon, but she barely managed to get to her room and sit upon her bed before an overpowering exhaustion overtook her. She got her shoes and spectacles off and lay down, telling herself that she would only rest for an hour. It was much later, when she heard her mother's gentle voice, that Sarah came to her senses again, and then unwillingly.

"Are you unwell, Sarah?" Lady Tamony asked, setting a cool hand on Sarah's forehead. "You do feel rather warm. Perhaps you're suffering from whatever ailed Julius yesterday."

"I'm fine," Sarah murmured, and sleepily struggled to sit up. "Have I missed tea? Why is it so dark?"

"Because it's well past dinner, my love," her mother said.

"But surely not. I can't have slept that long."

"But you did, dear. Come." Lady Tamony gently tugged her upward. "Stand up a moment and Irene and I will get you ready for bed. I've brought you something to eat."

Sarah protested that she didn't need to go to bed so

early, that she was perfectly capable of attending the poetry recital that they had been promised for at Lady Russell's.

"We've decided against going out tonight," Sarah's mother informed her as she pulled a fresh nightgown out of a nearby drawer. "I sent Lady Russell our apologies. Julius came home far too late to make himself ready, and—"

"Julius!" Sarah exclaimed, stepping out of her dress so that Irene could take it away. "He came home?"

Her mother looked at her curiously. "Of course. Why shouldn't he?"

Sarah blinked at her. Weariness had clearly stolen away all her senses. "Yes," she replied stupidly. "Yes, certainly. I was only concerned because he was so overtired yesterday. Is he well? Did he eat anything?"

"He retired to his room shortly after coming home," her mother said, her tone and expression slightly suspicious. "And begged leave to excuse himself from any further activities this evening, or from having dinner. I took him a tray before coming to you, but he assured me he wasn't hungry."

"What was he doing?" Sarah asked, lowering her head so that the remainder of her undergarments could be removed.

"Reading," her mother replied, helping Sarah into the nightgown. "He still seems somewhat weary from whatever he suffered yesterday. He didn't wish me to remain long."

"He'll likely sleep soon," Sarah murmured, standing still as her mother dealt with the gown's tiny buttons.

"Yes, I think that's so," Lady Tamony agreed. "Irene, you may go. I'll help my daughter finish readying for bed."

The maid gathered up Sarah's garments for pressing and left the room, shutting the door behind her.

"Sit and eat, Sarah," Lady Tamony said, indicating the writing desk where the tray was set. "I'll brush your hair."

Sarah did as her mother bade, though she scarce tasted the food. Just as she took a bite of toast she felt the touch of her mother's hands on her hair, gently pulling out the several pins.

"What's been going on these past several days, Sarah?" Lady Tamony asked. "It's no use telling me there's nothing, for I'm your mother as well as Julius's. I know something very unusual has been taking place."

Sarah set the piece of toast aside. "You're right, of course," she said, glancing at her mother. "Something has been happening. Something that has to do with the supernatural."

"I suspected as much," her mother said, releasing long ribbons of hair to fall loose about Sarah's shoulders. "And Lord Graymar is involved as well, is he not? Eat, dear," she added as Sarah looked at her again. "The soup has already cooled."

Sarah turned back to the tray and picked up her spoon. "How did you guess about Lord Graymar?" she asked.

"I'm not sure," Lady Tamony replied, pulling a brush with care through Sarah's unruly locks. "I know you wished to interview him for your book because of his family's history. Lord Llew is one of them, too, isn't he?"

"Mama, I scarce know what to say. Lord Graymar said you might be one of those who are sympathetic to his kind, and I believe he must be right."

Lady Tamony chuckled. "I don't know about being sympathetic. I would rather call it suspicious. But I quite approve of Lord Graymar, even if he does possess supernatural talents. He's clearly set his heart upon you and—"

"Mama! He hasn't done any such thing. Good heavens."

Lady Tamony smiled serenely and began to portion Sarah's hair into sections. "Your father and I have decided to consider him seriously if he makes you an offer. If you believe you would like being married to him, of course, although from what I've seen, when the two of you are together that's a question already answered. Sit still, dear, or I'll have to start all over again." She braided Sarah's hair with quick, deft movements.

Sarah didn't need a mirror to know how red her face was. She was trying to think of what to say when her mother went on.

"I wish I could say the same for the Earl of Llew, but I cannot. There's something in the man that I can't quite trust. Unfortunately, Philistia's fallen in love with him."

"Philistia!" Sarah repeated, shocked. "But she can't have. She only just met the man yesterday. Surely that's not long enough for any but the silliest girl to become infatuated."

"I confess the thought distresses me somewhat," Lady Tamony said, reaching for a bit of ribbon that she'd set on the table and tying the end of Sarah's thick braid. "But she came across him today while she was out, and Lord Llew gallantly offered to spend the remainder of the afternoon showing her some of London's more popular attractions. He brought her home before tea and—well, what could I do when Philistia looked at me in such a pleading manner? I invited him to join us again."

"I knew she'd gone out with only a maid, but could scarce believe it," Sarah said. "She's always been far too shy to go anywhere without one of us along."

"Yes, she has. Which leaves us to conclude that she went out with the hope of meeting Lord Llew. I can only pray that he had nothing to do with the matter, and has only been playing the gentleman in his attentions to Philla. There." She patted the braid with satisfaction. "Have you finished, darling? Wash your face and teeth and then you must get directly back into bed."

When Sarah had washed and slipped beneath the covers once more, her mother sat on the bed and gazed at her.

"Now, Sarah. What's going on? I know you don't wish to tell me, but it would be better for me to know in case your father becomes suspicious."

Sarah could see the wisdom of that. Of the two, her mother was by far the more unflappable.

"If I tell you, Mama, will you promise to trust me—and Lord Graymar—to make everything right? Will you give me your vow to not interfere or draw attention to His Lordship's powers?"

Lady Tamony reached out both hands to smooth them over the covers, tucking Sarah in more warmly.

"Yes, dear. I give you both my promise and my vow."

"All right, then," Sarah said, and began to tell her mother everything that had happened, starting with a confession about sneaking out of the inn near Glain Tarran so many weeks earlier.

An hour passed before Sarah's mother left the room, dousing the few candles and turning down the lamps. Sarah hadn't thought she'd fall asleep again as quickly, but a full belly and a clear conscience drew her downward into slumber once more.

She was wakened by the sound of a door opening.

Her sleep-addled brain said it was merely one of the maids, come to put her clothes away or check the fire in the grate. But as she came more fully awake she realized that the hour was far too late for the servants to be up and about. Everyone in the house would be asleep. Pushing up to peer into the darkened room, she murmured, "Mama?"

"It's me, Sarah," came Julius's voice. "Go back to sleep."

A moment passed as surprise rolled over her, followed by a shocking sense of realization. He was in her closet.

"Sweet merciful day." She tossed the covers aside and hurried across the room. "Julius, *stop*."

He ignored her, even when she moved to stand behind him.

"Where is it?" he asked, throwing aside the purse he'd been searching. "You always keep it here."

"My journal is hidden," she said angrily. "You'll never find it. Go back to bed."

He whirled about, his expression fixed. He was dressed in a shirt and trousers, as if he meant to go out.

"Give me the journal," he said, advancing upon her. "We must be quiet. I cannot wake the house."

"Oh, she thought of that, did she?" Sarah asked mockingly. "I'm glad to know Miss Daray didn't want you to be caught stealing. That would have been difficult to explain away."

"Give me the journal," he repeated.

"No." Sarah backed away. "Tell your mistress she can

have it if she releases you. Now go away or I'll scream for Papa."

"Give me the journal, Sarah, or I must force it from you."

He would do that, she knew. She'd seen earlier that he was willing to do what Serafina Daray had commanded.

"I'll make an exchange," Sarah countered. Moving around him to the closet again, she searched for the reticule she'd had earlier in the day, squinting in the dim light to see its contents. At last she drew out the vial that Rhys had given her.

She turned back to Julius. "I'll give you the journal if you'll drink some of this." She held out the vial.

He shook his head. "I cannot eat or drink anything save what my mistress gives me."

"But your mistress also commands that you bring her the journal," Sarah countered. "This is the only way you'll be able to have it, for I will not give it to you otherwise."

Julius advanced on her so quickly and unexpectedly that Sarah wasn't able to move back. By the time she realized his intent, he had her about the neck.

"We must be quiet, and so I cannot let you speak or scream. But you must give me the journal. *Now.*"

Sarah shook her head and, dropping the vial, tried to pull his hands away.

Julius released her as quickly as he'd set upon her, but Sarah's relief was short-lived. Grasping her by the back of the neck, he pulled her close, then brought the flat of his other hand sharply across her face with punishing force. The sound of the slap resounded throughout the room, but Sarah's following cry was stopped by that same hand closing over her mouth.

Tears filled Sarah's eyes, but Julius paid them no mind.

"Will you give me the journal?" he murmured.

She shook her head, clawing frantically to gain release. Julius was blind to her struggles. He lifted his hand and brought it down again, slapping Sarah so hard that flashes of light filled her eyes. She drew in a gasping breath just before the hand covered her mouth, muffling her sobs.

"Will you give me the journal, Sarah?"

She couldn't look into his beloved face, so void of emotion as it was. The world began to fade, along with her strength. Julius seemed to divine how near she was to fainting and lowered her to the floor.

"Give me the journal and I'll leave you in peace. I cannot go without it."

Streams of tears stung the sides of her face. Thoughts whirled through her mind—of Malachi, of how she could escape her brother's superior strength, of how deeply distressed her family would be if they should ever discover what was taking place. If only she could get him to let her go for a few moments . . . just long enough to clear her head . . .

"Sarah?" He gave her a shake. She marveled at how his voice remained so calm and controlled. Even his breathing was normal. "I'll strike you again if I must."

She wasn't going to be able to withstand many more blows, she knew. She had to find a way to escape him, no matter if it meant waking her family and exposing all of them to Julius's condition. He raised his hand to strike her again and Sarah balled up a fist. It would be difficult, but she had every intention of breaking her handsome brother's perfect nose.

Before either of them could send their fists flying, a flash of light illuminated the room, accompanied by a furious, unearthly roar. Sarah was stunned and blinded, yet the only emotion she felt was intense relief.

Julius was slower to react, stupefied as he was by the sudden appearance of such tremendous power. He tried to turn, but Lord Graymar moved far too quickly, grasping Julius by the front of his shirt and lifting him away from Sarah and into the air as if her brother weighed nothing. With a wrathful growl Lord Graymar shook his captive, only stopping for a brief moment when he heard shouts coming down the hallway. Turning his head toward the imminent arrival of the remaining Tamony clan and all their servants, Lord Graymar shouted, "Stop!" and they did. His Lordship went back to shaking Julius.

With an effort, Sarah pushed herself up, pleading, "Don't hurt him! He didn't know what he was doing! Please, my lord."

Uttering a string of oaths, Lord Graymar lowered Julius, who was weakly struggling, to Sarah's bed and held him there.

"The vial!" Lord Graymar shouted. "Do you have it?"

Blindly Sarah pressed to her knees and groped about the floor. "Here it is!" Her fingers closed about the small glass object. Unsteadily she rose to her feet and held it toward him.

Holding Julius with one hand, Lord Graymar opened the other, and the vial flew out of her grasp. Not looking away from the bed, he caught it and, with a flick of his thumb, unstopped it.

"A few drops will take care of him."

"He won't drink it," Sarah told him. "She's commanded him to take nothing from anyone but her, neither food nor drink."

"He's not going to have a choice," Lord Graymar said. Forcing her brother's mouth open with one hand, Lord Graymar poured the potion in with the other, then sent the tiny vial floating safely away in the air. He set his hand over Julius's mouth and pushed. The younger man sputtered and gagged but wasn't able to spit the potion out. Almost at once he began to calm and within the space of a minute had fallen fast asleep.

Sarah stood beside the bed, watching, until Lord Graymar slowly began to withdraw. Julius didn't move.

"He'll sleep until morning," His Lordship said, releasing a taut breath. "Perhaps to the afternoon."

"He didn't know what he was doing," Sarah whispered, trying not to weep. She was so happy to see the earl, and not merely because he had come to her rescue. "He wasn't Julius."

"No, he wasn't," His Lordship said, not looking at her. She heard his voice shaking. "And when the enchantment is broken, he'll not remember what he did to you."

"I'm glad," she murmured, then covered her aching face with both hands and began to cry.

Lord Graymar pulled her into his embrace. "Sarah," he said softly, pressing his cheek against the top of her head. "Forgive me for leaving you so vulnerable to such an attack. I protected the dwelling from magic mortals, but I never thought she might use Julius to harm you."

"She just wanted the journal. I don't think she meant for him to hurt me."

"Didn't she?" He took her chin in his hand to lift her tearstained face. He kissed her cheeks and eyes, then her lips, and murmured, "Wait here."

She regretted the loss of his warmth and strength when he walked away. In the hallway she heard Lord Graymar instructing those frozen there to forget all that had occurred from the moment they'd awakened and to return to their beds and sleep until he told them to wake. Then he came back to Sarah.

"Your family and the servants will sleep peacefully and safely until we've returned," he said.

"Returned?" she repeated. "Where are we going?"

He opened his heavy cloak and folded her within.

"To Mervaille."

Chapter 20

*H*e wasn't able to make his mind work properly. Or force his body to stop trembling. Sarah clung to him, her face pressed into his chest, shaking only a little more than he was.

God help him. He'd nearly killed Julius. It hadn't made any difference that the younger man was suffering beneath a powerful curse or that, in his right senses, Julius would cut off both hands before harming his beloved sister. Malachi had arrived to find Sarah weeping, in terrible pain, and he'd wanted to commit murder. If Sarah hadn't stopped him, he might well have done it.

"No one will harm you again," he said, moving his hands to press her closer. "Ever. I swear it before the Guardians."

"No, don't," she said in a small voice. "Don't make such a foolish vow. I won't let you."

"Sarah." It was the only word that escaped his lips before he had to stop speaking altogether.

"Where are we, my lord?"

"In my bedchamber." Lifting a hand, he set the fire in the grate alight and several candles in the room aflame.

She tried to look about, but he stopped her.

"Your face is badly bruised. And swollen." The fact of it filled him with equal measures of sorrow and rage. "Your—" He stopped to draw in a steadying breath. "One of your eyes is nearly shut because of it, Sarah. Let me heal you."

"I thought my vision was worse than usual," she said shakily, her attempt at humor only causing his fury to tighten.

He laid his hands lightly on her face, stroking and murmuring, drawing the heat and swelling out through his fingertips, letting them dissolve into nothingness in the air. Then he tilted her face upward, bending to press his mouth against the side of her face that Julius had struck, moving his lips over the skin until the stinging dulled completely.

He would have pulled back then, but her hands came up to grip the collar of his shirt and hold him still. Her mouth sought his, kissing him with the same longing that had lived in him since they'd parted from each other the night before.

It hadn't been his intention to seduce her with such immediacy during their first joining; in fact, quite the opposite. Malachi had envisioned a slow and thorough seduction, with food and wine and the sensual dance of the wit they so often engaged in. But she needed him now, not from physical desire or the want of pleasure but for surcease and healing.

"My lord," she gasped, her cold hands shaking as they pressed against his face.

"Yes, love," he said gently, taking her hands in his own to warm them. "I know what it is you crave. I can give you peace."

With a swift movement he undid the clasp of his cloak, letting it fall to the floor, then bent and picked her up into his arms, carrying her to the bed. It was an enormous piece of furniture and he rose up into the air to bring them both down into the middle of it. Settling Sarah's head upon the pillow, he kissed her deeply, willing her to calm.

But she was far too unsettled to let him be slow. Her slender body shook and her fingers dug into his arms.

"Please," she begged. "Please, my lord. I'm so cold."

"I'll warm you, sweetheart." Malachi reached down to unbutton his trousers, releasing his hardened member. Then he slid his fingers up along her thigh, lifting the skirt of her nightgown until he could touch her gently. She arched against him, her breathing heightened; her nails dug into him more fervently. Malachi kissed her. "Let me make you ready, love."

She shook her head. "Now," she said insistently. *"Now."*

He did as she asked. Lifting himself over her, he placed himself at the entrance of her and pushed forward. There was a brief resistance and then, with a gasp from Sarah, he pressed deeply in.

"Oh," she said, her voice filled with relief. "My lord."

It was a joining like none he'd before known. Not simply because he loved her, but because everything within her reached out to him as no other woman had done. As he began to move, she made the sweetest sound his ears had ever heard and, shutting her eyes, relaxed at last and opened to him completely.

"Sarah," he murmured. "I love you."

She smiled and opened her eyes. The Sarah who captivated all his senses was there once again, gazing back at him. All of the fear was gone, all of the hurt.

"It's like flying," she whispered, and her hands reached up to grip his shoulders. "Just as if we were flying again."

"Yes," he said against her lips as the rhythm of his body grew quicker. "Let me take you flying, Sarah. Like this. Hold on to me, and I'll take you into the heavens."

She dozed afterward, but only briefly. Malachi rose and finished undressing, then filled a nearby basin with water from a pitcher. Lifting Sarah's head from the pillows, he gently undressed her, tossing her nightgown aside, then washed the blood from between her thighs and afterward slipped her beneath the warmth of the sheets and covers. After cleaning himself he joined her there, drawing her warm, sleepy body into his arms.

"Thank you," she said, and he could feel her smile against his chest.

"I don't think there's much to be grateful for just yet," he said, kissing the top of her head. "That was not at all what I had planned. I'm not very pleased with myself."

She uttered a low laugh. "I confess I have little experience of such matters, my lord, but I thought it quite delightful. Far more than I had thought it would be."

"You have much to learn," he said. "And I shall make certain that you do. Then we'll revisit this conversation and see whether you've changed your mind."

Her hand slid up to touch his chin. "You mustn't say such a thing. I shall always cherish what you did for me. Thank you."

"You're welcome," he said. "I suppose we'll always be able to say that it was, at the very least, memorable."

"I'll never forget it." Her fingers stroked over his face, from his temple down his cheek, touching the stubble there. "Did all go well in Scotland?" she asked. "Were you able to make things right between the young man and his intended's family?"

"I don't know yet," he replied, pushing a few stray strands of hair from her face. "I left without so much as a word when I sensed you were in danger. I have no doubt that my cousins Niclas and Dyfed are wondering when I'll return."

She suddenly sat up, gazing down at him with dismay.

"Sweet merciful day. You left them without an explanation? Surely you must return at once, my lord. Your relatives will be lost without your guidance, and their wives want them home."

"Desdemona's filled your ears with her complaints, I see," he said. "No, don't frown at me, love. Surely you realized I'd know about your visit to Serafina."

"I assumed you'd find out," she confessed. "I had hoped to have a day or so to compose an explanation."

"Why?" he asked with genuine amusement, reaching to pull forward her thick braid. Untying the ribbon, he began to unravel her hair. "It's not in your nature to desert anyone you love, and I know how bold you are to enter forbidden domains."

"Then you're not angry with me, my lord? Or with Rhys for taking me? I made him do so, you know. He didn't wish to."

"I won't deny that I'm displeased," he said, his attention given to the rapidly diminishing braid. "I knew Serafina could not harm you through magic, but I wasn't glad when I realized you meant to so willingly place yourself in danger, or that my manservant agreed to aid you in the task. Desdemona, fortunately, had the presence of mind to go with you. I shall send her something pretty, and expensive, to render my thanks."

"You make it sound as if you knew the moment I went to Miss Daray's dwelling," she said suspiciously. "But that can't be."

"Of course it can," he said, spreading her unbound hair over her shoulder and arms, captivated by the glints of gold that shimmered in the firelight. "We are *unoliaeth*, Sarah. I shall always know what you are doing, whether you are at peace or not, regardless the physical distance between us."

She gazed at him in silence, her green eyes pensive. Malachi smiled with all the charm he possessed. He shouldn't have mentioned the *unoliaeth*. It was too soon. She hadn't felt the power of it yet, but she would, in time. It was inevitable.

"My lord," she began, and he could tell by her tone that she was about to say something foolish. Something about their union not being a permanent one. He expected it but wasn't in the mood to have the conversation just now. Not tonight.

Reaching up to cup her neck, he silenced her with a long, gentle kiss. Then he lay down once more and settled her comfortably in the crook of his arm.

"I wish you'd call me by my Christian name," he said. "Especially as we've become lovers."

"Have we?" she asked. "Become lovers?"

"Yes, sweet," he assured her. "I shall prove it to you again in a few moments, after you've had a chance to rest."

"Indeed, my lord?"

"Indeed, Sarah. And you must call me Malachi when I do, for although a man does enjoy feeling lordly while making love to a woman, I would far rather hear my name upon your lips. You may have noticed that I've been calling you by yours."

"I did," she remarked drily. "But I supposed that, being so great a nobleman, you might be in the habit of such things."

He laughed softly. "We've already disposed of the notion that I'm God, sweet. Perhaps we should have done with the idea that I'm the king."

"You're more powerful than he is," she said. "You're the Dewin Mawr. I'm a mere mortal, and not even highly born."

Malachi sighed and ran a lazy hand caressingly down the curve of her back. "Believe me, please, that neither my status as a nobleman nor as a sorcerer has any importance at all in my relationship with you. As it happens, I call you by your Christian name because my kind are not in the habit of using titles among ourselves, and as I am constantly obliged to do so with mere mortals, I find it wearisome to do with those whom I spend a great deal of time. As we are now spending much time together, Sarah, calling you Miss Tamony is most tiresome."

One of her fingers began to draw a lazy pattern on his chest. "You must take care to do so in public, my lord, lest the rumors about us begin to take on a completely different mien."

"I know how to behave when others are watching. Far more than you mere mortals do."

"I expect that's so, my lord," she admitted.

"Malachi," he prompted.

"Malachi," she repeated obediently. "I really mustn't keep you from returning to Scotland. I'm certain they need you, and now that Julius is asleep, I can—"

"It is night," he interrupted, "and my cousins need sleep, just as you and I do. Nothing more can be accomplished until tomorrow, when I shall return and face the trouble my MacQueen cousins have wrought. This isn't the first time one of the sons has lured a girl from the bosom of her naysaying family."

"I know," she said, her green eyes lighting with a familiar fire. "Their stories should make wonderful reading. I intend to write of Calum MacQueen in my next book, and of how he stole Aileen Drummann for a friend who was sick with love for her. Except that Calum decided to keep her for himself, though she wanted none of him, for she thought him a devil and a scoundrel and hadn't any use for his magic, especially when he used it to confound her father and his men when they came in search of—"

Malachi groaned and, grasping Sarah by the waist, rolled her over onto her back.

"My sweet love," he murmured, leaning over her. "Let's not speak of my relatives or your writing just now. We've but a few precious hours together. The last thing I wish to do is spend them talking of my ill-behaved family, past or present."

She slid her hands along his arms, up to his shoulders.

"As you wish, Malachi. But you shall have to show me what to do. I want to please you as well as your mistresses have."

"You please me far more than any of them ever could," he murmured, "and always will. But I shall be glad to be your teacher in such matters."

"Not half so happy, I think, as I am to be your pupil. I've been told," she said with a naughty smile, "that I'm quite apt."

He laughed. "I have no doubt of that, love. Before we've done I imagine you'll be teaching me."

Having enjoyed so much sleep the day before, Sarah woke long before Malachi did. She spent several moments gazing at him and pondering the significance of what had transpired. At the advanced age of twenty-six she, Sarah Tamony, had at last been someone's lover. And not any common someone's lover, but the Earl of Graymar's lover, the Dewin Mawr's lover, the incredibly handsome and amazing Malachi Seymour's lover. She was intensely pleased.

And then another happy thought occurred to her: *she was in Mervaille.*

Sliding from the bed, Sarah groped about for her gown, wishing she'd had the presence of mind to put on her spectacles before Malachi whisked her away. The thin garment was scarcely modest attire for exploring the house, and it was more shocking still to be barefoot, but the hour was so early that she imagined—and hoped!—none of the servants would see. Padding silently to the door, she slipped out of the room.

Sarah found herself in the midst of a long, dimly lit hallway. She considered going back into Malachi's room to collect a candle, but without her spectacles there was little help that such a small measure of light could provide. And she didn't want to risk alerting any servants to her movements.

It was a slow journey down the hall. Sarah was obliged to stand very near each portrait she passed in order to make sense of it, and her curiosity was such that every small table bearing even the most common objects was of interest to her. The first hallway led to another, and then another, until she reached a foyer that offered a number of options. One was a staircase that led both downward and upward, then there was a hallway that led, she supposed, to another wing of the house, and finally there was a pair of large, grand doors that proved to be more inviting than Sarah could resist. She hoped they were open. They were.

"Oh, my," she murmured as the doors swung wide to reveal a long gallery brimming with works of art and ending in one of the tall, grand windows like the one she'd seen in Malachi's study at Glain Tarran. It ran ceiling to floor and gave a glorious view of the garden and long lawn below and, beyond that, of the Thames and London itself. The sky was still dark, with heavy clouds allowing only a few stars to peek through, but it was the kind of darkness that would soon give way to dawn, so that even as Sarah watched it began to lighten to a luminous gray.

She didn't know how much time passed as she made her way about the gallery, save that her eyes were beginning to ache from strain, despite the ever-brightening sky. At the far end of the room she came across a portrait of two boys, one possessed of the Seymours' bright blond hair and brilliant blue eyes and one younger and dark haired. They were dressed in splendid finery, their faces clean and their hair neatly brushed. Sitting between them was a large, mottled spaniel with soft, flowing ears and an intelligent, if somewhat bored, expression. In fact, the entire trio looked bored, as if they longed to be allowed to tear off the confining clothes and go romping outdoors.

She looked at the boys more closely, a slow smile forming on her lips. "So that's what you looked like as a boy," she murmured. "And this must be Cousin Niclas. What a lovely dog. I imagine the three of you had many grand times together."

"Yes, we did," said a masculine voice, startling her. "And Samson was indeed a fine dog, though he possessed an unconquerable passion for chewing my father's favorite pair of boots, which nearly brought his happy life to an early end."

Sarah turned to find Malachi leaning against the wall, regarding her. He was dressed only in a pair of trousers and had his arms folded against his bare chest.

"Oh, my lord!" she said, and hurried toward him. His arms opened to enfold her in his warmth. "You gave me such a start! But I'm so glad you've come, for I'm having such a wonderful time. Will you tell me about all these paintings and who these people are?" She lifted on her bare feet to give him a rapid kiss, then pulled him toward the paintings. "I feel certain that some of these must be portraits of Seymours I've researched, for the faces and settings seem to match what I've learned. This gentleman, for instance." She stopped in front of a particularly large portrait of an older, rather stern gentleman garbed in tight silver knee breeches and a matching silver waistcoat topped by an elegant, heavily embroidered silk coat of deep blue, with voluminous quantities of lacy ruffles at his sleeves and neck. Atop his head was a gorgeous black wig composed of beautiful curls. He had a very proud, patrician expression, but he was so handsome, even in advanced age, that he could only be a Seymour.

"Is this not your great-great-grandfather?" she asked. "Lewes Seymour? The third Earl of Graymar?"

Malachi gazed up at the painting. "It is," he said. "How could you possibly have known? How could you have *seen* clearly enough to discern his identity?"

She grinned. "It took a great deal of time, for I mistook him for a woman at first. I'm hopelessly blind without my spectacles, and it's so dark. I should have brought a candle."

"But then you might have been caught sneaking about," he said. When she laughed he added, "You see, Sarah, that I'm beginning to understand how your mind works."

"Tell me about Lewes Seymour, if you please. He was once the Dewin Mawr, was he not?"

"He inherited the title from a cousin, just as my own cousin Kian will inherit it from me. The third earl was, I've been told, a terrible scalawag. But you could probably tell me more about him than I could you."

"I've heard several stories. He appeared outwardly stern and was famous for terrifying the villagers near Glain Tarran with but a look. But he was a contemporary of Charles the Second, another famous profligate, and, in fact, they were quite good friends who liked to . . ."

Malachi waited for her to finish, knowing full well that it wasn't shyness that kept her from completing the sentence.

"Go out carousing together with women of questionable virtue," he supplied at last. "Yes, that's true. Fortunate for magic mortals is the fact that we can control our breeding properties, else the country would be overrun with the progeny of Lewes Seymour's by-blows. My great-grandfather

Hollace Seymour was an entirely different sort of man, thankfully."

"Malachi," Sarah said faintly, stepping closer to stare at the painting. "It was Charles the Second."

He looked at her. "Was it, dear? In what way?"

She shook her head. "No, I mean . . . it's just come to me. He looked so much like this that it had to be him. Charles the Second."

"Darling, what do you mean? Who had to be Charles the Second?"

She turned to look at him, her eyes wide. "On the bell, Malachi. The one I saw when we stood in the fire. I told you there was a figure on it. It was Charles the Second." She grasped his hands, her voice rising with excitement. "We need only find where such a bell may be and we'll know where the *cythraul* will be arriving."

Interesting and welcome as Sarah's revelation about Charles the Second was, it wasn't sufficient to distract Malachi from the intention he'd come awake with—to make love with her once more before returning to the Tamony household. He took her back to his bedchamber, to his enormous bed, and laid her upon it. They made love slowly, touching and stroking with languorous pleasure. They dozed afterward, waking when Rhys scratched at the door to deliver a breakfast tray. Sarah hid under the covers, painfully embarrassed, until she realized that Rhys already knew that she'd been at Mervaille through the night. As Malachi told her, nothing that happened at either Glain Tarran or Mervaille escaped the manservant's knowledge.

An hour later they returned to the Tamony dwelling, where Malachi carried a still-slumbering Julius to his bed. He poured a few drops of sleeping potion down the younger man's throat.

"This will keep him asleep until late in the afternoon," Malachi said as he stepped back and stoppered the small vial. "When he comes to his senses he'll be eager to go to Serafina. She'll likely have instructed him to be at her town house in order to act as her escort to the Herold ball this evening—she generally puts her enchanted lovers to such use. The necessity to obey her will override her command to obtain the journal. Let him do as he wishes and depart. If your parents try to speak with him, try to stop them."

"My mother knows everything," she said. At his surprised expression she went on. "I told her last night when she asked me what was going on. She was amazingly understanding. I think you must be right about her being a sympathetic, for she'd suspected the truth all along. Although she was far from pleased to discover that Miss Daray and Lord Llew have magic, as well."

"I understand her concerns about Serafina," he said. "But why should she be displeased by Morcar?"

"It's Philistia," Sarah explained. "Mama believes she's fallen in love with Lord Llew. They spent the day together yesterday. We don't know how the circumstances transpired, but Mama suspects Philistia went out in search of the earl."

"Damn the man," Malachi muttered angrily. "I knew he'd cause trouble. But we've no time to worry over your cousin now. Morcar wouldn't be so incautious as to do more than seduce her. . . ."

"Dear God," Sarah murmured, her heart dropping to her feet. "Surely he'd not. She's a complete innocent, and of good family. Surely, *surely* he'd not ruin her."

Malachi took her hands in his and squeezed them gently. "I wish I could tell you that he'd not," he said, "but if Philistia is willing—and she certainly seemed to be taken with him—then there's nothing to stop him. She's not a child, after all."

Sarah gripped his fingers, hard. "I shall kill him if he harms her," she vowed. "It's one thing for Julius to be treated in such a manner, but not a young girl like Philistia!"

"I understand, love," he said reassuringly. "But we mustn't lose sight of the task ahead. There's nothing we'll be able to do for either of them if we forget the *cythraul*. I must return to Scotland; you must go and speak with Professor Seabolt about the location of the bell. Can you engage your mother to keep an eye over Julius? And to make excuses for him if your father becomes suspicious?"

"I'm certain she will," Sarah said. "She'll feel better if she can help in some way. And she's the only one who could possibly convince my father that nothing is wrong."

"Excellent." Gathering her into his arms, he kissed her deeply. "I'll return as quickly as possible, hopefully before the dinner at Lady Herold's."

"And I hope to have an answer from Professor Seabolt."

"After that," he murmured, kissing her once more, "perhaps we'll have a few spare moments to give our attention to other, far more pleasant matters."

It was the "other matters" that stayed in Sarah's thoughts some hours later as she sat among piles of books in Professor Seabolt's library, and made it so difficult to concentrate on the task at hand.

"Memorial bells . . . hmmm . . ." Professor Seabolt opened yet another ancient volume and began to search. "Charles the Second. Now where can it be? There must be dozens of them spread all about England, Wales, and Scotland, in universities, chapels, churches, and cathedrals alike."

"Don't forget the other clues," Sarah reminded, closing the book she'd been perusing and setting it aside to pick up another. "It's not at Glain Tarran, perhaps not even in Wales. I think we might discount Wales as a start and focus on those places where such a bell might have been hung. If we're wrong, then we'll shorten our borders to exclude only Glain Tarran."

Without looking up, Professor Seabolt nodded. "Or shorter still to encircle only the ceremonial grounds. But that would be a sorry sort of clue for the Guardians to send, would it not?"

"To discount only a small area from our search?" she asked, opening the new book to unleash a cloud of dust. "I should think so." She sneezed and waved a hand in the air.

"I can't believe that was their purpose. Surely it meant something else."

"Lord Graymar is of the same opinion," the professor said, his gaze moving rapidly over the pages before him. "The question is, what does it mean?"

A soft scratch came at the door.

"That will be Tego with our tea," Professor Seabolt said, glancing up to add, more loudly, "Come!"

The misshapen servant entered at once, bearing a silver tray laden with a tea service and what appeared to be enough food for ten people.

"Cook thought you might be getting hungry, sir, and miss," he said, clearing a table before setting the tray upon it. "I'll fix each of you a plate, shall I?"

"Very good, Tego," the professor said absently. "Now, here, Miss Tamony—" He sat forward and pointed to a particular spot on the page. "Here is mention of numerous dedications being made to Charles the Second for his renewed empowerment of the Anglican Church. Several of these dedications appear to include newly resurrected or repaired bell towers, made possible by Charles's financial support. One would assume that at least some of these might contain bells that were cast with his figure upon them."

Sarah sent a glance toward Tego, who, though his back was turned toward them, was clearly listening. She reached out to touch the professor's arm, to warn him to be silent, but he sat back, out of her reach, and, his eyes fixed upon the book, said aloud, "Unfortunately, there's no notation making a description of any bells. I feel quite certain, however," he added, at last looking up at her, "that one of these must lead us to the bell we're looking for. Ah, very good, Tego." He put aside his book and looked expectantly at the tray held before them.

Tego offered it to Sarah first, his expression blank. Professor Seabolt chatted on about the bell as Sarah sat in pained silence. She cast another glance at Tego as he made to depart and saw the smile playing on his lips. He turned to look at her as he moved toward the door, and she saw in his insolent gaze the answer to her question. He'd not only heard every word the professor had said but also tucked them away.

"Professor Seabolt," she said firmly as the door closed. "You must never speak so openly in front of him. Ever."

"Now, now, Miss Tamony, we've had this discussion before, have we not? I've told you that Tego's a wonderful servant, and perfectly trustworthy, as well."

"He's not," she stated flatly. "I know you make a habit of keeping such beings in your employ, but Tego's powers are dark—just like the creatures Serafina Daray keeps. . . ." She trailed off as realization struck. "Sweet merciful day," she murmured, gazing wide-eyed at the professor. She could hear Malachi's voice in her ears. *We all have spies . . .*

"What is it?" the professor asked.

"Nothing," she said quickly, uncertain as to whether she should voice her suspicion that Tego was one of Serafina Daray's spies. She was certain Tego had given Serafina the information from the journal, but if the servant knew Sarah had discovered the truth, Professor Seabolt might well be in danger. Malachi wasn't here to protect his dear friend. "Let's not speak of the matter further. We've more than enough to occupy our minds with finding the bell."

Another two hours passed before they'd compiled a list of potential places where the bell might be. Sarah wrote it on a single page and tucked it safely in her reticule. Tego could use magic to ferret the list from Professor Seabolt's memory, but she'd take no chance in leaving a physical copy behind.

She arrived home in plenty of time to prepare for the coming ball, with thoughts of how pleased Malachi was going to be with the progress that had been made. Her good mood lasted as she divested her outer garments, pulled off her gloves and took off her hat, and continued even after that, as Sarah went in search of her mother or

Philistia or both. She found her mother in the parlor, sitting before the fire, staring into the flames.

"Mama?" Sarah asked, closing the door behind her.

Her mother looked up, and her expression was such that Sarah didn't need to hear the words. Julius had gone.

Chapter 21

$\mathcal{T}$he Herold ball took on a nightmarish quality from the moment the dinner guests arrived. Lord and Lady Herold greeted these chosen few in an elegant parlor where drinks and hors d'oeuvres were served, and any onlooker who'd seen the assembly would have believed it to be nothing more unusual than a gathering of some of Society's most desirable individuals.

But Sarah knew better. Though Lord and Lady Herold were clearly unaware of the truth, at least a third of their dinner guests were magic mortals, and several of these weren't merely lesser wizards and sorceresses but extremely powerful. As they arrived in the room and segregated in separate corners, Sarah began to have the feeling that a terrible storm was gathering.

Malachi hadn't arrived yet, and Sarah couldn't help but worry. Perhaps matters in Scotland hadn't been resolved and he'd not been able to return to London. The idea made her shiver as she looked across the room, meeting the unfriendly stares of the dark wizards and sorceresses who surrounded Serafina Daray. Serafina, by contrast, smiled at one and all, her appearance as bright and glorious as that of a heavenly angel. Julius, sitting beside her, looked numb, almost lifeless. And very tired. Sarah was thankful that her parents weren't present to see him.

It had been difficult for her mother to manage keeping Sarah's father at home, for he loved great social events and had been looking forward to the Herold ball, especially the dinner, where interesting conversation might be found. But Sarah and her mother had agreed that until Malachi found a way to release Julius from Serafina's spell, it would be best to keep Sir Alberic and his son apart as often as possible.

"When will Lord Llew arrive?" Philistia murmured, not in the least interested in her male cousin's unusual behavior. Having seen Serafina Daray in all her formal finery, Philistia likely assumed Julius was too smitten to be distracted by his duller relatives. Her mind was also fixed, as it had constantly been, on the Earl of Llew. "He promised to come early. I've saved the first waltz for him. He must be the most marvelous dancer, for he's so tall and fit." She smiled at Sarah, her cheeks pinking. "I believe he's the handsomest man I've ever seen; don't you, Sarah? And by far the most charming."

Sarah looked at her cousin with renewed worry and wished even more for Malachi. She was almost tempted to believe that Philistia was laboring beneath an enchantment, too, save that she'd seen her cousin infatuated before and knew the signs. That there seemed to be something more intense this time was a problem . . . one Sarah didn't have time to ponder.

She was besieged by several of the other guests, all of whom wished to ask questions about her books. Fortunately, Sarah had managed to secret a pair of spectacles out of the house and put them on in the carriage, so that she could see everyone's faces. Philistia had protested the presence of the spectacles violently, for no lady ever wore them to a ball, but Sarah hadn't cared for such propriety. With her brother enchanted and her cousin infatuated, she needed all her wits about her.

The parlor doors opened and the butler announced the

latest arrivals. Sarah only heard a sudden rush of murmurs and the name "Seymour" and looked up expectantly. The sight of a tall blond gentleman briefly filled her with hope—until she realized that the gentleman at the door was accompanied by a small raven-haired beauty in an advanced stage of pregnancy.

Sarah had not yet met Dyfed Seymour but knew at once who he was. There was such a likeness between himself and the Earl of Graymar that they might almost have been brothers rather than cousins. He was by all accounts a lesser wizard, but Sarah supposed that his tiny wife's powers more than made up for whatever he lacked. It was unusual for a woman so pregnant as Desdemona Seymour to be out in public, especially at a ball, but she was so unlike other women as to be excused from Society's rules. And, Sarah suspected, Desdemona didn't particularly care what mere mortals said about her.

Dyfed Seymour escorted his wife with both hands, as if he'd prefer to carry her rather than allow her to wobble along. Everyone present watched as they made their way, fascinated by the young, attractive couple who'd not long been in Town. The open enmity between Society's other famous beauty, Serafina Daray, and Desdemona only made them more intriguing.

Part of the excitement that had surrounded the Herold ball had been due to the promised attendance of both women. The gossips would talk of little else for the coming week than what the two women had done and said. The fleeting but obvious look of disdain that Desdemona cast Serafina as she passed by was enough to send shivers of delight throughout the room. Serafina's frozen smile made the moment that much better.

Desdemona's arrival had increased tenfold the strength of magic that Sarah felt, and the tension as well. One wrong word, one wrong gesture, on either side and surely someone would erupt with anger and start some kind of magical war. Right in the midst of Lord and Lady Herold's elegant parlor. Dear God, how Sarah wished Malachi would arrive.

"They're coming this way!" Philistia whispered excitedly behind her fan. "Lord Graymar's relatives! If only he was here to make a proper introduction. She's so very beautiful, is she not, Sarah? And her husband looks so handsome and charming. Oh, and she's an *American*. Is that not the most shocking thing?" she added with scandalized delight.

Those about them parted at the Seymours' approach. Dyfed Seymour smiled and, bringing his wife to a halt, bowed. Philistia was perfectly right—he was quite handsome, with the refined features, blond hair, and brilliant blue eyes possessed by those Seymours who'd inherited a touch of elvish blood.

"Miss Tamony?" he said politely. "I'm Dyfed Seymour. I believe you know my wife?"

Ignoring Philistia's gasp of surprise, Sarah replied, "Yes, sir, I have that honor. How do you do, Mrs. Seymour? It's good to see you again."

Desdemona made a sound of impatience. "My back is killing me and my feet are swollen and I feel as if I'm giving birth to an enormous pumpkin. And don't begin calling me Mrs. Seymour, Sarah, else I shall be terribly put out." She glanced at the people still standing about them, all listening to her intently, and made a waving movement with one hand. It must have been an enchantment of some kind, for they walked away without a word. To her husband, who'd not spoken a word, she said, "I always take care, Dyfed. You know better than to worry."

To Sarah, Desdemona said, "Is this your cousin, then? You'd best introduce us before she grows so pale that she faints."

"Oh yes, of course," Sarah said, turning to indicate Philistia, who was staring at Desdemona with wide-eyed awe. "Philistia, this is Mr. and Mrs. Dyfed Seymour. Mr. and Mrs. Seymour, this is my cousin, Miss Philistia Tamony."

Dyfed Seymour bowed over Philistia's hand, murmuring his delight. Desdemona nodded. Philistia curtsied beautifully and replied that she was honored.

"I've heard a great deal about you in the past two days, Miss Tamony," Desdemona said.

A touch of color painted the younger woman's cheeks. "H-have you, Mrs. Seymour?"

"Yes indeed," Desdemona replied, her violet eyes glittering. "You've been in company with the Earl of Llew a great deal, have you not?"

Philistia paled again, especially beneath Sarah's immediate stare. She looked about nervously and said nothing.

"As it happens," Desdemona went on, a bit more gently, "I know His Lordship quite well. May I give you a friendly word of advice, even on such short acquaintance? You must be very careful when in company with him, Miss Tamony. The Earl of Llew is a powerful man, and very . . . ambitious."

Something sparked in Philistia's eyes, something Sarah had never seen in her shy cousin before. It was obvious the younger girl felt a deep sense of wonder at being in the presence of someone such as Desdemona Seymour, whose place on the ladder of Society was far higher than her own, and stood somewhat in fear of her, as well. Yet Philistia gathered herself up to full height—which wasn't much, considering how small she was—and said, in a quavering voice, "Lord Llew is a wonderful man. A very f-fine and noble gentleman. And he's my friend. I'll not hear a word spoken against him. By anyone."

"Philistia," Sarah said disapprovingly.

Tread lightly, Miss Tamony, Sarah heard Dyfed Seymour say. The words weren't spoken aloud, yet she heard them all the same. In her head. Her gaze shot to his, and he gave a slight nod. *There's a purpose to my wife's actions. Let her put the moment to good use.*

So that was Dyfed Seymour's gift, Sarah thought with some amazement. The ability to speak without words, making himself known directly to the minds of others. She nearly said aloud how marvelous it was, but Desdemona spoke first.

"I should never give you any reason for displeasure,

Miss Tamony," Desdemona said in a gentle tone that Sarah hadn't yet heard from her. She reached out a hand; Philistia put her own in it as if compelled to do so. "Forgive me if I've said something to overset you. Let us cry friends and find a quiet place to sit for a few moments so that I can rest my feet." She drew Philistia away as easily as if she'd placed the girl beneath a spell, though Sarah knew she hadn't. It was scarcely necessary, for magic mortals could be powerfully persuasive without the use of magic. "May I call you Philistia?" Desdemona went on as they moved away. "And you must call me Desdemona, will you? I so dislike the many formalities you English have. We're not so foolish in the States, you know. . . ."

Sarah would have followed, but Dyfed Seymour's hand on her elbow stopped her.

"I apologize for speaking to you as I did," he said in a tone that kept others from overhearing. "I could see at once that Malachi didn't warn you of my gift."

"No, he didn't," she said, "but it's wonderful. I've heard of it before, of course, in my researches, but never experienced it firsthand. It's delightful, I assure you."

"Thank you, Miss Tamony," he said. "You are kind, just as Malachi said you would be. And very beautiful, which both he and Niclas told me as well. Desdemona will take good care of your relative, so you've nothing to fear. She can be astonishingly polished when necessary, though it tires her. I have a message for you from my lordly cousin."

Sarah looked closely into his handsome face. "If it's that he's not returned from Scotland, I don't wish to hear it. I vow I shall run from the room screaming."

He laughed, his blue eyes alight with appreciation at these blunt words. "He and Niclas were delayed a few hours longer than myself. Malachi knew Desdemona would come in search of me if I didn't return this morning, and the last thing he wished to add to our difficulties was a temperamental American sorceress. He brought me home shortly after leaving you, then returned to finish dealing with our wild relatives. No, please don't look so unhappy,

Miss Tamony. He and Niclas have already returned to London, but only an hour past. They're readying themselves as quickly as possible—although the word 'quickly' doesn't apply when one considers Lord Graymar's insistence upon perfection—and will be here soon. Malachi asked me to reassure you."

She let out a tense breath. "Thank God."

He smiled and held out his arm. "Until he comes, will you do me the honor of allowing me to act as your escort? Desdemona will keep your little cousin occupied. She's sincerely worried about her, you know. The Earl of Llew is an unfortunate gentleman for any young woman to be in much company with."

"I'm familiar with the long-standing feud between the Cadmarans and the Seymours, sir," Sarah said, careful to keep her voice low. "Lord Graymar doesn't believe he'll attempt to use magic on her."

"I agree," Dyfed said. "There's no sense in him taking such a risk so long as your cousin willingly puts her trust in him. Malachi says she appears to be infatuated with Lord Llew."

Sarah sighed. "I fear that's so."

"Then I worry the more for her," he murmured. "Morcar Cadmaran is a dark, cruel wizard. He despises mere mortals and uses them for his own pleasure, just as Serafina Daray is doing with your brother. He'd not hesitate to do what he wishes to your cousin. Desdemona knows that far better than any of us do."

"But they both hail from dark clans," Sarah said. "Has he done something to anger her?"

A servant approached with a tray of hors d'oeuvres and Sarah shook her head at it. Dyfed waved the man away.

"Desdemona was brought to England to be Morcar's bride," he told her. "Her father sold her to the Earl of Llew for a large sum and made a binding contract that Desdemona wasn't given the opportunity to naysay. Then he abandoned her at Castle Llew and returned to the States, leaving her at Morcar's mercy."

Sarah glanced at Desdemona, who appeared to be conversing happily with a rapt Philistia. "I had no idea. I knew she was American, but never knew how she came to be in England." She looked at Dyfed. "How is it that she came to be your wife, rather than his?"

"We met quite by accident," he replied, smiling secretively, "and realized almost at once that we were *unoliaeth*. Unfortunately, Morcar had fallen in love with his betrothed and wasn't going to let her go easily. In typical dark wizard fashion, he imprisoned her in his family crypt at Castle Llew, where her powers were made useless."

Sarah nodded her understanding of this. Being surrounded by the dead, especially in a sacred burial ground, rendered magic mortals powerless. "It must have been awful for her," she murmured sympathetically.

"It was," he agreed, "but Desdemona is scarcely a wilting flower. My brother and I rescued her, and she recovered very quickly. But although Morcar eventually gave her up, she's never forgotten, or forgiven, what he did to her. None of us want to see your cousin harmed by him in such a terrible way. Desdemona was able to recover, even if she hasn't let her hatred for Morcar go. I fear your cousin may not be so strong."

Sarah didn't think so, either, but had no time to say so, for the doors were opened again and the Earl of Llew was announced, just as if their conversation had called him forth. He stood for a moment in splendid magnificence, allowing those in the room to admire him before he moved to greet his hosts.

Sarah looked toward Desdemona and Philistia and saw that her cousin had stood and was gazing raptly at the earl. Desdemona was staring at him, too. With hatred.

"This is the first time she's seen him since he at last set her free," Dyfed murmured, watching his wife, as well. "We stayed in Wales, waiting for permission from her father to wed, before coming to London for a Season."

"She's not going to do anything intemperate, is she?" Sarah asked worriedly. "Not in such a setting?"

Dyfed sighed. "I pray not. I'd feel better if Malachi and Niclas were here. We are decidedly outnumbered at present." He looked about, watching as Morcar coolly greeted other members of the dark clans who were present, even Serafina Daray, who smiled at him with feigned sweetness. But that was well matched by Morcar Cadmaran's overacted grandness. Sarah could scarce believe that anyone watching wouldn't recognize farce when they saw it, but the mere mortals present appeared to be completely unaware of the underplay taking place before their very eyes.

When he'd finished with his own kind, the Earl of Llew turned his attention to those mere mortals who were particular acquaintances. He was clearly a popular gentleman and was greeted heartily by all those who saw him, both men and women. Philistia had sat again but was giving very little attention any longer to Desdemona Seymour. She watched, her gaze filled with expectation, as the Earl of Llew slowly made his way toward her. By the time he arrived, Sarah and Dyfed had moved to stand protectively beside their respective relatives.

Sarah expected the Earl of Llew to maintain his careless, cheerful attitude when he greeted them, but there was something else in his eyes—a fleeting moment of unveiled pain behind the forced lightness when his gaze settled on Desdemona. It passed quickly and he was once again the charming nobleman whose company had been so pleasant at tea two days past.

"Miss Tamony," he said grandly, bowing to Sarah. "And Miss Philistia. I hope I find you well?"

Philistia had stood again and, smiling widely, said, "Yes, my lord. Very well."

His dark gaze returned to Desdemona. "Mrs. Seymour. It's been some years since we've crossed paths. You look very fine." He shifted his regard to Dyfed. "Mr. Seymour, well met. It appears that congratulations are in order. You will have a child soon."

Dyfed Seymour's handsome face remained serene, even angelic, quite in contrast to his wife's angry countenance, but his voice, when he spoke, was icy.

"Thank you, my lord. Yes, we expect our child to be born soon. This will likely be the last outing my wife enjoys until sometime later in the spring."

"I almost didn't come tonight," Desdemona said, staring so fixedly at the Earl of Llew that she might have bored holes into his face. "But when I knew that you would be present, Morcar, I determined that nothing could keep me away. You look much the same as I recall, though the eyes are an improvement. How do you enjoy seeing the world again?"

Lord Llew's countenance stiffened and his lips thinned. Philistia took a step nearer to him; Sarah put a hand on her arm to draw her back.

"It is as I had remembered it," he replied at last. "With one exception. And that I do not wish to gaze upon, for it is far too painful. Congratulations to you both again." He bowed and took his leave.

"Whatever can he mean?" Philistia asked, pulling free of Sarah's grasp. "Why did he go away so quickly?"

"Sit down, Philistia," Sarah insisted quietly. "You can ask him later, during the ball. Don't draw attention to yourself."

The doors to the parlor opened once more and Sarah's heart gave a leap of hope. But it was Niclas and Julia Seymour who had arrived, with still no sign of Malachi.

He'll be here soon, never fear, Miss Tamony, Dyfed said in his silent speech. *Be of good cheer. Our numbers are improving.*

Another ten long minutes passed before the Earl of Graymar at last made his grand arrival. When his presence was announced, Sarah could almost visibly see Lord and Lady Herold wilt with relief, for they'd held the dinner far too long already in the hope of his coming.

Sarah had attended a sufficient number of elegant events where Lord Graymar was also a guest to be used to his manner of making an entrance. She would tease him later about his need to ever create a scene, but for the moment she was so glad to see him that she merely wanted it over and done with. There was no hurrying His Lordship, however.

He stood, as he was given to doing, for a long, imperious moment just inside the open doors, his haughty gaze sweeping the room as he allowed those present to take in his elegant attire. The gaze stopped briefly when it lit upon his relatives, who politely looked back, with the exception of Desdemona, whose back ached far too much for her to look anything but disgruntled, then moved to Philistia and then to Sarah. She smiled at him in the teasing manner that always seemed to unsettle him in such public places. His mouth twitched, and then his gaze continued on.

He was dressed in his customary black and white, a gleaming quizzing glass dangling from his lapel and his cravat an object of perfection. He looked so handsome that Sarah could audibly hear the maidenly sighs that filled the room.

He greeted his hosts, who signaled to their servants that the assembled could now go in to dinner, and offered Lady Herold his arm to escort her. Sarah felt a pang of disappointment, for she'd hoped to have a moment to speak to him. But he was the highest-ranking member of Society present at the gathering and thus had duties to fulfill. She doubted she'd even sit near enough to converse with him.

Malachi smiled politely and nodded to his right as his hostess chatted merrily about the latest social on-dit. On his left, Lady Bellington was talking of fashion and asking whether His Lordship approved of the addition of so many unseemly frills to ladies' gowns. Across from him a fellow member of Parliament, Lord Bascolm, wanted Malachi's opinion on upcoming votes. Sitting next to Lord Bascolm was Mrs. John Stansmith, who was doing her utmost to signal to Malachi both her interest and her availability. Fortunately, sitting on her other side was a dark wizard, one of the handsome Thorne clan, who was ready and able to help her get past the disappointment of failure.

There was more than enough to occupy Malachi's

thoughts, but for the life of him, all he could focus on was the numerous men sitting near Sarah, all of them drooling into their cups in admiration of her beautiful person. He was displeased that neither Niclas nor Dyfed, who were sitting nearer to her, was doing something more to put a stop to such nonsense.

What had Sarah been thinking to wear such a gown? The vivid green and gold colors were charming, of course, and caused her hair and eyes, even with the spectacles, to stand out more markedly. But the bodice had been cut so low that her generous bosom was near to popping out. The gentlemen surrounding her were going to break their necks bending so near when they spoke to her. He was tempted to cast an enchantment that would make all of them temporarily blind, but that would only solve part of the problem. She was charming each of them in turn, smiling and laughing and relating all sorts of tales from her travels that had them utterly enrapt. God help him, if Phillip Fosby leaned any nearer to her Malachi would—

"Lord Llew appears to be smitten with the younger Tamony girl, does he not, my lord?" Lady Herold said, nodding to where the Earl of Llew and Philistia sat side by side, conversing quietly. "They've scarce looked at anyone else since sitting down. And she's had but two mouthfuls of food, I vow."

Yes, Malachi had noticed that, though he gave no comment. It was just as Lady Tamony had feared; the girl had clearly become deeply infatuated with Morcar. What surprised Malachi was Morcar's behavior. He'd not placed the girl beneath an enchantment; Malachi would have felt it if he had. And so he was obliged to treat her with a measure of interest, which Malachi supposed Morcar would find quite tiring, for he despised mere mortals and never showed any interest in them beyond their usefulness to him. But he looked as if he was actually enjoying Philistia's company.

It was far more than Malachi could say for Serafina Daray. Julius sat beside her, almost lifeless. He ate and drank perfunctorily but said nothing unless addressed by Serafina and then answered in one or two words.

"And the brother appears to have caught Miss Daray's notice," Lady Herold murmured. "If the rumors we've heard about you and a certain lady of some renown are true, my lord," she went on, "you might well find yourself related by marriage to both Miss Daray and the Earl of Llew. That would be quite a boon for the Tamonys, would it not? To bring together three powerful families in one Season. It would cause a remarkable sensation."

"Yes, it would," Malachi responded with a polite smile, though inwardly he thought, with violence, God forbid. What a dreadful contemplation. But of course it was impossible. Morcar would never consider marriage to a mere mortal; Cadmarans had but rarely mixed with anyone outside their own kind, and Serafina would rid herself of Julius as soon as she had no further purpose for him.

At just that moment Serafina caught Malachi looking at her and smiled in a wickedly seductive manner. She'd cast lures at him before, but despite her great beauty and human features, he'd never responded with more than a bored stare. There were those among magic mortals who had no qualms in mating with *animantis;* the Seymours were not among them.

It was not unusual when magic mortals were at social gatherings for one powerful *dewin* or another to place the mere mortals present into immobility. It was sometimes done in order to erase memories due to an unfortunate remark or ill-timed use of magic. More often, however, it was simply a way of putting mere mortals out of the conversation, and although Malachi could condone such cause once in a while, especially when something of import must be said, he found it insulting and cruel when magic mortals used it for insignificant means, either to make unkind comments regarding mere mortals or to play tricks on them.

During the course of the elegant dinner Serafina Daray

had attempted four times to use her magic to paralyze the mere mortals present. Malachi had no notion why, save that she had something particular to say to the magic mortals assembled. And each time less than a second passed before Desdemona countered Serafina's spell by voiding it, releasing their hosts and mere mortal guests from confinement. Serafina's fury at having her will thwarted was ill contained, as was Desdemona's amusement. Serafina attempted to shatter Desdemona's wineglass when she next picked it up, but Malachi had brought the small disaster to a halt before the first crack could unfold. Then he'd sent a warning glance at Serafina, who'd pointedly ignored him.

With a sigh Malachi steeled himself. It was going to be a long evening.

Chapter 22

$\mathcal{I}$'m glad to see that you had the good sense to wear your spectacles," Malachi said as he twirled Sarah about in the ball's first waltz. "Your mother's absence must account for your having them. If I'd known, I'd never have worn a quizzing glass, but I thought to match your deft use of the lorgnette."

"I had wondered about that, my lord," she said. "Having never seen you with one, I had thought you immune to such affectations."

"Affectations?" he repeated with mock insult. "I hope you do not mean to imply that I'm a slave of fashion, Miss Tamony."

She laughed. "You are very grand, Lord Graymar, and famed for it, as you know. But I must say you carry it off well. You looked especially stunning tonight, standing just so at the open doors so that all could admire your beauty. If every lady present had only sighed a little more strongly we might have had a hurricane in the room."

He had to press his lips together to keep from smiling. Attempting to look stern, he said, "You make jest of me, Miss Tamony. I'm wounded. Yes, I am, and there's no use trying to apologize for it now. Not after I went to the trouble to wear a quizzing glass. Rhys nearly wept when I asked him to fetch it."

"Did he?" Sarah said sympathetically. "Poor Rhys. I can just imagine it. But you know, my lord, we might have made a game of staring at each other from across the room if I'd worn the lorgnette rather than my spectacles. Perhaps we might have wagered on who could make the other laugh first. But I wanted to keep a better eye on Julius, and the lorgnette is hardly helpful for such a task." She looked to where her brother was dancing with tiny Serafina Daray. They made a handsome couple. "It breaks my heart to see him so. He's said not a word to either Philistia or me all night."

"Philistia doesn't appear to be worried over it," Malachi remarked, nodding toward where the Earl of Llew was dancing with the younger girl in his arms, so much taller than she that he nearly swept her off her feet at each turn. Philistia's pleasure was evident on her face. She laughed, and Morcar, much to Malachi's surprise, was laughing as well. "It may be a small comfort to you, love, but Morcar appears to enjoy your cousin's company, despite her being a mere mortal."

"He's been fixed on her almost from the moment he arrived," she said. "It's extremely odd."

"That has to do with Desdemona, in part," Malachi said. "He can't bear to see her so happy with Dyfed, and is likely doing what he must to divert his thoughts. Seeing her again, and large with child, must be painful for him."

"Did he truly love her? I find it hard to believe. He seems to have used up that emotion entirely on himself."

"I suppose that's true. Cadmarans have always found themselves worthy of awe. Morcar may be worse than most. But it's no secret that he's long wished for a wife. Some years ago he planned to kidnap one of my cousins, Ceridwen, and make her his wife, and was gravely disappointed by his failure. Then he found Desdemona and paid a goodly sum for her hand, and by all accounts appeared to be deeply taken with her. I believe he thought she was eager for the marriage, too, for they were both of high-ranking dark clans and well matched in powers. For her to choose a lesser wizard, and a Seymour, must have been quite a blow. I can almost feel sorry for him."

She raised her eyebrows. "Can you, my lord?"

"I can," he said, pressing her slightly nearer with the pressure of his hand at her waist. "I know what it is to be alone, and to wonder if that condition will last forever."

"Have you, Malachi?" she asked softly. "I find that surprising, but I suppose all mortals are vulnerable to such thoughts. There are those who would think your life perfect. You have had many beautiful mistresses and no wife to worry about."

"Any man who would prefer many beautiful mistresses to one loving wife is a fool," he stated. "I know whereof I speak. I do not know what Morcar might believe. But even if loneliness and desire drive him to be intemperate, he would never take a mere mortal wife. I only pray he'll not break Philistia's heart."

Sarah's brow furrowed as she cast another glance in the direction of the dancing couple. "Is there nothing that can be done to stop him?" she asked. "If he should ruin her . . ."

"She's no longer a child, sweetheart," he said. "Only Philistia can decide what transpires between herself and Lord Llew. If he had enchanted her, I might be able to approach the Guardians on her behalf. But she is ruled by her heart alone, and no one, either magic or mortal, can force that disobedient organ into submission save the owner of it."

When the dance ended, Malachi escorted Sarah to the punch bowl and thereafter, having chatted politely with a few acquaintances, said, "Let's go have a word with Serafina."

"Oh no," Sarah murmured. "That can't be a good idea."

"Don't be afraid, love," he encouraged softly, leading her inexorably toward the place where Serafina and Julius were resting following the dance. "She'll not cause you harm again."

Serafina was surrounded by her devoted magical sycophants. Her blue eyes lit at their approach, ready for battle, while Julius only stared and showed no sign of recognition.

The other wizards and sorceresses quietly took a few steps away, gazing at the Dewin Mawr warily.

"Why, Lord Graymar," Miss Daray said in her delicate, bell-like voice when they stopped before her. "You've come at last to speak with me. I had expected you long before now."

He lifted a hand and a kind of veil fell about them. Those outside of it moved and spoke just as before but far more dimly. They suddenly appeared not to be aware of those who stood within the veil.

"I would have come last night, Serafina," Malachi said easily. "To throttle you. You are fortunate that I was otherwise engaged."

"Yes, I know," she replied sweetly. "With Miss Tamony. I've discovered that the brother is quite satisfying. I hope you've found the sister to be the same." To Sarah she said, "How pleasant to see you again, Miss Tamony. You're looking well." She laughed.

Malachi lifted his hand once more, the barest movement. Serafina's laughter ceased and she made a choking sound. Her hands flew up to her neck, and she gasped, her eyes widening with panic. Her companions moved even farther back, murmuring. Malachi's hand lowered and Serafina nearly fell from her chair, gulping for air. Another movement of his hand and she sat bolt upright, her head flung back to meet his gaze.

"Do not assume, Serafina," he said quietly, "that because I have not punished you yet, I either cannot or will not. We have not dealt together much and so I have let you go about your way, so long as you've done nothing to draw my attention. But never mistake my forbearance for anything more. Your powers are great, but I am the Dewin Mawr. Never forget it again."

Her eyes flashed with fury. "I'll make *you* forget it, Malachi Seymour," she vowed, her voice raw and dark. Gone was the childish creature of moments before. "When I control the power of the *cythraul*."

"It's a pretty dream for you to hold near," Malachi said. "But I wouldn't cherish it overmuch, were I you. Until

one—or neither—of us comes out the victor in that contest, I remain your superior. And as such, I'm going to give
you certain commands to obey."

She opened her mouth to speak, and Malachi lifted his
hand, cutting off her intake of air once more.

"First, you're not to cause Miss Tamony harm again. In any
way, or by any method. Do you understand me, Serafina?"

She nodded vigorously and he released her. She gasped
for breath.

"Second, until I've found the way to release him from
the spell you've cast over him, you're to make certain that
Julius Tamony returns to his home each evening in good
time to keep his parents from worrying. He is to be unharmed and in excellent condition. You are to instruct him
to behave cordially to his family, and to eat and drink whatever is set before him."

She glared at Malachi, but didn't argue.

"Lastly," he went on, "you will leave Desdemona in
peace. She's likely to do something foolish if you push her
too far. Another time you can take such wild chances with
your life, but not until after the child has come."

With another wave of his hand Malachi removed the
veil. The sound and movement of the room grew louder,
clearer. Making a slight bow, he said civilly, "Enjoy your
evening, Miss Daray."

"Are you quite sure she'll not harm Julius?" Sarah
asked as Malachi led her away. "She's so angry, and he's so
close at hand."

"She'll not risk making another misstep that might draw
down my wrath," he said, patting the hand that rested upon
his arm. "Not unless she truly finds the way to gain the
cythraul before I do," he added. "But we must pray that it is
not so. Ah, here's our chance, while no one is looking." He
deftly pulled her out a pair of open French doors and into
Lord and Lady Herold's beautiful lamp-lit garden.

"Dear me," Sarah murmured, "you are clearly well
versed in such escapes, my lord. Dare I accompany you into

the darkness? You might very well attempt improprieties."

"Of course I will," he admitted. "I'd be an idiot not to, especially when you're attired in a gown composed in such a manner that it makes me want to remove it. Really, love, you shall have to let me choose your gowns after we've wed. I don't want other men ogling my wife's bosom."

"My lord—"

"Malachi," he corrected. "But we'll not speak of marriage now."

"I don't want to speak of it at all," she said, "for you know very well that we cannot marry, and I shall find it depressing to have to remind you. You really ought to tell me instead about how matters ended in Scotland. Did you manage to assuage the unhappy father? Are your cousin and his bride safe?"

"Safe and wed, legally this time, with witnesses on both sides. I stood up for the groom just to be certain. The bride's father may not be pleased that his daughter wed a magic mortal, but the dowry we agreed upon will soothe his loss. I never fail to be astonished at how agreeable people can become when filthy lucre enters the bargain. Here, shall we take this path?" He led her down one that was particularly dark. "It looks promising."

Malachi found a bench hidden within a cluster of bushes and with magic lowered the light of the lamps nearby.

"Will you truly find it depressing to have to refuse my offers of marriage, Sarah?" he asked, sitting beside her. "I shall, if you're too persistent in refusing me."

She didn't answer. Instead, she murmured, "I'm so glad you've returned," and kissed him.

Malachi responded with the hunger that he'd felt for her since they'd separated. Gathering her into his arms, he turned his head and kissed her deeply. They were breathing harshly by the time he managed to pull away. She tried to bring him back, but he took her hands from about his neck and straightened.

"No," he said, his voice shaking. "No. Gad, only let me think a moment. Now, Sarah, no." He gently pushed her questing hands into her lap. Then he scooted a few inches away. "If you're not careful, I'm going to forget everything and take you back to Mervaille. And then how will Philistia get home?"

Sarah made a sound of displeasure but obediently stopped trying to lure him back. "Very well. For Philistia's sake." She sighed. "I suppose I should tell you about my time with Professor Seabolt."

Malachi would have preferred to hear her sigh again, with far more privacy, but he said, "Yes," and made himself listen.

Primly folding her hands in her lap, Sarah told him of the list she and the professor had compiled, of their decision to exclude Wales from their compilation, and about Tego.

"Tego?" Malachi repeated. "No, I don't recall meeting him during my last visit to the professor's home. You believe he may be one of Serafina's spies?"

"I don't know," she said, "but his magic is dark—I felt that the moment I met him—and he found ways to make himself present as often as possible while I was with Professor Seabolt. It would explain how Serafina Daray learned about my journal."

"It would also mean that she knows we're looking for a bell with Charles the Second's figure on it," Malachi murmured. "I'll look into the matter as soon as possible. But not until tomorrow, for I've had a wearying day dealing with troublesome pests, and all my night hours are spoken for." He leaned forward and placed a gentle kiss beneath her ear.

Sarah dutifully remained where she was, hands folded. For Philistia's sake. He scooted nearer, slipping a hand about her waist. She ignored him. Turning her chin with the tip of one finger, he kissed her mouth. She tried humming to distract her mind. He kissed her again, causing the humming to fade. Just as Sarah's hands had unfolded, Dyfed's silent speech interrupted their bliss. Malachi lifted his head with a sigh and gazed into Sarah's foggy spectacles.

"Something's happened," he said apologetically. "We have to return indoors. Morcar's left in a hurry and your cousin seems determined to follow."

• • •

No one was certain about what had transpired, save that Morcar and Desdemona had gotten too close to each other and exchanged words, and Philistia overheard them. Desdemona refused to speak of what had passed and insisted that her husband take her home. Philistia refused to speak, as well, though she shot scathing glances at Desdemona, clearly believing the fault to be hers. She wanted to leave the ball, too, as quickly as possible.

"Whatever Desdemona said to Morcar," Niclas replied when pressed by Malachi, "it couldn't have been too terrible. He simply left. If anyone was overset, it was Desdemona. And the Seymour girl." He nodded to where Sarah was trying to soothe her younger cousin. "She actually asked him to take her with him, and did nothing to lower her voice. I fear there will be the worst manner of rumors flying about Town tomorrow. Worse still is that I felt her emotions. She's in love with him, poor girl."

"I feared it was so," Malachi said. "Were you able to tell whether it was deeper than mere infatuation?"

Niclas's expression was somber. "She's given him her heart. We'll not be able to spare her from the pain she'll suffer when he turns her aside."

"Poor child," Malachi murmured. "And all of Society will talk of nothing else, especially after the spectacle she made of herself this evening. Perhaps I should—"

"*No*, cousin," Niclas said firmly. "Philistia Tamony has my every sympathy—you know I speak the truth. But she's mere mortal. The Guardians frown upon the use of magic to alter memories for the sake of any but our kind."

Malachi absently toyed with his quizzing glass. "Even so," he said. "It would mean a great deal to Sarah. I shall remain and make some few repairs. Will you and Julia be so good as to see Sarah and her cousin safely to their carriage?"

Two hours passed before Sarah made her way down the hall to her own bedchamber. She was exhausted, having dealt first with her cousin's tearful unhappiness at being parted from Lord Llew and then, unexpectedly, with the sudden appearance of her brother.

. Sarah had never seen Philistia behave in such a manner. The younger girl was given to histrionics, and this was far from her first experience with believing herself to be in love. But tonight Philistia was beyond reassurance. She was hysterical. Sarah had tried everything, from gentle words to firm insistence. Nothing touched Philistia. One moment she vented her wrath at Desdemona Seymour for giving insult to the Earl of Llew; the next she was resolved to go to Lord Llew with the intention of consoling him yet refused, when pressed, to explain why that gentleman might need such a thing.

"But surely Mrs. Seymour can't have said anything so awful," Sarah said patiently. "And if she did, then Lord Llew is far too sensitive to have reacted in such a foolish manner."

"It was not foolish!" Philistia cried hotly. "She hurt him terribly. They were engaged to be married once—he told me so himself, and I could see the pain in his eyes as he spoke of it. She broke his heart, Sarah, and then tonight she laughed at him because of it. In front of others, and mocked his pain. I *hate* Desdemona Seymour. If you marry Lord Seymour I shall never, ever speak to her, no matter how often we find ourselves in company."

She'd gone into her room and locked the door, telling both Sarah and Lady Tamony to leave her in peace when they tried to reason with her.

"It's all right, dear," Lady Tamony said quietly, pulling Sarah from the door. "She's had a long evening. Both of you have. Let her rest. She'll be more reasonable in the morning. Come downstairs for a few minutes and help me reassure your father. He's never seen Philistia like this, and you know how he worries. I'm afraid he'll lie awake the night if we can't put his mind at ease."

They found Sir Alberic pacing in his study. Sarah had just begun to explain, in a careful and truncated manner, what had transpired at the ball to overset Philistia when the doors opened and Julius entered. He looked dazed, but he bowed politely and said, "Good evening, Mama. Sir. Sarah. I hope you are all well."

"Julius!" Sir Alberic said with relief. "Sarah was only just telling us what happened at the Herold ball. Come and give us your perspective. I'll pour you a drink. You look as if you could use a bit of something to settle your nerves. That bad, was it?"

"No, thank you, sir," Julius replied stiffly. "I fear I'm very weary. I'll go upstairs, if that's all right." He bowed once more and departed.

Sir Alberic frowned. "I'm beginning to think London doesn't agree with Philla and Jules. Perhaps we should leave earlier than we'd planned. The boy almost appears to be sickening."

"He's merely concerned about the publication of his book, Papa," Sarah said quickly, exchanging glances with her mother. "You'll remember how tense such a time is, especially with the first. I'm sure he'll be much improved once it's come out."

"Yes, that's so," Sir Alberic said thoughtfully. "Still, I can't like his color. Or Philla's hysterics. If we don't see an improvement soon I shall have no choice but to remove us from Town. Now don't look so downcast, Sarah. Lord Graymar will be welcome to come and visit just as soon as we've put the house in order. And you'll be able to begin work on your next book once we're in the country, which I know you're eager to do."

The words filled Sarah's thoughts as she made her way to her room. She stopped at her cousin's and brother's doors, briefly, and listened for any sound, but they were either already asleep or being exceptionally quiet, for she heard not so much as the scrape of a chair or the sound of a footstep. The lights had been dimmed in Philistia's room.

Sarah's own room was lit when she entered, but she'd expected that. It was why she'd assured Irene that she didn't require help in preparing for bed tonight and sent the bewildered maid away. Closing the door, Sarah took a moment to pull off her slippers and toss them aside before moving to the bed.

"If you've gotten my bedcovers dirty I shall be very angry," she told the man lying there. He had changed from the fashionable attire he'd worn earlier into far warmer and more comfortable clothes.

Malachi smiled and patted the place next to where he was so comfortably reclining, his blond head propped up on a number of pillows and his booted feet crossed at the other end.

"I took care to wipe my boots before lying down. You did take rather longer than I thought, and I've had a very long day. If you'd delayed a few more minutes you might have found me snoring. Come and sit, sweetheart. You look exhausted."

"I am," she said, sinking down beside him with a grateful sigh. "If my parents should find you here, however, it will hardly matter, for they'll strangle us both. It's a good thing I have the ability to sense the presence of magic, or the maid might have accompanied me."

"I would have made myself invisible if I'd heard two of you coming, or erased her memory had she seen me." He drew Sarah down until she was lying beside him, her head resting upon his shoulder and his arm about her waist. "Were your parents very glad to see your brother?"

"Yes," she murmured. "Did you bring him home, Malachi?"

"Let us say that I watched over him as he came." His hand slid to her hip. "My intention was to come for you as soon as I finished preparations at Mervaille—I had thought to have my cook prepare a proper Welsh feast for us—but I changed course and went to Serafina's dwelling in order to fetch Julius home. As it happens, your brother and a companion were departing as I arrived."

"A companion?"

"Serafina has set one of her own to guard Julius, but I

had expected she would. Will the house be settled shortly?"

"Yes, I believe so. Mama and Papa are retiring now, and the servants will be turning down the lights."

"Excellent. We'll wait until they've sought their beds before leaving so that I can place the house beneath a spell of protection. In the meantime, love, you'd best put on something warm and comfortable. We've another journey to make this night."

"Beyond Mervaille?" she asked, her weariness fading.

"Well beyond," he murmured, and bent to kiss her.

"Is it—?"

"Another clue, evidently." He sighed sadly. "We shall have to enjoy our Welsh feast another time. Perhaps we might make up for it while we wait for the servants to fall asleep."

Sarah sat up and looked at him in surprise. "With my parents just down the hall? Malachi Seymour." She said his name as if he were a mischievous child.

He grinned and, taking one of her hands, brought it slowly to his lips. "You have a naughty mind, Sarah Tamony. I only mean to help you . . . change into more suitable attire. You've no need to fear. I can lock the door and stop any sound from leaving the room." He pressed his mouth gently against the pulse in her wrist. "Will you let me play maid to you, love? I'll do my best to fulfill the role to your complete satisfaction."

Sarah did feel naughty. Her garments slid away beneath Malachi's skilled fingers, one after the other, and he touched and kissed and caressed until she could no longer hold on to rational thought. But neither could Malachi.

So lost were the two lovers in their mutual delight that neither of them, not even the most powerful wizard in Europe, realized that first Julius, and some minutes later, Philistia, quite without knowing about the other, had left their rooms, sneaked down the stairs, and, avoiding the sleepy eyes of the servants, left the house by way of the kitchen door.

Chapter 23

$\mathcal{F}$ast traveling was just as thrilling as Sarah remembered. It all happened so quickly; that was the most amazing thing about this kind of magic. The wind rushed about them, and when the air began to feel cold and damp, when she could smell the freshness of the earth, Sarah realized they were about to come to a stop. She heard music over the noise of the rushing wind, and laughter as well.

Trees, wagons, people, fires all came into view. Sarah felt the hard ground beneath her feet and knew that they had arrived at their destination. Malachi took a moment to steady her, then to release her from the confines of his cloak.

"Thank you," she murmured, setting her hat more firmly on her head and pushing up her spectacles. Turning, she looked through the trees to where a gypsy camp was alive with music and dancing. "Where are we?"

"Lancashire," he said, reaching for her hand. "Prepare yourself to meet some of my more interesting cousins."

"You have relatives who are gypsies?"

He sighed and pulled her toward the gathering. "My family consists of numerous odd and unusual individuals," he said. "You've already met Steffan and his men, and know what it is I speak of. Magic mortals are easily bored, and tend to seek entertaining lives. The Theriots aren't truly gypsies, but they choose to live as if they were, save when they're at their various estates and townhomes, behaving like the wellborn wastrels they are. They cause me no small measure of trouble when they get together and start roaming the countryside. You can't begin to know how often I've been called upon to pull their feet out of the fire. Ah, here is Christophe, coming to greet us. Don't let him frighten you," he said. "He's what might be considered a sort of wandering friend to all true gypsies, and can be rather exuberant and wild. But he's a good fellow and an extraordinary wizard of tremendous power."

A tall, broad-shouldered figure with dark unbound hair was striding toward them through the darkness. Sarah saw the flash of his white teeth as he smiled and the glint of a heavy gold ring in his ear.

"Malachi!" he cried. "Cousin! You've finally come. We've saved plenty of wine, and the fire will warm you quickly. Welcome, my lord." He enclosed Malachi in an enthusiastic hug, thumping him loudly on the back before letting him go. Stepping back, Christophe turned his wide smile on Sarah. "And this must be the woman that you—" He stopped, looked more closely at Sarah, then murmured, "Can it be? My little one?" He stepped nearer to better see her in the darkness, then gave a cry of gladness. "But it is! I could never forget the beautiful lady whose path I crossed in Florence. I thought I should never see you again."

Before Sarah could speak a word, the man had swept her off the ground and was whirling her about, sending her hat flying and loosening her somewhat tentatively arranged hair.

"Oh, my lord, please," she said. "It's wonderful to see you, as well." She pushed at his powerful shoulders to no effect. "I never thought to see you again, either."

"That night in Florence!" he said, setting her down but not letting go. "I looked for you everywhere afterward, but you had disappeared. You never even gave me your name, apart from 'Sarah.' You broke my heart, little one."

"I'm t-terribly sorry," she stammered, glancing at Malachi, whose brows had snapped down in displeasure. "I had no idea. It is very good to see you again."

"But how is it that you come to be in company with my cousin?" he asked, glancing at his relative before returning his attention to Sarah. "Never tell me that you're the one the spirits have sent their gift to? The red-haired seeker? But of course. It makes perfect sense, for you were so pleased when I took you to the gypsies in Florence. I always wondered at your boldness and bravery. Now I understand very well."

"It would appear," Malachi said stiffly, reaching out to slowly but firmly draw Sarah out of his cousin's grip, "that you are already acquainted with Miss Tamony. That will spare me the necessity of having to introduce you to my betrothed."

Sarah wasn't sure who reacted to these words with greater surprise—herself or Christophe Theriot. Malachi's fingers squeezed warningly on her arm, and she said rather shakily, "Yes, we met a few years ago. In Florence."

"So I perceive," said Malachi, his voice icy.

"Your betrothed?" Christophe repeated, clearly taken aback. "Malachi, you're to be *married*? After so many years?" He gave a laugh of sheer pleasure and then leaped upon his cousin once more, hugging him and kissing both cheeks before taking him by the shoulders and giving him a jolting shake. "I'd heard nothing of this! Do the other Families already know? What a celebration we shall have!" Turning, he shouted to those assembled around the fire. "The Dewin Mawr is to be wed! He's brought his betrothed to meet us!"

A loud cheer followed the announcement, and Sarah groaned. What on earth had possessed Malachi to tell such a bald-faced lie—to his own relative, no less?

Christophe had already turned back to them, his smile

wide. "And to think that you captured such a charming woman to be your wife. Sarah, my little one." He grabbed her up again and nearly squeezed the breath out of her. He kissed her full on the lips.

"*Christophe*," Malachi growled. But his cousin had already let her go and was hitting Lord Graymar on the back again.

"Of course you are jealous, Cousin. I should be as well, with such a beautiful woman for a wife. But come! Come to the fire and we'll see what the spirits have given us for Miss Tamony. Then you must stay for a proper celebration of your coming nuptials. We'll have music and wine, and I'll tell you of the night when I saved your lovely betrothed from a pack of hungry wolves intent upon gobbling her up." He laughed again. "I'll wager she never told you the tale, eh? Oh, you're going to have your hands full with such a wife as this, dear cousin. We Theriots will seem tame by comparison."

"Another fire?" Sarah murmured as they followed Christophe and his men.

"No, the message will be given differently this time," Malachi said. "The spirits seldom use the same method twice. Christophe contacted me to say that the Guardians had sent a message to him through water that was addressed to 'the redheaded seeker.' He thought it must mean Steffan or another one of our red-haired mystics, but I believe it must be you, love."

"Through water," she murmured thoughtfully. "Fascinating."

"Sit here, please, my lord and lady," Christophe said, indicating a wooden bench near the fire. "Warm yourselves and accept a cup of wine while I fetch the gift from our Guardians."

Pewter mugs were pressed into their hands, but Sarah only had a brief moment to savor the taste of the rich red wine on her tongue before Christophe returned and took the cup away.

"Here it is, my lady. It was sent to us upon the river that

runs close by, and put into my hands by the water faeries. You see what is written there, Cousin, in the ancient tongue."

He held out an object such as Sarah had never before seen. It was a perfectly round sphere made of what appeared to be blue glass, filled with swirling white smoke. On the top, arranged in a circle, were gold symbols similar to those on the Donballa.

"Oh, my," she murmured. "It's so beautiful." The amulet that lay between her breasts began to grow warm.

"It is what mere mortals sometimes call a crystal ball," Malachi said, stroking one finger lightly over the gold letters. "We call them *viatoris,* or messengers. It is rare to receive such a communication. You are most honored by such trust, Sarah. They have even given you a name. It's written here. To The Red-Haired One Who Seeks and Hears. It is a great compliment for a mere mortal, just as the gift of the Donballa is."

The moment was solemn. Sarah drew in a breath and asked rather shakily, "How do I read it?"

"Only the one it is addressed to can divine the way," Malachi said. "And each in their own way. You might start by looking into it."

Sarah's hands trembled as she took the sphere from Christophe. Bringing it near, she peered into the haze within the glass, watching as the white smoke twisted and swirled. It reacted to her touch, moving more rapidly as she brought it even nearer. But she saw nothing.

"You must find the way, Sarah," Malachi encouraged. "It's there, somehow."

Frowning, Sarah turned the globe all about, watching as the white smoke twirled violently within. She brought it so near to her spectacles that her eyes crossed, touched it to her cheek, then her forehead. Still nothing.

At last, very aware that she was being avidly watched, Sarah put it against her ear and listened.

"How strange," she whispered, and Malachi leaned nearer, saying softly, "What is it?"

"I can hear voices. Many voices. It's lovely."

"What are they saying?"

Sarah listened for a full minute before replying, " 'Be ready . . . be vigilant . . . for the charge laid before you . . . look to the sky on the half-moon . . . all become one . . . or all will fail. . . .' " She looked up. "Then the words repeat. That's all there is."

"It's enough," Malachi assured her. " 'All become one or all will fail.' That's the second time they've sent that message. It must be of far greater importance than I believed. And the half-moon. That will be the time of the *cythraul*'s arrival. Now we need only decipher the other clues and we'll know not only when but also where." He took the sphere when she held it out to him and with a gentle movement sent it floating into the air. It went higher, spinning slowly, then a little faster, until it suddenly broke apart in an explosion of light, sparkling for a few brief moments before fading entirely.

Christophe's gaze moved higher, into the early-morning sky. "The half-moon is but three days hence, Cousin. Can it be that the demon will come so soon?"

"If the spirits say it is so, then the demon comes three nights from now."

"Then we must make merry before the test comes, my cousin," Christophe said. To his people he said, "Hurry and bring more wine! Put more wood on the fire! My little Sarah will soon be the Countess of Graymar and lady wife to the Dewin Mawr. We must welcome her to our family as only the Theriots can!"

The Earl of Llew had seldom suffered through so unpleasant an evening or realized his loneliness quite so starkly. Not even when he'd been blind.

All mortals, magic or mere, tended toward denial in various forms, usually regarding some personal shortcoming or other. Morcar knew this and accepted that he suffered the same weakness. He had been raised to feel superior to others, to know how powerful he was even among magic mortals, to accept that he was beautiful and desirable. And although he knew, deep within, that he had failings, he pushed the thought of them far, far away and simply didn't dwell on them.

Seeing Desdemona large with Dyfed Seymour's child had forced them into vivid focus. She might have been Morcar's and the child his own. He'd dreamed of such things. Wanted them beyond anything else he could name. But Desdemona had spurned the heart he had laid at her feet because she'd preferred a lesser wizard—*a Seymour*—to Morcar.

Tonight, seeing her for the first time since the day he'd regained his sight, he realized why. It wasn't because Desdemona found him lacking as a mate. There was far more. He saw it clearly in her violet eyes. She thought him stupid, insipid, even dull. She wanted nothing to do with him, save perhaps to see him in pain. But that was a part of her dark nature that even being married to a Seymour couldn't change. She hated Morcar, and if he died on the morrow, would dance upon his grave.

He'd gone to the ball knowing that they must face each other at last and had thought that the pain would be bearable. And it might have been if Desdemona had played the part of a wellborn lady and behaved politely. But she'd not. She'd openly faced him with all the anger and hatred she felt, even speaking the words aloud to make certain he knew what was in her heart.

I would rather have been rendered forever powerless than live a single day as your wife.

He could still hear her voice and the sharp, biting manner in which she'd said it, still feel the pain that had knifed through him. More than that, he'd felt all those secret, self-denied failings rise up into his consciousness. The effect had overwhelmed him. Where Morcar usually might have found the strength to laugh her words away or pretend he didn't care, he'd instead given way to the pain and let it rule his heart. With all the social world watching, with so many magic mortals present whose good opinion he needed,

Morcar had let Desdemona Seymour's words drive him from the Herold ball in shame.

Now, standing alone in his darkened bedchamber, he was too disconsolate to care what anyone thought of him. Grimly he thought of how furious his father would be at such a sentiment. Cadmarans were rulers. Leaders. They did not show weakness before others, never before their own kind and certainly not in the presence of mere mortals.

But it scarce mattered now. The painful truth of the matter was that Morcar was not his father, nor his father's father. He was not . . . admirable. His own people, the dark Families, had no use for him beyond the protection his powers gave. If Serafina gained the power of the *cythraul*, those few clans who yet stood with him would abandon him in a moment, never looking back. Morcar had never been able to gain their real loyalty, as his forebears had done. Because he had never been worthy.

With a wave of one hand he started a blaze in one of the large chamber's two fireplaces, and moved toward a table set with various decanters to pour himself a drink. Just as he neared it, something stopped him. A feeling . . . a sound. A voice calling his name.

Morcar stood still and listened, realizing at once who it was. He told himself that he was aggravated at Philistia's insistence in pursuing him, but his heart felt something altogether different. The foolish girl might only fancy herself in love with him, but even misguided devotion was welcome to him now. The rest took but a moment to decide. Philistia Tamony was a mere mortal and inferior to his kind, which gave him every right to use her for his own benefit. And she wanted him so greatly that he'd not need to use magic to bend her to his will. She would give herself willingly and supply the comfort he needed. In return, Morcar would make certain that the loss of her virginity was as pleasurable as he could possibly make it. They would each gain something tonight.

He traveled into his garden and found Philistia standing just within the gate. She was startled by his sudden appearance but didn't cry out. She laid a gloved hand over her chest and drew in a sharp breath, but her expression filled with gladness at the sight of him.

Morcar opened the cloak he wore in silent invitation. Philistia gazed at him for a long moment, hesitating, then moved forward. She pressed against him, small and delicate and chilled by the night air. He enfolded her within the warmth of his heavy garment and took her into his bedchamber.

He said nothing as he threw off his cloak and began to remove hers. When she opened her mouth to speak, he brought his down upon it, kissing her with all the hunger and need he felt, willing her to answer. She did, opening to him with an immediacy that enflamed Morcar to an even greater desire.

He pulled away her garments one by one, letting them fall to the floor, and discovered with hands and mouth how exquisite her delicate body was. She was far more beautiful than he'd imagined or hoped, her skin white and smooth, like warm satin beneath his fingers. He explored her small, high breasts and the curves of her hips and thighs, delighting in the pleasure sounds his touch elicited. Philistia stood pliant beneath his kisses and caresses, and when he laid her down upon his soft feather bed she reached her arms out to receive him.

Morcar was rigid with desire and impatient for release, but she trusted him so completely, had opened herself to him so fully, that he made himself wait for her readiness. For the first time in memory, he wanted his lover to experience as much pleasure as he could impart without the use of magic. He wanted to see Philistia's sweet face when she reached fulfillment; only then would he allow himself to follow.

But it seemed impossible not to hurt her; she was so much smaller than he. Though he strove to be gentle, when Morcar at last pushed into her depths she uttered a sound of pain and clutched at his shoulders until her fingernails bit into his skin.

"Shhh, darling," he murmured, kissing her damp forehead. "Relax. I want to make you mine."

"Yes," she said. "Yours. Please, Morcar."

She squeezed her eyes shut as he pressed harder, breaking past the resistance, and her slight body stiffened beneath him. Morcar held still, waiting until she relaxed before he at last began to move, surely and carefully, watching as her eyes opened with unfocused wonder, as her expression began to reveal her increasing pleasure.

"I love you, Morcar," she said, and again, "I love you."

The words were meaningless to Morcar, and he let them fade from his thoughts, instead reveling in the pleasure humming in every pore of his body. He collapsed atop her with a hoarse sound, exhausted, replete with satisfaction. With an effort he rolled to the side and heard her gasp for air at the absence of his heavy weight.

He attempted to say something to her, to tell her that she'd pleased him very well for a mere mortal, but he couldn't call up the energy to do more than curve a hand about her small bottom as she nestled against his side. His eyes closed and he sighed deeply, and as one of her arms slid about his chest to hold him, Morcar fell into a deep and welcome slumber.

It was far too easy for her to become lost in the music and magic of the gypsies, Sarah thought with a measure of guilt. The women about her plied her with wine and laughter and extremely naughty words of advice to carry to the wedding bed they believed she was headed towards, very nearly making her forget that she and Malachi must return to London soon. But she was weak, and both the company and wine were so compelling and pleasant that Sarah almost couldn't think beyond the moment.

On the other side of the fire the men sat together, drinking and laughing and watching the women. She'd caught Malachi's meaningful gaze several times.

"Dance, Miss Sarah," one of the younger women urged. "You must dance for the great lord. Fill him with desire for you."

"Oh no, I really don't think it a good idea," Sarah said,

laughing, even as several of the women began to show her how to move in the correct manner. "I'm sure he wouldn't notice, save to laugh at my awkwardness."

"He has eyes," an older woman told her. "He'll notice."

"But you must call him to you," said the first, swaying her hips and twirling about. "You must have power over him, to call your lover when you desire him. Otherwise his gaze might fall upon another who calls as well, and he'll be lured away. Surely you don't wish the Dewin Mawr to look at another."

"Certainly not," Sarah replied with feeling. "But I shouldn't wish him to think that I . . ." She fell silent, wondering what, precisely, she did want him to think. Whatever it was, she knew it didn't involve him falling prey to the lures of other females. Sarah gave her attention to the women before her and began to copy their movements.

She was fortunate in the fact that the dance wasn't unknown to her. She had visited with gypsies in several areas of the Continent, and each tribe had been unique. But in certain aspects they were the same; in particular was their love of dance and music. This wasn't her first time at taking her place around the gypsy fire. It was, however, her first attempt at using the movements of her body to lure a certain man to her side. And if he didn't come, after she was about to make a complete spectacle of herself, Sarah supposed she might as well resign herself to eternal spinsterhood.

Her determination having been made, Sarah set her thoughts directly upon the Earl of Graymar and began to move her hips to the rhythm of the music. It took no longer than a few brief seconds before Malachi put his cup of wine aside, rose to his feet, cast off both his coat and vest—this to the cheers of the camp—and began to stride in her direction.

"You'd better have a care, my love," he murmured as he reached her, holding out his hands to set them on her waist. "I'll have to fend off every man in the camp."

"I had a feeling you'd be far better at this than me," Sarah said as he began to move with her in the dance. "We are not well matched in this particular dance."

"We are well matched in every way," he replied, pulling her nearer and turning her in a breathtakingly fast circle. "I should be happy to give you personal lessons in the movements. One day. Just now there is something I think you would like far better, and God alone knows when we'll have the chance again."

"What?" she asked hopefully.

"Hold tight, love," he said, wrapping his arms firmly about her just as their feet lifted from the ground. "Let's go visit the stars."

Morcar knew something was different even before he opened his eyes. Physically, all was well. Philistia Tamony's small, warm body was still pressed against him, cradled in the crook of his arm with her head pillowed on his shoulder. His own body was hard with desire, ready to possess her again and enjoy the intense pleasure that had made him mindless hours earlier.

But something had changed.

He was . . . happy. Happy in a new way. And content, as if he hadn't a care in the world. More than that, he felt a kind of inner lightness, as if some heavy weight had been cut out of his soul. He'd not been so relaxed and unperturbed since childhood.

The fact of it gave him pause. But only briefly.

He would ponder the matter later, he decided, moving his hand down the curve of Philistia's slender back to waken her. He wanted her again. She had satisfied him so well and showed such remarkable promise that he believed she might remain his mistress for the rest of the Season. That would give him sufficient time to train her to his liking and enjoy her endearing affection. But he would have to take care. If the aunt and uncle were to discover the relationship, they would demand marriage, likely hoping to land their niece a wealthy, titled husband. And that would never do. Philistia was a charming girl, as females went, but she was mere mortal and completely unsuitable as a mate for an extraordinary wizard.

Philistia murmured sleepily as he stroked his hand gently over her, bringing his other hand to her body to arouse her further. She stretched and yawned beneath his caresses and smiled even before she opened her eyes, whispering, "Good morning, my lord."

He kissed her soft, warm mouth and, turning to lie on his back, pulled her atop him.

"Good morning, sweet," he murmured, sliding his hands up her thighs. "Sit up, darling. Let me look at you in the morning light."

She did as he asked, smiling at him as if she had never known such happiness, as if he were the most wonderful man in the world to wake up next to. The thought filled Morcar with inexpressible satisfaction.

"Do you love me, Philistia?" he asked suddenly, surprised to hear himself ask such a thing. He could have forced her to say the words; he could have enchanted her to mean them. But she had said them freely last night, and their effect had been profound. It was the first time a woman had said such a thing to him without being either paid or enchanted to do so. "Do you?"

"I love you, my lord," she said softly, and bent to kiss him gently. "With all my heart, I love you. And will until my life has ended."

He found it difficult to breathe, suddenly. The tightness in his chest became an intolerable ache, and he had to blink to clear his vision, which for some reason had blurred.

She lifted her delicate hands and with cool fingers caressed his cheeks, then slid them upward to smooth the hair from his forehead. "I love you," she murmured once more, kissing him. Then again, and again, kissing him each time she said the words. Morcar lay still beneath her, letting the words flow over him, letting her touch push every other thought or sensation away. It was a spell, though he doubted she knew what she was doing. He was far too powerful a wizard not to recognize magic when it happened. She was casting a terrible spell upon him, the most powerful and unbreakable that could befall his kind, and though he knew it could mean nothing but misery for either of them, he was powerless to make her stop.

Soon he would be furious about it. Beyond furious. Now he could only lie beneath her kisses, captive, and let himself be taken by the magic she made. Grasping her by the waist, Morcar rolled until Philistia lay pressed into the soft mattress. Entwining her hands with his, he brought their bodies together, capturing her gasp in his kiss.

"Philistia," he murmured as he taught her his rhythm. "Tell me again. Don't stop."

She gladly obeyed.

Chapter 24

Serafina lay sprawled across Julius Tamony's naked body, smiling and replete.

"You're marvelous, love," she said, turning her head to nip him with her sharp teeth. "I can't seem to get enough of you." Sighing, she pushed upward to gaze into his weary half-closed eyes. "If only you weren't mere mortal, I might keep you longer. But we've only a few days, darling, and then you must be given to the *cythraul*. I shall miss our times together." Bending, she kissed his slack lips, then lifted herself from his body and lay beside him, caressing his chest with her fingertips. "Sleep now, Julius. I don't want to damage you before the *cythraul* takes possession. What an ill welcome that would be for the demon."

Obediently Julius's eyes closed and his breathing deepened. Serafina had meant it when she'd said that she would miss him. But having the power of the *cythraul* would more than make up for the loss. The thought, as she rolled from the bed and searched for her robe, filled her with anticipation.

She was the first to discover all the clues about the *cythraul*'s arrival. The two great wizards Malachi and

Morcar thought themselves so superior to any other magical beings that they'd not truly considered Serafina worth worrying over. How surprised—and sorry—they would be when she was the one who met the *cythraul* and leashed its power. And how foolish Malachi would feel when he realized that it was his incaution that had given her the final clue, for she was related to the faeries by blood and her spies were everywhere. Even in the forests where the Theriots made their gypsy camps.

She slipped the robe over her arms and tied the belt at her waist, then sat before her candlelit mirror to brush out her curls. The room was dark, lit only by the candles set near the mirror, but darkness didn't affect her vision. Gazing at her reflection, she turned her face from side to side, examining it for any sign of her *animantis* heritage. She seemed to have been changing of late, in small but worrisome ways. Her teeth had grown a bit sharper, and the tips of her ears seemed—at least to her—to be growing more pointed. The changes were so slight that only she appeared to notice them; her minions assured Serafina that she still looked entirely human.

A movement across the room caught her attention and she swiveled on her chair, casting a freezing spell toward the shadow-darkened corner. It bounced away uselessly, as did the next she sent, and the one after that. Swearing, she stood and raised both hands, ready to use the full force of her powers to stop the intruder, but before she could open her lips she found herself being wrapped and bound by invisible cords. Her arms were forced to her sides and her legs were pressed together. Her mouth was covered and stopped, and then her body was bent and pressed back until she sat on her chair once more.

Malachi moved out of the shadows and with the turn of one hand caused the candles in the room to give off greater light.

"Good morning, Serafina," he greeted calmly, the black cloak he wore settling about his shining boots as he came to a stop before her. "I shall release you from your bonds if you'll promise to cease your foolishness. You cannot touch me with your magic, and I so dislike seeing powerful beings go to such waste. Apart from that, I wish to speak to you, and it will be easier if you cooperate."

She nodded, and Malachi waved a hand to make her bonds disappear. Serafina sputtered with rage. Digging her nails into the chair's cushion, she demanded, "What are you doing here? I have a right to privacy in my own domain, regardless what the Seymours may think. The Guardians will hear of this."

"They already know," Malachi said dismissively, looking about the room with an air of distaste. "You needn't fear that I intend to make a habit of such visits. Poor Julius." His gaze fell on the sleeping man. "He'll be insensible with wretchedness if he recalls the hours he's spent here."

She laughed at that. "He'll remember nothing but pleasure, such as no mortal woman could give him, mere or magic. I might have taught you something about the ways of my kind, my fine lord, if you'd been brave enough to let me."

Malachi shuddered before turning cold eyes upon her. "The idea of lying with you, with any *animantis,* sickens me. The Seymours have made many mistakes in the years following the exile, but never that, thank God."

"That is all that we lack to be made perfect," Serafina said, rising from the chair to face him. "The seed of the Seymours. But I shall lay claim to it once I've gained the *cythraul,*" she promised. "Your seed, Malachi, growing within me." She set a hand over her stomach and laughed at his open revulsion. "Perhaps I shall even let you live long enough to see it born. To see what our child will be like. Or perhaps not." She smiled at the thought.

Malachi gazed at her for a silent moment, then said calmly, "I haven't come to be made ill. Or to suffer your idiotic speeches about what you'll do and how you'll do it. They are most tiresome to listen to."

"Then leave!" she cried furiously. "You have no reason to invade my dwelling. I did as you commanded and sent

Julius home to his parents. He was polite and kind, as you insisted he be, and then he came back to me. Nothing else has changed."

He looked at her closely. "But it has, Serafina. I've discovered your little trick, you see. Your little deception, carried out upon a dear friend of mine."

Her expression grew wary, and she shook her head. "I don't know what it is you speak of. No one can practice deception and the Great Dewin know nothing of it."

"I was lax," he confessed. "If you do indeed gain the *cythraul* the fault will be entirely my own, for I've allowed my mind to be occupied by other matters. But the fog has lifted, and I've come across the spy you set over Professor Seabolt."

The sudden intake of breath gave Serafina away. She stared at him and said nothing. Malachi smiled.

"Yes, Serafina, I've discovered your minion Tego and have removed him from his place of employment. He'll no longer be of use to you in bringing clues about the *cythraul.* Oh, he's a clever fellow, I grant you that. He nearly got away before I caught him, for he has that gift of sensing impending doom. Between Tego and your other spies I imagine you've far more clues than either Morcar or I have managed to collect."

"Where is he?" Serafina asked quietly, striving to remain calm in the face of Malachi's mockery. Tego was her most valued and loyal servant. She would be lost without him. "What have you done with him?"

"Your concern for so lowly a creature is touching, my dear," Malachi said in scoffing tones. "Given your fame for cruelty. But you've ever been faithful to those who are of your kind. It's the one thing I like about you."

"*Where is he?*" she demanded.

"Here," Malachi replied, putting a hand inside his cloak and withdrawing a small crystal vial. It shimmered with light and motion. With life.

Serafina felt an unbidden horror at the sight and lifted both hands to her mouth. It was an old magic the Dewin

Mawr had performed. A grave and terrible magic well beyond her own powers. There was nothing left of Tego but his essence, and if Malachi decided to unstop the little bottle in his hand and pour its contents upon the floor, Tego would be gone from her forever. The thought was too terrible to bear.

"The Guardians—" she began haltingly.

"Will not care in the least. Laid beside your own actions, Serafina, it is entirely just. You have gained the way to the *cythraul* by deceit and harm, by imprisoning an innocent mere mortal with the intention of allowing the demon to inhabit his body. Do you want Tego back?" He shook the bottle so that it gave off a stronger light. "You know what I want."

Serafina didn't have to think upon the matter. She hated being bested by Malachi, especially having her own deception turned back on her, but Julius Tamony could easily be replaced, both as a lover and as a vessel for the *cythraul*. Tego was vitally important to making her life possible.

"Return him to me first," she said firmly. "I must see that he is all right before releasing Julius."

Malachi shook his head. "No, Serafina. I am the Dewin Mawr, and my word is binding. You know that I will give Tego back to you if I say that I will. I do not have the same assurance of you. Release Julius Tamony and you will have your manservant back, just as he was, whole and in perfect health."

She did as he commanded, watching wrathfully as Julius Tamony woke from his stuporous slumber and, looking about, asked where he was. Malachi bid him to dress and he did, quickly, clearly frightened to find himself naked and in a strange place. He cast numerous glances at Serafina, begging her pardon in a pained fashion for appearing before her in such a state of undress, and kept pleading with Malachi to tell him what was happening.

The Dewin Mawr waited until the other man was dressed before quieting him with a spell. Then Malachi moved to the center of the room and set the crystal bottle

floating in midair. Speaking the incantation in solemn
tones, he gave a sharp clap of his hands, and the room exploded with light and sound. Serafina felt as if her sensitive
eyes would burst from the pain of so much brilliance, and
she fell upon her knees, weeping and blinded.

"Oh, God," she shouted out with agony, pressing both
hands over her face. "No more, Malachi. Please, no more."

Cool hands touched her shoulders, and a calm, gentle
voice spoke. "I'm here, my lady," Tego said, pulling her to
rest upon his shoulder. "I'm here. I'll take care of you.
They've gone."

Serafina's tears changed to those of relief; she didn't
care that the salt made her burning eyes sting the more.

"*Tego!*" she cried, grasping one of the arms he'd set
about her and hugging it tightly, pressing her face against it
and wetting him with her tears. "Tego, you're all right," she
managed against her sobs. "You're all right."

"Yes, mistress," he said, hissing the words more
strongly than ever. His arms tightened about her. "I'm well,
and will never leave you again." His voice was fierce. "Let
me care for you now. I'll make a salve for your eyes, and
you will rest. We must set our minds to destroying him.
The Earl of Graymar." He spoke with the hatred he felt.
"You must promise to let me do it, when the time comes. I
want to kill him with my own hands."

"Yes," she murmured, calming as he rocked her back
and forth. "You'll have that honor, Tego. Only don't leave
me. Never again, for any cause."

"Never, my mistress," he vowed. "There will be no need
once you have the power of the demon. But we must find
another to receive the *cythraul,* now that Julius Tamony has
been taken from us. We've only three days."

Serafina nodded and uttered a last, solitary sob. Her delicate frame shook, then quieted once more in his steady embrace. They were silent for a long while until Tego spoke.

"There is the cousin," he said thoughtfully. "The ugly
girl who follows Lord Llew about."

"She's far too small," Serafina said dismissively. "How could the demon possibly make use of such weakness?"

"But you are small, my mistress," Tego reminded. "And most powerful, nonetheless. No one would ever suspect."

Serafina considered what he said. "They'd not, would they?" she murmured. "Not if we're careful." Excitement began to grow in her breast. "But we must be far more cunning this time, Tego. We must make certain she's ours before either of them suspects."

"Completely ours, my lady," Tego agreed with a nod. "It will be done."

Morcar came awake with a jolt, as from a nightmare, sitting up before he knew that he was in motion. He was covered in sweat and his limbs were trembling. Beside him, Philistia stirred and made an irritable murmur, then turned on her other side and went back to sleep. Morcar slid from the bed and dropped his feet to the floor, running his hands through his hair as he struggled to control his breathing and put his thoughts in order.

They came at him all at once, and none more palatable than the other. A sense of dread settled over him, and for a long moment the world shifted completely out of place.

His life was ruined. That was the fact of the matter, and there was nothing he could do to change it. Philistia had forged an unbreakable enchantment and bound them together for eternity as *unoliaeth*—a oneness that could never be altered. They would not know happiness or contentment apart from the other from this moment forward. He, Morcar Cadmaran, one of the most powerful wizards on earth, was doomed to require the presence of a mere mortal woman, and not only in this life but in the next as well.

He stood and strode to the nearest window, flinging back the curtains to reveal the early-morning light.

"How can it have happened?" he asked aloud, his voice shaking as he fought back the tide of panic that threatened to overwhelm him. *"How?"*

But he knew the answer. It was because he'd wanted it to happen, because he'd desired love so greatly, at any and all costs, and had foolishly accepted the first woman to offer it.

Philistia Tamony. A mere mortal.

God help him, it was too awful to bear. Indeed, he told himself, he could *not* bear it. Would not. He would be despised by his own kind if it should become known that he was *unoliaeth* with a mere mortal. His own clan, the Cadmarans, would have nothing more to do with him. He would become a pariah and a curse, and they would turn to another to be their leader.

Serafina Daray. The thought only filled Morcar with greater displeasure. Aye, this dread thing that had happened would take away every resistance to Serafina's determination. Morcar would be left with no one to stand beside him, save, he thought furiously, Philistia Tamony.

He glared at the small figure lying upon the bed, focusing all his wrath and despair upon it.

"Wake up!" he shouted, striding across the chamber to grasp the edge of the bedcovers and yank them back. "Get up!"

Philistia came awake with a start of confusion. Sitting, she blinked and looked about. "What is it?" she asked with sleepy alarm. "Has something happened?"

"Yes, it has," he told her, not caring that she shivered in the room's chill morning air. "I want you out of here. Now. Get up and get dressed."

"W-what?" she asked, curling her knees beneath her and covering her bare arms with her hands. Her gaze fell for a brief moment upon the bloodstained sheets; then she looked up at Morcar. "Why are you so angry?"

"Because you're here," he replied cruelly, making the words purposefully harsh. "Are you so ignorant of the ways of Society that you don't realize a man of my rank doesn't enjoy waking up to find the whore he had the night before yet beside him? You've a great deal to learn, my dear. Now get up and dress yourself." He bent and picked up the nearest garment and tossed it at her. "I want you gone within the half hour."

Turning away, he moved to pull on the pair of trousers he'd discarded the night before. Her silence and lack of movement only infuriated him the more.

"Are you deaf, Miss Tamony, or incapable of understanding simple speech?" he asked, turning to pin her with an angry glare. "Do you want me throwing you out into the street naked?"

Her eyes had begun to fill with tears, but she obediently slid from the bed and began to gather her things. Silent, she dressed, not looking at him. Morcar forced himself not to watch. He pretended to busy himself about the room, starting a fire in the other grate and increasing the blaze in the first one to fill the lordly chamber with warmth. With a wave of a hand he summoned a servant, and when that man appeared he gave instructions for a hot bath and breakfast to be brought.

"And arrange for a hack to wait at the servants' entrance," he added as the servant bowed to leave. "My guest will be departing soon. I don't want her seen."

"Yes, my lord."

When the door closed, Morcar looked at her. Philistia was sitting in a chair near one of the fires, pulling on her boots. She was in disarray, her garments wrinkled and poorly buttoned, done up as they were without the help of a maid. Her hair hung free of any arrangement, long and uncombed. She looked so small and helpless, and Morcar's heart lurched within him. He ruthlessly pressed the feeling aside. He wanted to break the *unoliaeth,* to make her hate him so fully that the Guardians would take pity on the girl and set her free.

He knew how to manage the task. He was a master of cruelty; it had been taught to him from the cradle. "Fix your hair before you leave," he instructed coldly. "I'll not have people speaking ill of my new mistress. You must never be seen in public in such a state, Philistia, else I shall be very displeased with you."

"Yes, Morcar," she said in a quiet voice, though he could hear the tears she hid from him.

"I do not allow my whores to speak to me in such an informal manner. You will address me as 'my lord' or 'Lord Llew.' Do you understand me?"

She nodded this time, not looking at him. Standing, she moved to pick up a handful of hairpins that were scattered about the floor, then stood before one of the many mirrors in the room—Morcar had never tried to deny or hide his vanity—and began to put her hair up. Without the help of a maid, it looked awful. Morcar knew it would be better to send her back to her people looking her best, but he no longer cared what they thought or said or demanded. His life was ruined. Nothing else mattered.

"Are you finished, then?" he asked impatiently. "Good. Then leave. One of the servants will show you where the kitchen is."

Philistia slowly went to collect the dark cloak she'd worn the night before and, putting it on, drew the hood over her head to hide her tear-streaked face.

"Will I see you soon, my lord?" she asked softly.

"That's no concern of yours," he said curtly, opening the door to usher her out. "When I want you again, I'll summon you. You need only be ready to come when I call. Do not disturb me otherwise."

She moved to the door, then hesitated. "My lord," she whispered. "Why are you doing this? I didn't expect anything but—"

"But what?" he said fiercely. "Did you think I would fall in love with you simply because you gave a fair performance in bed? That I might marry you?" He laughed cruelly. "Surely you can't have been so foolish as to believe that bedding me would win you a rich and titled husband?" He moved nearer, gazing at her with all the fury he felt. "I've had far lovelier and more satisfying partners than you, my pet, and never fallen prey to their wiles. I'll keep you for as long as you please me, and when I'm done I'll throw you back into the pond like the worthless little fish you are. If you're quite good I might reward you with a pretty necklace, but that's the most you'll ever have from me, Philistia Tamony. Never hope for more."

She lifted her face to him then, and he saw at last the measure of pain he'd given her. Her cheeks were wet with tears, and her eyes filled with misery.

"I suppose it will do no good to tell you," she murmured, "but I have no need for a rich husband, for my parents left me very wealthy. I came to you last night because I knew Desdemona Seymour had hurt you, and I wanted to soothe that hurt. And I lay with you and g-gave myself to you because I love you. There was no other reason." Lowering her head, she added, "You need not see me again, my lord. I don't expect anything of you."

She walked out the open door and into the hallway, moving toward the stairs. Morcar pressed his lips together tightly to keep from calling her back and with every ounce of strength he possessed forced his body to remain still until he felt her presence leaving his home. Only then did he shut the door.

He raced to the window and gazed down, watching as she stepped out of the servants' entrance to the pavement, where a hack waited to take her home. But she didn't approach the waiting vehicle. Instead, Philistia turned and began to walk away, her head bowed as if she was grieving. Morcar stood, never moving from the window, watching until her small gray figure at last disappeared in the distance.

Sarah came awake at the touch of gentle fingers stroking against her cheek, though it took an effort to do so. She was so weary she didn't want to rise just yet.

"Go away," she murmured, grumpily pushing the hand aside.

A soft chuckle greeted the words. "I'm sorry to wake you, love, but there's someone who wishes to see you."

"Who is it?" she asked sleepily, cracking her eyes open to find Malachi standing over her. He looked as weary as she felt and was still dressed in the same garments that he'd worn when he'd brought her home from the gypsy camp. Had he even been home to Mervaille to sleep?

Turning aside, he motioned with his hand toward the door. "See for yourself," he said.

Sarah pushed into a sitting position and fumbled for her spectacles, which Malachi pressed into her hands. Putting them on, she saw Julius standing in the doorway, looking haggard and anxious. But his eyes, she saw with a leap of joy, were clear again. It was Julius who gazed back at her.

With a glad cry Sarah pushed the covers away and stood, hurrying to greet him with arms held wide.

"Oh, thank God," she said as he caught her in his embrace. "Thank God you're all right."

"Can you ever forgive me, Sarah?" he asked, his voice thick with tears. "I can't bear to think of what I've done."

"Oh no," Sarah murmured, pushing back to look at him. "You don't remember, do you?" She glanced at Malachi, who sat upon the bed. "I had so hoped he'd not remember."

"I didn't want to forget," Julius told her, wiping his wet face with the back of one hand. "I asked Lord Graymar not to alter my memories. Not until I can make things right. Will you forgive me, Sarah? I don't deserve it. I shall never forgive myself, especially for striking you."

"Don't be foolish," she said gently, stroking his hair back from his beloved face. "You didn't know what you did, and Malachi healed me at once. I'm only thankful that you're free and safely home again. And," she added with a jesting smile, "that you'll never again naysay me when I speak about magic."

"No, Sarah," he said, and began to weep anew. "Never again."

She hugged him and wept a little, too. Looking back to Malachi, she asked, "How did you manage it?"

He told her briefly of taking Tego unawares at Professor Seabolt's house, of using magic to trap his essence in a bottle, and of his visit to Serafina. By the time Malachi finished, Julius was nearly incoherent with exhaustion.

With Malachi's help Sarah got Julius undressed and into bed. The moment they returned to her bedchamber Sarah grasped Malachi by the lapels of his coat, pushed him against the nearest wall, and kissed him soundly. And then, before he could breathe or speak, kissed him again for good measure.

"You are the most wonderful man on earth," she told him. "And I love you very much. Thank you for bringing him home."

He laughed and pulled her closer. "You're welcome," he murmured, finding her lips with his own. "If I'd had any idea you'd be this glad I would have made the attempt far sooner. I don't suppose you'd agree to marry me by way of reward?"

She sighed and let him kiss her, then gazed up into his eyes and said, "It would be a very poor sort of reward, my dear. You can't really wish it, and if you would only take the time to consider how unsuitable a wife I should make a great lord—"

He kissed her again, not releasing her until she stopped resisting. His expression was set when he finally did.

"I'll not hear you, or anyone else, say such a thing," he told her. "You are entirely suitable in every way."

"I am a writer," she told him. "And a mere mortal. There is nothing I can do to change either. Only think how desperately unhappy you'll be when I press on with my writing, and how unhappy I'll be when you do all that you can to stop me."

He sighed and leaned his head against the wall. "Surely we can find a way around that troublesome problem. My love, I do try to consider myself not so vain as to believe that every woman in the world must leap at the chance to be my wife, but I confess that your refusals are most painful. Do you truly wish to be parted from me at the end of the Season?"

"Of course not," she said, slipping her arms about his waist and laying her head upon his chest. "I hope that we shall never be parted. I can't imagine wanting to live away from you now." She hugged him gently and added, "I'm sorry to have given you pain, my dearest. Will it help at all if I say that I'll be your mistress for the remainder of my life?"

"It would be a start," he said rather petulantly as the effects of exhaustion worked on his countenance. "But it's far from what I desire. And if you believe your parents would ever allow it, sweetheart, then you've clearly gone round the bend."

"Yes, that's so," she admitted, sighing. "I suppose it must be marriage, then, though I do feel terrible about doing such a thing to you. You don't harbor any real hope of trying to change me, do you, Malachi?"

He smiled at that, his spirits considerably revived by her agreement. "I should never be so foolish, my darling. Will you promise not to try murdering me in my sleep if I should stop the publication of your work?"

She looked at him very sternly. "No, I will not. You'd best escape such a fate this very moment by taking back your offer of marriage. I give you leave to do so."

"No, love, I'll take the risk," he said happily. "We are fated to be, you know. The Guardians gave you to me as a gift."

"A gift?" she repeated.

"When we stood in the fire with Steffan," he said. "They spoke with me alone, and told me that they had given you to me as *unoliaeth*. Do you know what the *unoliaeth* is, Sarah?"

"Of course I do. It means those who are fated for each other. But I thought such unions were determined before birth."

"They are, usually," Malachi concurred. "And such a union was never foretold for me, so that I believed I would never find a perfect mate. But the spirits took pity on me and changed their minds. They saw that I loved you and fated us to be together. And so you see, my love, you cannot be parted from me even if you should wish it. You'd be desperately unhappy."

"Will I?" she asked, smiling. "And you, my lord?"

"I should have been desperately unhappy with or without the *unoliaeth*. I loved you that first night at Glain Tarran."

That mollified her. "I loved you, then, too," she said. "My parents will be thrilled. Such a catch I've landed."

He laughed. "You make me sound like a fish."

"A fine, handsome fish," she murmured, sliding her hands up to his neck. "I shall never throw you back."

He readily met her kiss and began to wonder when he'd have another chance to be truly alone with her at Mervaille, but a disturbance at the kitchen door had him lifting his head.

"That's odd," he said.

"What is it?"

"It's Philistia." He was already pulling Sarah out the door and down the hall to the stairs.

"Philistia!" she said, hurrying behind him. "What's she doing out of the house? I thought you—"

"Yes, I did, but she clearly got past the spell I placed. Or snuck out before it was set, which is what Julius did. I do seem to be rather preoccupied these days."

"Was she with Llew?"

"Doubtless," he said grimly as they entered the kitchen.

It was a very good thing that the occupants in the house were still slumbering beneath Malachi's magic, for the moment the door was opened and Philistia saw her cousin, she burst into very loud tears and fell into Sarah's arms.

"Philla!" Sarah cried, shocked by her cousin's appearance. "What in heaven's name did he do to you?"

"N-nothing," Philistia said against her tears, letting herself be led into the house. "It wasn't him."

"By God it was!" Malachi declared wrathfully, following as the women made their way. "I shall have his head for this. Even the Guardians will refuse to protect him now."

"*No!*" Philistia pleaded. "Leave him alone. It wasn't his fault. I wouldn't leave him in peace. He didn't harm me. Please, my lord. Swear to me. Swear upon your honor."

"You're hysterical," he said, sweeping the slight, sobbing figure up into his arms. "You need rest."

Philistia flailed at him, deaf to Sarah's sharp command that she stop. "Swear to me!" she cried frantically. "I'll never speak to you again if you harm him! I shall leave! I'll never come back! Swear you'll leave him alone! Swear it! *Swear it!*"

"Very well," he said impatiently as she weakly struck him across the face. "I'll not harm Lord Llew. I swear it."

She subsided, collapsing against him and sobbing on his neck. She didn't resist as Sarah readied her for bed or when Malachi gave her a few drops of sleeping potion.

"This is becoming an embarrassing habit with my relatives," Sarah said as she gently washed Philistia's face and hands. The girl was so soundly asleep that she didn't stir. "I do hope you'll not be obliged to make entire vats of that mixture just for the Tamonys. Still, I wish you'd not given her your word regarding Lord Llew. He deserves a sound thrashing at the very least. Will he—will he have to marry her, do you think?"

"Yes," Malachi said with a sigh. "He will. He'll have no choice. There's been a powerful change in Philistia. I do not mean physically, though there is that, as well. I'm sorry for her. He's an evil, wicked devil."

"I was afraid it was so," Sarah said sadly. "She gave her heart to him, and now this. But, perhaps, if we take her away to the country her reputation might survive."

"Morcar will follow," Malachi told her. "He sent her away this morning very likely out of rage. I can only imagine how overset he is to find himself in such a situation. But no matter what he may be feeling now, he will soon be driven by an unconquerable compulsion to see her. They cannot be parted for long without becoming desperately unhappy."

"No," Sarah murmured. "No, Malachi, it can't be." His solemn expression filled her with dread. "Are you quite sure?"

He nodded. "They are *unoliaeth*, Sarah. Morcar Cadmaran and Philistia. It is far too powerful a change for me to mistake. How or why it came to be, I do not know. But it is. They will never know peace apart from the other now." He gazed at Philistia's small, slumbering form. "Poor child," he murmured. "She's been bound forever to one of the wickedest men alive, and there is nothing that I, or anyone, can do to set her free."

Chapter 25

$\mathcal{W}$ith but two days left before the *cythraul*'s arrival, Malachi was obliged to make the most of the time he had. The first matter at hand was returning to the Tamony dwelling that evening, refreshed from several hours of sleep and a good scrubbing by Rhys, to take Sir Alberic into his confidence. It seemed foolish not to do so, considering that the man's entire family had learned the truth about not only Malachi but also other magic mortals.

Meeting with Lady Tamony and Sarah in Sir Alberic's study, Malachi stated the basic facts, not sparing what Julius had undergone at Serafina's hands but taking care not to mention Philistia's circumstances. Soon Sir Alberic would need to be made aware of the *unoliaeth* that existed between his beloved niece and the Earl of Llew, but the time for such a revelation wasn't yet right.

Sir Alberic wasn't well pleased by what he heard; Malachi hadn't expected that he would be. But neither was he overset to know that magic truly existed or that the tales his daughter had written about were true. In fact, quite the opposite. "I always wished they were," he said, pleasing Sarah a great deal. That his only daughter was determined to marry a magic mortal, however, elicited a different response.

"I believe you to be a fine and true gentleman, my lord," said Sir Alberic, leaning back in his chair and regarding Malachi levelly, "and I have no doubt that Sarah loves you. But can she be happy, being married to a man whose first loyalties will always be to those who give him their allegiance? Your duties to these magical Families you speak of do not recommend you as a husband, I fear. I would prefer that my daughter be bound to a man who puts her first in his life."

"Sarah will always have that place in my heart, sir," Malachi vowed. "And any children that God may bless us with. And as Sarah is as brave as she is beautiful and intelligent, I intend to take her with me as often as possible when I am called away to fulfill my duties as Dewin Mawr. She will not be abandoned in favor of the magical clans, for I shall never be able to abide being parted from her for long."

Sarah beamed at him. "You see, Papa?" she said. "Nothing could be more perfect, or make me happier. Only think of the research I shall be able to do, and the sights I shall see."

"You might also be reassured, sir," Malachi added, "to know that Sarah has been unreservedly approved for inclusion in the magical Families. According to our laws, any union involving a mere mortal must be blessed by our elders before it can take place. No mere mortal woman has ever before been so quickly or readily accepted as Sarah was. There is great anticipation of our marriage, for they know what she will bring to us."

In the end Sir Alberic gave them his blessing, though Malachi could see that it wasn't easy for him to do.

"I'll write an announcement for the papers," Lady Tamony said, kissing first her daughter, then Malachi. "The wedding should take place at the end of summer."

Malachi would have preferred to have it immediately but was willing to be patient. "I'd be grateful, my lady, if we can be wed at my ancestral home in Wales, Glain Tarran," he said. "There is a beautiful chapel overlooking the sea, and the estate is large enough to entertain a large wedding party for several days. You may invite as many guests as you please. The weather will be ideal for such a gathering at summer's end."

It would be a very strange gathering, he thought silently, considering the number of magic mortals who would necessarily be invited. But that could not be helped. All Dewin Mawrs were wed at Glain Tarran and had been since time remembered. Sir Alberic and Lady Tamony, fortunately, were delighted by the suggestion.

Malachi was invited to stay for dinner.

"So you've a demon to confront and deal with," Sir Alberic said, setting aside his wineglass at the end of the first course. "And you've only a handful of clues to determine where it will arrive?"

It was astonishing how quickly the Tamonys had become fascinated with the *cythraul*. Malachi glanced at Sarah and realized how she'd come by her inquisitive nature.

"Hopefully they will prove sufficient to lead us to the *cythraul*," Malachi said. "Clearly the spirits believe they are, else we would have had more."

"With but two days to decipher them, I should be pleased to lend you whatever aid I might," Sir Alberic offered. "I know little of magic, most of it from Sarah's writings, but I do know a good deal about England's history, and Charles the Second has always been of special interest to me."

"That's good of you, sir," Malachi said sincerely. "I'd be honored for any aid you might give me in deciphering the clues."

Julius, who had grown suddenly quiet, set his fork aside and said, "I believe I know more."

They all looked at him.

"More clues," he said. "My memories are dim, but I believe that . . . she spoke of them. Miss Daray."

"Are you sure, Jules?" Sarah asked. "Your memories might not be reliable, considering the spell you were under."

"No, I'm not precisely certain," he admitted, "but I remember them talking. Miss Daray and Professor Seabolt's servant. You remember him, don't you, Sarah? That odd youth who gave us such a fright when he opened the door?"

"Yes, of course. His name is Tego."

"Tego." Julius gave a nod. "Yes, that's what she called him, so it must have been him. They spoke of the clues they'd gathered. I believe I might be able to recall at least one of them if I concentrate."

"That would be useful," Malachi said. "But you mustn't weary yourself, Julius. It will be some time before you've regained your strength."

"But time is just what we don't have now, it seems to me," Sir Alberic stated, pushing his plate aside. "Not if this demon is as powerful as you say. Two days will pass quickly, and you must be ready if you're to keep us all from grave harm. If Julius can remember anything useful at all, we'd best get to the task of putting our minds together. Let us retire to my study, if you please, Lord Graymar, and we'll see whether we can't assemble the pieces we have into a proper picture."

Sir Alberic's comfortably furnished study became the center of discussion over the next many hours for those involved in deciphering the clues. Malachi and Sarah were there almost without ceasing, while Sir Alberic, Julius, Professor Seabolt, Niclas, Dyfed, and even Lady Tamony took turns coming and going. Philistia entered on the first day to greet their visitors, looking wan. She said little and avoided meeting anyone's eye and retired to her room again as soon as was politely possible.

"There simply don't appear to be enough clues to narrow our choices down," Sir Alberic said grimly at the end of the first day. "The only definitive facts we know are that Glain Tarran is not the correct location and that the place that is has a bell with Charles the Second's figure on the premises."

"And," Sarah added wearily, "that there is a flower of some type, if Julius's memory about what he overheard is correct." She looked at her brother. "Are you certain they didn't say what kind of flower, Julius?"

He shook his head. "They only said 'flower,' but she seemed to understand what it meant. Indeed, she appeared to be quite confident in knowing the place where the spirit will descend."

"Aye, she has the advantage of successfully discovering clues that were sent to both Morcar and myself."

"I still say that the most important clue is the one that the Guardians gave to you twice," said Niclas, who had been quietly standing near Sir Alberic's extensive collection of books. " 'All become one or all will fail.' It sounds very much to me as if the Guardians intend for part of the test to include some manner of unity. Perhaps the time has come to approach the Earl of Llew and suggest joining forces."

Malachi cast him a look of fulsome displeasure. "No. He'd only use the chance to gain the *cythraul* for himself."

"That is the risk you would take," Niclas agreed. "But you have one thing in common. Neither of you wants Serafina Daray to gain such power. Would you not prefer chancing Morcar harnessing it? The demon is powerful, but Morcar would use it far less cleverly than Serafina, and is prone to making greater missteps. You'd have a better chance of besting him."

"I'll approach him only as a last resort," Malachi said. "Not before. Surely we'll be able to sort this out before tomorrow night arrives."

But as each hour passed, Malachi began to grow less certain. He sent greater wizards and sorceresses who gave him allegiance and who possessed the gift of fast traveling to the places in England listed by Sarah and Professor Seabolt to make certain that they contained bells bearing the likeness of King Charles the Second. Word returned that each place did. They were unable to scratch any of the possibilities from the list.

"It just gets worse and worse," Sarah murmured. "You can't be at all of these places at once. If you set guards, perhaps they could alert you in time when the demon arrives and you could use the fast traveling to get there."

"It may come to that," Malachi said. "But if Serafina is already present and ready . . ." He let out a tense breath. "I hate to think of it. If only we could understand what the spirits meant by the message they sent in the journal."

"It does seem too plain to assume it simply means Glain Tarran," Niclas said. "Or even, more closely, the ceremonial grounds."

"The ceremonial grounds," Sir Alberic said thoughtfully. "Perhaps that's exactly what it *does* mean. That those ceremonial grounds aren't the ones, but that the place where the *cythraul* will arrive is some other sacred Celtic land."

Julius gave a shake of his head. "There are no sacred Celtic grounds that contain English memorial bells. But I do think we might dispose of the idea that the place must have been sacred to ancient peoples. Can the clue not merely point to any sacred land, either ancient or modern?"

"Cathedrals, churches, chapels, and monasteries, then?" Sir Alberic said. He looked at Malachi. "It makes sense, and would cut the list down a bit."

"Perhaps," Malachi said thoughtfully. "But I believe the clue is yet more specific than that. The ceremonial grounds at Glain Tarran are quite definitively of Celtic origin. There has to be meaning there, somehow."

And so it went, as each hour slipped away. By the afternoon of the final day they had gone so many hours without slumber that they were beginning to lose their composure. Malachi's nerves had become so stretched that he was short-tempered, even with Sarah, who bore it patiently.

He was beginning to feel lost and, worse, powerless and desperate. Gone was his certainty that an answer would be given to him. He no longer believed that the Guardians would favor him with some greater explanation. A few more hours at best and he must go to Morcar Cadmaran with hat in hand, asking that they unite for the greater good. Morcar would be willing to make a bargain in order to stop Serafina, but Malachi feared the price of his agreement would be costly.

They had all gathered in Sir Alberic's study by late afternoon, including Lady Tamony, and sat in gloomy silence. They had relentlessly pored over the list, arguing for and against each potential place, giving up and starting all over again. They were exhausted and dispirited and out of ideas.

"Well," Malachi said at last, standing. "I must make my visit to Lord Llew."

"I'll go with you," Niclas said wearily, rising as well.

"And I," Dyfed put in.

"No," Malachi said. "The task is mine alone, especially as I've failed to understand the clues given to me. I—"

He stopped and frowned, his eyebrows lowering in concentration. "Kian is coming," he said, and the next moment strode to the study doors, flinging them open. Standing on the other side was a man who was clearly the twin of Dyfed Seymour, save that his long blond hair fell loose about his shoulders. He wore neither hat nor cloak but was dressed as casually as if he'd come straight out of his own dwelling. Everyone in the room rose, and Dyfed started forward, crying out gladly, *"Fy geffel!"*

Kian Seymour scarcely had the opportunity to draw in breath to speak before Malachi grabbed him by the front of his coat and dragged him into the room. "What the devil are you about, showing up in such a manner?" he demanded, the strain of the past hours tingeing his voice with a fearful sharpness. "The servants here aren't our kind, or even sympathetics. Any one of them might have seen you appear out of thin air."

"I apologize," Kian said, gazing at the assembled with a pleasant smile. "I was told to come at once and assumed— well, clearly I should have taken a moment to think. But the matter sounded urgent, so I kissed Loris and the baby good-bye and came at once. By the rood, you do look the worse for wear, I must say. Hello, Dyfed!" Pushing free of Malachi's grasp, Kian hugged his brother, then greeted Niclas and Professor Seabolt, whom he knew well. To the rest he said, "Pray forgive me for the intrusion. I am Kian Seymour, as you may have surmised. I believe some of you must be the Tamony family. And this, I would wager"—he bowed to Sarah—"is my future cousin, Miss Sarah Tamony. I had heard you were lovely, Miss Tamony, but I confess the reality is far more pleasant than expected."

"Be silent a moment, *cfender*," Malachi told him crossly, "and I'll make introductions." To the assembled he said, "This is my cousin Kian Seymour, the Baron of Tylluan. He is to be Dewin Mawr in my place, which, considering how ill we've done in discovering the arrival of the *cythraul*, may be soon. Kian, this is Lady Tamony and her husband, Sir Alberic. . . ."

Kian Seymour's bracing energy was a stark contrast to the dour exhaustion in the room. Sarah never knew how Malachi found the patience to make proper introductions, let alone address the younger man in so civil a manner.

"Explain yourself, Kian," he said. "Who sent you here, and for what purpose?"

"The purpose I do not yet know," Lord Tylluan replied, accepting the glass of wine Sir Alberic held out to him. "The Guardians sent me, through Steffan, who arrived and said that I must join you here at once. I went first to Mervaille, but Rhys sent me here. He's terribly worried. I take it that you've not yet discovered where the *cythraul* is to arrive."

"Why in the name of all that's holy would the Guardians send you here?" Malachi demanded. "Do they think me so incapable of dealing with the demon myself that they must send lesser wizards to aid me?" Small objects in the room began to tremble. "You are not yet the Dewin Mawr, Kian Seymour," he informed the younger man. "Your powers are nothing to mine."

Sarah stood and set a hand on his shoulder.

"My lord, you are weary and overset," she said gently.

"I am nothing of the sort," he snapped, shaking off her hand and stepping away. He began to say something more but stopped and looked toward the study's far wall. "Hell-fire and damnation. Christophe is coming, as well, and he's bringing Steffan with him. Make room, if you please, Harris."

Professor Seabolt moved aside just as the two men appeared, causing Lady Tamony to remark, "Oh, my," and Sir Alberic to say, "We had better move into the parlor. We're running out of room in here."

More introductions were made, with great impatience as Malachi forbore Christophe's and Steffan's determination to kiss the ladies' hands and make grand bows to the gentlemen.

"Tell me why you're here," Malachi said. "If the spirits sent you because of the *cythraul,* then—"

"That is precisely why," Steffan told him. "I received word this morning that we were to come at once and lend our aid. Desdemona should arrive soon."

"God's mercy," Malachi murmured. Dyfed stood and left the room without a word. "How many more are to come?"

"I cannot say," Steffan replied. "As many as are needed, for the spirits will make their wishes known to those who are chosen. We are to do your bidding. That is all I know."

"Then you may leave," Malachi stated. "Now. The *cythraul* is my burden, just as it was to those who came before me. It is a test in which to prove myself, and if I succeed, I succeed alone. If I fail, the fault will be mine as well."

Sarah moved toward him. "Think a moment before you send them away, Malachi. Consider how unusual it has been this time. None of the clues has been given to you directly by the spirits, but to you through me. They have never before been given through another, have they?"

"No." He looked more displeased than ever.

"And then there is that peculiar clue," she said gently. " 'All become one or all will fail.' You told me once, when you related the tale of the Donballa and Guidric of Maghera, that unity was not a lesson your kind has remembered." She touched his hand and held his gaze. "This is a test, my lord. Perhaps part of it is whether you are willing to sacrifice your own pride for the good of all men. If the Guardians sent others to help you, then they must have known that you would need them."

"There is sense in what she says, Cousin," Niclas said. "The world has changed, and will keep changing. We must change as well if we're to continue on in it. Perhaps the Guardians are showing you the way."

"It is the same lesson I learned when I dealt with the monster at Tylluan," Kian said. "Do you not remember, Malachi? I had to accept Loris's aid to be rid of the thing, regardless what my pride told me. If I'd remained stubborn, the beast would have run wild and caused every manner of destruction."

Malachi was quiet, his gaze held upon Sarah, who yet stood before him.

"There are a few hours remaining," Lady Tamony spoke into the silence. "Let us at least spend them more comfortably. With your permission, Lord Graymar, I'll order a light supper. I may require some . . . help in dealing with the servants, however."

Malachi scarcely wished to think beyond what Sarah had said to him. Her touch alone had soothed and quieted his inner turmoil. "Kian," he said, "go and enchant Lady Tamony's servants to forget all that they have seen or heard in the past many hours, or will see and hear until sometime tomorrow. Christophe, will you be so good as to go to Mervaille and bring Rhys to me? He'll be of help with all of us here. Have him bring a change of clothes, as well. Sir Alberic, may my family and I impose upon your hospitality a few hours longer? The number may grow shortly."

"For as long as you desire, Lord Graymar," Sir Alberic said. "We'll be happy to play host to all your family if they should wish to come."

Malachi laughed at that, as did Niclas. "Never say so, sir," he advised. "You have no notion of what that would mean."

Desdemona arrived before Christophe could return, pushing into the study with a very angry Dyfed at her back.

"No, I will not go home," she insisted as Julius stood to make a place for her near the fire. She looked him up and down and said, "You look just as fine clothed. What a handsome fellow you are. But you'll not remember me, I suppose, for we've not been formally introduced. I am Desdemona Seymour, and I am not leaving." This last was said to her husband.

Julius flushed hotly as everyone in the room looked at him. Making a bow, he murmured his pleasure at the introduction.

"You will not endanger our daughter by this foolishness," Dyfed said with ill-contained anger. "I'm taking you both home now. There is more than enough magic present to deal with the demon without you putting yourself into harm's way."

Desdemona merely made herself more comfortable. "If you think I'm going to sit at home while Serafina Daray gains the power of the *cythraul,* you are far mistaken, my husband. I'll be dead before I let that woman have the means to destroy us all. Including our daughter. Now be still and introduce me to anyone I don't already know. You British are so peculiar about such matters, after all."

An hour later Malachi had changed into fresh clothes and allowed Rhys to shave him, all in preparation for approaching the Earl of Llew.

"Niclas will go with me," he said once they had reassembled in one of the larger parlors, "and we will return as quickly as we can. There remains little time before the demon will arrive, and you must all be ready to travel the moment we return."

"My lord?" It was Rhys. He stood at the parlor door, his face ashen. "Miss Philistia is no longer in her room. She is nowhere in the house. The upstairs maid found this." He held out a folded piece of paper. Sarah hurried to take it from him.

"It's from Lord Llew," she murmured, scanning the missive quickly. Her mother peered over her shoulder. "Asking Philistia to meet him at his home."

"It can't be," Malachi said.

"But it is," Sarah insisted, holding the page out to him. "It bears both his signature and his seal. Do you not see?"

"I see what is here," Malachi replied, "but I cannot believe it's truly from Morcar Cadmaran."

"Why?"

"Because he's here. Now." Malachi nodded in the direction of the street. "The Earl of Llew is standing at your front door. Without Philistia."

The Earl of Llew had spent the past two days in hellish misery. From the moment Philistia walked out of his dwelling he'd been tormented by memories of the things he'd said to her, of her tears and the pain on her face, of her bowed head and the final words she'd spoken.

I don't expect anything of you.

He had tried to push the words from his thoughts, to push *her* from his thoughts, but it was impossible. No amount of drink nor any of the potions he possessed had the power to give him relief. He'd not been able to sleep or think or do anything at all save suffer. Because he'd hurt her and sent her away. Because he'd been a *fool.*

There was only one cure for such suffering, and Morcar had at last accepted what it was. He must find Philistia and plead for her forgiveness, and then he must make everything right, no matter what the sacrifice. He would cease being head of the dark Families. He would give up any hope of gaining the *cythraul* and cede his title and his lands, even Castle Llew, to a worthier Cadmaran. He would go where Philistia desired, live where she wanted to live, do whatever she bade him do. He would do it all gladly, so long as she forgave him.

And so he had bathed and dressed with special care and gone out in search of her, praying that he would find her at one of the numerous parties or dinners to which he had been invited that evening. Whatever pride he yet possessed hoped for the chance to approach her away from the Tamony household, for to go to her family would prove a humiliating experience. But she was nowhere to be found out in Society, and he at last climbed into his coach and gave the driver directions to her dwelling.

The Guardians, Morcar decided when he at last stepped to the pavement again, had clearly decided that having to throw himself upon her family's mercy wasn't sufficient punishment for his sins. He felt the presence not merely of Malachi's great powers within the elegant town house but also of many extraordinary magic mortals. Now Morcar's disgrace would be complete, having to beg Philistia to forgive and take him back before such witnesses. But he deserved it, he thought morosely as he trod to the door. He should be shot for having made her weep.

The door opened and he found himself face-to-face with Rhys, Malachi's most trusted servant, which was something Morcar had not expected.

"What the devil are you doing here?" he demanded crossly.

Rhys bowed and said, "You must ask His Lordship. Be so good as to follow me, please."

"I don't suppose you would tell me," Morcar said as he entered the dwelling and handed Rhys his hat, "but is Miss Philistia at home? I have come to speak with her."

"You must ask His Lordship," Rhys repeated, and led Morcar to the parlor where he had twice before enjoyed tea with Philistia and Lady Tamony. He felt the increase of magic as they made their way and wondered just whom Malachi had brought to the Tamony household and why.

The doors opened and Morcar had his answer. It looked like a veritable reunion of Seymour cousins. They even outnumbered the Tamonys. As he moved into the room, following Rhys's announcement, Morcar noted that the brother, Julius, appeared to have been released from the spell Serafina had placed him under. Morcar scanned the room hopefully, not caring overmuch that he was surrounded by enemies, but saw no sign of Philistia.

"Lady Tamony," he said, bowing to that lady, who was scowling mightily at him. "Sir Alberic. Miss Tamony. Forgive me for the intrusion. I've come to ask permission to speak with Miss Philistia. I realize how unseemly such a request is, especially at this late hour, but please believe me when I tell you that it is of the greatest importance."

It was Malachi who stepped forward to speak to him.

"You do not know where she is, Morcar?"

"She's not here?" Morcar asked, the hope of seeing her fading to despair. "Has she gone out then?" He looked about the room. They were all staring at him intently. Even that damned gypsy lord Christophe Theriot was present. And Steffan Seymour. What was going on? "I've searched every drawing room with a gathering already," Morcar said. "I didn't see her in any of them, nor was she expected."

Sarah Tamony came toward him, holding out a folded piece of paper. "This was just found in her room. She was here an hour ago, and now she's gone."

Morcar's hands trembled as he took the page and unfolded it, reading the words there. His entire body shivered with unbidden fear.

"I never wrote this," he said, finding it difficult to draw in breath. "My God . . . did she believe I wrote this?" He looked at Malachi. "She went out . . . you didn't even feel her absence? You let her go out in the dark of night *alone*?"

Malachi's expression was grim. "I accept that the fault is mine. We have been preoccupied with deciphering the clues of the *cythraul,* and I confess I paid no notice to those not present here." He waved a hand at the assembled. For the first time Morcar saw that Kian Seymour was there, and Desdemona as well.

"Lord Llew," Sir Alberic said tightly, "do you mean to say that you had nothing to do with my niece's disappearance? She apparently left in order to seek you out. Surely she must have had cause to believe the note was from you."

"Yes, she would have," he said, unable to keep the agony he felt from his voice. "I cannot explain to you now why that should be, save to tell you that I love Philistia. I love her, sir. I would not harm her. Never again."

"Again?" Lady Tamony repeated fearfully.

Morcar shook his head. "I will confess all my sins to you gladly, my lady, once Philistia has been safely retrieved. Malachi, you must help me. All of you—" His gaze took in the entire room. "Not for my sake, of course, but for Philistia's. She's overset and not likely to be thinking clearly. If we work together, so many of us, we can easily find her."

"We haven't the time, Morcar," Malachi said. "The *cythraul* comes tonight, very shortly. Or did you not realize it?"

Morcar didn't care about the *cythraul* any longer. He didn't care about anything or anyone save Philistia, out in the dark, alone, because she believed he had sent for her. And she had gone. After all he'd said and done to her, she had yet been willing to go to him.

"I'll go alone, then," he muttered, turning to leave. "I have to find her. God knows who wanted to lure her out, making her believe it was me—"

"That's exactly right, Morcar." Malachi put a hand on his arm to stop him, roughly pulling him back. "Only stop and think a moment about who would have cause to do such a thing. Who would know that Philistia would answer your call to come?"

Morcar accepted the fact that he wasn't a particularly clever or quick-witted fellow, but knowing that didn't help. He gazed at Malachi with a mixture of impatience and bafflement.

"The *cythraul* is about to arrive," Malachi stated more calmly. "It requires a mere mortal's body for its occupation else it cannot remain on earth. Serafina has gained enough of the clues that she's discovered when and where the *cythraul* will arrive. Do you not see that Julius, who she had planned to use as a vessel for the demon, is here among us?"

Morcar shook his head, utterly confused. "But surely she'd not use Philistia. Her body is so slight and powerless—the *cythraul* would reject the use of it."

"It will take what's been prepared," Malachi told him, "and I have good cause to believe Serafina lured Philistia out as a way of revenge. I forced her to set Julius free two days ago. Unless you can think of some reason why any other member of Society would wish to draw Philistia out into the darkness by the use of your name, I believe we must assume that Serafina not only has her, but has already taken her to the place where the *cythraul* will shortly arrive."

Clever he might not be, but Morcar did possess the ability to make decisions. "Then why do we stand here speaking like fools?" he demanded. "Let us go at once!"

"Do you know the place, then?"

"Of course I do," he snapped impatiently. "Do you mean to say that you don't? You, the great Dewin Mawr?"

"I know the time, but not the place," Malachi confessed. "And I shall be glad to let you rub it in my face as much as you wish later. We've not the time now. Where is the demon to arrive?"

"At St. Just-in-Roseland, in Cornwall. That is where I believe it must be, considering the clues I was given. One of them was given to me by Philistia. The cover of a book she'd borrowed from Hookham's had been changed to read *The Life of St. Justin*. This was written in English. Beneath it was a clue in the ancient tongue, which I've not been able to make sense of: All become one, or all will fail."

Malachi turned and met a sea of wide-eyed faces. He and Sarah locked gazes and she gave a silent nod.

"The other clue given me was a rose," Morcar went on. "I surmised that the place must be St. Just-in-Roseland."

"A rose," Julius murmured. "Of course. That was the flower Miss Daray spoke of. And the other clue, about sacred grounds at Glain Tarran . . . St. Just-in-Roseland is built nearly on top of a site that served as an ancient burial ground for Druid priests. Why, even the church there continued to embrace Celtic Christianity long after other churches accepted the recognized Church." He searched the list, which he'd picked up from a nearby table. "And it's listed here. The church tower contains a bell bearing the figure of Charles the Second. St. Just-in-Roseland *must* be the place."

"Serafina would have realized it immediately," Niclas put in, "for she was born in Cornwall."

"She's been laughing at us all this time," Malachi told Morcar, "knowing that neither you nor I had enough to go on to figure out both time and place. If only we'd come together sooner, we might have been ahead of the game." He sighed. "The Guardians are testing us, Morcar. Little though either of us likes it, they clearly mean for us to work together to defeat the demon."

"I care nothing about the *cythraul*," Morcar said. "I only want Philistia safely back."

"You'll never manage it without help," Malachi said. "Without all our help. The Guardians have brought us together to combine our powers." He nodded toward the wizards and sorceress sitting behind them. "What do you say, Morcar? Do I have your word that you'll lend your powers to sending the *cythraul* back to the spirit world?"

Morcar didn't have to consider the bargain—one he never would have dreamed of making only days ago. "If you'll help me regain Philistia, yes."

They clasped hands, sealing the bargain before the Guardians, and made ready for the fast journey to Cornwall.

Chapter 26

The group of extraordinary wizards and one sorceress, as well as Sarah, who reminded Malachi that he'd promised her she'd be allowed to view the spectacle, and Dyfed, who refused to let his pregnant wife go without him, arrived a short distance from the churchyard at St. Just-in-Roseland. It was a small edifice with a single bell tower rising into the dark night sky and a garden courtyard surrounded by walls. Just beyond the church was a large inlet where sea waves crashed against the shore.

"That must be where the bell is," Malachi murmured, nodding to the tower as he unfolded his cloak to allow Sarah to step free. "I should like to see the accursed thing once the *cythraul*'s gone, considering the trouble we had finding it."

"Silence," Steffan commanded, holding up a hand. "The demon has already come," he stated in dire tones.

"Philistia," Morcar murmured, his voice filled with fear. He quickly began to move in the direction of the church, stumbling on the uneven ground.

"Morcar, wait!" Malachi said fiercely, but it did no good. The next moment a great flash of light filled the walled courtyard, followed by a piercing scream and then a deeper, horrified cry. The group came to a halt.

"Gather together!" Malachi shouted, grabbing Sarah and pulling her hard against him. "Quickly!"

"Oh, bother," Desdemona muttered, slower than the others because of her ungainly belly. Dyfed swept her into his arms and carried her into the small circle that had formed.

Morcar alone pressed on, ignoring the command. If anything, he began to move more quickly than before. Muttering a curse, Malachi sent a wave of air that threw the larger man to the ground, and pinned him there with the same spell of protection that he cast about those circling him.

It was done just in time, for with another burst of light a figure rose into the sky from within the garden, floating in the air above them.

"Philistia," Sarah whispered. "Dear God."

The small, delicate figure was scarcely recognizable as Sarah's younger cousin, for she emanated a fierce power that caused her body, her skin and eyes, and even her unbound hair to glow as if a lantern had come alight within. Streams of light poured out of her fingertips and from the toes of her now-bare feet. The dress she wore had split at the seams and barely clung to the body it covered. Her eyes, burning like fire, gazed in all directions as her body slowly spun, taking in her surroundings. Sarah was certain the demon would see them standing just beneath it, but whatever spell Malachi had placed over them had clearly made them invisible even to such a piercing gaze.

The figure turned toward the sea, just beyond the garden gate, and floated downward. When its feet touched earth the ground shook and the air about them blew hot and fierce, but they were kept safe from harm. The *cythraul* began to walk toward the waves, which began to crash loudly against the shore at its approach. With each step it took, light flashed and the ground trembled.

With a quick movement Malachi brought down the barriers of protection and, grasping Sarah by the hand, moved silently toward the walled courtyard. Everyone, even Morcar, followed. The demon, farther away now, appeared not to notice. It kept moving toward the water.

"Where is it going?" Sarah whispered as they pushed into the walled garden.

"I don't know," Malachi said, pulling her into the darkness. "Demon spirits cannot pass through water, but a powerful one can command the waves. It may intend to destroy the church by water and return the land to its pagan state."

"No, my cousin," Steffan whispered from somewhere behind them. "Do you not remember what Julius Tamony said? This was an ancient burial ground for Druid priests long before the Christians claimed it. Unless it is stopped, the demon will call their spirits back to life to be his servants."

"Grand," Kian muttered. "And with no master to guide it I suppose the *cythraul* intends to set itself up as a god."

"But where is the one who came to claim the demon?" Christophe asked. "Where is Serafina?"

"She is dead," Steffan said, falling still of a sudden. "I feel it. And there is another one, as well."

"Dead?" Morcar repeated. "It's not possible. The *cythraul* is to serve the one who brings it a mere mortal for possession."

"This demon has a mind of its own, clearly," Malachi said.

They found the bodies in a small clearing. Malachi created a light to aid the glow of the moon. Serafina lay with her arms above her head, as if she'd been about to defend herself from the *cythraul*'s strike. Her servant Tego lay over her in a failed attempt to save his beloved mistress.

Kian knelt beside them and felt for life. "Steffan's right," he said after a quiet moment. "They're dead. It's almost too incredible to believe. Serafina Daray was an extraordinary sorceress. She arrived in time to meet the *cythraul* and brought a mere mortal for its possession. Why would it kill her?"

"Desdemona, we're leaving," Dyfed stated firmly. "Now. Take us home."

"Don't be foolish," she told him. "If we don't finish

with the demon tonight, none of us will be safe. Not if it could kill one of us so powerful as Serafina." She looked to where Malachi stood, solemnly gazing at the bodies. "But are there enough of us, Malachi? Should we not send for others? If we only had enough time, my father would come from America and bring all of our most powerful magic mortals with him."

Malachi met her worried gaze. "The Guardians saw fit to send only us. It must be enough. Now we must decide our course of action." He glanced at each of them in turn. "The *cythraul* will run wild unless it accepts a very powerful magic mortal as its master. It expects to be claimed by such a being. I do not know why Serafina, powerful as she was, was rejected. It may have to do with some other cause. Perhaps because she was a woman."

"Then the *cythraul* is an idiot," Desdemona said fractiously, rubbing her back where it ached.

"Whatever the reason," he went on, "one of us must try again. A man, this time."

"I'll do it," Morcar said.

They looked at him sharply.

"Never," Kian said.

"Not a Cadmaran," Dyfed added. "You'll use it for your own devices."

"I should be the one," Christophe said. "I have no wife yet, nor children."

"Neither do I," Morcar replied with anger.

"Nor I," Malachi put in more quietly.

"Philistia is my *unoliaeth*," Morcar stated. "It is for me to save her from the *cythraul*. I swear aloud before the Guardians that I care nothing for the demon's power. I want it gone far more greatly than any of you now."

"*Unoliaeth?*" Kian murmured. "You, Morcar?"

"With Philistia Tamony?" Dyfed added with disbelief, scoffing. "I don't believe it."

"It's true, however," Malachi said.

"Poor girl," Desdemona said beneath her breath.

Morcar ignored her. "I love Philistia. She is mine. I claim the right to rescue her from the *cythraul.*"

"You might die in the attempt," Steffan said quietly.

"Then I die," Morcar replied. "It is little enough after what I've done to her. If I can release her, I'll gladly wait for her in the spirit realm."

"Malachi, don't trust him," Dyfed argued. "He's a Cadmaran. Remember what he's done to us, how he has hated and harmed the Seymours since becoming the head of the dark Families. He's vowed to destroy you."

"Remember what he did to Julia," Kian added. "And to Desdemona. He unleashed the *athanc* at Tylluan and caused great harm. The beast would have killed hundreds of mere mortals if it hadn't been stopped. It did kill Loris," he added with greater heat. "If the Guardians hadn't shown me the way to retrieve her soul and heal her body, I would have lost my *unoliaeth*. Because of *him*." He glared at Morcar with unconcealed wrath.

"I do not forget," Malachi said soberly. "We have been at odds for most of our lives, Morcar. I have no cause to trust you. If I had not felt the power of the *unoliaeth* in Philistia, I would not trust you."

"I spoke my intentions before the Guardians," Morcar said. "We waste time comparing past deeds. I don't say I am a different man, or that I regret any harm I've visited upon my enemies. But while we stand here arguing, the *cythraul* takes Philistia farther away. If you'll not help me, then I go alone."

"I believe you," Sarah said suddenly, stepping forward. "Will this help?" She tugged the Donballa out into the light. The golden amulet shimmered with its own light, further illuminating the darkness.

"No," Malachi said firmly. "You are never to remove it, Sarah. You gave me your vow. It is all that protects you from the *cythraul*'s power."

"But will it help?" she pressed, moving to stand before Steffan, whose blind gaze had lifted to the skies. "The spirits empowered it to keep the wearer safe from the *cythraul*'s possession. Will it help Philistia now, though she's already been possessed?"

"Steffan," Malachi growled warningly.

"I cannot do other than speak the truth," Steffan said. "If the Donballa can be placed upon Philistia's physical body, the *cythraul* must depart and seek another. There is but one other mere mortal present," he went on, "and that is you, Sarah."

"I'll keep Sarah safe," Desdemona vowed. "If the demon can be forced from Philistia's body, Malachi and the others can surely send it back to the spirit realm. No harm will come to Sarah while both my child and I guard her."

"I have a terrible feeling about this," Dyfed murmured faintly, sounding ill. "I really think we ought to leave the Donballa here and send Desdemona and Sarah home."

"Never," Desdemona said. "Else you men will muck it up, as you always do without our help. Isn't that so, Sarah?"

Sarah was already pulling the Donballa from her neck.

"*No*," Malachi said tightly.

"She's my cousin," Sarah told him, struggling to maintain her composure. "But she means so much more to me. Philistia is as my own sister. If she should be lost when I might have done something—"

"She'll not be lost," Morcar stated flatly.

Sarah held the shining amulet out to him. "If you bring her back to us, my lord, I shall be thankful to you all of my life."

Morcar carefully put the Donballa in a pocket. He looked at Malachi. "We must hurry."

Malachi nodded. "Sarah, you and Desdemona remain well behind us, with Steffan and Dyfed. You'll know if we've failed, or if we've succeeded." To Desdemona he said, "If we fail, take Sarah, Dyfed, and Steffan and journey quickly back to London. Gather as many magic mortals about you as you can. Call your father to come from America, and every wizard in Europe who might be of help. Steffan will know how to contact them quickly. You will be the head of the Seymour family if Kian and I should perish, Desdemona, and your daughter after you."

"It won't come to that," she insisted. "Kian has not yet become Dewin Mawr, and you know what the prophecies foretold."

"Even so," Malachi pressed.

"It will be as you have said," she promised.

"We must hurry!" Morcar said. "She goes farther away with every moment that passes."

The demon stopped by the edge of the sea and gazed out to the fretful waves. It stood very still, emanating light.

Malachi and Morcar had moved a little ahead of the others.

"Act with care," Malachi said quietly. "If it was able to kill Serafina, it will kill you just as easily."

"I know what to do," Morcar vowed. "It is an evil spirit. I know far better than you how to deal with such beings."

"Yes, that's so," Malachi admitted. "But it will be a danger even if you manage to get the Donballa over Philistia's neck. Kian, Christophe, and I will move quickly to send it away, but you'll be very close and fully exposed."

"I don't care," Morcar said. "Only swear to me that you'll keep Philistia from harm."

"I swear it."

"Malachi," he said more uncertainly. "We have long been enemies, and you owe me nothing. But will you tell her . . ."

"What?"

"That I didn't mean the things I said to her when we last parted. That I loved her, even then, and it was fear of that love which made me so unforgivably cruel. Not that I expect she should ever forgive me for what I did. But tell her . . . I would have been the proudest man alive to have her as my countess. Above all other women."

"I'll tell her," Malachi said. "And then you must do so, as well, when you've both returned."

"I will," Morcar said, steeling himself. "Today and every day after this, God willing." He drew in a deep breath. Released it. "I keep remembering when we were boys, of a sudden. We were friends of a sort once, were we not, Malachi? During those times when all the Families came together every few years?"

"When we were very young, Morcar," Malachi said. "We used to run off and fish while the adults sat about dully making agreements and decisions. Do you recall?"

"Yes," Morcar replied. "Before we cared about who we were or the burdens that were to be laid upon us. I remember it."

"As do I. Fondly, as it happens." Malachi held out a hand.

"Take care of Philistia." Morcar took the offered hand and held it. "Make certain she's always happy and content."

"I will."

Morcar nodded, then released him. Turning, he began to walk in the direction of the demon. The sound of the ocean's crashing waves filled his ears; the smell of salt filled his nostrils.

The *cythraul* rose into the air at Morcar's approach, turning to face him as he came nearer. Its voice, when it spoke from Philistia's mouth, held the sound of a multitude.

"Who are you?" it demanded.

Morcar forced himself to keep moving. No dark spirit would admire fear at such a moment. He drew upon his years of being the leader of many dark beings to carry him through.

"I am Morcar Cadmaran," he said loudly, firmly, striding onward. "I come to claim the power of the *cythraul.*"

The demon regarded him for a moment, at last saying, "You are not as the other one. I do not bow to an unworthy creature."

Morcar understood at once why the *cythraul* had been so insulted by Serafina's claim upon it, despite her vast powers, or having brought a mere mortal for its possession. It had killed her for being *animantis.*

"I am *superum,*" he stated. "And made higher than you. I am worthy to be your master."

"You are a dark lord," the *cythraul* stated with approval. It began to drift to the ground.

"I am Morcar Cadmaran," he said aloud, never faltering in his stride. "You will bow to me and serve me."

Philistia's feet touched earth, though the demon's voice, when it spoke, was suddenly uncertain.

"You have dark magic," it said. "You are worthy to be my master. But I feel danger in you."

"You are to obey me," Morcar commanded, his heart beating wildly in his chest as he came closer still. The demon's power put off a fearful heat and light; he had to narrow his gaze and turn his face aside. Years of blindness had taught him how to act without vision. "You will kneel—"

"Stay back!" the demon roared. The sound made the air vibrate like thunder.

Morcar forged on, past the fury and fire. His skin and eyes began to burn, but he ignored the pain and put his hand into his pocket, pulling out the Donballa. The amulet's light burst forth with a blinding brilliance.

The demon's rage exploded, scalding Morcar's face and eyes and hands like boiling oil as he lunged forward. He grasped the Donballa's chain with both hands and forced it over Philistia's head, closing his mind to the hot pain and terrifying smell of his own smoldering flesh.

The demon left her body with an eruption of violence, shaking both ground and air and sending an explosion of wrath outward as it rose out into the sky.

All those present were thrown to the ground, their ears burning from the high-pitched wails the demon made. Desdemona crawled to Sarah and set an arm about her; Dyfed covered them both with his body.

"Now!" Malachi shouted, struggling to his feet. On either side of him Kian and Christophe pushed upward as well, their hands held aloft.

Their powers combined, they shouted the incantation as one, *"Exsulo!"*

What happened afterward none of them could precisely say. The demon's screams were so overpowering as to make them all insensible. The force of the spell shuddered over the land, throwing them to their backs, and the burst of light that heralded the *cythraul*'s exit was so bright they were blinded.

Malachi came back to awareness before the others, blinking into the dark stillness of night as his whirling senses cleared. He was wet and cold and lying on the damp earth. His ears were buzzing so loudly that it was several long moments more before he could make out any sound.

It took an effort to sit, to make his eyes focus. He saw that Kian and Christophe were stirring on either side of him.

And then everything else came back to him and he was on his feet, looking frantically for Sarah.

"She's here," Dyfed called. "Stop shouting, or you'll frighten her."

They were huddled together on the ground, not far away, Dyfed, Desdemona, and Sarah. The two women were sitting side by side, looking dazed. Dyfed had his arms about both of them.

"Their ears haven't cleared yet," he said a little too loudly, indicating that his own hadn't yet become normal.

Malachi knelt before her; Sarah put her arms about him and hugged him tightly. Kissing her, he rose and returned to his cousins, making certain that both Kian and Christophe were on their feet before turning his attention to finding Steffan.

He was on the rocks near the sea, kneeling beside Philistia, who was bent over Morcar's body, weeping.

Malachi moved toward them.

"He's dead," Steffan said as he came near. He set a gentle hand on Philistia's head. "She's all right. Or as well as can be expected. There are burns that must be healed. Terrible burns." His voice choked with emotion as Philistia's inconsolable tears touched his sensitive mystic's soul. "Morcar was killed when the demon left her body. The force was too great for him to absorb. He has gone to the spirit realm."

"Morcar." Malachi knelt beside them. The body was badly burned, the flesh that had been exposed to the *cythraul*'s fury melted beyond recognition. All Malachi could think was that he could heal these wounds if Morcar had survived. Malachi could restore him to his former beauty and make him whole, if only . . .

"We can bring him back," Malachi said suddenly. "Steffan—"

"No, *cfender*," Steffan said. "You know we must not."

"It can be done," Malachi insisted. "Kian brought Loris back from death. Do you not remember? Because he loved her so greatly and they were fated to be. The *unoliaeth* between Morcar and Philistia is no less strong. I'm sure of it. Can you listen to her grief and say it cannot be done?"

Steffan hesitated. Lifting his hand, he stroked Philistia's head. The strength of her pain left her incapable of speech.

"I sense that she is willing," he said. "Her love for him is great. But Kian is a powerful wizard, and it was that power that drew Loris's spirit back to earth. This girl is but a mere mortal, who hasn't the power to overcome death."

"We will lend her power, then," Malachi told him. "And I will heal Morcar's body so that he may live. Kian, Christophe! Come quickly! We've one more feat to perform this night."

"What is it?" Kian asked, kneeling beside Malachi.

Malachi told them; his cousins reacted with confusion.

"I'm sorry for the girl," Kian said, "but to bring a Cadmaran back to life? It is a foolhardy task at best."

"The world has changed," Malachi said, repeating Niclas's words. "We will change with it or perish. Let us make the first step by giving our enemy the one thing his heart has craved. But I cannot do this alone. Just as I could not rid the world of the *cythraul* alone. Will you help me, Cousins?"

"If they will not," Desdemona said, pushing her way through the men, "I will."

They all gaped at her. She looked at them with what little patience she had left. "Morcar set me free to wed Dyfed," she explained. "When he might have lawfully held me captive. After this we will each be free from debt to the other. And you may well believe, Cousins, that the Guardians would far rather let us have Morcar back than listen to what I have to say. My back aches like the very devil, and I'm not in the mood for argument."

She held out her hands. Malachi, Kian, and Christophe stepped in to make a circle. Steffan set his arm about Philistia and reached up to clasp his brethren.

At Malachi's word, they set out to do the impossible and retrieve the soul of the man who had been their enemy.

Chapter 27

*M*alachi closed the book he held and looked up at his wife, who stood nearby cradling their infant son. She was smiling at him knowingly, as if certain of what he was going to say.

"And?" she asked.

He sighed, defeated. "It's marvelous."

Sarah's smile grew well satisfied. "Aha," she stated, and that, thankfully, was all the conceit she put forth on the matter, though Malachi knew she might have crowed far more loudly. As much as he disliked admitting that he'd been wrong, the book she'd written about the magic mortals in England was just what she'd promised. No one would believe that what she'd written was true, and none of the magical Families had anything to fear from the tome's publication.

"Of course you must admit that my suggestion was helpful," he told her.

"I admit it gladly and fully. If you'd not insisted that I emulate Mary Shelley and write my stories as a work of fiction, the book never would have survived. You wouldn't have allowed it." She looked at the child in her arms. "I'm afraid it's true, Matthew, my love. Your father is a tyrant."

Malachi laughed and, putting the book aside, stood. "And yet I recall you telling me, my love, as you were writing this most excellent fictional account, that you'd never enjoyed writing so much before. I believe your exact words were that it was 'terribly freeing.'"

"Yes, I did say that, didn't I?" she said. "And so it was. I was able to create my own magical world and didn't have to worry about you looking over my shoulders the entire time. I was able to concentrate on my work, and you, my lord"— she handed him their son when he came near—"were able to concentrate on the Families." Smiling up at him, she added, "I believe we can both declare a job well done."

It had been a busy year, Malachi thought, gazing into his son's solemn, staring eyes—green, like his mother's. Matthew Alberic Lewes Seymour, Viscount Kendon, was three months old and already bore the sober expression common to dark-haired magic mortals. It had been prophesied at his birth, by Steffan, that Matthew would be a famed traveler who would journey to unknown lands. Sarah had been pleased, knowing how enjoyable traveling could be. Malachi, understanding the hidden meanings of prophecy, wasn't quite as thrilled. But he was confident, meeting his son's grave stare, that the world would be a safer place for Matthew than it had been for those who came before him, for the world was changing, and magic mortals with it.

A great deal had happened since the night of the *cythraul*'s arrival. Malachi and his cousins and, most important, Philistia had gone into the spirit world to retrieve Morcar's essence and bring him back to his mortal body. It had required all their powers, and the intensity of Philistia's love, to convince the Guardians to release him.

His body had been badly burned, and it had taken a great period of time and the most powerful potions Malachi could conjure to heal him. Morcar, short-tempered and impatient by nature, had borne up far better than Malachi expected, but he'd had Philistia to nurse him and was content so long as she was near. For her part, Philistia reveled in doing everything for the man, from fluffing his pillows, to bathing his forehead, to reading aloud in order to entertain him. She managed to bully him into drinking the potions Malachi insisted upon and, more astonishing, to make him remain in bed when he didn't wish to. Malachi had never imagined that Morcar could ever be so meek.

Malachi wouldn't go so far as to say that love had transformed Morcar, but it had significantly worked upon him. Rather than lose control of the dark Families, Morcar's grasp actually grew firmer, once he was recovered enough to face them.

The world was changing, Lord Llew informed those whom he'd summoned to Castle Llew, and they were going to change with it. There was to be no more enmity between the Families, regardless of whether their heritage was dark or not. They would all become one or they would all fail. The assembled hadn't liked it, indeed, had threatened revolt, but Morcar had held fast. In the end they'd given way. They'd not really had any other options.

It had been left to both of them after that, Malachi and Morcar, to call for a meeting of the Families to discuss a new and formal union. They had discussed and argued and fought for various concessions—all of which had made Niclas, who served as mediator, half-crazed—and had at last come to terms. The Families had agreed to decide upon one leader to give allegiance to and had chosen Malachi.

Morcar hadn't protested. In truth, he'd seemed relieved. He and Philistia had gone abroad for a few months, then returned to Castle Llew in the spring to begin preparations for the arrival of their first child.

Morcar and Malachi hadn't necessarily become bosom friends but, realizing the close relationship their wives shared, learned to be genial when in company. By mutual agreement they did not speak of past wrongs and strove to focus, instead, on the future. It wasn't easy, but change seldom was. Their hope was to form understandings with magical clans in other parts of the world, such as the Caslins in America. Desdemona scoffed at the idea, insisting that her father would never make such an agreement. Tauron Cadmaran, writing from the States, was of the same mind. But Morcar and Malachi weren't discouraged, for as Niclas liked to point out, it had taken hundreds of years for the Seymours and Cadmarans to at last cry truce; as Americans were far more stubborn, it would likely take hundreds of years more for them to come to their senses.

Sir Alberic and Lady Tamony had settled in Cambridge, where Sir Alberic had at last embraced a life of teaching. They visited Glain Tarran often and had spent a full month at the estate following Matthew's birth.

Julius had left England after the advent of the *cythraul* and returned to traveling. He'd spent time with Morcar and Philistia in Italy during the winter months and had come home shortly after his nephew's birth to see the child and visit with his parents and sister. Julius seemed, to Malachi, to be a different man. His book on Celtic history had been published to great acclaim the previous summer, but he appeared to care nothing for it. His travels were aimless and his interest in the Celts had died. More than that he would not say, and Malachi didn't press him. Julius would find his way, somehow. Perhaps all he needed was someone who could bring peace and contentment to his life, just as Sarah had done for Malachi.

He had long known that marriage would agree with him, but Malachi soon discovered he'd underestimated just how happy Sarah would make him. The feeling settled on him the moment they were declared man and wife and increased as each day passed. She brought so much to his life, to the realm where he carried such grave responsibilities as both the Earl of Graymar and Dewin Mawr, that, trite though it might sound, he didn't know how he'd once lived without her. And now she'd given him a child.

"The book is certainly a job well done," Malachi

agreed. "I especially liked the hero. Such a handsome, wise, and clever wizard he is."

"I thought you'd approve," she murmured.

"Very much," he said. "Though I must say that this particular work"—he gazed at Matthew—"is your finest."

"*Our* finest," she corrected. "It seems that we do very well, my lord, when we collaborate."

"Exceedingly well, my lady," he said. "I look forward to our next effort. If we succeed half as well as the first attempt, we shall be most blessed."

"We are blessed," she murmured. "I know a great deal about magic, but I didn't believe it would be the path toward bringing me such happiness."

"Nor did I," he confessed. "I've given my life to magic, and never thought of what it might give me in return beyond power and fortune. But it's given me so much more, Sarah. It's given me you, and now Matthew."

"And love," she said, rising up on her toes to kiss Malachi.

"Yes, sweetheart," he whispered against her lips. "It's the best magic of all."